CONQUERED BY DESIRE

The moment they stepped inside the tent, Drogo began to undress her. Eada laughed and tried to undo his laces even as he was tugging her clothing off. He gently tumbled her onto the sheepskin bedding before the fire and she greedily welcomed him into her arms.

"You are beautiful," he said when they had finally cast off all their clothes, studying her by the warming light of the fire.

"You are most fair yourself," she murmured, smoothing her hands over his chest.

Drogo began to slowly kiss his way down her soft body. "If I tell you that you taste as sweet as the richest honey, are you going to say that I too am sweet?"

She laughed and threaded her fingers through his hair.

"I would have thought you would be very tired," he said in an increasingly husky voice as she began to cover his chest with soft kisses and light, teasing strokes of her tongue.

"I think riding to battle has left me with very hot blood," she drawled and smiled when he shuddered beneath the kisses she covered his hard stomach with.

"You had nothing to do with the battle except to show us where it would be."

"Do you mean to talk me out of my boldness?"

When she slid her hand down to stroke him softly, he groaned and shook his head. "No," he whispered. "That would be madness . . ."

Books by Hannah Howell

ONLY FOR YOU * MY VALIANT KNIGHT *
UNCONQUERED * WILD ROSES * A TASTE OF
FIRE * HIGHLAND DESTINY * HIGHLAND
HONOR * HIGHLAND PROMISE *
A STOCKINGFUL OF JOY * HIGHLAND VOW *
HIGHLAND KNIGHT * HIGHLAND HEARTS *
HIGHLAND BRIDE * HIGHLAND ANGEL *
HIGHLAND GROOM * HIGHLAND WARRIOR *
RECKLESS * HIGHLAND CONQUEROR *
HIGHLAND CHAMPION * HIGHLAND
LOVER * HIGHLAND VAMPIRE *
THE ETERNAL HIGHLANDER * MY IMMORTAL
HIGHLANDER * CONQUEROR'S KISS *
HIGHLAND BARBARIAN *
BEAUTY AND THE BEAST * HIGHLAND
SAVAGE * HIGHLAND THIRST * HIGHLAND
WEDDING * HIGHLAND WOLF * SILVER
FLAME * HIGHLAND FIRE * NATURE OF THE
BEAST * HIGHLAND CAPTIVE * HIGHLAND
SINNER * MY LADY CAPTOR * IF HE'S
WICKED * WILD CONQUEST * IF HE'S SINFUL *
KENTUCKY BRIDE * IF HE'S WILD *
YOURS FOR ETERNITY * COMPROMISED
HEARTS * HIGHLAND PROTECTOR *
STOLEN ECSTASY * IF HE'S DANGEROUS *
HIGHLAND HERO * HIGHLAND HUNGER *
HIGHLAND AVENGER

Published by Kensington Publishing Corporation

HANNAH HOWELL

UNCONQUERED

ZEBRA BOOKS
KENSINGTON PUBLISHING CORP.
http://www.kensingtonbooks.com

ZEBRA BOOKS are published by

Kensington Publishing Corp.
119 West 40th Street
New York, NY 10018

Copyright © 1996 by Hannah Howell

All Kensington titles, imprints, and distributed lines are
available at special quantity discounts for bulk purchases
for sales promotion, premiums, fund-raising, educational,
or institutional use.

Special book excerpts or customized printings can also
be created to fit specific needs. For details, write or phone
the office of the Kensington Special Sales Manager:
Attn.: Special Sales Department. Kensington Publishing
Corp., 119 West 40th Street, New York, NY 10018.
Phone: 1-800-221-2647.

Zebra and the Z logo Reg. U.S. Pat. & TM Off.

ISBN-13: 978-1-4201-2233-6
ISBN-10: 1-4201-2233-9

First Printing: October 1996

10   9

Printed in the United States of America

One

"*Maman,* come look! There are hundreds of ships," cried the small boy as he stumbled into the house. "Come look, *Maman!* Never have I seen so many."

Lady Vedette of Pevensey could feel all the blood drain from her cheeks, and she grabbed her excited young son by his thin shoulders and shook him slightly. "Calm yourself, and tell me, most carefully, what you have seen."

"Ships. A very great lot of them," the tousled-haired boy of eight replied, pushing his blond curls off his round, flushed face. "They are fine, strong ships filled with horses, men, and supplies."

"The Danes?" she whispered, but a cold knot of fear had settled in her belly and she knew in her heart that it was not the Danes who now threatened England's shores.

"No, *Maman,*" the boy said, wriggling out of her hold. " 'Tis not the Danes. I saw the banners and remembered what my father told me. 'Tis William the Bastard." He cried out in shock and pain when his mother suddenly slapped him on the cheek.

"Never say that again, Ethelred. Never again. Do you hear me?"

"Yes, *Maman.*"

She pulled the tearful child into her arms and hugged him close for a moment then gently but firmly pushed him away. Her heart in her throat, she peered out a narrow window toward the sea. Everything Ethelred had said was true. There was no time to soothe the child.

"Gather your belongings, Ethelred. Do it now. Gather only what you most need and what is most valuable." As her son hurried away to do as he was told, Lady Vedette turned to her daughter, who sat at the table silenced by confusion and fear. "You must do the same, Averil. Gather together only what is most dear and necessary to you and what is most costly." When the pale Averil stood up but did not move, Lady Vedette gave her thirteen-year-old daughter a light push toward her sleeping chamber. "Run, girl. There is very little time left to us."

Even as Averil rushed off to obey her mother, Lady Vedette began to hurl commands at her frightened bond-slaves. One hurried away to prepare the cart while the other two helped her throw her belongings into sacks, baskets, and anything else they could find. All the while she gathered what she could, Lady Vedette prayed God would give them the time to flee safely. She concerned herself only with the things that would allow them to remain a family of means no matter where they went or who ruled England.

As they tossed all they had collected into a cart, Ethelred cried out, "What of Eada?"

Vedette grabbed her son when he tried to jump out of the cart and yanked him back in. "Eada must fend for herself," she said, tightly gripping the rough edge of the cart and staring blindly in the direction she had watched her eldest child walk earlier in the day.

"Mother, we cannot just leave her behind," Averil whispered, tears thickening her voice.

"We must. Look to the boats, children," she said, pointing toward the seashore where the lead boats of the huge force were already cutting through the shallows. "If we wait or try to search for her, none of us will get away."

As the cart began to move, Vedette looked toward the hills. "God protect you, Eada. I pray that those hills you so love can now hide and protect you."

Eada laughed as she watched her hounds play together. They loved to escape the confines of the town as much as she did. Although Eada did not actually dislike living in Pevensey, every once in a while she felt a strong urge to escape from the people, the noise, and the smell. She also liked to visit with Old Edith, a woman who had been banished from Pevensey years ago and lived alone, although she never told her parents about that. They would never approve.

As she rounded a corner and cleared the trees, Eada saw the old woman in the doorway of her small cottage and waved to her. Edith's return wave was weak for the pain in her joints restricted her movements. Eada sighed as she hurried toward the cottage, sadness weighting her heart and stealing some of the joy of being free for a little while. She knew that Old Edith would not live much longer. Even now, the knowledge of that was clear to see in the old woman's eyes. What helped soften Eada's grief was knowing how calmly Edith accepted it, had even begun to wish for it as it would put an end to her constant pain.

"You should not be standing out here," Eada gently scolded Old Edith when she reached the woman's side. "There is a chill in the air."

Edith nodded, stepping back into her cottage, Eada close behind her. "Winter will soon be upon us. I feel a need to watch its approach for I know that I will never live to see another spring."

"I wish you would not speak of it." Eada sat cross-legged by the center hearth.

Wincing as she lowered herself to the hard, dirt-packed floor, Edith asked, "Why? Death is but a part of life. I

am in the deep winter of my years, Eada. My body is worn
and my soul begs release from its crippled, pain-ridden
confines."

"Does it hurt so bad?" Eada gently placed her small,
soft hands over Edith's gnarled ones.

"I weep from the strength of it at every dawning, wondering why God is so cruel and what I have done to make
Him so angry that He forces me to endure for yet another
day. Come, my pretty flaxen-haired child, you cannot truly
wish me to linger when I suffer so."

"No, I do not want you to suffer, but I shall miss you,
dearest friend."

"As I shall miss you. That is my only regret. Now, how
fares your pretty family?"

"They are well." Eada frowned, her full mouth turning
down ever so slightly at the corners. "All save for my father. I fear for him, Edith. He went to join with King
Harold to battle Harald Hardrada and Tostig."

Old Edith shook her head. "Your father will gain
naught from that save for the cold, bitter taste of steel."

Eada shivered and wrapped her arms around her slim
body. In all the years she had known the woman, she had
never grown accustomed to the way Edith spoke so low
and firm at times. It was as if the woman saw things no
mortal could. The fact that her pronouncements almost
always proved true only added to Eada's discomfort. She
could almost understand what had prompted the people
of Pevensey to banish the woman.

"My father seeks to regain all he has lost by winning
favor with Harold," Eada explained.

A sad, sympathetic look settled on Old Edith's wrinkled
face. "I know, but he will fail. King Harold's sun has set.
He reaches for a destiny that can never be his. I am sorry,
child, but Harold will pull your poor father Waltheof
down with him. Did you not see what blazed across the
sky just recently?"

Slowly nodding, Eada fought to repress a shudder of fear. The thing in the sky was all anyone talked of. The fear it bred in people could be smelled in the air. Everyone was certain that it was an omen. They were just not sure what it meant or how it should be read. There were theories, and each one had its believers and its doubters. The only thing Eada was sure of was that she did not like it, and she prayed that it would prove to mean nothing at all.

"Only the blind did not see that fire moving across our skies," Eada said. "And even they must have known exactly what was up there because so many people spoke about it. In truth, many spoke of little else."

Old Edith nodded. "And each man, woman, and child, slave or freedman, had a thought on what it was and what it meant. I suspect that even the heathen at heart fell to his knees, eyes raised to God for guidance and help."

"That is the way of it. What do you think it meant?" she asked, a little reluctantly, for she knew she would not be able to ignore or push aside with scorn anything Old Edith said.

"Poor child. You want to know the truth yet, at the same time, fear it. Ah, me, there is good reason to fear, but do not let that fear steal away your wisdom and your strength."

"Edith, you are beginning to afright me far more than the fire in the sky did."

"Ne'er fear the truth. Ignorance holds the greatest threat. What you saw in the sky was Harold's brief reign being swallowed up by the flames of destiny. Riding to victory upon the bright tail of that fire is a new king, a Norman, one who will end the Saxon rule in this land."

"William the Bastard," Eada whispered.

"It would be wise if you were to cease thinking of him so," Old Edith suggested with a half smile that hinted at a beauty now stolen by age and hardship. "He will soon be your king."

"So my father will lose yet again."

"Poor Waltheof was ne'er destined to win. His line will survive and then rise above the weaknesses and failings of its forebears. Waltheof and those before him were only meant to plant that seed."

"Do you *see* all this, Edith?"

"*See* is, mayhap, the wrong word to use. I speak what I feel and it has the strong taste of truth. I do not have dreams or visions, if that is what you think. I have ideas, thoughts, revelations. I call them sendings. Sometimes even I am surprised by the words that flow from my mouth for I gave no thought to them. Sometimes I was intending to say something else entirely. The truth just comes. I cannot stop it, so I have come to accept it."

"I find what you say now hard to accept," Eada said as she absently tugged her gray tunic around her legs. "You speak of war and of the conquering of our people."

"That I do, and it saddens me. Howbeit, the Saxons were once the conquerors. They took all that they hold now away from someone else. Now comes their turn to be conquered, to have all they own taken away."

"They will fight."

"And they will die. God's will can ne'er be changed. We were blessed with a long reign in a fine land and we have built much that is good. God says 'tis now another's turn."

"Thus our people and all our ways must die?"

"No, child, merely change. You will be one of the ones who will fulfill that part of the prophecy."

"Me?" Eada cried as she clenched her small hands into tight fists, resisting the sudden urge to slap the old woman and demand that she cease to speak such nonsense. "I am but a small, thin female of only eighteen years."

"You should be wed."

The abrupt change of subject startled a laugh out of Eada, but she quickly grew serious again. "I was."

Edith snorted with disgust as she poked at the fire with a blackened stick. "That? That drunken boy who got himself killed ere he could even bed and seed his new bride? You are still a maid, so you are still unwed. I see that you still wear your hair loose as a maid does."

As she touched her thick, honey-blond hair, Eada smiled faintly. "As you just said—I am still a maid. It has caused some talk, however, for, still a maid or no, I am a widow." She shrugged. "I kept my hair bound until my mourning was done. That should be enough to still the tongues."

"More than enough. Your time is near though. Soon you will have a man, one worthy of you."

"And will he be handsome, brave, and strong?" Eada asked in a playful tone.

"You think I but say empty words, the same words many must say to you; but yes, he will be all three."

"And I will meet him after this war is done?"

"No. He rides with William."

All of Eada's good humor fled with a swiftness that left her chilled. She opened her soft lavender eyes wide as she stared at the solemn Edith in growing consternation. When Edith said such things, they carried the sharp sting of hard truth, but this time Eada did not want to believe it.

"A Norman?" she questioned, her voice soft and roughened by shock. "In one breath you tell me that the Normans will bring about the destruction of my people and wrest our lands away from us, and in the very next breath you dare tell me that I shall love a Norman. Am I destined to be a traitor then? Do you truly believe that such a weakness scars my soul?"

"Foolish, pretty child." Edith scolded. "Did I not also say that our people will not die away nor will all of our ways fade into legend? How do you think such a thing will come to pass? Not through our men," Edith said sharply, her colorless lips twisting with scorn. "They will just fight, cutting away at each other with their swords. They will plot, and lands will be won and lost. They will not be happy with some but will battle and bleed for more—only to see it all slip out of their hands. There is no Saxon future to be found in our men.

"The future is in our women, Saxon women," Edith continued, her voice growing stronger as she spoke. "In the wombs of our women will lie the future of our people. Their husbands will be of Norman blood, but the heirs will have good Saxon blood in their veins and, if the woman is wise, they will also have Saxon lore in their hearts. The women will learn the Norman speech, as they must, but will be certain that their children know the Saxon tongue as well." Old Edith smiled faintly at Eada. "I can see that you are fiercely fighting the truth of all I am saying."

"It makes sense yet—to bed down with the enemy?" Eada shook her head and nervously plucked at the gold brooch holding her cloak on her shoulders. "I cannot believe that we Saxon women must play the whores to ensure a future for our people."

"Not whores. Wives, ladies, the mothers of the future, and the guardians of the past. I see that you do not wish to listen to this, that you try to turn from the truth; but do not forget my words, Eada of Pevensey. Promise me that you will remember my words and think long and hard on all I have said."

There was an upsetting desperation in Old Edith's voice and Eada moved to gently hug the old woman, whispering the promise begged of her. "I have listened, Edith, and I will remember it all." She moved back to her place by the fire. "My heart but needs to ponder such solemn and sad news. Now, enough of these dark thoughts. Come, see what I have brought for you." Eada dug into the small sack she carried and cheerfully named each gift as she set it before her friend. "A pot of honey, sweet cheese, bread, and some very fine mead."

"Fetch me my knife and drinking bowls," Old Edith ordered with a smile. "We shall have ourselves a feast."

Even as she obeyed Edith, Eada asked, "You have so little, old friend. Do you not wish to save this?"

"When you reach my age, child, you cease to save every little thing," Old Edith murmured as she began to cut the bread. " 'Tis indeed wise to put something aside for the morrow, but not when one is as old as I am. The morrow may ne'er come. That is when you begin to think *Do it now, you old crone, for you cannot do it in your grave.*" She laughed softly. "Our Good Lord will not wait for me to finish these fine gifts when He finally decides to call me to His side."

Eada forced herself to smile as she joined in the small feast Old Edith set before them. She dearly loved the woman, but she now wished she had not made this visit. All the things Old Edith had spoken of could not be pushed from her mind and ignored. The words lingered in the forefront of her mind, distracting and disturbing her. What Eada found even more disturbing was the small voice in her head that kept reminding her of how often Old Edith was right.

She was just about to take her leave, needing to get away to think clearly, when Old Edith suddenly went very still, staring with a frozen intensity into her battered drinking bowl. Eada shivered, and it took her a moment to subdue the strong urge to flee from the tiny cottage. There was, after all, always the chance that Old Edith was suffering from some kind of seizure and needed her help.

"Edith?" she called, but the old woman did not even blink. "Edith!" she called in a sharper tone. "Are you ill?"

Blinking rapidly, Edith lifted her head to stare at Eada. There was such a wealth of sadness upon the old woman's face that Eada felt her heart begin to pound with fear.

She knew she was about to hear more news that she had no wish to know, but she still could not leave for there was still the chance that Old Edith might need her help.

"You should not have come here today, Eada of Pevensey," Edith whispered in a hoarse voice, but then she shook her head, a few dirty wisps of gray hair tumbling onto her deeply lined forehead. "No, I am foolish. There was naught else you could do. God's will brought you here. Nothing can alter our fates, not even these accursed warnings of what is to come. All we can do is prepare. I just do not know if I have had the time to prepare you or even if you will allow yourself to be prepared for what is to come."

"Edith," Eada snapped, then groaned and rubbed at her temples in a vain attempt to push away a forming headache. "What do you speak of now?"

"William again, child. The Normans and the end of Saxon rule begins today."

"Today?" Eada gasped and leapt to her feet. "Do you tell me that the war begins now?"

"And if I say *yes*, do you mean to run back home? Do you really think that one small woman can hold back an army? Can you make the ships turn and sail back to France?"

"I can see that my family is safe."

"Vedette will see that they are safe. That one is a woman who knows well how to survive. She will flee at the first sightings of the ships, flee to some place that is safe until the war is won. Then she will step out and start again, finding someone to care for her. You need not fear for her, child."

"She will not leave until I am with her. I must hurry so that she does not linger too long."

"She will not linger, not even for you," Edith said quietly as she followed Eada out of the cottage. "Beneath that sweet face, Vedette is a woman who has the strength to make a hard decision. She will see that if she flees without hesitation, she can save two children and herself, but if she waits for one errant child to return home, she could lose all chance of escape. It will hurt her to leave you behind for she loves you, but she will not wait for you. She will grab all she can and flee Pevensey as swiftly as she can."

"Nay," Eada whispered, but a voice in her head told her that Edith spoke the truth. "I do not even know if all of your warnings and prophecies are true," she suddenly cried and ran from the cottage.

Eada ran as fast as she could, her two hounds keeping pace. She was desperate to get home and find that Old Edith was wrong. She did not slow down until she was able to see the village and the sea it faced. Panting, her chest aching from the effort needed just to catch her breath, Eada stared in horror at the scene laid out before her, desperately trying to deny what she saw and failing miserably.

Pevensey swarmed with men. Ships clogged the shallow waters by the shore and the landing was crowded with men, horses, and supplies. Despite the abundance of all three, the ships kept pressing forward to be unloaded. Occasionally there was a cry of fear or pain as some poor fool tried to defend what was his against indefensible odds. There was also the occasional chilling scream of a woman as her hiding place was discovered and she tried to protest her almost certain fate.

Falling slowly to her knees, her panting hounds collapsing at her side, Eada stared at the constant activity in the town below. She prayed fiercely that her family was no longer there even though it hurt to think that they would really leave her behind. Pevensey was no longer safe. It was filled to bursting with an enemy eager to conquer.

Suddenly, as if yanked from a dream, Eada became aware that not every one of the invaders was lingering in

Pevensey. Small bands of men were mounting their own or newly stolen horses and riding away. She cursed as she realized what was happening and at her own stupidity for not considering the possibility the moment she saw the invaders. Soldiers would need to reconnoiter and forage. They could even be hunting down some of the people who had fled the town taking whatever was of value with them. Soldiers commonly lusted after the spoils of war, and if Pevensey had been stripped too clean, they would try to recapture that wealth.

Still cursing herself for staying so exposed upon the hilltop, Eada quickly searched out a hiding place. When she espied a heavy thicket, she ignored the sharp pull of the brambles and branches and plunged into it, urging her dogs to join her. She lay down on her stomach, ordered her pets to do the same, then placed a gentle hand on each dog's muzzle, silently commanding them to be still and quiet.

Edith was right, she mused, as she peered through the tangle of branches and watched a small troop of men approach. She should not have raced home. The old woman had never been wrong before, and Eada knew she had been a fool to doubt the woman this time. There was nothing for her in Pevensey now, had not been since the ships had first been sighted. Her mother would have gathered as much as she could as fast as she could and then fled. In her heart Eada knew her mother had not wanted to leave her behind but had had the wit and the strength to see that she had to sacrifice one to save all the others, that any delay would be costly, perhaps even fatal. Eada knew she would have done the same.

Like some unthinking child, she had run home to her mother at the first hint of danger. Now, instead of being safe with Edith, she was caught in the middle of an invasion. Instead of having the time to flee or to choose an adequate, comfortable hiding place, she was stuck in a thicket and she would be stuck there until nightfall. Only then might she have some small chance of slipping away unseen and getting back to Edith. The old woman would need help to elude the enemy. As she cautiously shifted her body in a vain attempt to get comfortable, she prayed vigorously that whatever Normans raped her home would find little there to enrich or comfort them.

Two

"No one is here, Drogo," announced Tancred d'Ullack as he picked up a wooden bowl from the floor and set it on the well-scrubbed table.

"Are there any beds?" Drogo de Toulon asked as he adjusted his firm hold on the slender, ashen-faced man who sagged at his side, and stepped further into the great hall of the house he had chosen to claim.

"Yes, and some very fine ones, too. Go right through that doorway at the far end of the hall. The one on the left."

Drogo picked his companion up in his arms, ignoring the man's groaning protests. "Come, Garnier, my friend, you will feel stronger after you have rested. Tancred," he called back to the younger man, who was just sitting down at the table, "have our belongings brought to this place and see if my man Ivo can find us some food."

"I shall never return home, my friend," groaned the man in Drogo's arms.

"Do you plan to die here then, Garnier?"

"No, but I plan to never set my boots in a boat again and, unless I learn to soar like a bird, I am destined to rot out my days in this accursed land."

Laughing softly, Drogo laid his slender friend down upon the first bed he found. A swift, but careful look around the small room told him that it had been hastily deserted. Clothes and the toys of a young boy were scattered around. His survey also told him that the room was extremely clean, and he began to relax.

"I should more closely study this bed," said Garnier, his deep voice hoarse and unsteady, "but I am suffering the *mal de mer* too badly to care if these Saxon fleas eat me alive."

"I would be most surprised, Garnier, if there are any fleas about. The people who held this house were very clean."

"Some distant family of yours, mayhap?" Garnier teased, and he managed a weak smile.

Drogo briefly returned the man's smile, accepting the gentle jest aimed at his own strong inclinations toward cleanliness, a preference that many found a little strange. "Rest, Garnier," he murmured. "Rest is what you need."

The moment Garnier closed his eyes, Drogo returned to the hall and found the central hearth already being tended by his man Ivo. Ivo was big, dark, and somewhat slow; but he tended to most of Drogo's and his men's needs as well as any woman. Displeasure tightened Drogo's finely carved mouth, however, when he saw the young girl huddled close by Ivo's side. A quick glance at Tancred, who was sprawled comfortably at the table, elicited only a shrug.

"Ivo, where did the girl come from?" Drogo asked his servant as he approached the man. "Was she here? In this house?"

Ivo shook his head, his thick black hair tumbling onto his face. "Outside."

"Ah, then you have brought her to us for our amusement." Tancred leapt nimbly from the bench he had lounged on and strode closer; but when he reached for the girl, Ivo suddenly placed his large, muscular body firmly between the much smaller Tancred and the terrified girl. "I see; you have not, then."

"Mine," Ivo growled as the girl huddled behind him. "I found her."

"And were you the one who beat her?" Drogo asked, frowning as he studied the girl's thin, bruised face.

"No. The others did. I stopped them and took her."

"Oh, *merde.*" Tancred sighed with a blatantly false dismay. "We shall have some deaths to explain away." He again approached the girl, reaching out one slender hand, and said quietly when Ivo tensed, "I only mean to look at her."

"I did not kill the men," Ivo said, never taking his gaze from Tancred as he defended himself to Drogo. "I only hurt them."

"She is a bond-slave, Drogo," Tancred said and pointed to the earring the girl wore. "That earring is how the Saxons mark their bond-slaves. And it appears that she is a disobedient one," he added in a soft voice when he saw the still-raw lash marks on her back revealed by her torn gown. "She could be more trouble than she is worth."

"Mine." Ivo put his arm around the wide-eyed girl's thin shoulders and held her close as he fixed his dark gaze on Drogo. "You can give her to me."

Drogo grimaced and absently rubbed his hand over his broad, mail-covered chest as he realized he could have a serious problem on his hands. "Ivo, she belongs to someone."

Ivo nodded. "A Saxon. You will fight them soon and win. Then, everything will be yours and you can give her to me."

"Such lovely simplicity," Tancred drawled, his grey eyes bright with laughter.

"Enough of your jests, Tancred," Drogo muttered as he frowned at Ivo. "Ivo, you may have her for now, but she must work and she must behave. We have no time now to waste upon a lazy or disobedient bond-slave. Do you understand?"

"Yes," Ivo replied, and he nodded slowly. "I will watch her."

"And one more thing. Now, heed me closely, Ivo. The girl belongs to someone. That earring tells us so. We are here to fight the Saxons for William, but that does not mean that everything will then belong to us. If someone comes to claim her and there is trouble over the matter, she may have to be returned to her masters."

"I understand. If someone comes to claim her, I will tell him that she is mine. We will talk on it."

When Tancred laughed, Drogo briefly glared at him, then looked back at Ivo. He decided it would be easier to just wait and, if someone came to claim the girl, he would deal with the problem then. "One last thing, Ivo," he said, as the big man moved to search the house for supplies, the girl close at his heels. "I will take her away from you myself if you hurt her too badly." He did not really believe Ivo would hurt the girl for he was a relatively gentle giant, but he felt a need to give the warning.

"No, I will not hurt her. Her name is May," Ivo added in a quiet tone as he took the girl by the hand and led her out of the hall.

"I am not sure it is wise to keep her with us," Tancred said as he and Drogo sat down opposite each other at the big table.

"Then you go and take her away from him," Drogo said as he tugged off his heavy leather-and-mail gauntlets.

"No, thank you, my friend. I am most fond of keeping my head just where it is. I just fear that she could bring us trouble. By the look of her back, she is a much-whipped slave."

"That does not mean she is any trouble. She could be a little slow of wit, as Ivo is, and had a master with no patience. Mayhap the lady of the house had the girl whipped because the master found her too comely. We will wait and see how she behaves. A servant can do well by one master yet plague another to madness. Also, she now owes Ivo for he rescued her. That might help."

Tancred shrugged his slim shoulders. "As you wish. It is a pity that he could find no wenches for us, though."

Drogo laughed as he tugged off his mail hood and the padded hood beneath it then combed his long fingers through his sweat-dampened black hair. "You look for wenches despite spending your last days in France rutting day and night? I should think that you would be in need of a rest."

"I rested on the journey here. I wonder what sort of wenches lived in this fine house?"

"Clean ones," Drogo murmured as he ran his hand over the smooth, clean oak table. "And how can you know that any wenches lived here?"

"While you tended to our belly-emptying friend Garnier, I wandered through the house. There are women's gowns in two of the sleeping chambers. They did not have time to take all of them. Ah, good, wine," he cried with pleasure when Ivo set a jug and two wooden goblets on the table.

"They took a lot of things, though. This is a wealthy man's house, yet there is little of any value within it."

"There will be plunder to be had elsewhere," Tancred said cheerfully as he poured them each some wine. "Since you are so close to William, we will be certain to get our share of it."

"Ah, and I thought you had joined this battle for the glory of it and for love of me."

"And so I did. Also, William's cause is a just one. But, I will not turn aside any gain either."

Drogo smiled faintly, but made no reply. He shared Tancred's feelings. William's cause was a just one and there would be glory to be found in fighting for it. If they were victorious and could hold onto that victory, there would also be rewards. Drogo had considered that when he had agreed to join William. He was close to William, although not as close as others. His position was strong enough, however, to promise him a healthy bounty of some kind and even a voice in what that bounty might be. In France, there had been little William could give him and, with three brothers between him and his father's titles and lands, there was no hope of an inheritance.

Inwardly, he sighed, wishing that he were not so prone to thinking matters over. Harold of England had earned whatever fate befell him. He had pledged to accept William as his king then broken that pledge. Unfortunately, Drogo could too easily see how badly others would suffer for Harold's treachery. That knowledge made it difficult for Drogo to maintain any real peace of mind.

Even the woman who lived here must suffer, he thought as Ivo set bread and cheese upon the table. The woman clearly cared for her home and had worked to make it a fine place to live, yet she had been driven from it, able to take only what she could grab in a few, hectic moments. Drogo doubted that she cared who sat upon the throne, and she certainly had been given no say in the matter; but she had still lost her home and could easily lose far more in the troubled days ahead.

"Drogo," called a rough voice.

Pleased to be dragged free of his morose thoughts, Drogo smiled at the man standing in the doorway of the house. "Come inside, Serle. You are most welcome to share in our bounty. The larder here was not completely emptied."

"Nor were many others," the older man said even as he sat down next to Tancred. "There is not enough for so many men, however. We are to rest here for a while as many of the men did not suffer the crossing well. Where is that pretty courtier Garnier?"

"He rests," Drogo replied and smiled faintly. "He did not suffer the crossing well either."

Serle laughed softly then murmured his appreciation of the wine he sipped from the bowl Ivo brought him. "Who is the woman?" he asked when he noticed May, who still shadowed Ivo's every move.

"A bond-slave called May. Ivo rescued her and now claims her."

"And out there lie a few men who can lay claim to broken heads, eh?" Serle grinned, revealing that his front teeth had not survived his chosen life as a warrior.

"Not broken beyond mending, I pray. I have no time to become tangled in some quarrel. Has there been no sign of the English? Are we to be allowed ashore unopposed?"

"It appears so. We now have a few of the Saxons in our grasp. They have told us that Harold has gone to face Harald Hardrada, yet another who tries to unseat Harold from his stolen throne. It will be a most bloodied throne the victor finally sits upon."

"The victor will be William, of course," Tancred said as he wiped his slightly full lips with the back of his hand.

Serle looked at Tancred and his weathered face creased with a faint smile. "Ah, the confidence of youth. Come, my boy, do not forget that we are only a few thousand men facing a whole country. We have set ourselves down in a strange land and only a few of us speak the tongue of these people. Do not strut about thinking that we are already the victors or your slender body will soon feed the Saxon worms. Nor should you think that all will be settled and done once William gets his buttocks on that throne."

"But, William will be the king."

"And that is all, eh? No, my boy. We will still be a small army of French in the midst of a sea of Saxons. Would you let a man take your land with only a small protest? I think not. William may gain the throne, but it will be a long time before he truly holds the country. I have lived three-and-forty years and I have never seen a king sit easy upon his throne. And the men who hold whatever bounty William might gift them with had best keep their swords and their wits honed and sharp."

"You begin to make me wish I had remained in Normandy."

Serle shrugged his broad shoulders. "That king knows little peace, either; and you, as most of us, could hope for little reward save honors when fighting for him. Here, there is a chance for some gain."

"Now that you have thoroughly discouraged my friend," Drogo said, laughter trembling in his deep voice, "can you tell me why you have sought us out?"

"To enjoy Ivo's fine cooking," Serle replied, only half in jest as Ivo set a hearty venison stew before them. "Would the promise of that not be enough to bring any man to your door?"

"It would," Drogo agreed as he began to eat. "You, however, could not have known that there would be a meal to enjoy. We did not. And I think this fine stew was already brewing for Ivo has not had the time to cook one. So, tell, what brings you here?"

"William calls for supplies. He asks for men to ride out and grasp all they can so that all of his men might eat well. I have come looking for some men to ride out with me."

"And you have found them. As soon as we have filled our bellies, we can begin the search for what is needed to fill the bellies of the rest of the men."

"And we are to look for Saxons. I have no wish to be caught with my back to the sea."

Drogo nodded in heartfelt agreement before turning his full attention to his meal. As soon as they were all done eating, he ordered Ivo to watch over Garnier and hold firm to the house. He did not wish to lose such a fine place for he could not be sure how long they might have to rest in Pevensey. Even if they lingered for only one night, however, he wanted to do so in comfort.

Just as they stepped out of the house, a youth raced up to them. Drogo doubted that the boy was even old enough to grow a beard, but someone had at least armored him well before sending him out. The youth had a mail hood, surcoat, and gauntlets, as well as a fine sword. The warhorse he led was of a good, sturdy build and almost looked too big for the slender boy.

"Who are you, boy, and what brings you to me?" Drogo asked.

"I am Unwin, sir, and I should like to join with you," the youth replied.

"You appear too young to be able to pledge your sword where you will."

"The man I rode with died of a fever but hours before we sailed." The youth flushed. "When William discovered that I was alone, he told me to find another knight to serve or he must return me to France."

"There are many knights here, Unwin."

"And all are well served. I was told that you and your men have neither pages nor squires, only a brute called Ivo. Please, sir, I need nothing as you can see. My family armoured me well before sending me to this battle. I will serve you well."

"You have never been in battle, have you?"

"No," Unwin admitted reluctantly. "But, I am well trained. I need this battle to gain my spurs, Sir Drogo."

"Or to get your head taken from your shoulders," Serle grumbled then smiled crookedly when the youth stiffened.

"I can fight," Unwin snapped.

"I am sure you can; and if your family has taken such time and spent so much coin to send you along with William, then fight you must," Drogo said, ignoring the way Tancred rolled his eyes. "You must know, however, that we have no pages or others to serve us because we have no lands, no titles, and no coin. You join a poor group of knights, lad. We have come here to fight for William in the hope of gaining some or all of what we lack."

"As have I, Sir Drogo."

"Then join us, if you will."

Drogo smiled faintly at the way the youth grinned and quickly mounted his horse. It had been a long time since he had felt such eagerness. Unwin still held only visions of glory and wealth. If the boy survived the battles he would soon face, that sweet, blind eagerness would quickly fade away. If the boy were to survive, he would have to grow hardened as the rest of them had.

As he, Tancred, Serle, and the youth rode out of town, Drogo carefully looked around. The area swarmed with men pleased to be on solid ground again and eager for war and gain. Neither the ominous fire that had streaked across the skies at Eastertide nor the way William had faltered upon landing could dim their confidence. Drogo prayed that this was not all the result of an empty and useless bravado. He did not want to think that he had come to England only to die.

Three

Eada gave a convulsive start and then heartily cursed her own foolishness. She could not believe she was so lacking in wits as to fall asleep in the midst of an invading army. Such idiocy could easily have cost her an opportunity to escape.

As she began to ease her head out of the shrubbery in the hope of getting a closer look at her precarious situation, she suddenly tensed. She felt the approach of the horsemen before she heard or saw them. Eada flattened herself against the ground and gently pressed a hand over each dog's muzzle. When she saw the riders and they drew near enough to overhear their conversation, Eada grimaced with distaste and anger.

Her mother was Norman born and had taught all her children how to speak the language. Eada suddenly wished her mother had not educated her so well. She also wished that her mother had spared a little time to tell her what a Norman soldier looked like. A little knowledge might have made the men look less frightening. When the soldiers paused before her hiding place, Eada got a very close look and shivered.

All four mounted men wore tunics of mail, two with loose sleeves that reached only to their elbows and two with longer, more closely fitted sleeves. Three had mail leggings. With their mail hoods pulled over their heads and topped by metal helmets with a strip that jutted down over their noses, they made for an unsettling sight. Eada knew that the padded clothing they wore beneath their armor, the stallions they rode, and even the armor itself added a great deal to the impression of size, but she suspected they were still goodly sized men when stripped of all those trappings. If William the Bastard had a whole army of such well-armored giants, then Harold had little chance of defeating the Normans.

"Are there no women in this land?" complained Tancred.

"We look for food, Tancred," Drogo said, skillfully stilling the suddenly restless stallion he rode.

"Man does not live by bread alone."

"When you reach my age, a full belly grows more important than a rutting," Serle said. "A man will not die from the lack of a woman to plow."

"There are times when I think he can, Serle, old man." Tancred sighed dramatically. "My belly is full, and now my staff aches to be stroked."

"And yet the man sits a horse when in such a condition. Now there is bravery."

Men, Eada thought with disgust as the Normans laughed. *If they are not waving a sword about, eager to chop off heads, then they can only think of wielding their other weapon. If they cannot pierce a man's flesh with their steel, they seek to pierce a woman's flesh with their staff. In that, at least, it is evident that Normans do not differ at all from the men they seek to do battle with.*

"Your mount is most uneasy, Drogo," Tancred said, frowning as Drogo had to steady his horse again.

"He is," agreed Drogo. "Either the journey here has made him unusually restless or a dog lurks near at hand."

Eada tensed, her grip on her dogs' muzzles tightening slightly. She briefly wondered why hearing the deep voice of the man called Drogo should cause such an odd sensation to ripple through her. It felt like anticipation, but she told herself it had to be fear. When the men began to move on, she sighed with relief. The sigh caught sharply in her throat when she realized the direction the men were riding in. If the Normans veered neither left nor right, they would arrive at Old Edith's door.

For a moment Eada fought back the stomach-knotting panic that rushed over her. Old Edith would never try to fight the Normans, so there was no reason for them to harm her. The woman was also far too old to stir their lusts. Such assurances only dimmed Eada's fears a little, however, for she loved Old Edith too much to be so practical.

As she forced herself to be calm and hold onto enough of her wits to remain cautious, Eada slipped from her hiding place. She curtly signaled her dogs to be quiet as they joined her in following the men. The Normans were not traveling at any great speed, but Eada found that she had to maintain a steady trot to keep up with them. She also found it difficult to keep them in sight yet remain hidden from their view. Only once did she fear she had been seen. She quickly sought out a thicker shelter within the trees only to nearly lose the men for her fear of discovery made her very slow to take leave of that shelter and continue the chase.

"Something wrong?" Drogo asked Tancred when the man looked to their rear and lightly grasped the hilt of his sword. "Did you see something?"

"No," Tancred replied as he slowly relaxed. "I but had the feeling that we were being followed. There is nothing there. I think I have listened too much to Serle's talk of an enemy lurking all around us."

Serle quickly began to defend the wisdom of his warnings, and he and Tancred fell into an amiable brangle. Drogo could not cast aside his own uneasiness so quickly, and the lingering fretfulness of his mount only added to it. He continued to glance behind them for several moments. When he failed to see anything he forced his attention back to the route they traveled and his companions, sternly telling himself that he must not allow caution to become an unreasonable fear of every shadow.

Minutes later, a small, poor cottage came into view. Just as the Normans began to rein in their horses, an old woman hurried out of the cottage. Drogo tried to warn her to stop, but she dashed in front of them, waving her arms and shouting. He watched in horror as she fell beneath the hooves of the rearing warhorses despite all their efforts to calm the beasts. When the horses were finally steadied and Drogo began to dismount, his companions cautiously doing the same, the old woman lay still upon the ground. Her limbs were twisted into grotesque positions, and blood stained her rough gown.

"No," Eada moaned as she stepped free of her hiding place and watched her friend fall. "No," she repeated but screamed it this time, the small word becoming a long wail of grief.

Drogo and his men immediately drew their weapons only to gape at the slender girl running straight toward them. An instant later, they had to scramble to control their horses again for the two large hounds loping alongside the girl frightened them. Drogo cursed for neither the girl nor the hounds paid them any heed, running directly to the old woman's side.

After softly ordering the young Unwin to firmly secure the skittish horses, Drogo carefully approached the girl and sheathed his sword. He halted, then crouched when the hounds looked his way and bristled slightly. Once certain that the dogs would not attack if he gave them no reason to, he studied the girl, who wept over the dying old woman.

Despite the smudges of dirt and scratches on her face and the tears in her gown, Drogo found the girl beautiful. Her hair was the color of sweet honey and flowed in thick waves to her slim hips. Full, ripe breasts, heaving gently as she wept, made him painfully aware of how long it had been since he had held a woman. Her voice was low, husky with grief, and it stirred him although she spoke a language he found harsh. He watched in hungry fascination as a tear rolled down the ivory cheek of her small, heart-shaped face. Drogo had to grit his teeth to suppress the urge to kiss that tear away.

"Oh, Edith, why did you do something so mad?" Eada hesitated to touch Edith's broken body for, although she ached to do something, she was sure she would cause the woman untold pain if she tried to move her.

"I tried to stop fate," Edith replied, her voice little more than a hoarse whisper. "No, that is not the full truth. I but followed fate's path. This is what was meant to happen. I knew today would bring my death. Come, take hold of my hand, child."

"It will hurt you."

"I feel nothing. That is strange, is it not? I believe the chill of death steals away my pain." She smiled when Eada tentatively took her gnarled hand between her young, soft ones. "Now, heed me well, child. There is no time for arguments or explanations."

"You should not waste your strength in talking now."

"No? Silly girl. I cannot speak from the grave, can I? And that is where I go now. Your man is here, Eada of Pevensey. He crouches near at hand and stares at you."

"He murdered you." Eada fought the sudden, almost-overwhelming need to look at the man at her side.

"Bah, the poor fool was but God's tool. I leapt in front of a warhorse." Edith laughed, but it quickly became a rasping cough which brought the warmth of her own blood into her mouth. "Do not blame the man for this, child. He is no murderer of old women. I saw the look of horror on his face as I fell beneath his horse. Do not fight him, Eada, for he is your destiny. But, do not surrender too completely. Ah, but my Eada never would. You have such spirit, and wit. More than most men want in a woman."

"Edith, I cannot—"

"You can. You will fight it a little, but God's will cannot be changed. Just remember all I have told you on this day. Now, in my cottage in the large chest there rests a smaller one. Take it. Once I had a finer life, a man, and a child."

"Where are they?" Eada asked, wondering if Edith spoke the truth or had become lost in the delirium of approaching death.

"Close. God blessed me with a child when I was nearly too old to bear one; but with that precious gift He gave me the knowledge of things to come. Few people can bear that. I lost all—my man, my child, my home, and nearly my life. Take the box, child, and read the truth I have hidden within it. And take my other gift to you now as well, although you may well curse me tenfold for giving it to you."

Before Eada could ask the old woman what she meant, Edith gripped her hands with a strength that astonished her. She met Edith's steady gaze and was captured by it. The old woman's eyes seemed to grow larger until Eada felt lost in them. She began to feel light-headed, nauseated, but still could not free herself.

"Always think, Eada, but always follow your heart." Old Edith's voice pounded in Eada's mind. "And always remember this old woman who loved you."

"I could never forget you," Eada whispered, her voice choked with tears. As she bent to kiss Edith's cheek, she heard the breath of life flee the battered woman's body and her hands were abruptly freed.

Her hand shaking, Eada tenderly closed Edith's eyes. She felt painfully alone. In the course of but a few hours, her home had been lost to her, her family had fled to a place unknown to her, and Old Edith had died right before her eyes. Eada started to rise only to feel her legs weaken and her head swim.

When the Norman crouched by her side moved to catch her as she stumbled, she finally looked right at him. For one brief moment she was held captive by the dark eyes staring at her through the helmet, then rage filled her, pushing aside her pain and unsteadiness.

"Murderer," she cried and leapt at the man she saw as the cause of all her grief and confusion.

Even as Drogo reached out to try and catch hold of her, he thought wildly that her large lavender eyes were beautiful as they sparkled with fury and hate. When she slammed her body into his, he tumbled backwards and fell to the ground. He cursed when his helmet fell off and rolled out of his reach, but his full attention was swiftly captured by the furious woman who leapt upon him.

Eada got a firm grip on his sweat-dampened, thick hair beneath his loose mail hood. Cursing him with every breath, she repeatedly banged his head against the ground. Just as the pressure he was exerting on her wrists began to loosen her grip upon his hair, she felt strong arms encircle her and she was roughly pulled off of the man. The Norman who now held her did so in such a way that she could only flail uselessly with her feet.

A low snarl halted her indulgence in that fruitless activity. Eada saw that her hounds were ready to attack the man despite not being fighting dogs. A quick glance at the other men—including the one she had just attacked, who stumbled to his feet, rubbing and shaking his head—

revealed that they all had their swords drawn. They were ready to cut her pets down at the first hint of an attack.

"Call the dogs off, child," Serle growled in her ear, musing that she was a nice little bundle of female to hold. "They have fine, sharp teeth, but they will be dead before those teeth can cut through the mail we wear."

Although the man spoke to her in French, a language he could not know she would understand, Eada felt she could still obey his command without revealing her knowledge. It was clear what had to be done. "Ligulf. Ordway." She said the dogs' names in a sharp voice, and her pets grew still. "Good dogs. Easy now, lads." She breathed a sigh of relief when the dogs ceased to bristle.

Since she had grown still, the man holding her slowly released her. Her anger gone, she moved toward Edith, easily pushing aside the need to study the man Edith had said she was destined for. Although small, she was strong, and she picked up Edith's broken body with ease. Eada heaved a sigh of sadness when she realized that her old friend was little more than skin and bones. She entered the cottage, intending to prepare Edith for burial.

Drogo gaped after the girl then shook his head. He would never have believed that such a tiny woman could have the strength to carry even the frail old woman. Neither would he have expected such a tiny woman to attack him with such fury. One thought that did trouble him was the girl's presence at the cottage. His horse had acted like it had scented her dogs just outside of town and had continued to act that way all the way to the cottage. Drogo could not believe that the girl had followed them the whole way from Pevensey. Unable to answer his own questions, he shook his head again and forced his thoughts elsewhere.

"We must dig a grave for the old woman," Drogo told his men. "Tancred, you were trained to be a priest so you must know what needs to be said."

"Well enough," Tancred agreed reluctantly as Unwin and Serle moved to search out something to dig a grave with. "I will need a moment or two to recall it clearly."

"There is time," Drogo murmured as he watched the girl step from the cottage to fetch some water from a barrel.

Tancred smiled when he saw how Drogo watched the young woman's every graceful move until she disappeared back inside of the cottage and then drawled, "Was it not you who reminded me earlier that we search for food? You will leave the girl here, of course."

Drogo picked up his helmet and looked at the hounds. "Her beasts may remain here."

"Those animals will not desert her unless you cut their throats," Serle said as he strode back from behind the cottage.

"Serle, tell him what we have found," a pale Unwin urged the older man.

"Calm yourself, boy. There is no need to dig a grave, Drogo, nor to make a marker if I guess the meaning of these scratches correctly." Serle handed Drogo a small plaque of rough wood.

The training he had received during a few long years spent at a monastery gave Drogo the skill to read the scratches even though the words were somewhat strange. He felt superstition stir to life within him. "It says Edith of Chichester and this day's date," he whispered, fighting for calm.

"Sorcery," Unwin hissed, and he crossed himself.

Serle snorted in contempt. "I have known of many men who knew just before they rode off to battle that they were facing their last fight. Since those men were Christians, I can only assume that God must choose one person now and again to warn them that their time is nigh. I have never seen one this well prepared though."

"The foresight the old woman possessed may well be

why she lived alone, far from the village," Drogo mused aloud. "Such a thing can breed hate and fear. I wonder what the girl was to her?"

"Are you worried that she could bring you trouble when you take her with you?"

"And who said that I planned to take the girl, Serle?"

"The way you stare at her tells me. I began to fear that you would grab the girl ere the old woman had finished dying."

Drogo colored faintly. Serle's words crudely but accurately described what he felt. All that held him back was a distaste for taking an unwilling female. He had seen the tragic results of a man's brutal lust and, despite how badly he ached for the girl, he would wait. When she suddenly appeared in the doorway of the cottage holding the shroud-wrapped body of the old woman, he ruefully admitted to himself that such patience would be hard to grasp.

Serle walked over to the girl and held out his arms. "Let me carry the old woman, child. The ground is rough and you will not wish to drop her. So, too, can I place her more gently in her final bed." Not sure she understood him, Serle struggled to embue his rough voice with the meaning of his words and the kindness he intended.

After a brief moment of hesitation, Eada nodded and let him take Edith's body. She followed him as he strode to the readied grave. When Eada saw the plaque, she sighed. Edith had not lied. The woman had indeed known that her time was at an end. When one of the men began to murmur a prayer, Eada was grateful but wished that her dear friend could have had a sanctified priest and been laid to rest in holy ground. The woman had lived alone and now had to be buried alone. It seemed grossly unfair to Eada.

The Normans left her alone after the burial although she knew she was being closely watched. Eada busied herself piling rocks on the grave to protect the body from scavengers as well as more clearly mark the gravesite. She was only partly aware of the increasing noises around her.

When she finally turned from Edith's grave and looked toward the Normans, she scowled. Three of the men had stripped to their shirts and were chasing Edith's animals. The man she had attacked, the one the others called Drogo, stood by, still fully armed. He was watching her, however, and not being much of a guard. Finally, disgusted with the knights' inept attempts to collect up Edith's farm animals, Eada strode over to them. Standing by the pen, she put her hands on her hips and wondered where these men had sprung from. They knew nothing about the very animals who kept their tables weighted with food.

"Did you just pop out of the ground, oafs, that you know so little about the creatures that feed you?" she snapped in English as she strode into the middle of the men and pushed them aside. "Never have I seen such nonsense. You may be able to ply your swords with some skill, but I pray you have brought your servants with you. You will surely starve if it is left to fools such as yourselves to provide food."

"Do you think she means to try and stop us from gathering this food, Drogo?" Tancred asked as he backed away from the angry young woman.

"I think she insults you," Drogo replied.

"That much I knew, but does she do so because we do such a poor job or because she tries to keep us from taking anything?"

After watching the slender woman for a moment, Drogo answered, "Because you do such a poor job of it. Come, arm yourselves," he ordered the men. "I have seen no one, but that does not mean it is safe here."

"I will collect that pony and cart I saw," Unwin said as he hurriedly redonned his armor with Serle's help.

Eada leashed and caged the last of Edith's stock and

ed her gown. Torn and dirty
though it is, no pauper would own such a gown. Perhaps
you should think longer on what you plan to do."

Drogo did, but only for a moment, and then he
shrugged. "She is Saxon, the enemy."

"Her family might ride with William."

"Then why is she out here at this poor cottage? I am
taking her with me, Serle. I fear reason will not stop me."

Although Drogo smiled at Serle's curses, he ignored
them and strode into the cottage after the girl. He had
to bend to get through the low doorway, and it took a
moment for his eyes to adjust to the dimness inside the
cottage. The girl knelt by a chest, holding a smaller one
in her arms, and the look she sent his way was not a
welcoming one. He thought of the old woman they had
just buried and suddenly feared that he might never be
able to overcome the girl's anger.

Four

The huge chest Edith stored her few possessions in creaked loudly as Eada opened it. A small, ornately carved chest sat atop the old clothing and blankets inside. For a moment Eada was afraid, but she harshly scolded herself for her own foolishness. Despite that, she still shuddered as she picked up the small chest. She was almost glad when the Norman entered the cottage, distracting her, but she still glared at him. It was easy to blame him for all the turmoil she suffered.

Eada realized that she had already ceased to think of the large man as Old Edith's murderer. She knew in her heart that it had been just a horrible, tragic accident, but she still resented him. From the moment he and the rest of the Normans had set foot upon English soil, her life had been drastically changed. Her family was gone; her father was quite possibly doomed, and now Old Edith was dead.

Even worse than all of that, Eada decided crossly, was the fact that the man disturbed her. She could not stop herself from wondering what he looked like beneath his armor. Her anger and grief had prevented her from really looking at him during the brief time she had attacked him and he had lost his helmet. She found that she was intensely curious to see if he were as handsome as Old Edith had said he would be.

She quickly cursed herself for being a fool. It did not

matter if he were handsome. He could be as ugly as a toad. The man would take her whether she wanted him or not. He was a Norman, one of a large army that had landed in England with every intention of conquering it. If he chose to conquer her, too, there was not very much she could do about it. Eada decided she would simply not make it too easy for him. If it really were her destiny to belong to this tall Norman, then so be it; but she would ensure that he had to work hard for his prize.

"Well? What are you standing there for, you great fool?" she snapped.

Drogo decided that her language added a new sharpness to an insult; and although he did not understand her, he knew she was insulting him. If the tone of her voice had not told him so, the look on her pretty face would have. He crossed his arms over his chest and looked down at her, wondering idly why his desire should be so strongly roused by such a foul-tempered little female. Drogo then found himself wondering what he would feel if she smiled at him.

"You will come with us," he ordered and held out his hand.

She looked at his hand as if he waved something vile in her face, then stood up, still clutching the small box, and walked out the door. Drogo watched the sway of her slim hips and fought the urge to slap her attractive backside. He followed her out of the cottage, still uncertain if Serle were right when he had said the girl understood what they were saying.

When the Norman reached for her to set her on his horse, Eada neatly eluded his grasp. She hurriedly mounted the cart pony's back and wondered crossly how the fools had planned to get their stolen bounty back to Pevensey if they all rode their own horses. The stallions would never allow such a collection of noisy animals anywhere near them. Eada called softly to her hounds as she urged the pony forward. It angered her that Edith's animals would soon fill Norman bellies, but she suspected that her dear friend had known that as well.

Drogo glared at Serle when the man laughed then hurriedly mounted his horse. He was going to have to do something about the girl's impudence. Even now, something inside him told him that he would be keeping her close by his side for a long while. Many men would envy him her beauty, but they would also laugh heartily at a man who had so little control over his woman. The girl had clearly not been taught that man was the master of women.

"Er, Sir Drogo?" Unwin asked a little timidly as he rode up beside the older knight. "Do you take the girl, too?"

"Of course. She is my prisoner," Drogo drawled.

"Oh. I see. Your prisoner." Unwin's tone of voice made his doubts very clear.

"Yes, my prisoner. Do you not see how she quails before our manly strength? Do you not see how she rushes to obey my every command? Look closely, boy, and you will see how her slim back already begins to bow beneath the acceptance of her enslavement." He grinned at the young man, who quickly grinned back as he realized he was being soundly teased.

Eada bit back a laugh then scolded herself for softening so quickly. A sense of humor was compellingly attractive in a man, however. It had always been one of the things she had looked for in a person. She soon decided that the men's raillery grew unnecessarily crude and fought to keep her face averted, hiding her blushes. If the men saw how she colored, they would know that she could understand them, and she was not quite ready to give them that knowledge.

Just as they entered Pevensey, the four knights encircled her, even though their warhorses needed a great deal of convincing before they would draw near so many common animals. Eada wondered briefly if they made a show of bringing food and a prisoner but an instant later felt almost sorry for maligning them. It was clear to see that they had moved closer to protect her from the harsh consequences of being a young woman within reach of a seven-thousand-man army.

Her guardians quickly got rid of their horses, and Eada decided that had been a mistake. Four easily unsettled warhorses inspired far more caution than four well-armed men and two hounds which were not much inclined to bite anyone. She was just about to kick one particularly annoying man right in his leering face when everyone suddenly grew quiet. When the crowd of men slowly parted to allow one man and his small entourage to approach the cart, Eada instinctively knew that she was about to meet William the Bastard.

The man smiled faintly at Drogo and said, "When I saw such a crowd gathered, I thought you had brought us some fanciful beast, Drogo." He briefly glanced at Eada. "Although, when one considers the rarity of this particular creature at the moment, I suppose you have."

Eada carefully studied William as Drogo explained what had happened during his brief foraging sortie. The man who claimed the right to sit on the throne of England was not very impressive in appearance or stature, yet there was something deeply compelling about him. She could see the strength in him, a strength supported by wit, determination, and ambition. It saddened her to acknowledge that, but it was clear to her that William of Normandy could easily accomplish all he planned unless God decided to deny him the prize he sought. She was abruptly pulled from her musings about the red-haired Norman baron when Drogo picked her off the pony's back and set her down at his side.

"Amfrid," Drogo said to the nervous, bone-thin man

at William's side, "will you tell this girl that William of
Normandy is her new king?"

When Amfrid did as he was told, Eada looked at William and calmly said, "Not yet. Harold still holds the
throne. You, my lord, are still only a Norman lordling
standing on the edge of England looking in."

"What did she say, Amfrid?" William asked when the
man stared at Eada in openmouthed horror.

"It does not matter, my lord," Amfrid stuttered in reply.
"She is but some foolish girl."

"Amfrid, she is one of the people I intend to rule.
Now, tell me what she said."

His voice high and unsteady, Amfrid dutifully repeated
Eada's words. For a moment Eada feared that she had
indeed been a silly girl. William's face darkened and
Drogo looked torn, as if part of him wanted to hide her
and part of him wanted to beat her soundly. Then, to
Eada's surprise and the obvious astonishment of others,
William began to laugh.

"Ah, Drogo, my old friend, do not look so dismayed,"
William said. "She but spoke the truth. Ask her, Amfrid,
And when I do hold the throne? Go on, ask her. She speaks
the truth with no pretty dressing and I will hear it."

After Amfrid had carefully translated William's question, Eada replied quietly, "Then you will be my king and
I will kneel to you. I but ask that you forgive me if I weep
at your crowning." She waited for Amfrid to repeat her
words in French, then continued. "I am but a little
woman in a little town and will dutifully kneel to whomever sets the crown upon his head. I am Saxon, however;
and though I know none of the men of any consequence,
they, too, are Saxon which makes them my kinsmen in
blood and heritage. To gain all you seek, you must now
spill the blood of my kindred.

"Yes, I will honor the crown, especially since I have
heard it said that it was promised to you; but I will weep

for the loss of Saxon lives, for the loss of Saxon lands, and, I think, the loss of much else that is Saxon." She curtsied then walked back to the cart, not waiting to see how her words were accepted.

"I am sorry, my lord," Drogo finally said when he was able to shake free of his shock and dismay and speak coherently.

"Do not apologize for words that have come from the heart. They have even moved my dear friend Amfrid. That child neither insulted me nor threatened me. She simply and eloquently explained what she felt, and I can well understand those feelings. 'Tis rare to find one who can explain it so clearly and with neither anger nor bitterness."

William smiled suddenly and lightly slapped an uncertain Drogo on the back. "I think you may have captured yourself a troublesome bundle, my friend."

William's good humor eased some of the unease knotting Drogo's stomach, and he smiled faintly. "Most troublesome, but I intend to tame her."

"And watch her most closely," William said, quickly growing serious again. "As she so graciously told us, Drogo, she is Saxon and, until I am crowned, she will not see me as her king. She is small and very pretty, but that does not mean that she cannot be dangerous as well."

"I will not be blinded by her loveliness, my liege."

"Good. Now, have your men take a share of the bounty you have gained and then put the rest with the supplies."

Drogo bowed slightly then watched as William walked away to disappear into a crowd of men near the town well. From the moment he had set eyes on Eada, he had given little thought to the fact that she was Saxon, one of the enemy. He was not sure he appreciated William's reminding him of that fact. A hint of suspicion now stirred in his heart and he wished he could banish it.

As he looked toward Eada, he sternly told himself not

to be such a fool. He had invaded her land, taken hold of her town; and in the fighting that was sure to follow, he would undoubtedly take the lives of some of her people. It would be wise to hold onto some suspicion. He was responsible for other lives as well as his own, and he could not allow a pair of beautiful eyes to beguile him into ignoring any possible threat.

When he finally caught sight of Eada, he cursed softly. She stood flanked by her growling hounds and encircled by nearly a dozen leering men. Although she held her ground, glaring bravely at the men, it was a dangerous situation. As he pushed his way through the men to get to her side, he mused crossly that some of the trouble she would bring was the lust and envy of the men. He might well spend a great deal of his time trying to stop his fellow Normans from stealing her away.

The moment he reached Eada's side, he grabbed her by one slim arm and confronted the men. With a sweeping glare, he proclaimed Eada his and his alone. He knew that his belligerent stance at her side also announced that he was willing to back that claim with a sword or his fists. As soon as the soldiers began to back away, Drogo turned his attention to Eada, absently patting the hounds which had been ready to defend her.

"William is right," he murmured. "You will be trouble. If I keep you, it is akin to taking an enemy into the very heart of my camp; and now I see that I may well have to watch my companions-in-arms as closely as I watch you."

Eada looked at him, hoping her expression held the look of sweet ignorance she strove for. She resented the implication that she was not to be trusted, but could not reveal that without revealing that she understood every word he said. Although he was an invader, her enemy, she would never stoop to betrayal, deceit, or treachery. If she fought him, she would do so openly. She also knew that, even if she spoke to him in French with all the eloquence of a troubadour, he probably would not believe her.

She met his steady look and quelled a start of surprise. Behind the frowning concern and the faint hint of unwarranted suspicion was wanting. It was the same look she had seen in the other men's faces, yet not so harsh or alarming. Instead of fear, she felt her body warm with welcome.

Perhaps they were destined, she mused. It was the only explanation for responding favorably to a lustful look from a man who intended to fight her people and help conquer her country. She knew she was not the sort of woman to warm to a man simply because he was strong and handsome. There was the problem of his suspicion, however. If he feared she was the sort to slip a knife in his back or feed him to his enemies, their destiny would be difficult to fulfill. Eada knew he would bed her without hesitation, but she was confident that Edith's prophecy was not for her to be a mere leman, one of the many poor, bedraggled souls who often trailed along behind an army. Old Edith had promised her a soulmate. Eada wondered just how hard she might have to work to gain that prize.

A group of men awkwardly shepherding a small flock of sheep down the road caught Eada's attention and she cursed. "And where might they be taking them?"

The way she was glaring at the sheep gave Drogo a hint of what she had just said and he replied, "We need to feed the men." He pointed at the sheep and rubbed his flat stomach in an awkward attempt to make her understand.

"If you feed your soldiers too well this late in the year, you will face a long, hungry winter, fool."

Drogo shook his head. Her tone was cold, angry, but he had no idea what she had just said. He was either going to have to learn her coarse language or teach her French. Although what she had said to William had disturbed him,

it revealed a sharp mind, and he realized he wanted to
enjoy that almost as badly as he wanted to bed her.

"Tancred," he called to his friend as he shook aside
the confusion he felt over his strong, unwavering attrac-
tion to the slight woman at his side. "Stay and guard this
bounty of ours for a moment or two. I will send Ivo to
you so that he might choose what we require. The rest
must then be placed with the other supplies."

"Since the beasts are all tethered, I think I can do it,"
Tancred drawled, and then he looked at Eada. "And I
think you had best hide away your own bounty. The men
eye her with more greed than they eye the food."

"They understand that she is mine."

"Oh, they understand that. You made it very clear. That
does not mean that they will now all stay away. Some of
them might think to challenge you, especially if you continue to dangle the prize in front of their eyes."

"I do not fear them nor will I turn away from a fight."

"I know that. No insult was meant. William, however,
might prefer that his soldiers save their strength for the
battle with the English."

While Drogo laughed along with his companions, Eada
rolled her eyes. The men had probably earned the arrogance they now displayed, but that did not make it any
less irritating. Eada also knew that, no matter how much
she might resent it, she was going to need their protection. One glance at the thousands of Normans and mercenaries swarming over Pevensey verified that. Even if
Drogo were not the one Old Edith had claimed as her
destined mate, Eada suspected she would have accepted
his claim to her anyway. From what little she had seen so
far, Drogo seemed to be a good, honorable man. Far better to be the leman of one good man than a whore to
the whole of the invading army.

"I wonder which one of these dogs has laid claim to my
home?" she murmured as she looked around, trying to

see if anyone walked toward her house. "It would be nice if I could at least get a clean gown." She patted her dogs, glancing up at Drogo and catching him staring at her.

"It would be better if we spoke the same tongue," Drogo said.

Eada wondered if he were trying to trick her into confessing that she knew French. It would make some things much easier if they could talk openly. She was also not confident that she could maintain her air of ignorance for very long. For the moment, however, it gave her a small advantage and she intended to cling tightly to that for as long as she could.

"And since I know exactly what he will ask of me, I see no need for words or any great understanding between us." She could tell by the frown upon his face that he recognized the bitter tone behind her words. He had a keen ear and that could prove to be troublesome.

"I will not hurt you."

After glancing around to make sure that the English-speaking Amfrid was not close by, Eada decided to answer Drogo directly. He could not understand her words or know that she understood his if she guarded her expression. "You mean to make me your leman, your whore. If Old Edith was right and you are my destiny, it is certain that you do not know it. You are but acting like any warrior who sees what he wants and just takes it."

Drogo shook his head. "I wish I could understand you or that you could speak my language. There is anger in your voice and, unless I can reason with you, I cannot soothe it. Nor can I still the fear you must feel despite your brave stance."

She looked at the Normans casually plundering the town and noticed how few of her fellow Saxons she saw. "Even if we spoke in the same tongue, nothing you could say could fully banish my anger, my sense of hopelessness, or my fear. You have come to conquer and, though we are destined to be mates, in doing that you must hurt me. And even if I spoke in the most eloquent French, I do not think you could ever understand how I feel about all of this."

When she tried to pull free of his grasp, he gently tightened his grip on her arm. "No, you will stay with me."

Still pulling against his hold, Eada pointed toward the cart. "I must get the chest Old Edith gave me."

Eada breathed a silent sigh of relief when he eased his hold enough to allow her to pull him along as she went to the cart. It dismayed her a little that she had almost forgotten about the gift Old Edith had left her. She quickly soothed her pangs of guilt by reminding herself of all she had endured since waking that morning.

A shiver of unease tickled her spine as she picked up the chest. Old Edith had said that it held the truth. Eada decided she had had her fill of Old Edith's truths. So far, they had brought only confusion and sorrow. As she clutched the small, ornate chest in her arms, she decided that this particular truth could wait. She needed time to muster up the courage to look at it.

"You have not opened it," Drogo murmured. "I did not see you do so in the cottage and I am sure you have not tried to since then. Are you not curious about what she gave you? Or, mayhap, what you have stolen?"

It was hard not to respond to the accusation that she had helped herself to the possessions of a dead woman. Eada found that deeply insulting. If he made too many remarks like that, she was certainly not going to keep her knowledge of French secret for long. Such insults demanded a quick, angry reply.

Her thoughts on how she might vent her anger were abruptly ended when Drogo reached for the chest. "Do not touch it," she snapped, holding it out of his reach. "It is mine."

Drogo was surprised at the vehemence of her response.

He was also dismayed by her continuing utter lack of submissiveness. Although he did not wish to have her terrified of him or completely defeated in spirit, a little deference would be better. It would strengthen his claim to her in the eyes of the other men.

"I think you forget that you are a prisoner," he said, wishing she could understand him. "Nothing is yours alone any longer."

"*This* is mine. There is nothing in this of value or of interest to you. Old Edith granted me this with her last breath, and no French knight will lay his hands upon it."

The old woman's name was all Drogo recognized out of the softly hissed barrage of words. It was enough to make him step back, however. The old woman had clearly left the girl some meager inheritance, and he would honor that. He would find some other way to assert his authority over her.

"Come," he ordered as he took her by the arm and started toward the house he had claimed.

Eada hurried to keep pace with his long strides. She was uncomfortably aware of how tall he was, and how strong, as she was pulled along by his side. Destiny had chosen a great deal of man for her.

All of her concern over his size, strength, and how she might be able to resist complete domination by him fled her mind as she realized which house they were striding toward. She had to nip the inside of her cheek to keep from gaping. The tall Norman who planned to conquer her as well as her country was leading her to the door of her own home. Eada decided that the fates which had chosen him for her had a perverse sense of humor.

Five

As Eada stood in the great hall of her home, the first thing she was aware of was how thoroughly her mother had emptied the house of all that was of value. She was certain the Normans would not have hidden away such treasures as the pewter goblets or the silver platter, but they were not anywhere to be seen. Eada prayed that her mother had been successful in getting their valuables to a safe place. There would be a real need for such things when England's fate was finally decided. She just wished she had some way of discovering where that haven was.

"Ivo, go and collect our share of the bounty we found," Drogo ordered his servant.

Eada looked at the big, dark man Drogo spoke to and frowned when she saw the thin, dark-haired girl who huddled close by his side. She moved quickly and caught the girl by the arm when she tried to leave with Ivo. Ivo turned and stared at her, his look so fierce that Eada almost stepped back.

"Ivo," Drogo said, placing a gentle but restraining hand on his servant's shoulder. "This woman is Saxon. She will not hurt the girl. I swear this. I think it is also wise if the girl does not venture outside."

Ivo nodded, and after one last look Eada's way, he left. Eada breathed a sigh of relief and looked at the faintly trembling girl. "What is your name?"

"May."

"I am Eada. Whom did you belong to, May? I see that you are a bond-slave."

"I was held by Eldrid, son of Hacon."

"You poor girl," she murmured in honest sympathy, for those men were well known as brutes. "I can see that the swine beat you often." When the girl relaxed, her trembling fading away, Eada eased her hold on her.

"I was beaten because I wept when Eldrid raped me, and then his wife beat me because he kept lying down with me."

"May he rot in hell. And he left you behind when he fled?"

"No. He and his family tried to gather up all they owned when they saw the Normans, but they were too greedy and did not leave in time. When the Normans began to take their things, Eldrid's wife stuck a knife in one of them, and then the Normans killed them all."

"But not you? Where were you?"

"I was hiding in the wagon, but they soon found me. One man struck me, and then Ivo came. There were four men there; but Ivo beat them, and then he claimed me."

"He was kind to save you, but do you wish to stay with Ivo?" Eada was not sure if she could do anything to help the girl, but she would try if May was desperately afraid or unhappy.

"I think Ivo is slow-witted, but he is a good man. I think he is also a freeman, and that too is good. He wants to keep me and he is gentle with me. It might be foolish to push him away or try to leave." May shrugged, a faint wince marring her thin face as the gesture pained her back. "In truth, I like him."

Eada smiled faintly and kissed May on the cheek, her smile widening when the girl stared at her in open-mouthed shock. "Then you must stay with him, May. I fear we are all no more than loot or bounty at the moment, free for the taking. If we are fortunate enough to be claimed by a good, gentle man—and I think we have been—then it would be best to try and make him want to hold fast to us." Eada wondered briefly if she would have the wisdom to heed the good advice she was giving May.

"You, women," called Drogo as he moved toward the table. "Come and help me shed this armor." He sighed with frustration when both women stared blankly at him and then tried to signal his wishes to them.

"I fear I cannot understand their speech, mistress," May whispered, a meek, apologetic tone to her timid voice.

"The fool wishes us to help him take off his armor," Eada explained.

"You can speak their tongue?"

"Yes, but I do not feel like telling them so. Not just yet." Laughter shook her voice as she watched Drogo struggle to let them know what he wanted by acting it out. "I believe I have let the poor fool stumble about for long enough. Come, May, let us help him ere he injures himself."

Drogo muttered his relief and gratitude as each piece of his armor was removed. When Eada felt the weight of his mail, she was not surprised that he had been so eager to get it off. She carefully set it down on one of the chests which lined the west wall of the great hall. The armor he wore interested her less and less, however, as the man beneath became clear to see.

He was still big, even after she and May had helped him remove the thick, padded tunic he wore beneath his mail. Even when he was finally seated on the bench at the head table wearing only his linen tunic, he still possessed the broadest shoulders Eada had ever seen. He was lean, but his dark skin was stretched tautly over hard muscle.

Inwardly deciding that his body was the finest she had

ever seen, Eada looked at his face and silently sighed. For
a man, he had almost-beautiful eyes; and she now understood why, every time he had looked her way, those eyes
had caught and firmly held her attention. They were
nicely spaced and set beneath finely drawn, slightly arced
brows and encircled with thick lashes. Of a brown so dark
they were almost black, his eyes exerted an almost frightening pull on her. She had to tear her gaze away to look
closely at the rest of his face. A strong, straight nose cut
its way down through high, wide cheekbones to a firm
yet slightly full mouth.

"If Edith saw this face upon the man she knew I was
destined for, it is no wonder that she was certain I would
accept him," Eada mused.

Her only complaint about him was his hair. It was a
rich, glossy black, thick and wavy. It was also cut in a way
that made her wince. Eada decided it looked as if someone had stuck a bowl over his head, cut around the rim,
then taken the bowl away and brutally shaved off the
whole back of his head. She much preferred the long,
proudly displayed hair of Saxon men and wondered how
long it would take Drogo's hair to grow back.

"He looks like a badly shorn lamb," Eada muttered,
and May giggled.

Drogo looked at the two grinning women and knew he
had been insulted again, but he decided to ignore it. After a rough, dirty passage across the water and a long day
spent in full armor, he had a need far more pressing than
scolding Eada for her continued impertinence. He repeated the word bath as he struggled to mime the act of
washing.

"If I did not hear him call for a bath, I would think
he suffered the curse of fleas," Eada said, and she
grinned when May laughed. "Ah, and that gives me an
idea."

Eada smiled sweetly at Drogo and nodded, then hur-

ried into the kitchen at the far end of the hall. Her
mother had not taken any of her herbs and potions, and
Eada quickly found the medicine she sought. She put
some of the dark, strong-smelling paste in a small wooden
bowl and, walking to where Drogo sat expectantly, solemnly placed it on the table in front of him.

Drogo scowled at the dark muck in the bowl, cautiously
sniffed it, coughed, and then cursed softly. *"Merde!* I know
what this foul brew is for. It is a cure for vermin. I have
never been afflicted by them. I want a bath, woman, or,
by God's merciful eyes, I might soon suffer that curse."

His obvious inclination toward cleanliness pleased
Eada, but she played dumb for a little longer. Finally,
acting as if she suddenly understood his gestures, she mo-
tioned for him to follow her. She led him to a lean-to off
the kitchen, even more pleased when he showed great
delight in the bathing room her family had been so proud
of despite the gentle ridicule of their friends.

As he looked around the room, Drogo murmured his
surprised pleasure. The lean-to enclosed a well, and a
long wooden tub stood to one side. There was a drain in
the masonary floor to aid in the emptying of the tub. So,
too, was there a brazier to warm the room. Since it was
next to the kitchen, filling the tub with heated water
would not be difficult. He touched the tub and nodded,
a broad smile on his face.

By the time Eada brought in the first pot of hot water,
Drogo's impatience was evident. He had already put some
water from the well into the tub and was clearly in a hurry
to scrub away days of sweat and dirt. Eada gasped when,
as she poured the hot water into the tub, he flung off
the last of his clothes.

Eada had seen men naked before, but she quickly decided that she had never seen quite so much naked man.
Drogo was dark all over, lean and finely honed. A neat
triangle of tight black curls adorned his broad chest, ta-

pering into a thin line that went down his rippled stomach to his groin, where it thickened again. A light coating of hair covered his long, well-formed legs. When she realized that staring at him was clouding her mind with wanton thoughts, she glared at him. She hurriedly emptied the last of the water into the tub, refilled her cauldron at the well, and stomped out of the room.

It was not easy, but Drogo swallowed the laughter trembling in his throat. The way Eada had looked him over had pleased him, for the appreciation he had read on her face meant that his attentions might be welcomed. It had also aroused him, and it had taken every drop of his willpower to subdue any blatant response by his body. The way she had suddenly glared at him, however, as if her interest in him were all his fault, was highly amusing.

When Eada walked past May, who was taking the man even more hot water, she briefly thought about warning the girl, then shrugged away the thought. May would not be shocked by the sight of a naked man. Her confidence wavered badly when, a few minutes later, May dashed back into the kitchen looking very flustered. Eada realized that she loathed the idea that Drogo might have acted lustfully toward the girl; and the fact that May was a young, timid, much-abused girl had little to do with it.

"Did Drogo touch you?" Eada demanded as May hung her refilled pot over the kitchen fire to heat the water.

"No, mistress. I fear I was shocked, for I have never seen such a man. My master and his friends never looked like that. I swear, all the man did was touch this pot and say what I assume was *more hot water.* I think he wants to be sure that we understand him."

When Eada carried yet another pot of water into Drogo, she was severely tempted to pour it over his head as he lolled in her tub. He held out the soap and signaled that she should scrub his back. She struggled against the urge to hit him over the head with the pot then sighed. Courtesy

demanded that she assist him. He was not insulting her
with his request. Eada was very unsettled, however, to be
caught washing his broad, smooth back by his fully armed
comrades who suddenly appeared in the doorway. She
prayed that they had not seen the appreciation she felt as
she touched Drogo reflected in her face.

"Here is comfort," Tancred drawled as he stepped into
the room and looked around.

"Come and make use of it," Drogo called, waving his
friends inside.

How generous of him, Eada thought crossly. *He does not
have to heat all the water.*

"I had best be the last to bathe, my friend," Serle said,
and he smiled crookedly as he and the others began to
remove their armor. "I believe my companion on the
boat has gifted me with a few of his livestock."

The way Serle scratched told Eada what he suffered
from. She knew she could act as if she understood his
gestures and not reveal her understanding of what he
had said. As she hurried to fetch her mother's medicine,
she decided she was willing to risk discovery if it kept
such vermin away.

"Now, here you are, Serle," Drogo said with a hint of
a laugh when Eada returned with the bowl she had pre-
sented to him earlier. "The girl intends to physic you for
that curse."

"It is a foul-smelling potion," Serle grumbled as Eada
rubbed it into his hair.

Eada tugged off Serle's tunic and rubbed the thick
medicine into the hair on his chest and beneath his arms.
There was one other place where fleas were sure to nest,
but Eada decided that courtesy only went so far. She ignored the men's laughter as she lightly tugged on Serle's
braies and then set the bowl in his hands. Forcing herself
not to blush, she refilled her cauldron and left the room.

For what felt like hours, Eada and May heated water,

added it to the tub, and scrubbed backs. When Ivo returned, he was quick to come to their aid; but then he,
too, succumbed to the temptation of a hot bath in a tub
that was big enough to hold a man of his great stature.
By the time all the men were clean and their clothes
scrubbed, Eada was exhausted. She slumped on the rough
bench in the corner of the room and smiled faintly at
May, who was washing out the tub.

"Now it is your turn, mistress," May said.

"You must be heartily sick of fetching water." Eada desperately wanted a bath, but was reluctant to ask May to
do any more work.

"Not so sick of it that I cannot do it for you. And if I
might use the water when you are done, I should like to
bathe as well." When Eada nodded, May picked up the
bowl of ill-smelling lotion Eada had smeared on Serle and
asked softly, "Does this work?"

"It does. Let me fetch you some clean clothes, and
then I will help you rub it into your hair."

After her bath, Eada felt in a more charitable mood.
She sat with May near the kitchen fire. They took turns
brushing each other's hair as it dried and watched Ivo
prepare the evening meal. It had taken a lot of cajoling
to get May to wear one of Averil's gowns, but Eada could
easily see how pleased the girl was. She just hoped she
would be allowed to sit quietly with May and not have to
deal with Drogo for a while. There had been no time to
think since she had been captured, and she sorely needed
to do some hard, clear thinking.

Drogo frowned and glanced around as Ivo set the
roasted lamb on the table. "Has that woman finished her
bath yet?"

"Yes," Ivo replied. "She is done. She and May are dry-
ing their hair."

"Well, tell her that she is to come here and eat with us."

"Er, Drogo?" Tancred said as Ivo strode away. "Are you certain the girl is one who will know how to dine at a high table?"

"More certain with each moment," Drogo replied. "In truth, I begin to think this is her home."

"What makes you think so?"

"She knows where everything is and she took clothes for herself as if it were her right. I will not be surprised if those clothes fit her perfectly."

"She is too young to hold such a house," Serle said. "There must be others in her family."

"I am certain there are," agreed Drogo. "Somehow they fled without her." He looked toward the kitchen and murmured, "I also begin to think that you are right about her understanding French, the question now is—how can I be certain of it unless she tells me so? There is a puzzle."

When Ivo returned to the kitchen only to stand and stare at her, Eada realized he was trying to think of how to tell her something. She was just deciding that she would not play the game of not understanding French for too long, at least not with him, when he picked her up, tucking her under one big arm like a sack. He strode out to the hall, set her down on the bench next to Drogo, and pushed a wooden plate in front of her.

"Eat," Ivo ordered as he filled a wooden goblet with wine.

"Ivo," Drogo said, his deep voice choked with laughter. "I told you to tell her to come, not to fetch her here."

"I do not speak Saxon." Ivo shrugged and returned to the kitchen.

Eada briefly wished she had four goblets of wine within reach so that she could pour one over the head of each guffawing male. Instead, she decided to ignore them and helped herself to some of the lamb, bread, and carrots.

Her snubbing of the men lasted only until a fifth man suddenly appeared in the doorway that led to the sleeping quarters. Eada wondered crossly just how many Normans had invaded her home.

"Garnier," Drogo called out in welcome. "Have you recovered then? I can see that you have bathed."

As he smoothed his hand over the clean grey tunic he wore, Garnier approached the table and smiled sheepishly. "Ivo and some female scrubbed me while I lay abed as weak as a babe." He nodded toward Eada, a question lighting his dark hazel eyes. "It was not that one, for I would remember."

"It was Ivo's woman, May," replied Drogo, and then he patted Eada on the head. "I found this pretty little piece myself."

Beneath his hand, Drogo felt Eada tense, and he wondered if he had found the way to force her to reveal her knowledge of French. She had already revealed that she had a temper and an ample amount of pride. If he goaded her hard enough, she would break. As he invited Garnier to join them, Drogo decided he would keep prodding her temper and pride until she lost control. It would be enjoyable to return a few of the insults he knew she had hurled at his head, and if she truly did not understand French, no harm would be done.

"She is most fair," Garnier agreed as he sat down across the table from Drogo. "I had not realized that Saxons could breed such beauty."

"Hair like warm, sweet honey," Drogo said, stroking her hair. When she hissed and slapped his hand away, he added, "And a temper like soured wine."

"What is her name?"

"Now that you ask, Garnier, I realize that I have not yet discovered it." He looked at Eada, saw the anger glittering in her eyes, and felt certain that his plan was working. "What is your name?" Pointing to each man, starting with himself, he said, "Drogo, Garnier, Unwin, Tancred, Serle—and you are?"

"Eada," she replied, struggling and failing to keep all her anger out of her voice.

"Eada, hmmm?" He frowned and shook his head as he pushed his empty plate aside and sipped his wine. "One of those strange Saxon names. Saxons do not know how to properly name their women." He sighed and saw by the sudden widening of Serle's eyes that the older man had guessed his game. "I suppose one can expect no better from such a harsh tongue."

Eada was concentrating on her food, and Drogo winked at his friends. Their swiftly hidden smiles told him that they understood as well. There was only one thing Drogo regretted about what he was doing. If Eada did understand him, his little game would undoubtedly make his wait for her a very long one unless he was extremely clever in his explanations and suitably contrite in his apologies.

"You do not think William shall make us learn the language, do you?" asked Tancred, his expression one of well-feigned horror.

"God's teeth, I pray not," Drogo replied. "It sounds too much like grunting or a heavy clearing of the throat. Most unpleasant to the ear."

As they continued to malign the Saxon tongue, Eada fought valiantly to control her temper. She thought nastily that her speech was better than theirs, for they all sounded as if they spoke through their noses. It would also prove difficult for them to rule England if they scorned the language of its people; and that, she decided, would be justice. As the wine continued to flow, the talk turned to her; and Eada wished she had not lingered in the hall but had fled to her room the moment she had finished her meal. So personal were their remarks, Eada was not sure she could control the fury building inside her.

"We shall be well served if England holds more such beauties," Tancred said.

"Just pray that their tongues and temper are sweeter than this one's," Drogo replied.

"I am not concerned with what they *say.*"

Drogo laughed. "Nor I, when the candle is snuffed. Although with a piece as fine as this, I would miss much if I but rutted in the dark."

"I thought prisoners were supposed to be made to tell you the secrets of the enemy," Unwin said, a wide grin brightening his beardless face.

"Well, boy, mayhap if I pump hard enough at one end, words will pop out the other." Drogo laughed heartily with his friends, his amusement growing when he heard Eada grinding her teeth. "Ah, but usually all that the women cry is *More, Drogo, more.*"

"How he boasts!" Tancred hooted with laughter. "This one will no doubt scream *less, less.*"

"I think not, my friend." Drogo patted Eada's leg. "Once I spread these pretty thighs and fill her, she will grow sweeter."

Eada's control snapped and she flung herself at Drogo, yelling in French, "Norman swine, I will break your fat head!"

"Look out, Drogo!" Tancred cried, but his warning came too late.

When Eada slammed into him, Drogo tumbled back off the bench onto the hard floor. He knew what she would do next, but was a breath too late to stop her. As her small hands painfully gripped his hair and she began to bang his head against the floor, he cursed and grabbed her wrists. Careful not to press so hard he would break her delicate bones, he started to exert enough strength to break her hold on him.

When the force of his hold caused her to loosen her grip, Eada was angered more. A big, strong arm suddenly encircled her waist and she was yanked off Drogo. She hurled curses at Drogo as a frowning Ivo carried her to her bedchamber, a wide eyed May hurrying ahead of them to show him the way. Eada's curses only stopped when Ivo dropped her on her bed so abruptly the breath was pushed from her body. By the time she caught her breath, Ivo was gone and only a wary May remained.

"I should have broken that Norman dog's head," Eada hissed.

"You spoke to him in his own tongue," May said.

"I know it," Eada snapped, and she indulged in a brief tantrum, pounding her fists and heels on the bed. "That bastard tricked me." She sighed as she gained control of her wild emotions and sat up. "Those men spoke of me as if I were some baseless whore. I see now that it was all a game. Drogo meant to enrage me and make me reveal that I could understand him. I fell into that snare like a blind hare."

"So now you must speak to him."

"I think I shall not speak to that oaf for at least a week."

"M'lady, he intends to bed down here with you. See, there sits his chest."

"How did he know where to put it?"

"I believe he but chose the best chamber for himself." May frowned as she looked around the room. "Did your parents not use this chamber?"

"Mother did not like to sleep in this big bed when Father was away, so we would change rooms until he returned. Well, I think I will ready myself for bed," she said, as she stood up and May hurried to help her. "Mayhap I should just sleep in one of the other rooms."

"All the beds have been claimed, m'lady. That youth Unwin was offered the last one just before the meal was served."

"So, my home is full to bursting with cursed Normans,

and if the weather turns poor, there will undoubtedly be more to come." Eada shook her head. "These men are careful, but others might not be; and Mother worked so hard to make her home a fine one. Ah, well, there are more important matters to worry about, such as staying alive. It will not be this peaceful for long."

"M'lady?" May asked as Eada slid into her thin night rail and crawled into bed. "Do you know what that man Drogo will want from you?"

"I am not that ignorant, May," Eada replied. "I know."

"If you wish, I could take your place in this bed. With the candle snuffed, he would never know the difference. My maidenhead was torn from me but days after my first flux, so it would matter little to me."

It was a clever idea and would probably have gained her at least one night's respite, but Eada found that she could not agree to it. What troubled her was that her refusal was not fully born of a distaste for using May in such a way. She simply loathed the thought of Drogo bedding down with the comely brunette. Although she dreaded the idea of being no more than the man's leman, she did not want another woman to take her place.

"No, May. I wish I could say I refuse your gallant offer all for your sake, but I fear do not." She looked at the small box she had earlier had May set on the table by her bed, then reached out to cautiously touch Old Edith's gift. "I also refuse because, although I do not wish to be used by any man, I do not wish this man to use another. The woman who gave me this told me that Drogo was the mate I have waited for, and even though I tried to fight that truth, I fear she was right." She smiled at May. "I also think that your very large protector would not like it either."

"No, I do not think so either. M'lady, what is in that chest? If it holds valuable things, mayhap I should hide it away."

"I do not know what rests inside. Strange, but I feel most wary of looking. Old Edith told me it held the truth, but I think I am too weary of her truths to face another at this time." Eada snuggled down beneath the covers. "I believe I will go to sleep now. Let that big fool find only a limp body at his side. And who can say? Mayhap I have made his head throb so badly it will kill his lusts."

Six

"Drogo, are you all right?" Tancred asked, but his laughter tainted his obvious concern.

As he slowly sat up, Drogo rubbed his aching head and smiled ruefully at his laughing friends. "I shall have to break her of that little habit. You were right, Serle; she does understand French."

"And speaks it," Serle replied as Drogo stood up and brushed himself off.

"Most colorfully. What is that?" Drogo tensed when he heard a soft scratching at the heavy oak door then relaxed when it was followed by barking. "Eada's dogs. They left us at the door when we returned here. I am glad that they are safe. Someone could have easily thought them dangerous and slain the beasts." Ivo returned to the hall just as Drogo opened the door, and the two wolfhounds trotted in. "Here, my big friend, this should please you."

Drogo smiled at the delight that shone in Ivo's face. The man had wept like a small child over the pets he had been forced to leave behind in France. As all animals did, the dogs went to Ivo without hesitation. Drogo bolted the heavy door and returned to his seat at the table.

"Why do you linger in the hall with us?" Tancred asked in surprise as Drogo poured himself some wine. "I would have thought you would be eager to seek your bed—your nicely full and warm bed."

"I believe it will be a most chilled bed for me tonight," Drogo said.

"Oh, yes. Perhaps. Howbeit, I think she is clever enough to have guessed by now that you only played a game."

"That knowledge will not really soothe her temper."

"No, mayhap not." Tancred laughed and shook his head. "She has a strange manner of attack for a woman."

"Yes, although I prefer it to scratching nails and biting. I think she must have had an unusual childhood. Although I have fought the idea, I grow more certain that she followed us from just beyond the village to that old woman's cottage. Throughout the journey there, Faramond acted as if he scented dogs."

"And you, too, felt as if someone followed us, Tancred," Unwin said.

"I did," agreed Tancred, but he shook his head. "The girl would have had to trot or run all the way and stay out of sight."

"The dogs were panting," Serle murmured.

"The only way you can be certain is to ask her," Garnier said.

"True," agreed Drogo. "Howbeit, tonight I think what little she might have to say to me is not something I truly wish to hear." He grinned when his friends laughed. "I may come to regret that she can speak French."

"Mayhap you should make sure that she has no weapons," Unwin suggested, the expression on his face one of grave concern.

"There is no need," said Serle.

"You sound most certain of that, old friend." Drogo frowned in curiosity.

"I am. That girl will never strike out so unless her very life is threatened." He reached across the table and picked up a small dagger next to Eada's plate. "This is more than an eating knife. She had it on her and has probably had it on her the whole time she has been with us. Tell me, Drogo, why it does not now rest in your flesh."

Drogo took the dagger and studied the ornately carved handle. "This is no peasant's knife."

"Neither is this the home of a poor man."

"No. He may not be a lord, but he has a full purse."

"Her gown was no peasant's shift, either."

"Serle, I have seen all this for myself."

"She speaks French."

"Serle," Drogo repeated, a touch of steel hardening his deep voice. "Cease this tedious game and just say what rests so heavily on your mind."

"You have grabbed yourself a high-born maid, Drogo. I ask again that you think well on what you are planning to do."

"And I tell you again that reason and thinking carry little weight in this matter. I have tried it; but there is a part of me which throbs so badly with wanting, it drowns out the voice of caution. She is trouble—beautiful, tempting trouble. I know this. I simply cannot bring myself to care."

"Then can you not care for her fate?" Serle asked quietly.

"I do. Yes, I know many would say that what I plan for her will dishonor her. Yet which is worse? The same fate would greet her outside these walls if I set her free, mayhap even worse. She was trapped within the heart of the enemy. I will at least be kind to her and keep her safe."

"Safe? You intend to take her with you while you battle your way across England to London. How can you promise to keep her safe?"

"Why do you argue with me about this?"

Serle shrugged. "Although I am a man and can understand why you hunger for her, I am also old enough to see her as a child. Something prods me to try and make

you turn away from what you plan. If you do not, have
no fear that I will plague you with each step we march.
Once you have made your decision, I will stand by it and
aid you in keeping whatever promises you make."

"I have made my decision, old friend. I made it the
moment I set eyes on her."

Drogo saw May return and silently hurry to Ivo's side.
With a nod to his friends, who did not look certain about
his actions, Drogo rose and went to the bedchamber he
had chosen. He had little hope of gaining the prize he
ached for tonight, but he still looked forward to simply
sharing the bed with her. He prayed that Eada was in the
bed where she belonged and would not force him to hunt
her down.

The room was dark when he entered. Awkwardly, yet
quietly, he found and lit the candle near the bed. He was
relieved to see Eada curled up beneath the covers, for he
was weary and had no wish to chase her down. It only
disappointed him a little to see that she was asleep. He
would not be able to begin the seduction he had planned,
but he would be saved her anger for a little while. Drogo
knew that the weariness now weighting his body would
let him sleep despite the unsatisfied desire knotting his
insides.

He shed his clothes, letting them lie where they fell,
and eased his body beneath the coverlet. It took only a
moment before he decided he had grossly overestimated
the strength of his weariness. The strength of his desire
was far greater. The mere scent of her was enough to
tighten his loins. He was painfully eager for her and she
was much too near to ignore.

Turning onto his side, he reached out to stroke her
hair, savoring the soft, silken feel of it beneath his fingers.
He admired the slim line of her back and fought against
the urge to strip the covers away and look his fill. Drogo
knew it was not only a lengthy celibacy that made his

desire for her so strong. That only made control a little more difficult to grasp. Eada of Pevensey alone fed his passion until he felt bloated with it.

Drogo slipped his arm around her tiny waist, grimacing when she murmured in her sleep and cuddled closer to his warmth. His body's reaction was immediate and powerful. He found himself briefly, but heartily, regretting that he was not the sort of man who could just take what he ached for without a thought for the woman's feelings.

There was trouble ahead, and Drogo knew it. The war had not yet begun, but it could not be averted. He was in England to fight the Saxons; he would undoubtedly kill Saxons, and Eada was a Saxon. Wisdom demanded that he not allow himself to trust her fully, and it told him that what lay ahead could easily cause her to hate him. Every instinct told him it would be for the best if he just took what he ached for and left her behind when the army moved on.

He sighed then cursed as she sleepily wriggled even closer. It was going to be a long, uncomfortable, and sleepless night. Even more distressing was the knowledge that he would ignore all wisdom, all good sense and instinct, and do his utmost to keep her as close to him as she was now.

"No, no. Edith! Oh, Edith," Eada muttered as she fought the harsh memory of her friend's death which disturbed her dreams.

Drogo cursed softly as one of her small flailing fists caught him squarely on the chin. He swiftly pinned her thrashing body beneath his and shook her. She stilled slightly but did not open her eyes, so he shook her again.

Eada blinked then hurriedly wiped away the tears dampening her cheeks before scowling at the man who had shaken her awake. "What did you wake me for?"

He hastily swallowed the first answer that rose to his lips as he stared into her sleep-clouded lavender eyes. "You were having a nightmare. I thought you might wish to be freed of it."

When Eada realized she had spoken to him in French not English, she cursed herself for so quickly forgetting her resolution to treat him coldly and give him only silence. Worse than that, she was also forgetting that she was supposed to be furious with him. In fact, all she could seem to think about was how pleasant it felt for their bodies to be so close, the warmth of his large, strong frame infecting her blood with its heat. Even though her thin night rail lay between them, she was far too concerned with the fact that she could feel his nakedness. She decided she was not really thinking clearly at all.

After all, she mused as she studied the strong lines of his face, *what do I know of this man who so effortlessly stirs the wantonness in me? He is big, handsome, Norman, and here to conquer my land and my people. He is good to his big, slow servant Ivo, when few others would have such patience. He has not raised a hand to me despite the times I have attacked and insulted him. He is obviously quick of wit, for he guessed the game I played when feigning ignorance of French, and I know I played the game well until I foolishly allowed my temper to take control of me. And he has not raped me, yet I am certain that he wants me. Even now I can see the hunger in his dark eyes. He is also a man who favors cleanliness as do I.*

Inwardly she sighed as she thought of Edith, her grief over the woman's death still deep and sharp. Edith had told her that this man was the one she had been born for, had even hinted that he was a man who would appreciate both her spirit and her wit. Talk of destiny was all fine and good, she thought crossly, but it should not mean that she must warm to him after only a day's acquaintance nor spread for him as easily as some whore. Despite that admonition, Eada had to admit to herself that she was warming to him, alarmingly so. Her body had already softened in welcome beneath the weight of his.

She closed her eyes as she fought to gain control of her errant passion by not looking at him. It did not help. She became even more aware of the tantalizing clean male scent of him, of the feel of him. Her mind's eye revealed images of their bodies entwined, sensuous images which were not at all conducive to chilling her rapidly heating blood. Destiny had decided that they were soulmates and clearly did not see the need to allow her any time to truly know the man or to adjust to the turmoil she had suddenly been dragged into.

Drogo felt the softening of her lithe body beneath his. He dropped his gaze to her full breasts and saw as well as felt the increasing unsteadiness of her breathing. Gently he pressed more of his body against hers and felt her tremble. That sign that she was not completely cold to him was enough to loosen what little control he had kept on his desire since first setting eyes on her. It took all his strength to hold back, to remind himself that they were still little more than strangers. Moving too quickly could put a swift end to the subtle welcome of her body. *Gently, slowly,* he told himself over and over again as he began to brush light, tender kisses over her face.

Eada felt the warm softness of his mouth against her cheek and shivered. She struggled to put a halt to the feelings flooding her body but found such restraint almost impossible. She wished he would grow rough, even violent, in his passion, for she knew that affront would give her the strength to fight him. The gentleness of his seduction made her too willing to succumb to the tempting heat he stirred within her.

"No," she whispered, turning her head when he touched his lips to hers, but he cupped her face in his big hands and gently but firmly turned her back to him.

"Yes," he murmured against her full, shapely mouth as he teased it with soft, nibbling kisses. "Come, you knew from the moment I took you from that old woman's cottage that this was meant to be."

"No, it does not have to be so."

"Ah, my pretty, honey-tressed Saxon, it does. It has had to be since I first set eyes upon you."

Her reply was slain by his mouth as he pressed her for a fuller kiss. She tried to remain cold beneath him, but her body refused to obey her mind's pleas. Eada released a soft cry of helplessness as her mouth softened and her desire rapidly responded to his. She was not even able to refuse the invasion of his tongue, the gentle strokes within her mouth robbing her of what little resistance she had been able to muster. When he eased his heated kisses to her throat, she simply tilted her head back to allow him greater access then cursed her own meek surrender.

"You mean to take the land and the power from my people," she said, her voice thick and husky. "Must you rob me of my honor as well?"

Inwardly Drogo winced, but he replied, "You have told me *no,* have requested me to cease. Let that soothe your honor. All who have seen you know you are my prisoner and know just what I shall steal from you. They will not judge you because of this. You are but a tiny woman, and although I know you could put up an astonishing fight if the fever you now curse did not steal away your resistance, you could never win. Even your own people will see the truth of that."

Drogo was unlacing her night rail, touching each newly exposed patch of skin with a kiss, and Eada found speech difficult. "My people will see me as a traitor."

Although he ached to simply rip the thin gown from her body, Drogo continued to move slowly. He did not really want to discuss the right or wrong of doing what he craved to do, for he knew it was wrong. Talking aided him in reining in the desire raging through his body, however. He also hoped that he might yet find just the right words to ease and defer all her future regrets and recriminations.

"Some people will think that any Saxon who does not kill a Norman, even if the man is sleeping and unarmed, is a traitor. Most will think little ill of you and of the other women who will soon be held in Norman arms."

"Held with no thought to where her heart may belong or the man she might belong to?"

He glanced at her face and cursed the dark, for the shadows made it difficult to correctly read her expression. "And does any man hold a claim to you, Eada?"

"No. I am a widow."

"Good. It means I need not make you one now."

His soft, cold words shocked Eada. She struggled to reply but a moment later lost all her ability to even think of a response. He gently cradled her breasts in his big callused hands, brushing his thumbs over the hardening tips until they ached. When he replaced his thumbs with his tongue, she cried out and clutched his broad shoulders. She trembled inside and out from the strength of the desire he stirred in her, a desire so powerful she was unable to fight it.

As Drogo smothered her breasts in kisses, he quickly removed her night rail. Tense with anticipation, he eased his body back on top of hers and groaned with pleasure as their flesh met. He covered the crown of her breast with his mouth and drew the nipple deep inside. A soft growl of need escaped him when she moaned and moved, rubbing invitingly against his body.

Eada lost all ability to think and all interest in doing so. She gave herself over completely to the feelings raging through her body. Greedily, she ran her hands over the lean, muscular body she had admired from the first time she had seen it. She did not care that the body she held was Norman or that the hands stroking her would soon wield a sword against her people. He was simply a man, a big, beautiful man, and she ached for him.

Drogo sensed Eada's surrender and fought to keep that knowledge from severing what little control he clung to. The feel of her small, soft hands moving over his skin made that all the more difficult. He wanted to immediately and fiercely bury himself deep within her warmth, but he knew it would be a grave mistake if he succumbed to that urge. It was important that he give her pleasure, as much pleasure as he could, and not simply because he wanted to. By giving her pleasure he knew he would further ease whatever regrets she might have when the clouds of desire fled her mind. It would also ease any possible renewed resistance from her.

He stroked her, kissed her, and whispered sweet flatteries against her downy, soft skin. Eada felt as if some madness had seized hold of her. It was the only explanation for why she was succumbing to the pleasure of his touch so quickly and completely, her passion flooding her so strongly and hotly.

If fate had decided she should be with this man, it had certainly found the surest way to make her follow the right path. Such heady passion was hard to fight. Part of her resented being pushed and led into something that could bring her pain and heartbreak. A moment later, she knew there was no hope for a return to sanity as he slid his hand up the inside of her thigh and stroked the very heart of her aching need for him. The cry that escaped her lips held both regret and desire as she opened to his touch, silently welcoming the intimacy.

When Eada made no attempt to stop him at that final barrier, Drogo groaned. His body shuddered as the hunger he felt for her gained force in one swift, heady rush. She was fire beneath his hands, hot, wild, and inviting.

Unable to restrain himself any longer, he prepared to possess her.

As he eased into her, he felt her suddenly tense, and he joined their bodies with one greedy thrust. He gasped in surprise when he felt himself tear through something he had not expected to find. She had said that she was a widow and so should not have had a maidenhead. He quickly grabbed hold of her when she cried out and tried to pull away. Almost desperately, he struggled to soothe her and restore her passion. He did not think he had the strength to stop now if she remained cold to him, and yet he did not wish to continue if she were unwilling or in too much pain.

The burning pain Drogo had inflicted when he had plunged into her body tore away the passion clouding Eada's mind, and for one brief moment, she was able to think clearly. She was stunned. All her prideful plans to resist had been swept away with an embarrassing swiftness.

Even as she began to castigate herself, however, her passion returned. As Drogo stroked and kissed her, her lost maidenhead and the pain of that loss grew less and less important. He had not killed her desire, merely brushed it aside for a minute. The need he restirred within her as he soothed and aroused her soon had her arching against him. She was not sure what would happen next and simply moved instinctively, trying to draw him deeper inside of her. Everything within her drove her to try and quell the hunger gnawing at her. Her body craved something and moved in an effort to get it.

Drogo was left gasping when Eada moved against him with an unskilled eagerness. The feel of her acceptance was exquisite. Uttering a harsh cry, he began to move. He was determined to give her as much pleasure as he could before he could no longer restrain his need for release. Eada quickly matched his movements, thrust for thrust. She wrapped her lithe limbs around his body, and he lost all ability to hold back.

As Drogo's lovemaking grew fiercer, Eada felt more exhilarated. It increased her passion tenfold to feel the loss of control in his large, strong body and know that she had caused it. It was a heady thing to know that she could stir him as much as he did her.

Suddenly, she cried out, clutching at him in a wild attempt to draw him even closer. Pleasure tore through her body in waves, thrusting her into an oblivion that was both frightening and dizzingly beautiful. She was faintly aware of Drogo's almost painful grip on her hips and of the way he drove deeply within her, holding himself there as he cried out her name. Her last clear thought was that she could easily be tempted to do anything and everything just to hear him say her name like that again.

Seven

Awareness returned slowly to Eada and she immediately regretted its appearance. Several conflicting emotions tore at her. Everything she had felt seemed to confirm Old Edith's prediction. That, however, could not alter the facts that Drogo was the enemy to all that was Saxon and that she had lost her much-protected maidenhead to a man she had known only a few hours. She lay numb and silent as Drogo gently cleaned them both, washing away the remnants of the innocence he had stolen from her with such ease.

Drogo slid back into bed a little warily. Eada looked stunned, and he suspected it was not for the same reasons he felt that way. He sighed inwardly as one fat tear rolled down her still-flushed cheek. A moment later, his suspicion that it was the harbinger of a flood was confirmed. Ignoring her tense resistance to his touch, he tugged her into his arms and held her close as she wept. He was somewhat disappointed that she would react so after all the pleasure they had shared, but he could understand it.

"Come, little one, this weeping changes and helps nothing." He combed his fingers through her thick, tousled hair.

"I know." Eada desperately tried to stop crying, but it was a few minutes before she began to succeed. "It is just a bit difficult to discover that one is no better than a whore."

"You are no whore."

"No, perhaps not, for I required no coin to spread for you with such dismaying ease. A whore would at least have the wit to ask for some boon."

"Eada, I cannot explain why your passion so quickly and fully matched mine, but that does not make you a whore. That would only be so if you rose from this bed and lay down with any of my men with ease." The mere thought of Eada doing such a thing turned Drogo's stomach, knotting it with anger. "You would do it but the once."

Yet again there was that hard chill to his voice that made Eada shudder, but she decided not to question him about it. "No, I could not do that. If nothing else, I believe I feel traitor enough now."

"Woman, you are no traitor. A small woman like you can do nothing to stop what is to come. Harold chose his fate for himself. I am but sorry that such things always make the innocent pay dearly as well." He began to idly smooth his hands over her slender curves and felt his need for her stir with renewed life.

"Harold had no right to choose or promise anything," Eada said as she relaxed beneath his gentle stroking.

"He was heir to the throne."

"Maybe the old king chose him, maybe not. It does not matter. Only the *witena gemot* can choose the king."

"The wita—what? And what nonsense do you speak of? No one chooses a king."

Eada looked at him and smiled sadly. "You know nothing of the land you seek to conquer, do you? I think you will take a lot more from my people than their land. The *witena gemot* is a group of wise men who decide who will rule us. They can also take that throne away. Harold's brother Tostig was an earl, but he failed in his duty to his people and he was deposed, sent into exile, and another took his place."

"That is madness."

"And so you will end this custom. And soon, you will end lives. Your sword will drip with the blood of Saxons, of my people."

"I fear it will, although I intend to spill as little blood as I can. I take little pleasure in the death a battle brings, Eada, but a man like me has only two choices—the sword or the church. I abided in a monastery for a while, but that life was not for me. Since I have three brothers older than I, there is no chance that I will gain the right to rule my father's lands. And thus, I took up the sword."

Eada knew that everything he said was the truth, that his choices were indeed few, but she still asked, "Must you take up that sword against *my* people?"

"My sword is pledged to William. I follow where he leads me and must fight whomever he fights. It is the path all men must walk. If William had broken a promise he had made to Harold, then Harold would have sailed for our lands and many a Saxon would have come with him. They would have been seeking exactly what I do— loot, especially a piece of land. That is what all men seek. All I can try to do is to build my future on as little blood and sorrow as possible."

His soft deep voice and the soothing-yet-arousing movement of his big hands on her skin soon had Eada pressing against him, absently snuggling closer to him. A part of her was appalled at her easy surrender and urged her to pull away, but it was not strong enough. It could not conquer how good it felt to be held by him, to feel his warm skin close to hers. She was painfully confused in her mind and her heart, and she was alone. Despite everything that was wrong about being his lover, it felt right to cling to this big man, to find comfort and strength in his arms. She needed him, and no matter how much she cursed what she saw as a weakness, it did not change that fact.

"If you begin your future on blood, you must sustain it with blood," she felt compelled to say.

He did not really wish to linger on such weighty matters. With her slender body pressed close to his, he was finding it difficult to think of anything but making love to her. The truth of her words also made him feel uncomfortable. Drogo grimaced at his own vagaries. He had wanted her to speak French so that they could talk and learn about each other, and now he wanted her to be quiet. He had wanted to know what she thought, and now he just wanted to hear her cry out his name in the throes of passion.

"I know that, little one," he said. "I do fear that this land will be well soaked in blood and that there will be much grief to bear, but I cannot stop it."

"You could put your sword down." She tentatively smoothed her hand over his taut stomach and felt him tremble faintly.

"Even if I could sheath my sword, refuse to fight, and still maintain my honor, that sword would only be picked up by another. At least I shall wield mine with mercy. Come, sweet child, this is no time to think such dark thoughts."

Since Drogo's body was taut with arousal and he was nibbling at her earlobe in a way that had her blood running hot, Eada could easily guess what time he thought it was. Even though she did not really wish to be, she was stirred. Her fears and concerns could not be so easily pushed aside, however. All too clearly she could see what lay ahead of them and began to fear that she had been bequeathed Old Edith's foresight.

"Mayhap it will not be as bad as you fear," Drogo said as he trailed soft kisses over her throat.

"No? Would you allow all you hold dear to be taken from you and stand by meekly, head bowed, offering no fight? Would you willingly step down from being a leader of men to become a follower? Would you ignore your oath of allegiance to a man simply because another man with an army of landless, hungry knights and mercenaries behind him has said that that man is not your rightful king?"

"No, I would not, but I think you knew my answers before you asked the questions."

"I cannot give you the lies of hope you seem to want. I pray that, if I ask it of you, you will treat me with the same courtesy."

When he responded by holding her more tightly against him, she returned his hug. She was a little dismayed by her actions, but the soft kisses he brushed over her face quickly soothed her troubled mind. He sought to comfort her as well as restir her passion. Eada realized that part of her inability to resist him was because he was a good man.

"Why did you hide the fact that you could speak French?" he asked in a quiet voice as he stroked her hair, savoring the thick silken feel of it beneath his fingers.

She shrugged. "I was a captive surrounded by the enemy. I had just lost my dear friend and did not know where my family had gone. I had nothing. Nothing except the fact that I could understand every word you said and you did not know it." She idly trailed her fingers over his ribs and asked, "How did you guess the truth? I thought I had hidden it very well."

"You had. It was Serle who first suspected it. And this is your home, is it not?"

"It is. This is the home of Vedette and Waltheof."

"Vedette? Your mother is French?"

Eada nodded. "She was the one who taught me to speak your language. Her family is in Normandy. My father conducted some trade with them and that is how he met her. She is not fully French. She carries some Saxon blood and that is how she came to speak both languages. It was a skill she felt all of her children should share."

"And your family has fled to safety?"

"My mother, sister, brother, and the servants have fled. I can but pray that they find a safe place. My father is with Harold, and Old Edith told me that he is doomed. You need not fear that he will fall beneath your sword, for Old Edith said he was already doomed and she has never been wrong. I think my father will fall or has already fallen in the battle with Harald Hardrada and Tostig."

"I am sorry. You truly believe in the old woman's visions?"

"Yes. Only once did I completely doubt her, even called her a foolish old woman. She told me that I would marry my betrothed but that I would never be his wife. She would not or could not explain that, and so it sounded like empty babble." Eada shook her head and laughed, a touch of sadness weighting her humor. "She was right. I did marry, but the fool got into a fight at the wedding feast and died so—"

"You were never a wife. That is how you could say you were a widow and yet still be a maiden. I am the only one who has ever tasted your passion." Drogo knew the intense satisfaction he gained from that knowledge was probably a warning that his feelings had already gone a lot deeper than passion, but he shrugged aside all thought of that.

He grasped Eada lightly by the chin and turned her face up to his. Eada looked into his dark eyes and suddenly felt tense, a growing fear knotting her stomach. The word that suddenly formed in her mind made her shiver, a cold sweat breaking out on her skin. A soft curse escaped her as she abruptly pulled away from Drogo, clutching the covers to her in a vain attempt to regain the warmth she had been enjoying.

"What is wrong?" demanded Drogo as he sat up, hesitantly reaching out to touch her arm and frowning at how cold she was. "Why do you suddenly fear me?" He had found the look of terror that had passed over her face painful to look at.

"I do not fear you," she said, confused by what had just happened to her.

"Eada, I saw the way you looked at me."

"It was not you I saw," she whispered, not resisting when he slowly pulled her back into his arms.

"You make no sense, *ma petite*. You were looking at me. What else could you have seen?"

"I am not certain."

He frowned and felt her forehead and then her cheeks. "You have no fever."

Eada laughed shakily. "I almost wish I had just fallen ill. The frightening dreams of a fever would be an almost-welcome explanation."

"I will fetch you some wine. A drink will soothe you."

She watched him as he climbed from the bed and walked over to a table by the far wall, the candlelight draping his body in unsteady shadows. Fate had chosen well for her. Drogo was strong, handsome, kind, and honorable. If she could convince him to allow his hair to grow, he could be a man who could take a woman's breath away. Eada just wished that fate had brought him to her during a less-troubled time.

It was shocking to have fallen into his bed so quickly, but she had no time to consider the right or wrong of it. Until the rule of England was settled, she was alone, and that was dangerous. Her only chance to survive the turmoil ahead was to find her family, which was not only impossible in a land torn by war but would only be helpful if her family had found a safe haven, or to find a protector. Fate had made the choice for her by sending her Drogo and she decided it was foolish to keep questioning it. Soon women all over England would be held in Norman arms, willingly and unwillingly, she thought with a strong touch of anger. She knew she ought to be grateful that she had been found by the man Old Edith marked as her soulmate and that her bedding brought her pleasure. Eada was just deciding that it would un-doubtedly be a long while before she was grateful for anything when a soft laugh from Drogo pulled her from her thoughts.

"Why do you laugh?" she demanded as he returned to bed and handed her a goblet of wine.

"When I went to pour the wine, you were frightened and chilled. Now you look flushed with anger," he replied and he shook his head. "I but turn away for a moment, and your humor changes completely."

"Do not fear. I am not usually so quick to change tem-pers," she murmured and took a long, steadying drink of wine. "It has been a long, upsetting day."

"Did thoughts of your old friend put that look of fear upon your face?"

"No. I but thought that I saw something."

"That brings me little comfort, for you were looking at me."

"I was; but as I said, it was not you I saw."

"What else could you have seen?"

Eada studied him as he took her empty goblet and set it aside then tugged her into his arms. She prayed with all her heart that Old Edith had not passed her strange gifts along to her, but there was no denying what had just caused her to be so afraid. It was suddenly of great in-terest to her to see how Drogo would respond if she told him the truth about the cause of her fear.

"I saw someone else," she replied, watching him closely as she spoke.

Drogo frowned. "There is no one else here. Only you and me, and you were looking right at me."

"I know, but then you disappeared into a thick mist— not fully, but you were no longer clear to see. Behind you lurked a man draped in black—whether in a cloak or a monk's garb, I do not know. When I saw him, my mind spoke only one word, but it spoke it so loudly that my head throbbed. It said, *Enemy*. You have an enemy."

"I have many enemies for I live by my sword," he replied, but he began to feel uncertain. "There will soon be many more as I do not believe many of the Saxons I will meet will cry me a friend."

"The enemy I saw stands behind you. You do not march toward him; he slithers at your back. He is a shadowed threat at your back."

"Tancred also stands at my back, so you need not fear for me."

"Tancred was not there."

"Come, this is but your fears come to life."

"Is it? How odd that my fears should wear a mark like the half moon upon his right cheek."

Eada was not surprised when Drogo suddenly tensed, pushed her back, and stared at her, his eyes wide and his expression a mixture of disbelief and fear. She knew in her heart that what she had seen was a warning. She did not like it, prayed that she would have no more, but knew that it should not be ignored.

"You saw a scarred man at my back?" Drogo demanded, unsettled by what she told him, for he believed her; yet he heartily wished she had kept her vision a secret. If she had the gift of foreseeing, it could cause them even more trouble than they already faced.

She nodded. "It was all that was revealed from beneath the black he had shrouded himself in. Do you know such a man?"

"I do. Sir Guy DeVeau. I have done him no wrong, yet he hates me and makes no secret of it."

"Sometimes there is no reason for a man's hatred. Or a woman's. No reason the person who suffers from that hate can see, at least. It is born in the hater's mind and heart, places no one else can look into."

"True," he murmured, astonished by her wisdom. "Yet

there has to be some cause for such a strong, dangerous emotion."

"It could be born of a slight so small, an insult so insignificant, that you do not even know you have committed it. It could even be born of envy."

"Yes, and it is something I cannot cure or soothe."

"No. That would require some show of humility," she drawled, feeling as surprised as he looked that she would tease him.

Her surprise increased when she giggled at his expression. Such levity seemed ill-placed when danger lurked on all sides. Eada decided that she had simply had enough of anger, worry, and fear for the day. Danger and tragedy would still be lurking close at hand in the morning. It could not hurt to just ignore them for a little while.

A soft screech of laughter escaped her when Drogo suddenly, gently wrestled her onto her back, pinned her to the bed, and lightly tickled her. She slipped her arms around his neck and smiled at him, enjoying the feel of his strong body pressed close to hers. It was possible that Drogo also wished to ignore the troubles surrounding them. She grew serious as she wondered if he also intended to ignore her warning about an enemy.

"What will you do about Sir Guy?" she asked even as she tilted her head back to allow him free access to her throat.

"I intend to watch him closely," Drogo replied, and he slowly dragged his tongue along the rapid pulse in her slim throat, enjoying the way she trembled slightly beneath him.

"And will you have your men watch him as well?"

"I am honored that you are so deeply concerned about my safety."

"Do not be," she said, the coolness of her tone belied by the way she stroked his back. "As was revealed this afternoon, you are all that stands between me and a lustful army of Normans. I would be a fool if I did not do all I can to insure that you continue to stand there." She caressed his calves with the soles of her feet and smiled crookedly when he looked down at her.

"At least you recognize me as your protector. Maybe soon you can show me a little deference before the men." He began to follow the delicate lines of her small face with soft, lingering kisses.

"Ah, deference," she murmured, her growing passion making her voice husky and unsteady. "I have never been very skilled at showing deference. Would it help if I ceased to bang your head against the floor?"

Drogo chuckled against the curve of her neck. "It might, and where did you learn such a trick?"

"From a boy, a childhood friend. I fear my lack of deference caused me some trouble in my youth. Ere I became a woman, and even a few times after that, I got into battles. He showed me how to strike first and quickly with a telling blow. Even when the ones who stood against me knew *what* I would do, they could never be certain of *when* I would do it."

Even as Drogo prepared to ask her what had happened to that boy, he bit back the question. Since William's army had either captured, killed, or chased away everyone in Pevensey, it was a question that could easily restir her anger. He was enjoying her good humor almost as much as he was her passion, and he did not want to do anything to ruin it.

"He went to London," Eada said in a soft voice then met his startled look with a faint smile.

"Can you read what is in a man's mind as well as what lies in his future?" he asked, only half-jesting, for her warning about Guy had been both welcome and unsettling.

"No. In truth, I pray I cannot see what lies in the future. I would prefer to think that that vision was simply a sharp-

ening of my senses inspired by a very real danger and one
that is very close at hand."

"The old woman could see things."

"Yes, but how could you know that?"

"It was but a guess. She lived alone, far from the town,
and there is usually a good reason for that. There was
also the fact that she had prepared her own grave as if
she knew she was going to die."

Eada shivered and held him closer. "We are speaking
of somber things again. I do not want to speak of them
or think of them now."

"You wish to pretend that we are in a sun-drenched
meadow, deer grazing quietly at the forest's edge. The
sweet song of birds is the only sound to break the peace
of the fields."

As he spoke, his deep, rich voice soothed her worries
and nudged aside her fears. She closed her eyes to allow
the tranquil scene he painted to form more clearly in her
mind. Eada could almost smell the sweet grasses he said
were enfolding them as they made love. The touch of his
warm lips against her skin and the gentle caresses of his
big, callused hands enhanced the magic of his words. She
felt both calmed and inflamed. Forgetfulness could be a
very good thing she decided as she curled her limbs
around him and welcomed him into her body.

Eight

"Leaving Pevensey?" Eada asked in confusion as she hastily finished her breakfast of bread and honey.

She had woken up to Drogo's lovemaking. Sated and groggy after their passion was spent, she had risen, dressed, and joined the men for breakfast. This abrupt return to the cold, harsh world of armies and marches left her confused.

"Yes," answered Drogo as Unwin helped him don his armor. "It is time to move on. This is not a good place for a battle. I begin to think that William had not really intended us to land here, but was aiming for a port farther up the coast. He now says we are to march to Hastings."

"Mayhap it would be best if I stayed here. May, too. It would only slow you down if you had to drag us along."

Drogo watched her closely as he strapped on his sword. If she thought that one night in his arms was all he wanted, or all she needed to do to be free of him, she was in for a surprise. He saw no signs of guile or anger in her expression, however, only confusion and a hint of fear. Drogo pushed aside his sudden suspicions, feeling guilty for even having them, and wondered how he could convince her that she needed to stay with him.

"It will be too dangerous for you to stay here," he said finally.

"I think it would be dangerous for me to march along

with an invading army," Eada responded. "That could easily place me in the very midst of a battle."

"You could find yourself in the midst of a battle here, too, but with only a few men between you and whoever attacked."

"The attackers would be Saxons, my people."

"We are not Harold's only enemy. And who would protect you and May from the men left behind? Once I am gone, I do not believe my claim to you would be heeded or honored."

Eada cursed softly, for there was no denying the truth of all he said. "It would seem that there is *no* safe place for me, not in England, not in Pevensey, not even in my own home."

"There is one place where you will have some chance of being safe."

"With you."

"Yes. With me. Ivo will take the cart and pony to carry our supplies. You and May will remain with him. There will be the baggage of a whole army, servants, youths in training, even some armed men to protect it. And when we camp, you will again be with me." He walked over to her, touched a kiss to her forehead, and started toward the door. "You may take your hounds. And I should hurry and collect what you feel you need, for we shall be leaving shortly."

She watched him leave, the other men hurrying out behind him. There was no argument she could make, although she dearly wished she could think of one. It irritated her, but Drogo was right. She would be safest traveling with the army. Unless William was soundly defeated or swept to victory with just one battle, England would soon be a very dangerous place for a woman, especially a woman alone. She suspected that the only way she could return to her home again was if her father emerged from the war victorious or if William suddenly decided to give up and sailed back to France. Either one would require a miracle, and Eada felt sure that England would be seeing few miracles in the years to come.

As Eada stood up, she caught sight of May standing at the far end of the table and looking uncertain. "Come, May, let us see how much we can gather before we are forced to leave."

"We shall be safe with Ivo and the others," May said as she followed Eada to her bedchamber.

"Yes, I think we shall be, but we shall have to watch our people suffer. But I must try and save myself now. I cannot stop this war and I would make a very poor warrior, so I shall have to endeavor to survive and, if fortune smiles upon me, mayhap I can aid a few of my people as well."

"Are you certain that you need so much?" Drogo asked as he rode up alongside the cart and scowled at the contents, an odd collection of chests, barrels, and sacks.

"Most of what you see here is to enhance your comfort," Eada replied as she got into the cart and settled herself on a sack of grain next to May. "Wine, bedding, food, and other comforts. If you wish, we could discard—"

"No." Drogo smiled faintly. "We can always discard something later if the cart becomes too heavy to travel over the road with ease."

"Or steal another cart," she murmured.

Drogo opened his mouth to protest the word *steal* then frowned as he suddenly noticed how the men passing by the cart were casting hard, curious looks at Eada. "I think I had best tell William that you speak French."

Thrown off guard by the abrupt change of subject, Eada asked, "Will that be a problem for you or for me?" She began to wonder if her little game, prompted by stubbornness and pride, could now put her in danger.

"I do not think it will be a problem for either of us. Not

if I tell William before others can whisper the news to him, slyly twisting their tale until it smells of some treachery."

She nodded as she suddenly understood his concerns. "Your enemies could easily use it against you, making what was but foolishness sound evil."

"Yes, and there are ones who would like to cause me such trouble, mayhap lessening me in William's eyes." He looked back at Eada. "Stay with the cart and with Ivo," he ordered. "Do not stray from Ivo's reach."

"I will not flee," she said. "Where would I go?"

"It is not your escape I fear, for I believe you have the wit to know you are safest where you are now. No, I give this warning because we now ride amongst the Saxons. I do not wish you to be mistaken for some fleeing villager."

She tensed as she realized what he was not saying. "Now the killing truly begins."

He sighed and rubbed his chin. "*My* men do not cut down the unarmed and innocent or lay waste to all in their path, but others are not so merciful. The mercenaries will certainly be brutal. I have also heard talk of some retribution. Two of our ships went ashore in another village, and many are certain that the men were killed. If they find such a village and the tale is true, those people will pay dearly." He shook his head. "It does us no good to talk of this, for neither of us can stop it. Just stay in the cart or at Ivo's side. I ask it only to keep you alive."

Eada nodded and watched Drogo ride off to rejoin the others. He was right. It did no real good to speak of the horrors to come, of who was right and who was wrong. She knew Drogo was a merciful man and, in the end, he had no more power than she did.

The stinging smell of smoke roused Eada from her sleep. She winced as she straightened up, deciding that sleeping on a sack of grain in a moving cart was not something she would do often. Rubbing the small of her back, she looked around. It was already late afternoon, and she was sure they were nearing Bulverhythe Harbor. They would have to ride around that just as they had had to ride all the way around Pevensey Harbor, so it was possible that they would soon stop to camp for the night. The smoke, she realized, was drifting toward her from Hove or Bexhill and she shivered.

"God have mercy on them," she whispered and crossed herself.

"I think God has shown mercy on us," May said, her voice soft and unsteady. "You have slept, and I have been saved from seeing the horror all around us."

"It has been bad?" Eada asked, briefly clasping May's hand in hers.

"Halisham, Herstmonceux, Ninfield, and Hove were all struck at least as hard as Pevensey was."

"That was hard enough."

May nodded. "From what I have heard, Ashburnham has been laid waste, and I fear that fate awaits Bexhill. The footsoldiers who march along the coast have just reached it. I cannot be certain for I but grasp names spoken, know where the villages lie, and see what the soldiers do."

"And smell the smoke." Eada cursed softly. "With such wanton destruction, even those fortunate enough to avoid the swords and arrows could still be doomed. The winter to come will be hard with all of their stores emptied or burned." Eada looked to the carts behind them and saw that prisoners had been taken. "Have you spoken to the prisoners?"

"No, but we have been close enough many times and I have heard some of what they say to each other. That is how I learned a little more than the names of the villages. How can the men we are with be so good and kind yet ride with men who can do such cruel things?"

"All men do evil in war. A village suffers even when our own men march through it or camp nearby. Warriors are the same no matter which king they march behind. Some just have a little more mercy and honor in their hearts than others." Eada tapped Ivo on the shoulder. "Are we going to stop to camp for the night?"

"Yes," Ivo replied even as he nodded. "I do not know these roads, and it would be dangerous to travel them in the dark. They are rutted and the mud is thick."

"They were passable until an army marched over them," Eada muttered, but she kept her voice too low for Ivo to hear for she did not wish to confuse him or hurt his feelings with her complaints.

"When we stop, you can teach me how to talk to May."

Eada glanced at him and grimaced inwardly when she saw the earnest look upon his face. She really doubted that he had the ability to learn English, but she could not say that. "Mayhap it would be better if I taught May how to speak your language. She and I will be together more and talking more. You will be too busy helping your liege lord." She patted him briefly on the shoulder. "Then, when you are not so busy, May will be able to teach you all she has learned."

"Yes, that is a good idea."

She sighed inwardly with relief. Although teaching Normans English would help fulfill Old Edith's prophecy that everything Saxon would not die, Eada did not think she wanted to start with Ivo. That would require more patience than she had at the moment. When all their fates had been decided, if they all survived and were still together, she would do her best to teach every Norman in her reach how to speak English, even Ivo.

Even though she wanted to ignore it, to remain blind to all of the tragedy, Eada looked at the prisoners riding in the carts and stumbling along the muddy road. They all looked terrified, some wearing the empty expressions

of horror and grief on their pale faces. It did not surprise
Eada that most of the prisoners were women, many looking as if they had already suffered the pain and degrada-
tion of rape. Many soldiers considered women part of the
loot due the victor. The only other reason they would
take a prisoner would be for ransom, but there was no
reason to do that in this war. If William lost, his men
were doomed; and if he won, few Saxons would have anything left to pay a ransom with. What the Normans had
not already taken they would soon claim as their rightful
due under the new king.

After watching the mournful prisoners for several miles
and smelling the taint of smoke in the air from yet another burning village, Eada's spirits were very low by the
time Ivo stopped to make camp. She silently helped him
prepare a meal, absently noticing that May was equally
subdued. It was not until she heard the sound of a man
in armor approaching that she was able to shake free of
the fear and the grief weighting her heart; but when she
looked up, it was not Drogo standing before her. The
man turned to look at Ivo and Eada tensed. On his right
cheek was a scar, the same scar she had glimpsed on the
man in her vision. She did not need Ivo's muttered greeting to know that this was Sir Guy DeVeau.

"Which one of these women is Sir Drogo's whore?" Sir
Guy asked, his voice soft and cold as he stared at Eada.

Eada stiffened with outrage as a scowling Ivo pointed
at her. She ached to respond to the insult but forced
herself to remember that, despite the kindness of Drogo
and his men, she was a prisoner, a Saxon in the midst of
an enemy army. This time she would have to swallow her
pride, for acting out in anger could not only endanger
her but Drogo and the others as well.

"You can speak French?" Sir Guy looked Eada over
with an insolence that had her clenching her fists.

"Yes," she answered, spitting the word out between clenched teeth.

"I need you to speak to my prisoners," he said, as he grabbed her by the arm and started to pull her toward his camp.

His grip was so tight Eada nearly gasped from the pain, but she fought to hide it. She waved Ivo back when he stepped forward. Sir Guy would not tolerate a servant's interference, and Eda saw no point in Ivo's putting himself at risk. She wanted to talk to the man's prisoners anyway. Even if she were unable to comfort them, she could at least find out what had happened in their village.

At his camp, Sir Guy pushed her toward two terrified women and a boy of about fourteen. All three were badly bruised, and the older of the two women sat on the muddy ground clutching her two small children. A quick look at Sir Guy was enough to tell Eada that he intended to stay close enough to hear what she said. That made no sense if he could not speak English, and Eada briefly wondered if he could and sought to trick her. She decided she would carefully guard her words until she was sure of what he did or did not know.

"Tell them that they are to serve me," Sir Guy said. "They are to cook for me, clean, mend, and whatever else servants do. And tell the women they are to warm my bed."

Eada refused to blush as she repeated his words. When she saw the anger flare in the youth's blue eyes, she quickly took him by the hand. She moved around the camp touching things and making him repeat the French word for each item until she felt the tight fury in him begin to ease.

"What is your name?" she asked.

"Godwin of Halisham. My father was a shepherd. They cut him down in his pasture as he tended his flock. My mother was slain as she fed our chickens. You are not Norman?"

"I am Eada of Pevensey. My mother had some Norman blood. That is why I can speak their language. Now, who are the women?"

"The younger one with the red hair is Elga. She is from my village. The older, dark-haired one is Hilde. Those are her children. Welcome is but two, and Eric is not yet four."

"And you are not yet fourteen I would guess."

"A good guess. Was Pevensey laid waste?"

When she saw a frowning Sir Guy step closer, Eada started to prepare a meal and the youth quickly helped. "He will not be fooled by this for long," she murmured. "Pevensey was damaged and many were killed, but I know little else. I was captured outside of town. Now, heed me, Godwin, and try to make the women understand, too."

"Can you not talk to them?" he asked as he stoked the fire.

"I have little time and I picked you because you appear to be the strongest." She began to prepare a stew and tried to act as if all she were doing was giving him instructions. "Do not fight this man. He has no mercy. He will kill you without hesitation and simply find more Saxons to serve him."

"It is cowardly to just give up, to just meekly bow before him."

"Bow. Bow and survive and help those poor women and the babes to survive, too. That should be your only battle and, believe me, it will be a hard one. Yes, you have a lot of courage, but it is still trapped inside a boy's body and that boy is surrounded by battle-hardened men. Saxons will soon die in the thousands. Why not try to defeat the enemy by living?"

"You have said enough," Sir Guy snapped, grabbing her by the arm and yanking her away from Godwin.

Eada could not fully restrain a gasp of pain as Sir Guy's gauntleted fingers dug into her arm, but she quelled Godwin's move to help her with one sharp look. "There are better uses for good Saxon blood than feeding the flies."

"I told you, you have talked enough."

She ducked when she saw Sir Guy swing at her, but was not quick enough to completely avoid his blow. His hand slammed into the side of her head with enough force to cause her ears to ring and make her fall to her knees. Out of the corner of her eye, she saw Godwin move; but before he took more than one step, Sir Guy was pulled away from her so abruptly the mail of his gauntlet scratched her wrist as he was forced to release her.

Holding the side of her aching head, she looked up and nearly gaped. Drogo now stood between her and Sir Guy, his sword drawn and his face white with fury. Sir Guy quickly recovered from his surprise and drew his sword, an odd smile curving his thin-lipped mouth. Eada stumbled to her feet and backed away, knowing there was nothing she could do, that she could even make matters worse if she interfered. The moment Drogo drew his sword, she had lost all chance to end the confrontation.

"See to the women," she said to a startled Godwin and was pleased when he immediately went to the terrified women, escorting them out of harm's way and then standing guard over them.

"So gallant, Sir Drogo," said Sir Guy. "You leap so quickly to the defense of this Saxon whore."

"This woman is under my protection," Drogo said, his voice hoarse with anger. "There was no need to strike her; and even if there had been provocation from her, you had no right."

"No right? She is a Saxon—"

"—lady," Drogo snapped, interrupting Sir Guy before he could utter yet another slur against Eada. "She is probably as well born as you, but you must have known that.

Or did you think that all peasants in England were taught to speak French?"

"I gave her no thought at all."

"Here, here, my young knights," said a coarse, deep voice. "So hot of blood."

Eada tore her gaze from Drogo and looked at the older knight who calmly stepped between the two younger men. She had not yet learned how to tell who was higher born, but the reactions of Sir Guy and Drogo told her that this battle-scarred, grey-haired knight sat a lot higher at the table than they did. Both men eased their battle stances, lowering their sword points slightly as they faced the man.

"Lord Bergeron—" Drogo began.

"No, Sir Drogo, there is no need for explanations. I saw all that happened." Lord Bergeron stepped closer and placed a hand on each man's shoulder. They quickly obeyed his silent command to sheath their swords, although neither looked pleased to do so. "Young Sir Guy was hasty, and I am sure he regrets not leaving the girl's discipline in your capable hands, Sir Drogo. It is not worth wasting good Norman blood, however. We have been on these shores but two days and a great many days of fighting lie ahead of us. Let us not waste our strength here. Go, Sir Drogo, and take the pretty little girl with you. Sir Guy and I will have a word or two, hmmm?" Lord Bergeron slipped his thickly muscled arm around Sir Guy's slender shoulders.

After bowing to the older man and casting one last cold look at Sir Guy, Drogo grabbed Eada by the hand and started to walk back to his camp. Eada stumbled along behind him, but managed one last look back at Sir Guy and Lord Bergeron. The older man was doing all the talking and Sir Guy's tight, pale expression told her that the words he listened to were not to his liking.

"I am sorry," she whispered when she looked at Drogo and caught him frowning down at her.

"You should have stayed with Ivo as I told you to."

"I had little choice. Sir Guy is a Norman knight. You also told me to remember that I am a prisoner, and neither Ivo nor May could safely deny the man what he wanted. The man strode into your camp, said he needed me to talk to his prisoners, and took me with him. Despite his insulting manner, I said nothing and did as I was told."

"So he struck you because you were so obedient?" Drogo stopped and lightly touched the bruises on the side of her face.

"He seemed to think I was saying too much to his prisoners."

"And what did you say to them?"

"I told the women exactly what he told me to tell them and then I spoke to the youth Godwin. I told him that the only battle he should fight now is the one of survival, not only for his own sake but for the sake of those two terrified women and the babes."

"And that is all you said to them?"

"Yes. It would be foolish to try and stir rebellion in the hearts of a boy, two frightened women, and two babes when we are in the midst of thousands of armed men." She sighed when he only smiled faintly at her tart words. "Sir Guy hit me because I did not stop talking when he told me to. All that was not what I said I was sorry for."

"Then what are you sorry for?"

"Because I think what has just happened has made Sir Guy hate you even more than he already did." She cursed inwardly when Drogo offered her no argument.

Nine

Eada grimaced, shifted slightly in Drogo's arms, and struggled to go back to sleep. Curled up in Drogo's arms but unable to make love because they had no privacy, she had found sleep annoyingly difficult. She did not want to be awake, but the voice in her head would not shut up. Something pulled at her, demanded that she leave her safe, warm haven; and she cursed as she finally accepted that she would not get any more sleep until she answered that voice. Fully awake, her decision made, she suddenly realized that what she could hear in her head was weeping and a cry for help.

Drogo murmured a protest as she eased out of his hold, but to her great relief, he did not wake up. Her hounds whined a greeting as she tiptoed past them, and she signaled them to be quiet. She did not hesitate to think about where she was going; she knew. The cry in her head led her. So intent was she on following that cry that she was only faintly aware of her hounds trotting silently by her side, but their presence eased some of her trepidation.

When she found herself in the shadowed woods, she reached out for her dogs. Although the bright moonlight helped her to see where she was walking, it also heightened the unsettling eeriness of the shadows around her. She caught hold of her dogs' rope collars, and her painfully rapid heartbeat slowed.

Just as she began to think that the voice in her head had been no more than the remnants of some frightening dream, she saw the woman. She was huddled at the base of a tree, and it was impossible to tell if she was alive or dead. It was not until Eada reached the woman's side that she saw the swaddled child held in the woman's arms. Even as she soothed her nervous dogs with a pat, Eada knelt by the woman's side, smiling a greeting when her eyes slowly opened.

"Are you hurt?" she asked.

"Mortally," the woman replied, her voice a raspy thread of sound.

Eada needed to open the woman's cloak only a little to judge the truth of that. The pale gown beneath the cloak was soaked in the blood from several wounds. She felt the woman's face and found only the coldness of approaching death.

"Who are you and where are you from?" Eada asked.

"I am Aldith, wife of Edward of Bexhill." Aldith eased the blanket away from her child's face. "This is Alwyn, my son. He was born when the fire crossed the sky, a day after Easter."

"A powerful omen to be born under."

"And mayhap a good one, for he is one of the few who may survive the slaughter at Bexhill." Aldith touched a kiss to the baby's forehead. "I give him to you. Come, we both know that I am dying. I beg you to ease my passing by promising to care for my child."

"I promise," Eada said and silently prayed she would not have too much difficulty in convincing Drogo to let her keep that vow.

"May God bless you."

The words were said with Aldith's dying breath. Eada gently closed the woman's eyes and felt torn between grief and an inability to decide what to do next. She wanted to bury Aldith and wanted to grab the child and race back to camp, away from the shadows of the forest and the presence of death.

She sensed someone approaching even before she heard her dogs growl softly in warning. As the crack of a twig sounded in the stillness, Eada moved to shelter the baby with her body. When she looked up, she found herself staring at the point of a sword. She tore her gaze from that threat to look at the one who held it. Inwardly she breathed a sigh of relief when she saw the fair hair of the youth and his rough attire. He was Saxon and probably her age or only a year or two older. She knew she was not out of danger, but she felt she had a better chance of saving herself than if some Norman had found her.

"Would you kill one of your own people?" she asked.

"I have seen you with the Normans."

"I am Eada of Pevensey. I fear I was cursed with the chance to be one of the first Saxons captured. Would you kill me for that bad turn of luck?"

"I am Brun of Bexhill," he announced, but he eased his offensive stance only slightly. "Aldith was my cousin. If I believe you and you are lying, I could soon be rotting beside her and that is not a fate I wish to share."

"No. I would guess that you crave a chance to kill Normans."

"You would not sound so disparaging if you had seen what those cowardly dogs did in Bexhill," he snapped. "Mayhap taking a Norman between your thighs has stolen away your loyalty to your own people."

"Swine," she said almost pleasantly, her fear that he would hurt her fading away. "What man or men I have taken between my thighs does not concern you. I intend to survive this bloody, male folly. And now, I intend to see that this babe survives as well."

"He is my kinsman, not yours."

"You clearly intend to fight Normans. The babe will be safer with me." She tensed, saw her hounds look back to-

ward the camp, and hissed, "If you do not intend to surrender your sword to me, you had best leave this place
now."

"Surrender? Never. And why should I run?"

"Because a very large, battle-hardened Norman is coming this way." Eada was suddenly certain that Drogo had
woken up, found her gone, and had come to look for
her. "Do not think to whet your sword upon him."

"I am not without skill."

"You are not old enough to learn all that he has learned.
Go and save yourself for a bigger fight than this, if you
must fight at all. Just heed this one thing—if you decide
you have fought enough and that life is more precious
than death in an already-lost battle, surrender to one of
these men." After taking one quick glance behind her to
be sure Drogo was not yet in sight, she clearly named him
and each one of his knights. "Or to me."

"I will never surrender."

"There is no time to argue that. Just remember those
names. Now, go, for if Sir Drogo sees you holding a sword
on me, he will kill you before I can even cry halt. And,"
she added quickly as, after a brief hesitation, Brun
sheathed his sword and started to leave, "if you need aid,
call to me."

"Call to you?" Brun's voice was little more than a whisper in the dark for he had already disappeared into the
trees. "Unless you are with me, what can I gain from
calling to you?"

"There is no time to explain something I am not sure
I understand myself. Just do it. Call to me. It brought me
to your cousin. It might bring me to you."

The only answer she got was a faint rustling as he
moved away through the trees. Eada sighed and picked
up little Alwyn, who continued to sleep sweetly, blissfully
unaware of the tragedy around him. She had not been
able to save the child's mother; and Brun was so angry,

so eager to kill Normans, she suspected there might not be any saving him.

"What has happened here?"

Although Eada had been waiting for Drogo, she was still startled when he spoke. His voice sounded frighteningly loud in the moonlit wood. When he stepped up beside her, she looked warily at him. The anger tightening his face began to ease as he studied Aldith's body.

"Is she dead?" he asked, finally releasing his grip on his sword hilt.

"Yes. Somehow she dragged herself here from Bexhill, which has been laid waste." Eada shook her head. "There was nothing I could do to save her."

"How did you know she was here?"

Eada grimaced. "I heard her call for help."

"I heard nothing."

"I heard her in my head," she said, watching him closely as she stood up, Alwyn held close to her chest. "Her voice was in my head and it pulled me here."

She cursed inwardly when she heard the defensive tone in her voice. What he thought or felt about the strange things happening to her should not matter, but they did. That annoyed her for she did not want to care about his opinion of her—not now, not when they stood on opposite sides of a bloody war, and especially not when she stood next to the body of a young woman slaughtered by the Normans.

"You heard her call to you within your head, but not with your ears?" he asked.

"Yes, within my head."

"Then you can see what is to happen, know what lies ahead."

"No. I *heard* her. I did not see her or know what I would find when I followed the voice."

He made a sharp, dismissive gesture with his hand. "You *heard* her and you *saw* Sir Guy. Call it what you will, you know things others do not and cannot. Did you plan to keep this a secret from me?"

"There was no secret to keep. I do not understand this any better than you do. I have never had such things happen to me before. Not until I met you. Mayhap you brought this curse with you from France."

"I do not think so," he drawled, and taking her by the arm, he started to walk back to camp. "There is no need for you to be afraid to tell me such things."

"I am not afraid."

Drogo ignored her sulky protest. "I do not understand such things, neither how nor why they happen, but I do not condemn them."

"But you fear them. Everyone does. That fear is why Old Edith lived and died alone."

"And that is why you must be careful. Yes, perhaps I do fear it, but that fear is born of uncertainty, not some idea that the devil works through you or some other foolishness. But you know how others will think and, I say again, that is why you must be careful. You must be secretive."

"Do you expect me to ignore what I see or hear? Should I have just pretended that I did not see the warning about Sir Guy or hear that poor woman's cries for help? Am I to push such things aside and do nothing?"

"No, but you must learn how to act so that people do not begin to question how you know such things."

"I am hoping that these things will not happen often, will, in fact, stop happening; but you are right, and I will try to do as you suggest."

"So obedient," he murmured and met her cross look with a smile. For a moment they walked through the wood in silence, but then Drogo asked calmly, "What do you intend to do with that baby?"

"This baby?" She sighed when he looked at her. "I

promised the woman I would take care of him. His name is Alwyn, and he is about six-months old."

"And you plan to fulfill that promise as we battle and march our way to London?"

"You could leave me behind in some safe haven and then you'd need not fear for the babe's safety."

Drogo ignored that. "It will not be easy; but you have May to help you and, perhaps, we will find a safe place to leave him until this war is over. Our problem now is to think of a reasonable explanation for how you could take a walk in the wood and return with a baby. It will not take long for people to wonder how you found him when no one else recalls hearing or seeing him."

She watched him when he paused just outside of camp and frowned down at her. He was obviously trying to think of a tale no one would question. Eada said nothing, not wanting to disturb his thinking, especially when she had no ideas to offer.

"I think we shall just say that you slipped into the wood to relieve yourself and got lost in the dark," Drogo finally said. "While you were wandering about trying to find your way back to the camp, you stumbled upon the child and his already-dead mother. Not wishing to leave the child to die, you picked him up and continued to wander until I found you."

It was a good story and would be easy to remember, but Eada felt compelled to say, "I never get lost."

"This time you did—hopelessly so," he replied as he took her by the hand again and walked into the camp.

Eada was embarrassed to find everyone awake, waiting for their return. She knew that, except for May, who rushed to her side, most of that concern was for Drogo, who would not have been in the wood if she had not slipped away without telling anyone. If there were a next time, and she heartily prayed that there would not be, she would have to remember that she could not just run away without a word.

"What a sweet-faced child," May said as she lightly touched Alwyn's thick, blond curls. "Where did he come from?"

Eada dutifully repeated the tale Drogo had concocted, feeling guilty about lying to May. At the moment, however, all the men were close at hand, listening, and she was not sure if Drogo wished her to hide her skill from May and the men as well as from everyone else. When May shyly asked if she could take the baby, Eada placed the child in her outstretched arms. She watched May closely as the woman walked back to the rough blanket-bed she shared with Ivo, cooing and cuddling the small child every step of the way.

After glancing around to see that everyone had returned to their beds, Eada murmured to Drogo, "I think May has suffered the loss of a child—whether one of her own, a young sibling, or one she cared for, I do not know, but she *has* lost one."

"More visions?" Drogo asked as he pulled her toward their bed then sat down and yanked off his boots.

"No." She sat down next to him, tugged off her small boots, and slipped beneath the blanket. "It was just something I sensed in the hungry way she took possession of the child. She was gentle, but she grasped that baby like a starving man grasps a scrap of bread. At first I thought she rushed to my side because she had been afraid for me, but although I do think she was concerned, that is not why she ran to me. No, in truth, she did not run to me; she ran to the child."

"Then, perhaps, she will care for the child," Drogo said as he slipped beneath the blanket, curled his arm around her waist, and tugged her close against him. "That would allow you to keep your promise to that woman yet not have to care for the child yourself." He nuzzled her hair, sorely regretting their complete lack of privacy and the inability to leave the protection of the army in search of a private place. "Unless you want the child."

"There was no time to become attached to the baby. If May truly wishes to care for Alwyn, she can, for I am sure he will be much loved. Poor Aldith can rest easy about that." Eada sighed. "I just wish I could have given her a burial, no matter how hasty or meager."

Drogo pressed a kiss to her shoulder. "I will send Ivo and Tancred out to attend to her before we leave." He fought to subdue his hunger for her as he rested his cheek against the top of her head. "Rest now, Eada. There is little time left before the dawn when we must continue on to Hastings."

She put her hand over his and closed her eyes. "And what will happen in Hastings?"

"We will wait for Harold to bow to William and accept him as his king."

"Then you will wait a very long time."

Eada cursed, subtly rubbing her backside as she hopped out of the cart and then held the baby as May climbed down. They had left the camp at dawn just as Drogo had said they would, hesitating only long enough to bury Aldith. This time, they would set up a more permanent and, Eada hoped, a more comfortable camp.

As she helped May and Ivo empty the wagon, she looked toward the castle the Normans were hastily erecting. It was no more than a wooden fort on a mound raised from the dirt dug out of an encircling trench, but that was equal to what many of the Saxon lords lived in. What troubled her was the mark it made upon the land, a Norman mark of power on Saxon land. What saddened her was her unshakeable conviction that it was but the first of hundreds.

"Do you think they intend to wait here for Harold?" said a young male voice from behind her.

As Eada turned to face Godwin, she tried to hide the dismay she felt when she saw that Sir Guy was making his camp right next to Drogo's. "It appears that that is their plan."

"Do you think Harold will come?"

"It would be justice if he hesitated. The way these men are clearing the area of food, there will soon be very little to eat. So, if Harold waits long enough, these Normans will be starving and the winter will set in and then they will flee back to France."

"Which would be a nice, bloodless way to end the war," he said and smiled faintly.

"But it will not happen," she said after briefly returning his smile.

"Do you know something I do not?" Godwin asked, frowning and combing his fingers through his roughly cut, long, fair hair. "What you said to me before and what you just said leaves me feeling that you know what lies ahead."

"Not really. There was an old woman called Edith near Pevensey who knew such things, though. She said that the Normans would win."

"She was a seer?"

"I suppose. She called them *sendings*. She heard things, and she was never wrong when she said something would happen. Well, she said that the Normans would rule us."

"And that is why you want me to save myself and the women and the babes. You feel that the crown already belongs to William. Is that why you are so good to the Norman who captured you?"

Eada grimaced and shook her head. "For all I tell everyone else to bow and survive, I have too much pride and anger to heed my own advice. No, Old Edith told me that fate had chosen Sir Drogo as my mate, and I soon had to accept that, as always, she was right. Sir Drogo does not know that," she added, glancing sharply at Godwin, who nodded, silently agreeing to keep her secret. "Sir Drogo and his men are good, kind, and honorable men; so, since some Norman would undoubtedly have grabbed me, I am glad that it was him." She glanced behind Godwin to look at the two women preparing a fire. "How are they?"

"Not well. We were not taken by a good, kind, and honorable man. Sir Guy treats us all like the meanest of slaves—and it is worse for the women, of course. Last night he bedded Elga and handed poor Hilde to a fellow knight to use as he pleased." Godwin sighed and shook his head. "I ached to kill him, but I fought to recall your advice. This morning, Hilde forgot to feed or tend to her children, so I had to; and I realized that, although I do not think I can save the women, the children need me."

"Yes, Sir Guy would not care for them if the women died."

"No. In truth, I think he would kill them or leave them for the wolves."

"Yes, he holds such cruelty in his soul. It is good to have you near to hand to talk to, but I do wish Sir Guy had not chosen to camp here. There is bad blood between him and Sir Drogo. I fear there may be trouble."

Godwin nodded. "Sir Guy hates Sir Drogo—deeply. Sir Guy should be closely watched. The kind of hate he holds is a sickness." He shyly patted Eada on the arm. "Do not worry on this. Sir Drogo is a strong, skilled knight. Now, I must begin to work or Sir Guy might catch me idle and talking."

Eada smiled fleetingly and left him. She busied herself laying out Drogo's things in the tent Ivo had erected on a small mound at the far end of their camp. Since Drogo's men had their own shelters and even Ivo had a small one he would share with May and the baby, she and Drogo would be alone again. When that thought made her shiver with anticipation, Eada lightly scolded herself for being a wanton.

"Mistress," May called as she cautiously entered. "Young Unwin has come to say that Sir Drogo will return within the hour."

"Is there somewhere I could wash?" Eada asked, grimacing at her mud-stained gown. "After two days in that cart and sleeping upon the ground, I feel very dirty."

"Ivo has prepared something for Sir Drogo." May caught Eada by the hand and tugged her out of the tent. "If we shelter it with blankets, you can wash in comfort."

Eada took one look at the vat set near the brook edging their camp and knew that Ivo had foraged while she had been busy elsewhere. It troubled her, but she pushed her unease aside and said nothing to Ivo. He was doing what all armies did, including the English, and she knew he would not steal so much that people would starve. Others would undoubtedly take what he had left behind, making Ivo's kindness useless, but she could do nothing about that.

As soon as the vat was filled and encircled by blankets, Eada took her bath. It felt good to get clean and she allowed the pleasure of the bath to push aside her concerns. When Drogo returned, she wanted to be clean and in good spirits. This could be the last time they had together before the real war began.

Ten

"What is to happen now?" Eada asked Drogo as they sat with the others by the fire and enjoyed Ivo's hearty venison stew.

"We wait," Drogo answered as he accepted the wineskin from Tancred, and he took a deep drink before handing it to Eada.

"Wait for what?" Eada took a drink of wine and passed it along to Unwin, who sat on her right.

"For Harold. William has sent a messenger to Harold in London. Harold will either send a messenger back or come himself."

"You do not still think he will come to bow before William, do you?"

"No, although it would save his people a lot of grief and destruction."

Eada glanced around at the hundreds of camp fires covering the land and sighed. "Not too much. You have brought thousands of men here and they all seek some gain. And even if Harold hands the crown to William, there will be all the Saxon earls, lordlings, and thanes to deal with. William will want to give his loyal men land, and he will have to take that land from someone. Not everyone will give it up easily."

"You sound very accepting."

"I am simply trying to be for there is nothing I can do to change matters." She tore off a chunk of the bread

May had baked and passed the rest to Drogo. "Nothing can stop this. William will win."

"I wish I could be as sure of that as you are."

She shrugged. "Your time at the monastery might make it difficult to believe in omens and dreams. Old Edith said that the fire which moved across the sky at Easter marked Harold's end and that William was riding that tail to the throne."

"So, Old Edith *was* a witch," exclaimed Unwin.

Eada gave the youth such a cross look that he blushed. "Just because someone hears or sees what is to come does not make her a witch. Could it not be God's hand at work? That poor old woman never hurt anyone, man or beast. I think people drove her away out of envy, because she was chosen to learn such truths and they were not. Would you have called our King Edward a witch?"

"Of course not."

"He had a dream, too, you know. He had it on his deathbed." Eada was unsettled by how quickly and intently everyone's interest was fixed upon her. "It is said that he awoke out of the fever's madness and recounted a dream. He had met two monks he had known in Normandy, monks who had died a long time ago. They said that the country was cursed because of the evil done by our earls and our churchmen. They prophesized that in one year plus a day after Edward died, the land would be scarred with war and fire. Only when a green tree, felled halfway up its trunk and that piece taken three furlongs away, should put itself back together without any aid from man and grow leaves and fruit again, will God cease to punish us."

"It sounds as if you are to be punished forever," Drogo said after a long moment of heavy silence. "Once cut, no tree can grow back together, especially not if one part of it is taken so far away."

Eada smiled faintly. "I did find that difficult to believe

myself. It would require the log to grow feet and walk
back."

"And what evil have your earls and churchmen done?"

"Well, I am certain someone must have done something bad or wicked."

"Without a doubt," he drawled and smiled when she
laughed softly.

"So, all of this means that the battle is already won,"
said Unwin.

"If one holds faith with dreams and prophesies, then,
yes," responded Serle as he idly poked at the fire with a
long stick. "I would still watch my skinny backside, boy,
as we march to London to crown William. No one has
dreamt or seen that the English will lay down their weapons and welcome us with open arms. And no one has
said that young Unwin can walk through the arrows and
battle-axs unhurt."

"I intend to fight whenever I must," Unwin declared
stoutly, and he grasped the hilt of his sword.

Serle looked at the youth with open amusement and
made a gently demeaning remark about little boys and
hot blood. Eada shook her head and laughed softly as
Unwin rose to the bait. She had not known the man long,
but it was easy to see that Serle loved to tease the younger
knights. Her attention was drawn away from the ensuing
argument when Drogo put his arm around her shoulders,
tugged her closer, and touched a kiss to her ear.

"Shall we leave these children to their play?" he whispered.

Eada suddenly found herself fighting the urge to blush
so fiercely that she could only nod in reply. She did not
really understand why she felt so shy and slightly embarrassed about what everyone would think as Drogo led her
to his tent. It was no secret that she and Drogo were
lovers, and not one of his men had treated her as anything less than a lady because of it.

Once inside the tent, Eada busied herself tidying the already very neat inside. She heard the rope-strung cot creak as Drogo sat on it, but forced herself not to look his way. She needed time to calm herself. Since they were already lovers, had already spent one long heated night in each other's arms, she felt that her sudden shyness was foolish and wanted to hide it from Drogo until she had completely conquered it.

When, a few moments later, she felt Drogo's hand on her arm, she gasped. She had been concentrating so completely on calming herself that she had not heard him move. Praying that the shadows cast by the tallow candles would hide the blush she could not subdue, she turned to face him.

"Why so timid, *ma petite?*" Drogo asked in a soft, gentle voice as he lightly ran his fingertip over the fine line of her cheekbones. "You blush like the sweetest maid." He smiled faintly when she scowled at him.

"It is most annoying. I do not know what troubles me," she grumbled as he took her by the hand and led her to the cot. "It is not as if I am an innocent."

"One night with a man does not fully steal your innocence." Drogo sat down, tugged her forward to stand between his legs, and began to unlace her gown. "I have the feeling that you could bed down with the whole of William's army and still hold that sweet hint of innocence. It is too deep a part of you."

She trembled as her gown slid down her body. Even in the dim light of the candles she could read the hunger on his face and it roused her own. Eada knew it was not simply fate forcing her to its will, either. It was heady, intoxicating, to know that she could stir this man to such passion.

Briefly, as he continued to slowly undress her, she scolded herself for succumbing to the sin of vanity, but that fault was easily shrugged aside. She was not vain, had never even considered her appearance something to be concerned about. The proof that Drogo wanted her, badly, was there to see in the way his breathing had increased, the way his features had tightened, and the way his hands shook as he slowly removed her chemise, the last of her covering.

Eada reached out to thread her fingers through his hair. Her shyness and embarrassment were gone, pushed aside by her own passion and the way Drogo so reverently undressed her. When he pulled her even closer to touch a kiss to each breast, she sighed with pleasure. She then grimaced as her fingers reached the abrupt end of his hair and scraped over the stubble of his shaved head.

"Are you going to let your hair grow?" she asked, making no attempt to elude him as he wrapped his arms around her, fell back upon the cot, and pulled her down with him.

"You do not like the way my hair is cut?" he asked.

Since he was covering her throat with lightly feverish kisses Eada knew she had not insulted him. "No. I do not like it. It looks as if you had a shepherd cut it and the poor fool forgot that he tended a man and not a sheep." His warm breath caressed the hollow of her shoulder as he laughed.

"You wish me to have flowing locks like your Saxon men?"

"I think you would look very handsome."

"And now you try to bend me to your way with flattery?"

When he grinned at her, she grinned back. "Is it working?"

Drogo laughed as he smoothed his hands down her small, sleek back. "It might if vanity had not already begun its work."

"What do you mean?" She wriggled around until she straddled his body with hers and then gently rubbed herself against his hardness, savoring the gasp of pleasure he could not fully subdue.

"Many of the Normans have eyed those flowing Saxon locks with envy. This shorn head serves little purpose. One still sweats in one's armor and, with no hair to protect a man from the roughness of his hood or helmet, the skin ofttimes grows raw. There are many good reasons for a man to let his hair grow, but most men will make their decision because of simple, sinful vanity."

"I suppose having no hair does lessen the chance of getting vermin."

"No, for half the hair is still there."

Eada gasped with surprise when he swiftly turned and neatly settled her beneath him. "You will land us upon the ground. This cot is the largest I have ever seen, but I am not sure it is large enough for such swift, unplanned movement."

"If it can hold me as I thrash about with a fever—"

"When did you have a fever?" she asked and then felt foolish for the alarm she had just experienced. It was clear that he had survived that illness with no scars or weaknesses.

Drogo smiled against her collarbone when he heard the concern in her voice. It pleased him to know that she felt more for him than a heedless passion. He realized that the speed with which they had become lovers had left him uncertain. Although he did not know what the future held for either of them, he knew he wanted more than desire from Eada. It was wrong, probably even callous, to want such emotions from her even as he fought his own feelings, but he could not help himself. There was a greed within him, a gnawing hunger to know that Eada cared for him.

"I but caught one of the many fevers a warrior often finds upon a march or the battlefield. Ivo never left my side and I believe I owe him my life. He nursed me well."

"He is very loyal to you. Has he always been your servant?"

"Since we were small boys together." He framed her breasts with his hands, teasing her nipples into an inviting hardness with his thumbs. "I do not really wish to talk about Ivo, my past illnesses, or his healing skills." He stroked the tip of her breast with his tongue. "I do not believe that I wish to do much talking at all."

Eada laughed, her amusement swiftly changing to a soft gasp of pleasure when he began to suckle. She curled herself around his strong body, arching into him. Talking about anything swiftly became impossible.

Her mind finally cleared of desire's haze, Eada looked at the man sprawled on top of her, his dark head resting on her breasts. She felt both stunned and frightened by the revelation that swept over her. She loved him. Since she had first looked into his eyes and felt drawn to him, she had thought only on fate, destiny, and passion. Eada suspected that she had started to love him then. Although it neatly explained why she had so quickly become his lover, this was far more frightening than being a pawn of fate. This was also an appalling time to fall in love, even if the man she loved was a Norman, one of the victors. The fact that Drogo *was* William's man only made it a lot worse.

Briefly, Eada cursed Old Edith's prediction and doubted her own shattering conclusion. A moment later she felt guilty and sincerely apologized to her old friend. Edith had only told the truth as it was sent to her. It had not been the woman's fault if that truth caused someone trouble. She also knew that she could not talk herself out of being in love, no matter how much she might want to. She loved Drogo, and the wise thing to do was to accept it and decide what she would or would not do next.

One thing she would not do, she decided as she idly toyed with his thick hair, was tell Drogo. She felt sure that the man cared for her, but dared not judge why or how much. Passion and a deep sense of responsibility could make him act in a way that appeared to be caring. Until she knew for certain what he did or did not feel for her, she was not going to bare her heart and soul to him. The man held enough power over her now, through passion and her deep need to be safe. Eada saw no reason to give him even more. The man had also made no mention of a future that included her. Although it hurt to remind herself of that, Eada knew she could not let herself forget it.

When he suddenly lifted his head to look at her, she felt a blush warm her cheeks and inwardly cursed. The man could not read her thoughts, so she had nothing to feel guilty or embarrassed about. When his eyes narrowed slightly, she knew he had noticed her discomfort even in the dim light, and she hurried to think of some explanation.

"Is something wrong?" Drogo asked as he propped himself up on one elbow and lightly touched her cheek.

"I just remembered something about my journey into the wood last night, something I forgot to tell you." Although she had not really forgotten, had simply decided he did not need to know about Brun, Eada decided that the tale would now serve a good purpose. She definitely did not want to tell him what she had really been thinking.

"Something else happened that night?" He frowned at her when she lightly bit her bottom lip, then he tensed. "There was a man out there."

"How can you guess these things with such accuracy?" she demanded sulkily. "There was nothing in what I just said that would tell you that, and I know that you did not see a man. There was only me, the baby, and the dead woman in the clearing when you arrived."

Drogo did not reply to her question, treating it as no more than a muttered complaint. He did not want to answer her, for his statement that she had met a man had not been a clever guess or knowledge born of skillful deduction. For one brief moment, he had scorned all her talk of hearing a woman's cries for help and suspected that she had really crept away to meet some Saxon spy or lover. Drogo was heartily glad that he had not had the time to say any more than he had, for he knew he could have delivered a serious insult to Eada.

"I but guessed," he said finally. "It had to have been a Saxon man, because a Norman would have killed you or brought you back to camp."

"Yes, it was a Saxon man. A youth, my age or a year or two older. He was Aldrith's kinsman. He had obviously been near the camp for he knew I was from there. He burns to kill Normans, to avenge the slaughter in Bexhill."

"I am surprised he did not wish to kill you. Not only does he find you next to his dead kinswoman, but he knows that you abide with his enemy."

Eada could tell by the way Drogo watched her that he was not making an idle statement. He knew exactly what the youth had done, probably because it was what he would have done under the same circumstances. Drogo was simply waiting to see if she would tell him the truth or try to push him aside with a lie. She knew she would have been angry, even insulted, by his suspicious attitude except that she had contemplated telling just such a lie or not telling him anything at all about that part of her meeting with Brun.

"You know that he thought to kill me. I saw his sword point before I saw him."

"And that should clearly show you the danger of wandering about alone."

"Most clearly, but if you wait for me to vow that I shall

never do so again, you will be dust in the earth before it happens." She touched her fingertips to his lips when he started to talk. "And do not weary your tongue telling me about the dangers awaiting a woman alone. I am no fool. I know all about them."

"Yet you will not vow to take care—"

"No, I will not, for it is a vow I know I will break, which will distress me and displease you." She nervously curled a lock of her hair around her finger again and again. "It is most difficult to explain. When I heard that woman's cries in my head, I did try to ignore them; but I could not. I was pulled toward her. I was afraid to enter the dark forest, knew it was neither safe nor wise, yet I could not stop myself. Although I pray it will not happen again, if it does, I know I will do the same. My head was so filled with her voice and the urgency to answer her that there was no room for another thought, for caution or hesitation."

Drogo gently eased the much abused lock of hair from her fingers and pressed a kiss to the palm of her hand before pulling her back into his arms. He did not fully understand what she meant about hearing the woman's cries in her head, but he could easily sympathize with her uneasiness. He knew he was praying as hard as she was that her vision about Sir Guy and the incident with the woman in the wood were rare occurrences. People's superstitions and fears could turn such gifts into curses, bringing danger and even death.

"Perhaps these things are caused by the turmoil around you," he murmured, kissing her ear and smoothing his hands down her back. "All the body's humors are strengthened when the scent of battle is in the air. Grief, anger, fear, and all the other emotions roused by war are strong ones. I think you are also feeling a need to help your people in whatever way you can."

"Yes, I am," she agreed softly as she cuddled nearer to

him, pressing her ear to his chest so that she could hear the soothing, steady beat of his heart. "It would be easier to bear if I knew that this strange skill was a gift from God, one He has granted me only for this time of war to allow me to help my people and then it would go away."

He smiled faintly as he reached out to snuff the candle on the stool by the bed. One moment she speaks of her new skill as a gift from God and, in the next, is wishing it gone as if it is some annoying fly. Drogo also wished her strange skill would fade—for many reasons. He could not have Eada rushing off to answer voices or trying to save someone from a fate she had been told of. The chance of others discovering her *gift* was greater than he liked. And although he still did not know what the future held for them, he reluctantly admitted to himself that he did not like her *gift* because it made him feel as if there were a part of her he could never hope to understand. It separated them in a way he could not explain, and he loathed it.

Eada began to grow heavy against him, and he realized that she was going to sleep. He briefly considered restirring her passion so that they could make love again, then brutally subdued his own selfish desires. She had suffered through a great deal of grief and hardship since he had found her and there was undoubtedly a great deal more to come. She needed the rest to keep her strength. He grimaced as she murmured in her sleep and curled her lithe body around him. It might be noble to let her rest, but it was going to be very uncomfortable.

As he idly combed his fingers through her hair and closed his eyes, he thought on what the future might hold for them. The most satisfying vision was that they would all survive the war, William would be crowned king, and he would gain the land he sought, a rich piece of land that could support them all. Then he could retire to his

demesne with Eada. She was wellborn and he had made
no bonds with another woman, so he could take her as
his wife.

His mind refused to linger on that pleasant dream,
however. It quickly showed him the other paths fate could
send him down, and none of them led to a future for
him and Eada together. She would not be his leman once
the war had ended and he could never ask her to, which
meant that they would have to part. The thought of that
left Drogo feeling somewhat frantic, and he tightened his
hold on her.

What became clear to him was that his future held only
one real certainty. Sometime soon, he would be faced
with a hard choice. He was not high enough in William's
court to gain a rich demesne, so he would need to find
some money. Eada had none. As far as he knew, she had
no dowry at all; and even if she did, one way or another,
the war would take it.

It was both irresponsible and blind, but he decided to
stop thinking about the future. He would settle the matter
when and if he had to. Thinking about it only brought
turmoil, a hundred possibilities, and no certainties. Eada
also asked for no promises, so it was foolish to worry over
what he might and might not be able to give her. For
now, he would simply enjoy Eada, he decided as he
brushed a kiss over the top of her head. He had no doubt
that she would keep him completely and, often, delight-
fully occupied in the days to come. All she asked of him
was that he keep her safe and, as Drogo forced himself
to relax, allowing sleep to fold over him, he prayed that
he had the wit and skill to fulfill that modest wish.

Eleven

Eada wrapped her arms around herself, clutching the cloak she wore closer to her body, but that did not end her shivering. It was not the chill October morning that made her shudder but the sight of thousands of men preparing for battle. After a fortnight of messages between William and Harold, long enough for her to nurse a small hope that matters would be settled peacefully, the time for battle had come.

The English had arrived in the night. She did not have to see them to know that they were prepared to fight. She could hear them. Their shouts of *Olicrosse!* and *Godamite!* cut through the morning mists. The steady chant of *Ut! Ut!*, combined with the beating of their shields, made a frightening martial din.

She looked at Drogo and his men. They had stood at arms for most of the night. That had been terrifying enough, but when the priest had come to take their confessions, she had had to hide in the tent. It would have helped no one if she had wept with helplessness and fear as she had felt inclined to.

Something she did not care to look at too closely made her sure that this was the day that the fate of England would be decided. For a while, she had cherished the dream that the decision would be made peacefully, but she had never wavered in the belief that that decision would be made in favor of William. Now, as she watched and listened to the preparations for battle, she could only pray that the decision was made with as little bloodletting as possible.

The cause of the fear and grief knotting her insides was twofold. She mourned the Saxon loses to come and was terrified that someone she knew or loved would soon die. It grieved her to watch Drogo go to battle with her people and it terrified her to think of how, in only moments, Drogo would face battle-axs, swords, and arrows. Soon the people she loved would be doing their utmost to kill the man she loved. She was so filled with confused emotions that she felt choked with them and her head throbbed painfully. When Drogo walked toward her, she tried to smile, but the sad look upon his face told her that it was a poor effort.

"Perhaps you should confine yourself to my tent until this is over," he suggested as he cupped her chin in his hand and brushed a kiss over her trembling lips.

"I will still be able to hear it all," she whispered, her strained emotions stealing the strength from her voice.

"I ache to comfort you, to take the sadness from your eyes, but I know I cannot. Even if I swore to fight no Saxon, tossing aside all honor, it would not help you."

"No, for the battle must still be fought." She reached up to touch his cheek. "Be careful. I know you are a strong, skilled knight, but you fight for honor and gain while my people fight to survive as a people, for their laws, their customs, and their homes."

"Do you think they know that?"

"How can they not know? William is a Norman and he will try to make England like Normandy. One does not have to believe in omens and prophesies to know that."

Drogo nodded then gave her one short, fierce kiss and walked away. Eada stood, unable to move or speak, as she watched him mount Faramond and ride away with his men. She bit her tongue until it hurt to stop herself from calling after him, begging him to return.

When a pale, tight-lipped May, holding a cooing Alwyn close to her chest, stepped up beside her and took her hand, Eada clung to her tightly. Despite the sounds of thousands of men preparing to do battle that drifted back to them, the camp was strangely quiet. Norman and Saxon alike were subdued and tensely awaited the battle and its outcome. If the Normans lost, they would all have to flee or fight the victorious Saxons, who would overrun the camp looking for bounty and revenge. Eada suspected she was the only one who had no doubt about the outcome of the battle.

"Sir Drogo will be safe, mistress," May said, awkwardly patting Eada on the shoulder.

"Your words might be more of a comfort if you did not look so afraid," Eada drawled, smiling faintly at May's discomfort.

"I confess that I am not sure what I am afraid of. The men we ride with appear to be strong, skillful knights, all the protection any woman could need. I do not really tremble with fear for their lives, yet tremble I do." She shook her head and gave Eada a furtive, faintly embarrassed glance. "My man is not even riding into battle."

"There is a lot to fear today, May, even if Ivo does not carry a weapon. I, too, tremble yet I feel certain that the Normans will win. Today is a day scribes will write about until we are all dust. The importance of the battle may be what makes us all tremble. This will decide who rules this land and we have never been a part of such a weighty decision before." Eada reached out to lightly pat little Alwyn's back. "Do you have any family who may suffer on this day?"

"None that I know of. I was left alone and taken as a bond-servant while still a child. There may be a Saxon warrior or two who is kinsman to me, but I know him not and I doubt he knows of me. You have family—"

"Old Edith believed that my mother, brother, and sister would survive."

"Then try to be at ease, mistress. Ones such as we do not have the power to end the bloodshed. We can only save ourselves. And you have already saved others. This sweet babe, young Godwin, and probably the babes he cares for all owe their lives to you. Let that be enough."

Before Eada could reply, an ashen-faced Godwin rushed up and grabbed her by the arm, clutching her tightly as he said, "You must come with me, mistress."

"I am not sure I should enter Sir Guy's camp."

"He is not there. He has left his captives alone." Godwin's brief smile was little more than a bitter twisting of his lips. "Where can we go when we are surrounded by Normans and a battle lurks but a short walk away? Please, you must come with me."

Even as she allowed him to tug her toward Sir Guy's camp, she asked, "What do you need me for?"

"When Sir Guy left, I entered his tent to clean it and I found poor Hilde."

"Poor Hilde?" asked May as she hurried along behind Godwin and Eada.

Godwin did not reply, simply lifted the flap to Sir Guy's tent and nudged the two women inside. Eada softly echoed May's cry of horror. Hilde lay sprawled on the smoothed dirt floor inside the tent, staring sightlessly up at the dawn through the hole that allowed the fire's smoke out. Her wrists had been slashed and the knife she had used lay in the pool of blood surrounding her lifeless body. She was naked and the bruises marring her pale body revealed that her final days had not been easy to endure. Eada was not sure which horrified her more, the sight of a woman who had committed the grave sin of suicide or that Sir Guy could be so cruel that he could push a woman to put her immortal soul at risk just to escape him.

"Has anyone else seen this?" she demanded of Godwin as she took a deep, steadying breath and warily approached the body.

"No. Elga has not returned from the camp of the Norman who won her favors with a toss of the dice and I have kept the children away." Godwin shook his head. "Suicide is a mortal sin. I did not know what to do. Shall I fetch a priest? There are plenty of them wandering about."

"Do not fetch a priest until we have Hilde cleaned and readied for burial."

"Now that I think, a priest will not attend one who died by her own hand."

"One will attend to Hilde for we are *not* going to let anyone know that she killed herself," Eada said as she grabbed a blanket from a pile in the far corner of the tent.

"But she cannot be buried in consecrated ground."

"Today I think only Normans who are killed in battle will rest in consecrated ground and probably not all of them. Most of the men who die today will be hastily buried or left to rot upon the battlefield. I do not think a priest will trouble himself to ask too many questions about one poor Saxon captive." Eada spread the blanket out on a clean part of the dirt floor then moved back to Hilde's side.

Godwin helped Eada lift Hilde off the blood-soaked dirt and lay her face-down upon the clean blanket. "She should not be tended to by a priest, Eada," he said, "for she died by her own hand, unshriven."

"I do not see this as a suicide but as a murder."

"I really do not think that Sir Guy cut her wrists."

"He might as well have." Eada looked at Godwin. "It was because of what Sir Guy did to her that poor Hilde did this. She probably thought that her soul was already so steeped in sin that committing this grave one made no difference."

"But if we lie to a priest, do we not risk our own souls?" asked May.

"I do not ask you to lie," Eada replied. "We shall clean her and wrap her in this blanket for burial, and we shall tell the priest that she died of grief. I do not condone what she has done, only understand it, and now I wish to protect her children." She nodded when Godwin's eyes widened with sudden understanding. "We are in the midst of a war; no one needs to know *how* she died. The children do not need to bear the burden of her sin, one I feel certain she committed in blind despair. For the children's sake, I am willing to carry this secret to the grave."

"As am I," said May. "I will fetch what is needed to clean her and leave Alwyn with Ivo. Do you want me to ask him to dig a grave? I think I can make myself understood about that."

"Yes, May, if he is willing. We can do it if we must." As soon as May left, Eada turned to Godwin. "We need to clean away this blood-soaked earth." She grimaced. "Anyone who sees this will easily guess what has happened."

"Eada?" Godwin lightly bit his bottom lip as he hesitated, then asked, "If one of us still knows or cares for her children as they age and one day they ask about their mother, are we to lie to them?"

"That is a question I cannot answer. It must be decided when and if the time comes and then one will have to consider if the children really want to know the truth or can accept it. They may never even ask. My concern is for now, and *now* those children have suffered enough, as has poor Hilde."

"Agreed. Having the priest tend to her may not help though. God knows what Hilde has done."

"True, so let us leave the forgiveness or punishment of her sins in His hands."

"One more question before we begin this work. What if Sir Guy decides that he need not feed or tend the children now that their mother is gone?"

"She did not tend to them while she was alive, not since Sir Guy took her captive. You have cared for them."

"I know, but I think he took little notice. Now he may think that there is no one to care for them."

"If Sir Guy casts them out, put them into our camp. May and I will tend to them. May will probably gather them to her as abruptly and as tightly as she did Alwyn. Her man Ivo also appears most happy about that and so reveals that he holds a great love for children."

"And Sir Drogo will not mind?"

Eada grimaced. "I do not think he will be happy, for he is a poor knight, but he will not cast them aside. Come, let us get to work before someone else stumbles by and this dark secret is out before we even have a chance to keep it."

It proved to be hard work to clear the dirt floor of all sign of the tragedy. Godwin had to sneak buckets of blood-ied dirt out of the tent and dump them in the surrounding wood then bring in clean dirt to replace it. May had re-turned, cleaned Hilde, and dressed her for her burial be-fore Eada and Godwin had repaired the floor. Godwin then hurried away to find one of the many priests who had filled the camp at dawn, giving each Norman knight the church's blessings, taking confessions, and insuring that no knight would die unshriven upon the battlefield.

When the priest arrived, Eada found the grief she felt for the forlorn Hilde pushed aside by anger. The priest was young and filled with self-importance. Duty forced him to tend to Hilde, but he made it very clear that he felt such service to a Saxon was demeaning to him. What guilt Eada felt over lying to him about how the woman had died faded quickly. She had to bite her tongue to stop herself from reminding the young man that pride and vanity were sins.

Ivo appeared just as the priest was leaving and Eada smiled at the younger, smaller man's obvious fear. The priest lost all of his arrogance as he warily edged around Ivo and fled the tent. A dosing of fear and humility could only do the priest some good, Eada decided as Ivo picked up Hilde's body and they all followed him out of the tent. She and Godwin paused only long enough to collect Hilde's two sad-eyed children.

The burial was at the far western edge of the huge camp in a spot beneath some trees that was already marked by several graves. It was not until Eada helped the others pile some rocks on the grave that Eada realized that the sounds filling the air around them had changed. The battle had begun. Blindly, she took a step toward the harsh noises only to be stopped by a big hand clasping her by the arm. She looked at Ivo in surprise for she had not heard him approach.

"You must stay here with me," Ivo said, frowning down at her.

"Yes, I know." She sighed and rubbed a hand over her face. "I was not thinking. I just heard the battle and moved toward it."

"If you draw too near, you will be killed," said Godwin as he brushed off his hands and took little Welcome into his arms.

"I know that, too." She smiled at young Eric, who clung tightly to the hem of Godwin's jupon. "I do not think the children understand what has happened."

"No, but I will try to explain it to them. It may be a blessing that their mother has shunned them for so long, too sick in her mind and her heart to tend to them. They have turned to me."

Ivo briefly placed one of his big hands on Eric's fair

head. "If Sir Guy wants them to leave, May and I will take them. We like children."

After Eada translated Ivo's words, Godwin smiled and nodded his gratitude, but said to Eada, "That eases my mind, yet I pray that Sir Guy will continue to be blind to them. I have grown fond of them." He winced, briefly looking toward the battle which poisoned the air around them with the sounds of weapons and death. "May we abide with you for a while? I think this day will be hard to endure and I would prefer not to be alone."

Eada hooked her arm through his as May took a shy Eric by the hand. "Yes, stay with us. If nothing else, you will be one more to help keep me from doing something foolish."

"Your man will return," Godwin said as they all walked back to Drogo's camp.

"I pray you are right. I always dreaded Old Edith's *sendings,* but now, I deeply wish for your words to be a prophecy."

Drogo cursed, ripped off his helmet, and wiped the sweat from his face with the blood-spattered sleeve of his tabard. There was a pause in the fierce fighting and he sorely needed the brief respite. Eada had spoken a wise and sad truth when she had said that the Saxons would fight. The battle was hard and bloody, the dead too numerous to count. His men had survived the long hours of battle, bloodied and exhausted but unhurt, but too many other Normans had not.

What troubled Drogo was how the Norman knights had retreated again and again before the solid line of Saxons on the small rise. The Saxons stood like a human wall that William's army hurled itself against, failing to climb it or knock it down. Norman arrows had taken a heavy toll upon the Saxons, but the men did not waver. Soon it would be night and the fighting would have to stop. If something did not change soon, the day would end in neither victory nor defeat. Harold could gather more men, but William could not. Although Drogo knew he would welcome an end to the fighting, he dreaded the thought that all the dying and the killing done this day would lead to nothing.

"Do you think we will lose?" Tancred asked as he stepped up beside Drogo.

Drogo glanced at his friend, who was pale with exhaustion, then shrugged. "Only God can answer that. All I pray for now is that it ends soon, before I can no longer lift my sword."

"We have lost many of our number."

"Too many. If we do not win the day, then, yes, I believe we will have lost the war, for we cannot replace our dead as swiftly as our enemy can."

Tancred swore and put his helmet on again. "I did not come all this way just to run back to the sea. I know my reasons for fighting are not as high and honorable as the Saxon's—they fight for hearth and home—but we ride beneath the Pope's banner and carry holy relics. If we cannot win even with the Church's blessing, then so be it I will die here, sword in hand." He looked at Drogo. "And your woman said we would win."

"She said that William will be king. She did not say when or how. This may not be the battle which sets the crown upon William's head." Drogo tugged Faramond closer and, after redonning his helmet, hauled himself back up into his saddle. "Come, let us hurl ourselves back into this bloody melee before our strength is gone." As Tancred and the others mounted their horses, Drogo looked toward the ridge the Saxons defended with such ferocity. "The enemy's numbers have lessened so that I believe we can reach the ridge this time. It appears that the ends of the ridge can no longer be defended."

As Drogo rode toward the western edges of the Saxon line, his men close behind him, he saw Harold's banner and the tight knot of his housecarls fighting around it. The English king had not moved from his stand at the crossing of the two roads which wound over the ridge. Drogo had to admire the man's strength and skill in battle. For one brief moment he had a clear view of Harold, and what happened next caused him to stop so abruptly that his men rode past him.

One of the hundreds of arrows fired by the Norman archers struck Harold in the eye. He fell to his knees; and his valiant housecarls, the best of his army, struggled to protect their king as the Normans, scenting this chance for victory, converged upon them from all sides. Drogo saw William and his men gallop toward the fallen king, slashing their way through his dying guard. It was not long before Harold, blind and helpless, was left alone and unprotected.

Even though the battle still raged around them, Drogo relaxed as he waited for William to accept Harold's surrender and thus end the battle. He gasped with shock and a strong hint of revulsion when William and his three companions killed the helpless Harold. Only faintly aware of how, with the capture of Harold's banner and his death, the battle began to rapidly end as the English scattered and retreated into the forest, Drogo watched four Norman knights butcher a crippled man. Harold was hacked to pieces, cut through the chest, beheaded, disembowelled, and thoroughly mutilated. Drogo knew it would be a long time before he could forget William's part in such an ignoble deed.

"Look, Drogo, the English flee to the forests like rabbits," cried Tancred.

Although he understood Tancred's joy, for there was a part of him that shared it, Drogo looked around solemnly. "Their king is dead. If any of them were unfortunate

enough to see how he died, they must believe that a sur-
render will never be accepted with mercy and honor."
He heard a grunt of agreement from Serle on his left.
"You witnessed Harold's death?"

Serle nodded, only briefly breaking his close guard on
the men still on the field to look at Drogo. "I will now
work to make myself believe that William was but caught
firmly by the bloodlust of a long, fierce battle."

Drogo closed his eyes for a moment, struggled with his
disgust and dismay, and then nodded. Serle was right. William would soon be their king. They could not let him
know, by word or by deed, what they truly thought of his
part in Harold's slaughter. He, too, would try to forget the
matter or, at least, find some way to excuse William's actions.

"I intend to cast aside my honor for a while," Tancred
said as he turned his mount back toward the Norman
battle line. "I mean to join the others in picking over the
dead. I am too poor to stand upon my honor and watch
all the loot being taken away by others."

"And the dead cannot use it," agreed Garnier as, with
one last look at the fleeing Saxons, he, too, turned around,
Unwin and Serle quickly doing the same.

It took Drogo a moment to quell his embarrassment
and a touch of shame before he could follow his companions. He could not allow his pride to make him forget
that he was poor. Drogo consoled himself with the knowledge that if he knew the dead man's family, he returned
all valuables to them and, unlike others, he never hurried
the dying of a man just to take his possessions. As he
joined his men in gathering what he could, he found
himself praying that Eada would not condemn him for
what he was forced to do.

Twelve

"King Harold is dead."

Her own voice, deep, solemn, and strange to her ears, and the gasps of May and Godwin brought Eada out of her own thoughts with an abruptness that left her unsteady. The words that had just forced themselves from her mouth were repeated once more inside her mind and then faded. She was confused and terrified by what had just happened yet knew in her heart that what she had just said was the absolute truth.

She looked at May and Godwin, saw the fear and shock on their faces, and suspected that she looked much the same as they. In an attempt to ease the concern Ivo so clearly felt, she repeated her words in French. He frowned then nodded, accepting her statement as fact with no apparent fear. They were seated around the fire in the center of Drogo's camp and had been trying to pretend that a massive battle was not being fought within a short walk from them. She had certainly put a harsh end to their meager efforts, she thought ruefully as she nervously smoothed the skirts of her soft grey gown.

"Are you sure King Harold is dead?" Godwin finally asked, absently rocking a sleeping Welcome in his arms, then he frowned. "How can you know that? You cannot see the battle from here."

"No, I can see nothing and, at times, I can hear very little." She cursed and frowned at them. "I heard it in my head and I feel it." She placed her hand over her heart and looked down at it. "Something told me that King Harold was dead, and the grief and pain of that great loss immediately filled my heart. No, I did not see our king die, but I know that he has." Eada hastily brushed tears from her eyes and forced herself not to cry.

"I was right. You *are* a seer."

Although that was a far kinder word than witch, Eada still winced. She was not doing well in obeying Drogo's reasonable command that she hide her skill. "I do not know what I am. I do not understand what has changed within me, or why, for these things have never afflicted me before. I begin to think that my old friend Edith gave me more than that mysterious box when she died. It seems strange that one could pass on such a skill, yet I have no other explanation for what now besets me."

"In such troubled times, such a skill could prove to be most helpful. I would not trouble myself over the how or the why."

"Easier to say than to do, Godwin, but you are right. We are now a vanquished people. Knowing things others do not and getting warnings of dangers before our conquerors do could prove to be a saving grace. I shall try to think of it as such and cease to curse and fear it."

"There may be an answer within that box," suggested May.

Eada shivered slightly, still unable to even think of the little chest without suffering a touch of fear. "There may be, but I fear my courage still fails me. I pick it up; I look at it, and then I falter, unable to look inside. Do not fear, May. I will open it. I know that soon my curiosity will overpower that fear."

May nodded then looked toward the battlefield, her bottom lip trembling as she fought back tears. "What shall we do now?"

"Survive," said Eada. "I cannot say it often enough.

Life will certainly be more difficult and very different, but I believe we can all learn how to live and work beneath Norman rule. Ones like us shall not suffer as much as those who hold lands, wealth, and power."

"Are you *very* certain that our king is dead?" Godwin asked.

"*Very* certain," replied Eada.

"Did he die bravely?"

It troubled her that she could be so certain of Harold's fate when she had not seen even one sword-stroke of the battle, but Eada heard herself answer firmly, "Bravely, but not easily. Our new rulers showed him no mercy and did not act with honor."

It surprised her when both Godwin and May accepted her words without question. She also felt comforted by their calm belief in her. At least with them she did not have to hide her skill or fear how they would treat her. It was good to know that there were others besides Drogo with whom she could be completely honest.

"Are our Normans still alive?" asked May.

Eada had to bite back a smile over the way May referred to Drogo and his men as *our Normans*. "Yes, I believe they are. Everything within me says that they survived the battle, but that could be born of hope and not of my new skill." She shrugged. "I wish it too much to completely trust what my heart and mind tell me. I have not had this strange gift long enough to know what is a true *sending* and what is just my own hopes and fears."

"You want Sir Drogo to survive."

"I do and not simply because we are lovers. He is a good, honest, and fair man. If I must be troubled by a Norman, I want it to be by him."

"And not a man like Sir Guy," muttered Godwin as he slowly stood up. "I do not suppose you have seen him die? Slowly and in great pain?"

"No, I fear not. Do you return to your own camp now?"

"Yes. If Harold is dead, then the battle will soon end. Even if he is not, the night comes and that will end the fighting. I had best be in Sir Guy's camp and prepared for his return."

Eada watched him leave, gently shepherding Hilde's children in front of him. Godwin held the promise of being a very good man. She prayed that Sir Guy would not end that promise with his cruelty.

A moment later she followed Ivo's lead and began to prepare for Drogo's return. She had known the fate of the Saxons long before the battle, yet she felt weighted down with sorrow. As she worked, she struggled to banish such feelings. Although she knew she would not be able to celebrate Drogo's victory with him, she would not condemn him for it either.

The victorious Normans began to return to camp, and Eada went into Drogo's tent. She built a small fire in the hollowed-out ground that marked the center of the tent and began to prepare Drogo's meal. It was probably cowardly to hide, but she suspected it was the only way she could hope to keep her composure. Wrapped in the privacy of Drogo's tent, she could ignore the celebration of the Norman victory. By the time Drogo joined her, she wanted to be, if not happy, at least resigned and calm. Eada prayed that he would not want to talk about the battle, for that could easily break her hard-won control.

"Where is Eada?" Drogo asked even as Ivo stripped away the last of his begrimed clothing.

"She waits in your tent." Ivo emptied one last bucket of hot water into the vat as Drogo stepped in. "She knows you have won. She told us that King Harold is dead."

Drogo grimaced then nodded as he began to scrub off the dirt, sweat, and blood of battle. He was both relieved that, somehow, Eada already knew what had happened and annoyed that she had revealed her unsettling gift before others again. It frightened him to think of what could happen to her if anyone outside their own small group discovered her unusual skills. He could no longer guarantee her safety if the cry went out that she was a witch.

"William is the king now?" Ivo asked as he scrubbed Drogo's back.

"Yes, although he will not be crowned until we reach London and that could be many months from now. For now, we will bury our many dead and wait for the English nobles to come and declare fealty to William."

"Do you think they will come?"

"No, but I cannot truly judge what these people will do. I only pray that there will be no more of the slaughter I saw today. It would be best if Eada did not venture near the battlefield. Many of the Saxon dead will probably be left to rot upon the battlefield, and it is not a sight for her pretty eyes."

"No one will bury the Saxons?"

Drogo could see how that distressed Ivo, and as he stepped out of the vat and began to rub himself dry with a blanket, he patted his big servant on the back. "Their kinsmen will either be too frightened or too far away to tend to the dead. That is often the way. And we will spend days burying our own dead before we march on. Do not let that trouble you, Ivo. You cannot bury them all either."

Ivo nodded as he helped Drogo put on clean hose and a jupon. "I buried one Saxon today." He slowly told Drogo about Hilde.

"That was most kind of you, Ivo. Now, you can return to your woman. I do not think I will require your aid again this night."

As Drogo walked to his tent, he thought about what Ivo had just told him. He felt certain that there was far more to the tale of Hilde's untimely death. He had only seen

the woman occasionally in Sir Guy's camp, but although
it had been evident that she was not hale in her mind, she
had not looked as if she were about to drop dead.

He slipped into his tent, saw Eada kneeling by the central fire, and sighed. There was no real outward sign of
her grief and sadness, yet he knew it was there. He walked
over, sat down beside her on the sheepskin, and wondered
what, if anything, he should say as he silently accepted the
bowl of lamb stew she served him. It had pleased him that
she had not been there to see him return covered in the
dirt and stench of battle, but he realized that had not dis-
pelled what now sat between them like a living thing, only
delayed it. As he ate, he watched her and struggled to find
the right words to cross that emotional distance that had
suddenly sprung up between them.

Eada ate her food even though she was finding it hard
to swallow. She knew Drogo was staring at her; she could
feel it. Her attempt to appear calm and unconcerned was
evidently not working or had completely confused him.
One glance at his thoughtful face told her that he was
considering talking about the battle, and she dreaded
that. She was too full of emotion to discuss the Saxon
defeat yet. There was little chance she would be able to
control what she said, and she feared she would spit her
anger and grief at him or even insult him, neither of
which he deserved.

What she had to do, she decided as she set her bowl
down, was distract him. When he also set his bowl down
and turned to face her, she suddenly knew exactly how to
do that. She would seduce him, allowing passion to push
aside his concerns and questions. The thought made her
tremble faintly with a mixture of uncertainty and anticipation. Seeing how he had come through the fierce battle
hale and unmarked had made her eager to make love to
him, but she was not sure she had the skill or the courage

to be the seducer. In their short time together as lovers, it had been Drogo who had begun and led the lovemaking.

"Eada," Drogo began hesitantly. "Ivo told me that you already know who won the battle and the fate of your king."

"Yes," she whispered, feeling the emotions she only lightly controlled ripple through her. "But I have known who would be the victor from the beginning." She took a deep, steadying breath, edged closer to him, and slid her arms around his neck. "I am pleased that you escaped the battle unharmed."

Drogo trembled when she began to tease his lips with hers. He was desperately hungry for her, had been from the moment he knew he would survive the battle. It had not been easy to subdue that craving, but he had, for he had been uncertain of her mood and had not wanted her acceptance of his passion to be anything less than wholehearted. The light touch of her soft, warm mouth snapped his control, his need for her rushing to every part of his body with a speed that left him reeling. Even though she had reached for him first, her mood was still solemn, still somewhat distant, and he ached to dispel it.

"Eada, we should talk," he said, his voice thick and hoarse as she covered his throat with kisses and moved so that she was sitting on his lap.

"I know, but I do not want to." She unlaced his jupon, smiling faintly when he hurriedly aided her in tugging it off him.

"Is that why you do this?"

"It is one of the reasons." She ran her hand over his broad, smooth chest then pressed a kiss to the hollow of his throat. "You also have a fine strong body and I truly am glad that it remains so."

He ached to ask her why she was so glad but bit back the words. Now was not the time. He also fought the urge to wrench control of their lovemaking from her small, soft hands and rush to gain the release his body cried out for. Whatever her reasons were for doing so, it was intoxicating to be made love to by Eada and he wanted to savor that for as long as he could.

Eada felt her uncertainty and hesitation fade with each kiss she gave Drogo and with each tremor of pleasure that shook his strong body. He felt good, tasted good, and smelled good. The feel of his smooth, warm skin beneath her lips and hands made her passion soar. That that passion overshadowed her grief, anger, and sorrow only enhanced her pleasure in it. She was not only keeping Drogo from talking but herself from thinking, and she savored the respite.

She left no spot unkissed as she removed the rest of his clothes. As she tossed aside his braies, leaving him fully naked before her, she touched a kiss to his erect manhood. The way he shuddered and groaned, his hands clenching in her hair, told her that he found that highly pleasurable. Caressing his muscular thighs with her hands, she kissed him again and slowly stroked him with her tongue. The praises he gasped out in a thick, unsteady voice encouraged her to continue her intimate attentions.

Drogo stared down at Eada as she pleasured him with her mouth and felt as if his blood had caught on fire. When she obeyed his whispered request and took him into her mouth, the feelings that tore through his body were so strong they were almost painful. He suddenly understood why men would pay large sums for such a pleasure, yet he knew what they paid for could never equal what Eada was giving him, freely and with apparent delight. When he knew he could no longer control himself, he pushed her away. He tried to hold onto her, aching to immediately bury himself deep within her, but she stepped out of his reach.

For a brief moment after he so abruptly ended her intimate caresses, Eada feared that she had been too bold.

Then she looked closely at his face and felt all of her desire return in a dizzying rush. He had not rejected her, simply stopped her before he was so lost to his passions he had no more control. She stepped away when he reached for her, amused that he seemed blind to the fact that she was still dressed. Eada also felt sure it would be safer for her clothes if she undressed herself, for Drogo looked ready to tear her gown from her body.

Her desire making her bold, she slowly undressed. Drogo had already unlaced a lot of her clothes making disrobing easy. When she finally stood naked before him, she smiled, excited by the way he watched her and by her own daring. Slowly, she stepped closer to him.

When he reached out to grasp her by the hips and pull her nearer, she laughed softly. Eada murmured her pleasure as he covered her stomach in fevered kisses, all the while caressing her backside and thighs with his big, callused hands. Shock intruded on her passion when he took his kisses even lower. Despite how she had pleasured him with her mouth, she had never thought he would or could do the same to her. With one slow stroke of his tongue, he took away her shock and her passion returned with such force she had to clutch his broad shoulders to keep standing. She no longer thought about the deep intimacy she was allowing, only how good it felt.

Her release but a heartbeat away, Eada tried to break free of his hold. He ceased his intimate kisses but did not release her. Slowly, kissing his way up her body, he pulled her down until she almost straddled him. He teased her mouth with soft kisses as he eased their bodies together. When they were fully joined, he cupped her face in his hands and gave her a deep, tender kiss that left her gasping.

His hands on her hips, he held her still as he turned his attention to her breasts. Eada threaded her hands in his hair and tried to remain still; but when he drew the hardened, aching tip of her breast deep into his mouth, her body refused to obey her wishes. Drogo echoed her groan as she moved upon him, and his lovemaking rapidly grew fierce. Shaking with her need for release, Eada welcomed his sudden roughness. When the culmination of her desire finally ripped through her body, Drogo followed within a heartbeat. They clung to each other, rocking back and forth as their bodies ruled the moment.

It was not until they lay curled up in each other's arms on the sheepskin that Eada actually began to think about what she had just done. She had been too lethargic, too weakened by her own passions, as Drogo had made them a more comfortable bed by the fire and gently cleaned them both off. Now her mind filled itself with uncomfortably clear memories of all she had done to him and what she had allowed him to do to her. A flush of embarrassment and shame heated her cheeks, and when Drogo looked at her, she was unable to meet his eyes.

"Do not grow modest and pious now, sweet Eada," he said as he grasped her by the chin and turned her face toward his. "I am not a demanding man and will not expect such heated play each time we lie together, but do not let shame or embarrassment steal away all promise of such lovemaking." He brushed a kiss over her lips.

"Do you intend to tell me that we did nothing we should be ashamed of?"

"Yes." He grinned when she laughed. "I know what the priests say, but I cannot believe that God punishes lovers, and we have done nothing thousands of lovers have not done thousands of times. Do a penance if you must, but do not let fear of sin kill your passion."

"Since you have lived in a monastery, I suppose I should believe you, as who would better know what is sin and what is not. Of course, there is always the chance that you seek to soothe me to serve your own purposes."

"A very good chance," he drawled and laughed at the

way she scowled at him, all the while her eyes sparkled with laughter. "The monk who taught what little I know did not believe passion was a true sin unless it brought evil or was the cause of adultery."

Her sense of shame banished, Eada relaxed, idly smoothing her hand up and down his side. Neither of them mentioned that their passion was not sanctified by marriage and that that in itself was a sin. That would not hurt anyone but her, so Eada decided it had to be a small sin.

All thoughts on how much she may or may not have sinned ended abruptly when she saw how serious Drogo looked. Eada tensed as she guessed that he wanted to talk about the battle or, at least, how she felt. Although she had thoroughly enjoyed her attempt to distract him from any such discussion, she was annoyed that it had only worked to delay the matter, not make him forget about it completely.

"I do not wish to talk about the war," she said, briefly wishing that she did not sound so sulky. She had wanted to sound firm, commanding.

"Are you certain you cannot read or hear what is in my mind?" he asked, only half-jesting for, yet again, she had guessed exactly what he wanted to say.

"I swear I cannot see inside your head." She lightly pressed her fingers to his mouth. "If you fear I will condemn you for the Saxon loss, do not. Nor will I belabor you with anger or grief. You did only what honor demanded of you. Today, with defeat still so fresh in the air, I do not want to talk of it, for my heart is sore and my soul is torn all ways with strong emotion. I do not wish to spit that out at you, for you have not earned it."

"There is one thing I feel I must beg forgiveness for—Harold's death. You saw it?"

"No, I just knew he had died and I knew it was not a good death."

Drogo held her close and prayed that some day he would be able to shake from his mind the sight of William and his men butchering Harold. "I do not understand why William and his men acted so dishonorably, and that is what they did. Harold was blinded, an arrow in his eye, helpless. They rode in upon him and cut the man to pieces. No offer of mercy or call to surrender was made. I am deeply ashamed by their act of murder and cruelty."

Eada fought back tears over Harold's ignominious end. "Why? You did not do it. You would never have acted so shamefully."

"William is my liege lord. His shame is mine. Searle says I must forget what I saw, that he will work to convince himself that William was but caught in the wild, unthinking bloodlust of battle. He told me to do the same."

"Wise words. Heed them and do as he says as quickly as you can. William will now be king. It could cost you dearly if he knew what you thought of his killing of Harold. If it aids you, then remind yourself that Harold's death was fated. There could not be two kings upon English soil."

Drogo nodded, kissed the top of her head, and settled himself more comfortably on their sheepskin bed. "How did Hilde die?"

The question was asked so quietly and so abruptly Eada replied without thought. "She cut her wrists and bled her life away in Sir Guy's tent."

"Suicide? Ivo said you had a priest tend her."

"I told the priest she died of grief. It was the truth. Let God decide if she sinned. Let Him punish or forgive her. We have told no one, not even her children."

"There is no need for anyone to know," he agreed, smiling when she hugged him in gratitude for his compliance.

"What happens now, Drogo?"

"We wait for the English nobles to come to William, to accept him as their new king."

"They will not come."

He sighed with resignation, not questioning her certainty. "Then we will march to London and I will pray every step of the way that I do not see another day like this."

Thirteen

"No! I will not listen to you!"

Eada covered her ears. When that did not silence the cry she heard, she wriggled beneath the blanket and put the pillow over her head. Drogo had left her to sleep while he went to meet with William. After a long night of lovemaking and the exhausting trial of waiting a full day to find out how the battle had ended, she had heartily welcomed a lazy morning spent curled up in bed. She deeply resented the voice keeping her from her much-needed rest. She also knew that her attempts to silence it were useless, even foolish. The cry did not come from without but within, and the only way to stop it was to answer it. Eada threw the pillow off angrily and sat up.

Cursing softly, she rose and dressed. The voice in her head pulled her toward the battlefield, the very last place she wished to go. She knew she would find only horror there and that nothing could ever prepare her for what she would have to see. Angrily, she pulled her hair back and secured it with a leather thong then, grabbing up a small bag she had filled with bandages and healing balms, she marched out of Drogo's tent.

Ivo and May were nowhere in sight, and Eada cursed again. She knew Drogo would be angry if she went alone, but there was no one in camp to take her and she could not wait. The cry in her head was too desperate, too demanding.

"You can cease now," she muttered as she started to walk toward the battlefield. "I will find you soon." Although she wanted the voice to be silent, the pain and the fear in the cry deeply affecting her, Eada also hoped that she did not have the skill to send a message as well as receive it. "I just pray that I can return before Drogo discovers what I have done," she said fervently as, after checking to be sure that no one would try to stop her, she walked away from the soldiers' camp.

May gasped softly, grabbed Ivo by the arm, and pointed at Eada, who was already too far away to call to. "Look there, Ivo, Eada has left the camp—alone." She cursed when she realized that, since Ivo could not understand English, all she had done was draw his attention to what looked like an attempted escape. "Wait," she cried, tightening her grip on his arm when he tossed aside the kindling they had gathered and started after Eada.

"Drogo said Eada must stay in camp," Ivo said, frowning down at May but hesitating in his pursuit of Eada.

Eada had not had enough time to teach her much French, but May began to struggle with what little she did know. To help May to make herself understood as quickly as possible, Eada had stressed simple commands, the words for common objects, and a few select verbs. May was finally able to get Ivo to understand that he was to just follow Eada, staying near enough to help her if she stumbled into any trouble, but not to just drag her back to camp. As she watched Ivo go after Eada, May prayed she was right in thinking that Eada was responding to some sending or vision. She refused to even consider the possibility that Eada was plotting some treachery or was trying to escape. That would only bring them a great deal of trouble.

* * *

Eada's first sight of the battlefield nearly brought her to her knees. She pressed her hands over her mouth, altering her cry of horror into a smothered groan of pain. The dead were everywhere she looked. Norman bodies were being carried from the field to be buried, but the Saxons were left where they fell. Only a few Saxons wandered in the field in search of their kinsmen. The mutilation caused by swords and battle-axes caused bile to sting the back of her throat as she fought back a choking nausea.

The voice in her head pulled her free of the shock which held her motionless. She cursed when she realized she would have to walk the length of the battlefield to the forest beyond. As she walked, she tried to keep her gaze fixed upon the trees and not look at the devastation she passed.

When she entered the wood, her sense of urgency grew and she tasted fear, yet she knew it was not her own. Whoever drew her to him was desperate and terrified. She came to the bank of a small river, the dead thick upon the ground, and knew she had reached her destination, yet she saw no one alive. For one brief moment, she wondered if she could now hear the voices of the dead then hastily calmed herself. Someone needed her help but was too afraid to show himself.

"I am here," she called, her voice trembling as her own fears grew, born of standing in the midst of so many dead. "I cannot help you if you do not let me see where you are."

"You would see me if you would but look down," said a deep male voice from very close by.

"There are only dead men upon the ground," she replied as she fought for the strength to look at the corpse-littered ground surrounding her.

"It should now be clear that not all of us are dead."

Trembling slightly, Eada looked at the dead, idly noticing that most of them were Normans. At least in one place, her people had clearly won. Just as she began to wonder if she were losing her mind, had not really heard anyone at all, she saw movement in what looked to be a pile of dead Normans. She grit her teeth against a rising nausea as she moved closer; then, seeing that one body at the bottom of the pile was dressed as a Saxon, she began to push and pull aside the dead Normans. She gasped with surprise when, after heaving aside a body, she found a filthy, blood-soaked Brun staring up at her.

"You have decided that you are tired of killing Normans?" she asked as she pulled him away from the dead.

"I have decided that I do not want to die," he answered, his voice hoarse with pain.

Eada nodded, and tearing a strip from her undertunic, she soaked it in the chill of the river and crouched by his side. "I am glad," she said, as she gently bathed his face. "I have seen enough Saxon dead this day to haunt my dreams the rest of my life." She tried to unlace his jupon but found the blood-soaked ties stiff and hard to work with. "Are you badly wounded?"

"Two clean sword cuts. One to my right side and one in my left leg. My right arm was badly beaten by a mace, but I do not believe it is broken. I have left a lot of my blood in this dirt."

After checking the wounds he spoke of, Eada sat back on her heels and sighed. "I cannot tend these wounds here."

"I have come to take you back to camp now," said a deep voice.

Eada stared up at Ivo in openmouthed surprise. "You followed me?"

"Sir Drogo said you must not leave camp," Ivo replied as he calmly disarmed Brun, who was struggling to reach his sword to defend himself.

"This man called to me. He has surrendered."

"He cannot surrender to us. We are not knights. He must surrender to Sir Drogo."

"Sir Drogo is with William. It will have to wait, but this man's wounds can wait no longer to be tended."

"Sir Drogo will be angry."

Although she was not sure what Ivo thought would anger Drogo, her coming to the battlefield or adding another to those he was responsible for, Eada nodded. She stared up at Ivo, saying nothing and waiting with a hard-won patience for his decision. Eada just prayed that Ivo would make that decision before they were discovered by the Normans who collected the dead from the battlefield.

"Look there, Sir Drogo," called Sir Guy as he rode up next to Drogo and pointed to the wood at the far end of the battlefield. "Your little Saxon whore has obviously tired of your lovemaking and flees."

Already in a foul mood because he had had to endure Sir Guy's company as he rode back to camp, Drogo saw Eada disappear into the wood and struggled to subdue a sudden rush of anger. He felt and heard his men draw closer even as he caught sight of Ivo striding right behind Eada, and he turned his attention back to Sir Guy. Sir Guy had a true skill for making everything Drogo said or did carry the taint of treachery, and he wondered how the sly little man would twist this insignificant incident. Drogo knew that was not Eada's fault, but he could not fully suppress his irritation that she might have given the treacherous, hateful man one more thing to whisper lies about.

"My man Ivo is with her," Drogo said, his voice cold and hard as he struggled to remain courteous to a man he knew would stab him in the back if given half the chance. "She is probably searching the field for her kinsmen or friends, just as others do."

"Of course. We must see if we can assist her in her search."

Drogo cursed as Sir Guy and his two equally treacherous companions turned their mounts and started to follow Eada. "Tancred, you stay with me. The rest of you can return to camp. This should not take long."

As Drogo hurried to catch up with Sir Guy, Tancred close by his side, he silently and viciously cursed the man. In the meeting with William, it had become blatantly obvious that Sir Guy intended to do his utmost to discredit Drogo. He was too much the coward to make any open accusations but indulged in an unrelenting campaign of whispered lies and innuendo. Drogo doubted that he could even relieve himself without Sir Guy trying to twist it into something suspicious or some insult to William. At the moment, it did not appear that the man was gaining any believers except for the few who had always followed him. It worried Drogo, however, for these were troubled times and the men who tenuously held the power were often quick to scent treachery, real or imagined.

When Drogo first saw Eada by the murky river, he discovered that he too could have a suspicious mind. She knelt by a young, handsome Saxon, tenderly holding the man's hand in hers. Drogo had to battle a surge of jealousy when, as Sir Guy and his companions dismounted, swords in hand, she moved to protect the youth with her own body. He slowly dismounted and cautiously approached her.

"So, you found one of the dogs still alive," said Sir Guy. "Move away, woman, and let me end his miserable life."

"No," Eada cried, and she looked pleadingly at Drogo as he reached her side. "He has surrendered."

"We are not troubling ourselves with prisoners, certainly not from amongst those who raised their swords against us," Sir Guy snapped. "This fool chose to fight with Harold. Let him die with his king."

"No, he is a kinsman," she cried, trying to protect Brun even as she shifted out of the way of the sword Sir Guy poked at her.

Drogo drew his sword and thrust it between Sir Guy's and Eada and the helpless youth. He was furious that he was placed in the position of stopping Sir Guy from killing one of the enemy, but he had seen enough of the helpless slaughtered. Neither did he believe it was right to kill a man who had offered up his sword in surrender. As he met Sir Guy's glare with an icy calm, he found himself thinking petulantly that, if Eada were determined to save Saxons, she could find ones who were not so handsome.

"Put your sword away, Sir Guy," he said. "He is but a wounded boy."

"He is a Saxon," Sir Guy protested angrily, but after one long look at Tancred and Ivo, who stood firmly behind Drogo, he sheathed his sword and curtly signaled his companions to do the same. "You are very kind toward our enemies."

"When that enemy is wounded, unarmed, and has surrendered—yes. He threatens no one, and he is my woman's kinsman."

"You gather around you an increasing number of useless Saxons. One might begin to wonder why."

"Since they are useless as warriors against our king, I do not see why it concerns anyone. Ivo, can you carry the boy back to my camp?"

Ivo nodded and picked Brun up in his arms. After one long, hard look at Sir Guy, he strode right by the man and his increasingly uneasy companions. Drogo grasped a wide-eyed Eada by the arm and pulled her to her feet. He stood watching Sir Guy until the man hissed a curse and remounted, his friends quickly doing the same. A moment later, they were gone.

Drogo tossed Eada onto the back of his horse and silently mounted behind her. He was glad that she held her tongue as they rode back to camp. He knew she did not deserve any of the anger churning inside him, but he also knew he could easily flay her with it if they spoke before he was able to control it.

The moment they reached his camp, Eada slid off his horse and hurried over to where Ivo had settled the Saxon youth. Drogo fought to dispel a sudden, sharp pinch of jealousy. The youth was badly wounded and had suffered through a night with no treatment of those wounds. He did, however, intend to find out how Eada had found the youth and exactly who he was. Instinct told him that the boy was not really her kinsman. Drogo also wanted to hear from the youth's own lips that he had surrendered, for, young though he was, he was still a Saxon warrior.

Eada sighed with relief as she finished washing and slipped her clean gown on. It had taken a long time to clean, stitch, and bandage Brun's wounds. She had then left him in Ivo's care and rushed into Drogo's tent to scrub away the scent of blood and battle. And to hide from Drogo, she ruefully admitted to herself. She had felt his gaze on her from the moment they had returned to camp. She had also felt the anger he struggled to control.

She felt absolutely no guilt about helping Brun, and she felt sure that Drogo did not really fault her for that either. Leaving camp alone had not only been disobedient but foolish and dangerous. That, however, would bring no more than a stern reprimand and, perhaps, a heavier guard. The anger she saw in Drogo was caused by Sir Guy and the fact that, however inadvertently, she had somehow made matters between the two men even worse. As she brushed her hair by the small central hearth, she decided that she needed to know exactly what was going on between Sir Guy and Drogo.

When Drogo entered the tent, Eada gave him a tentative smile as he sat down facing her. He was still angry and, although she did not fear him, she was unsettled by it. Since she did not know the full cause of that anger, she was uncertain about how to soothe it.

"Who is that youth?" he asked. "I do not believe he is your kinsman."

"No, he is no kin to me at all," she admitted, feeling a distinct pinch of guilt for having lied to him. "I said that to try to save him. He is Brun, the youth I met in the wood when I found the baby."

Drogo felt himself relax. Her reply soothed the small lingering suspicion he held that something secretive was going on. He knew it was a suspicion born of his own jealousies, but he had not been able to fully conquer it.

"He called to you?"

"Yes. I am sorry that I did not wait for Ivo. I did look for him, but he was not in camp and I was desperate to silence the voice in my head. It carried such pain and fear, and those feelings were beginning to spread through me. Did you really think I would go willingly to that battle-field?" she asked in a soft voice, shivering as she remembered the horrors she had seen.

"You may have thought to find someone you knew, a friend or a kinsman," he replied and then shrugged. "Did Brun really surrender?"

"He did not actually say so, but he called to me. I told him to do so if he decided he needed help and that, perhaps, there were a few things he cherished more than killing Normans. He said he had decided that he did not wish to die."

"That is not really a surrender. I will talk with him. I want to hear the words of surrender myself so that I can attest to them in all honesty if anyone asks about Brun." He combed his fingers through his hair and sighed as he felt his stomach begin to unknot, his anger finally leaving him. "I believe I will also get him to pledge himself to me and, when and if the need arises, to William as well. Is he highborn?"

"Higher than I, I think, although not wealthy. He told me that his father was killed as he tended their flock in the fields. Good blood does not always bring an easy life. The fine quality of his weapons marks him as one of good family, however."

Drogo nodded then grimaced. "Do you mean to gather forlorn Saxons to your breast all the way to London?"

"I cannot ignore a cry for help."

"Neither can I, and I could never ask you to do so anyway. It is just that filling my camp with Saxons could prove troublesome."

"Because of Sir Guy."

"Yes, because of Sir Guy. He was easy to ignore before because he simply hated me. Now he tries to destroy me."

"How can he do that?" Eada remembered Sir Guy's words about Drogo's kindness to his enemies, words that had been meant to be insulting, but now also seemed ominous and threatening.

"In a most cowardly way. He twists and tangles everything I say and do until it appears treasonous. He whispers suspicion and lies into every ear he can reach. He blackens my name and questions both my honor and my courage, yet not in a way I can fight. There are no open accusations or insults made, and so I cannot challenge him. That means that I cannot prove my innocence in battle."

"William cannot believe any of Sir Guy's lies, can he?"

"I would like to believe that William would treat Sir Guy's words with all the scorn they deserve, but I cannot be certain of it. Treachery and danger lurk in every shadow. William has faced betrayal so often, he sometimes sees it everywhere. This is the greatest battle he has ever fought, and a crown is the prize. For every man who wants William to be king, there is one who would rather see him dead. Sir Guy's lies could turn William against me.

It is a small chance, but I cannot ignore it. What troubles me and infuriates me is that I do not know how to fight against this. I can only deny what he says as lies."

"It is sad, but I fear your word may not be enough. In his heart, I am sure that William trusts and honors you; but sometimes, one forgets to listen to one's own heart. I will try to do and say nothing to help Sir Guy. I certainly do not wish to be the one who puts the dagger in his hand, the dagger he will then bury in your back."

Drogo nodded as he stood up. "I can ask no more. Except, perhaps, that you think of a sure but honorable way to shut his mouth." He kissed the tip of her nose then started out of the tent. "I will now go and talk to that boy."

Eada cursed and moved to start cooking the evening meal. Whispered lies were a hard thing to defeat. She had seen before how completely they could destroy a person and dreaded such a fate befalling Drogo. And once the lies had wreaked their havoc, the truth no longer mattered. Eada vowed she would try to be more careful in all she did and said. She refused to give Sir Guy the weapon he needed to destroy Drogo.

After helping Brun drink from the wineskin to seal the oath he had just made, Drogo sat down and studied the youth's somewhat sullen, pale face. "I did not ask you to swear to like me," he drawled. "Only to obey and serve me."

"You cannot expect me to find the taste of defeat a sweet one," Brun said in heavily accented French, revealing his high birth.

"No, I expect no Saxon to embrace us with joy. You are wellborn?"

"Yes, but poor. My father held lands but had to do all the work himself. As you saw, I had weapons but no armor.

You need not fear that I will have too much pride of blood. I may be cousin to kings, but I still had to clean our stables. My father had hoped that my skill with a sword would help us regain the riches his father had lost."

"You have good blood, a fair face, and wit enough to speak both English and French. You may yet gain more than your father had."

"There is one thing my father had that I do not think I will ever attain, not under Norman rule, and that is freedom."

Drogo wanted to argue that flat statement but could think of nothing to say. What little he had learned of Saxon ways told him that the youth was probably right. Freedom as a known Saxon would not be allowed under Norman law.

"I do not know what laws you have lived under," he finally said, "so I cannot agree or disagree. If you remain in my service, you will not be treated badly," he felt compelled to add even as he wondered why he felt a need to gain the youth's respect, if not his friendship.

"I begin to believe that that is the truth."

"Eada said you called to her?"

"Yes. She told me to; and after a night of lying with the dead, waiting for some Norman to find me and cut my throat, I decided to try it. I had not understood that she had such a gift. If I had, I would have called to her sooner."

"That gift she has is to remain a secret." Drogo shook his head. "More people know of it than I can like now. No others need to hear of it. It would stir fear and put her in grave danger."

"Not all Saxons could accept it either."

"I have an enemy in this camp, a man who seeks to destroy me. He could try to do that through Eada if he discovered her strange skills."

"He will never gain that secret from me. I would never betray Eada."

Drogo found it irritating that the youth vowed to protect Eada with a great deal more fervor that he vowed to serve him. At the moment, such intense loyalty was important, however. He prayed that he could learn how to successfully play Sir Guy's games before it was too late and all the loyalty and praise in England could not save him.

Fourteen

"We are beyond the battlefield. You may open your eyes now."

Eada cautiously took her hands away from her eyes and looked around, then smiled her gratitude at Drogo, who rode beside the cart. William had waited five long days for the English nobles to come and accept him as their king, but no one had come. The army now rode to London, and Eada dreaded to think of what would happen to all the innocents who would be in their path.

"It was foolish," she said, "but I saw the dead once and did not wish to see them again. No, especially not after they have lain there, forlorn and unburied, for five long days."

"That was not foolish." Drogo reached out to gently caress her cheek. "I am battle-hardened, but even I found the sight hard to stomach."

Eada looked at the cart directly behind them. Ivo had *found* it to carry a still-weak and healing Brun as well as the bounty Drogo and his men had collected. Serle drove it, seemingly content to take a job that had appalled Unwin. He nodded at her when he caught her looking his way, and Eada returned the greeting.

"Do you think Brun is all right?" she asked Drogo.

Drogo hastily swallowed the flash of jealousy that assailed him. He had been fighting that unpleasant emotion since Brun had joined their group. Each time Eada tended to the wounded Brun, it unsettled him, despite the fact that she spent every night in his arms. Telling himself that she was simply tending to Brun's injuries, her softness toward the youth stirred only by his pain, did not stop the attacks of jealousy. Drogo too easily saw Brun's youth, beauty, and the bond of Saxon blood the boy shared with Eada—all things he could never hope to equal. The only thing he could be grateful for was that Eada had not yet noticed his jealousy.

"He is as comfortable as he can be," Drogo replied. "You can cease to worry about the boy," he added and then gently spurred his horse forward, riding ahead to rejoin Tancred, Unwin, and Garnier before he said something he would regret.

Eada frowned as she watched Drogo disappear into the crowd of mounted knights they followed. There had been an odd tone to his voice, and his leave taking had been abrupt. In the last few days, she had noticed an occasional moodiness in Drogo and she did not believe it was all due to the sly games played by Sir Guy.

"May, have you sensed an odd humor in Sir Drogo?" she asked and waited patiently for May to raise her gaze from the sleeping Alwyn she held in her arms.

"He is but jealous of Brun," May answered, constantly glancing back down at Alwyn.

"Jealous? Drogo? No, that is foolish. He does not care for me in that way," she added softly.

"A man does not have to love to be jealous. You are Sir Drogo's woman and yet you tenderly nurse a very handsome young man. You worry about Brun and speak to him in a language Sir Drogo does not understand so he cannot know all you two say to each other. Sir Drogo has a strong passion for you. That is something he may fear to lose."

"May, I am Sir Drogo's captive, as is Brun. With such power in his hands, how could Drogo fear such a thing?

And if he does, why has he not told me to stay away from Brun?"

"Sir Drogo does not treat us as prisoners or serfs. He is kind and has a most generous spirit. He might want to command you to stay away from Brun, but he would never do so. And he would never do anything to Brun either."

"And so he just broods and leaves us all to wonder what ails him?"

"That is the way of some men." Her gaze fixed steadily on Alwyn again, May brushed one of the child's thick blond curls off his forehead. "And I think you are the only one who believes that Sir Drogo holds you prisoner."

Eada grimaced and slowly nodded. In fact, she rarely thought of herself in that way. It was not really Sir Drogo who held her captive but the war. Drogo did not simply command her to do something; he always gave her the reasons for what he asked. Even with the lovemaking he did not demand anything, and she knew in her heart that she could say no at any time without fear of reprisal. That was not the way of a captor or a master.

May's opinion that Drogo was jealous quickly consumed her thoughts, pushing aside all musings on her position as a captive. She was not sure she could or should believe it, yet it did explain his moodiness. For one brief moment she considered testing him, increasing her attentions to Brun until Drogo was pushed to openly reveal his jealousy. She then hastily discarded the plan, appalled that she had even thought of it. She was not good at such deception, nor did she want to be. It could also prove little more than the fact that Drogo was jealous and not what she really wanted to know—which was why. If it were only a sense of possessiveness that spawned his jealousy, she did not really want to know.

When she looked at May, intending to ask a few more questions about men and their strange ways, Eada frowned. May was intently watching Alwyn again. The woman did it constantly, only relaxing her guard when the boy was awake. Eada reached out and touched May on the arm, provoking a brief startled look from the woman.

"He is asleep, May. He cannot go anywhere," she said quietly.

"I just wish to be sure that his sleep does not become death," May whispered.

"Is that what happened to your baby?" Eada smiled with sympathy when May looked at her in wide-eyed surprise.

"How did you know that I had a child and that he died?"

"The way you so greedily took hold of Alwyn when I brought him into camp told me that you had suffered some loss. The way you have clung to the child since then only confirmed my suspicions."

"I gave Hacon a son a year past. Despite the hate I held for the man who sired him, I loved my child. All was well. My babe grew, ate, cried, smiled, and all any hale child would do for two short months. Then, one morning, I woke to find him cold in his little bed. He had died in the night, died without a sound to warn me of his passing. I think Hacon always believed that I had killed my baby, but I swear I did not."

"I believe you, May," Eada said, briefly hugging May. "Hacon was a fool. You could never hurt a child. But, May, not every child dies; and watching them as you watch Alwyn will not save them. If God plans to take this child into His arms, you cannot stop Him—no matter how tightly you cling to the babe."

May smiled crookedly as she idly smoothed the blanket the child was wrapped in. "My heart and my mind know that, and yet—"

"Yes. And yet. But think, May: You sleep little. I can see the weariness you suffer in your face. You cannot rest when the babe is awake, and you watch him all the while he sleeps. That will soon make you ill, and then you will be unable to care for Alwyn at all. You do not want that, do you?"

"No. I already feel as if he is my own child. But I am so afraid."

"May, this child is older than your babe. He has already lived six, nearly seven months without your constant guard. I think he is probably safe. Why not keep yourself hale and strong so that you can tend to his hurts and his ills when they do afflict him and not spend all your strength watching for a danger you cannot see or stop?"

"You are right and I will try. I did not really understand how completely I had allowed my fear to rule me." She cast Eada a wary look. "Are you sure you do not mind that I have taken the child?"

"No, not at all. I had no time to grow fond of the child. I do not even feel as if I am breaking my promise to his poor mother. The baby is safe and much loved. That fulfills my vow even if I am not the one doing it."

"And you do not think that his kinsman, Brun, will try to take him?"

"No. I am certain he will not. He will wish to remain known to the child, but he will not take him away from you. Once, while I was tending his wounds, I saw Brun watching you and the child. He told me that he was glad that Alwyn had found a new mother." She patted May's shoulder when the woman sagged with relief. "Now, do you think there is anything I can do to end Drogo's jealousy, not that I fully believe he suffers from it?"

"You cannot ignore Brun, for he still needs his wounds tended and you are skilled at that. Is that another gift the old woman gave you?"

Eada shrugged. "I do not know. It may have always lurked within me. I was never tested before. If this is another of Edith's gifts, then I thank her for this one. And you are right; I cannot ignore Brun."

"No, but you could only tend his wounds and no more until your man sees that there is no danger of your leaving him for another."

"I do not understand why I must change what I do because the fool has a suspicious mind, but—" She held up her hand to halt May's soft protest. "—I will do it. I have had a bellyful of dark looks and sharp remarks." She snuggled into the arrangement of grain sacks, pillows, and blankets that cushioned their ride. "I will cease to worry about the fool now, for I am tired." She flashed a quick grin at May. "And I would appreciate it if you would not ask why." She echoed May's laugh as she closed her eyes. "Wake me if Brun needs me or if we stop."

The sharp scent of smoke intruded on Eada's dreams and she coughed. She struggled to ignore the smell and all it meant and stay blissfully lost in her dreams of sweetly flowering fields and a passionate Drogo. The sound of May coughing ended her fruitless attempts. Afraid of what she might see, Eada slowly opened her eyes.

They were stopped in the midst of chaos. Fear gripped the followers of William's army for they knew something was happening but did not know what it was. Eada accepted the waterskin Ivo thrust at her and took a long drink before handing it to May. As she looked around, Eada realized that they could not get away to a quieter place for they were tightly encircled by carts.

Ivo began a heated argument with one of the men surrounding them; but as Eada started to translate the angry words for May, she grew still. Voices crowded her mind, their pleas for help deafening. Tears stung her eyes as she realized that she was hearing the screams of terrified children. Without a thought for her own safety and ignoring May's cry, she leapt from the cart. She did not know where she was going or what she would find when she got there. All she was certain of was that children were in grave danger and they needed her.

Eada could hear the battle before she saw it. The moment she caught sight of the burning cottages and the people desperately trying to flee William's mounted knights and mercenaries, she knew this was no battle. It was hard and greedy men destroying homes and slaying the innocent in their hunt for riches. She allowed the cries in her head to banish her fury and concentrated on finding the ones in danger.

Wrapping her cloak tightly around herself she stayed to the shadows, trying to remain out of the sight of the men reveling in their destruction. It was as she approached the church at the far edge of town that she realized why she had been called. Several women and a large group of children were trying desperately to reach safety, hoping a sanctified place would protect them. Between them and the haven they struggled to reach was Sir Guy and half-a-dozen men. Eada cried out a protest and raced forward when Sir Guy raised his sword and cut down a woman who protected two children with her life.

"You bastard," she screamed at him as she put herself between the terrified women and children and the hard-eyed Sir Guy. "Are you such a weakling and a coward that you must fight unarmed women and babes?"

"Drogo's whore," he said, as he glared at her, his voice a cold hiss of hatred. "You have erred now, whore. No one will fault me for killing you here. You are easily mistaken for just another Saxon pig."

She neatly avoided the swing of his sword, darted in closer, and grabbed him by the leg. He could not strike her without cutting himself. Taking full advantage of his hesitation, she used all her strength to yank on his leg and succeeded in unhorsing him. He leapt to his feet and faced her, his face bright red with fury. Eada took her gaze off him only long enough to see that his companions were staying back, not interfering in what they saw as mere amusement.

"I shall enjoy killing you," Sir Guy said as he and Eada circled each other, he looking for the perfect time to strike and Eada doing her best to stay beyond his reach. "I shall leave you so bloody and torn that your fool of a lover will never recognize you."

"Such bravery. It takes skill and courage to cut down one tiny woman."

As she hoped, her insults infuriated him and he charged her blindly. She neatly avoided his attack. Sir Guy stumbled to a halt near some of the women he had been trying to murder, and they took quick advantage, delivering a few telling blows before they had to flee his sword. When the men with Sir Guy laughed heartily, it only enraged the man more and Eada could see how badly Drogo's enemy ached to kill her.

She struggled to hide her fear. There was no way she would win this confrontation. A few of the women had already begun to edge closer to the church and sanctuary, using the distraction she had caused to try to save themselves. Eada prayed that they would be safe within the church, for she suspected she would soon be dead and she wanted to believe that her death had at least saved a few people.

"Guy," ventured one of the men watching the unequal battle, "I am not sure it would be wise to harm Sir Drogo's woman. He is much favored by William, and displeasing him could well anger William."

"Sir Drogo will not hold his place of favor much longer," Sir Guy snapped.

The cold, arrogant way he smiled at Eada made her angry. He truly thought that he could defeat Drogo with his petty lies. She clenched her hands into tight fists and wished she had a weapon with which she could cut out his lying tongue before it did any real damage to Drogo.

"You are a fool if you think your lies can hurt a man like Drogo," she said, fighting to keep her fears out of her voice and maintain a tone of deep scorn. "No one heeds them. All they see is a man who is too much of a coward to fight Drogo as a man should fight. You tiptoe about, whispering lies and gossip like an old, bitter woman."

"You beg for a slow, painful death, Saxon whore." He was breathing so hard from the force of his anger that he stuttered.

"Such brave talk and yet you stay out of my reach."

A hoarse cry of pure rage escaped him as he charged her. Eada felt his sword cut her skirts as she moved out of his way, but she stuck her foot in front of him. To her surprise, the childish tactic worked and he fell on his face in the mud. She leapt on him, desperate to disarm him before he could harm her. As he tried to throw her from him, she ripped off his helmet, got her hands beneath his mail hood, and tightly gripped him by the hair. Putting all her strength into her attack, she banged his head against the ground. He let go of his sword as he tried to grab her wrists and loosen her hold. The moment she felt he was too groggy to stop her, she leapt off him and lunged for his sword.

A brief sense of victory coursed through her veins as she curled her hands around the hilt of his sword. Then he fell on her. She could sense that he was still dazed from her attack and used that momentary weakness to wriggle out of his hold. When she turned to face him, however, his sword in her hands, one of his companions suddenly moved to interfere. The sword was wrenched from her hands even as Sir Guy staggered toward her.

Eada cried out in pain as he hurled himself toward her, and she hit the ground hard. His body landing on top of hers only increased her pain. Out of the corner of her eye she saw the women try to help her only to be stopped by one of Sir Guy's men, who put his horse between them and Eada.

When Sir Guy put his gauntleted hands around her throat, Eada knew she had to escape his hold fast or she would surely die. As his grip tightened and it became increasingly difficult for her to breathe, she wedged her leg between his. With all her rapidly fading strength, she rammed her knee into his groin. He screamed, ripping his hands from her throat and clutching himself. Eada punched him in the throat, and as he gasped helplessly for air, she shoved him off her and staggered to her feet.

Weak and breathless, her throat bruised and aching, she fought to steady herself. Just as Sir Guy began to pull himself to his feet, she kicked him in the head. He sprawled on his back in the dirt, but before she could do him any more harm, another of his men moved to his aid. It was evident from the serious look upon the man's face that he realized this battle was no longer a simple amusement. He put his horse between her and Sir Guy and impeded her every attempt to get around him.

As Sir Guy began to recover and stand up, Eada cursed as she watched her chance to win being stolen away. Her only consolation was that most of the children were already inside the church. Several of the women lingered in the doorway of the little building, obviously hoping they could find some way to help her.

"You are all cowards," Eada said. "Not only do you cut down children and women at the very door of a chapel, but you aid a man to win what is an already-unequal battle."

"I begin to think that you are anxious to die, woman," said the man on the horse. "It is not wise to spit such insults at men who could kill you with but one blow."

"Can they? Then why do I still stand while your fine Sir Guy is the one pulling himself out of the mud?"

The man looked down at Sir Guy, and Eada saw his mouth twist with a grimace of disgust. "I wonder as well. Come, Sir Guy, do you wish the tale told that you died at the soft hands of a tiny Saxon woman?"

"I will not die by her hand."

Eada felt herself grow still and, despite all her efforts to keep her full attention on Sir Guy, the words in her head demanded that she heed them. She was unable to cast off the distraction forced upon her until she stared at a fully recovered Sir Guy in horror, the truth her mind had just made her see making her blood run cold. He was right. He would not die by her hand. No matter how hard she tried to scorn the message she had just been given, she could not. But if he were not to die by her hand, then there was no chance at all that she would survive this confrontation.

She fought the strong urge to flee. There was nowhere to go. Sir Guy and his men could run her down and murder her before she could even reach the edge of the village. She cursed herself for having run into the heart of danger without a thought. Ivo and Serle had been with the carts and they could easily have helped and protected her, yet she had said nothing to them. Now she could not even hope for their aid.

"I think we should end this, Guy," said the mounted knight, who remained between her and Sir Guy. "There is now calm in the village, and many are beginning to look our way."

"What does that matter?"

"This woman is well known to be Sir Drogo's woman. I do not believe you will be able to claim that you mistook her for one of the villagers anymore. It will be said that you killed her. I warn you again—Sir Drogo is well favored by William, and I do believe the man will be much angered if you kill this woman."

"Let him cry to the king. Few will heed him. She is

just a Saxon whore, and they will tell him to catch himself another and be silent."

"They may allow him to openly challenge you."

"And then I shall have the pleasure of cutting him down."

Eada could tell by the way the mounted knight frowned that she was not the only one who felt Sir Guy was no match for Drogo. It was past time that Drogo ended Sir Guy's threat, but she had the sinking feeling she would not be alive to see that well-earned death. Nothing she could think of offered her a chance to escape or survive. At best, she was just going to delay her death. As the mounted knight edged away, Eada tensed, preparing herself for the attack she knew was about to come. She was determined to make Sir Guy fight hard for his victory.

"Ivo," May screamed, finally pulling her man's attention away from the argument he was apparently enjoying. "Eada has run off." When he immediately scowled and looked around, she breathed a sigh of relief. He had understood her odd mixture of French and English.

"Where is she?" he demanded.

"She went toward the smoke," May answered, pointing toward the signs of a fire, and then she quickly pointed toward where she had last seen Serle and his cart. "Get Serle. He can help."

May stared toward the smoke as Ivo leapt from the cart and pushed his way through the crowds in search of Serle. Eada had gone white, cried out, and then fled toward the very danger everyone in the baggage train was worried about. She knew Eada had had some sending, heard some cry for help, but she wished the woman had paused long enough to at least take Ivo with her. May was sure another village was being laid waste and Eada would look like just another Saxon to the men wreaking the havoc. May cried out in surprise when Serle suddenly grabbed her by the arm, pulling her attention to him.

"She went to the village just ahead?" Serle asked, speaking slowly and using the simplest words he could in the hope that May could understand.

It took a few minutes of French, English, and signals to tell Serle what had happened. May heartily wished she could be certain that he really understood her. He looked concerned, said something to her that was obviously supposed to comfort her, mentioned Drogo to Ivo a few times, and then, leaving Ivo behind with the carts, disappeared into the crowd. She sighed and rubbed her forehead, managing a weak smile for Ivo when he patted her hand in a gesture of comfort. May decided that when Eada returned, and she refused to think of any other possibility, she was going to work harder on her French.

"She did what?" Drogo asked in a tight voice after a scowling Serle found him and the others.

Standing with a large crowd of knights encircling William and watching another small village suffer beneath the brutality of mercenaries and bloodthirsty knights, Drogo was not in a good humor. Not only did he not understand why such destruction was necessary, he was deeply disappointed that William did nothing to stop it. These people were no threat to them and did not really have anything worth taking. All Drogo saw was the murder of innocents and wanton destruction, but he struggled to hide his distaste from William. Now Serle arrived to tell him that Eada had run blindly into the midst of that deadly melee. He wondered how he had missed seeing her.

"I think she may have had a vision or something," Serle said quietly when he was certain that only Drogo, Tancred, Unwin, and Garnier could hear. "If I understand May correctly, and she is getting much better at making herself understood, Eada went very white, cried out, and then fled toward the village."

"Eada seems determined to get herself killed." Drogo started back to where they had left their horses, the others hurrying to keep pace with him. "I know she is moved by the cries for help she hears, but she must learn to wait until someone can go with her or, by God's sweet grace, I will tie her into the cart." He mounted and looked at Serle. "You had better return to Ivo and help guard our goods. The fact that we are Normans will not protect us from thievery. I will take the others and see if I can find that mad woman before some fool blinded by the scent of blood does."

Fifteen

Her breath coming in short, swift gasps and her whole body aching, Eada faced Sir Guy with all the defiance she could muster. They had circled each other and lunged and retreated until she was dizzy with exhaustion. The women cried out words of encouragement, but inspiring though they were, they could not restore her swiftly waning strength. Sir Guy no longer responded to her insults, and his attack was cold and well planned. She had been nicked by his sword several times and she began to wonder if she were as good at eluding him as she thought or if he were just toying with her, killing her slowly as he had threatened to do.

Suddenly he lunged at her again, and although she avoided the full thrust of his sword, he cut her side. She cried out in pain, clutched the freely bleeding wound, and staggered as she turned to face him. Eada wondered why her voices had not told her that she would die.

"Sir Guy," cried one of his companions, "I think we had best flee this place."

"Not now," he snapped. "I finally have this whore at my mercy."

Eada was stunned when a shape suddenly hurled itself through the air at Sir Guy's back. She barely retained enough of her senses to move out of the way as the two men hit the ground hard. It was only then that she recognized Drogo. She looked up and saw Unwin holding the reins of Drogo's horse and Tancred and Garnier flanking him, keeping a close guard on the men who had ridden with Sir Guy.

She looked back at Drogo to see him and Sir Guy now standing and facing each other. Sir Guy's companions had retreated, silently telling Drogo's men that they would not interfere. Both Drogo and Sir Guy were pale and hard-eyed with fury, and Eada shivered. She felt that Sir Guy was deserving of death, if only for the woman he had so coldly slain; but she suddenly thought that it might not be a good thing if Drogo killed the man, at least not yet.

Just as she looked to Drogo's men, wondering if she could get them to stop the fight, a man on a huge white horse rode almost calmly between the two combatants. It was a moment before she recognized the old knight who had stopped the two men from fighting before. Lord Bergeron had a wonderful skill for showing up at just the right moment, she thought wearily as she slowly sat down in the dirt.

"Again I am called upon to stop two of William's knights from killing each other," the older Lord Bergeron murmured as he leaned forward on the pommel of his saddle and studied Drogo and Guy. "Did neither of you heed my words?"

It took all his strength to control his fury enough to sheath his sword; but after taking one, long, shuddering breath, Drogo did so. "I fear anger seared your wisdom from my mind," Drogo drawled, glancing sideways at Lord Bergeron, and was relieved to see the man grin.

Lord Bergeron looked down at Eada, his head cocked to the side in a gesture of curiosity. "You were in the middle the last time, too, although it looks as if you have fared far worse this time."

"I am still alive, my lord," Eada said, and she looked toward the Saxon woman Sir Guy had killed. "That is more than some are."

After a brief, scowling look at the dead woman, Lord Bergeron returned his attention to Eada. "I could begin to think that you are a great source of trouble."

"You could, my lord, but I think you know that it is much more complicated than my disobedience and Sir Guy's ability to see insult in every word." She was startled when he grinned at her. "These women and children sought the sanctuary of the church; and when Sir Guy arrived, I felt they might need some help in reaching it."

"Of course." Lord Bergeron looked down at Sir Guy. "I believe we must have ourselves another talk, boy."

Knowing that that was the signal to leave, Drogo grabbed Eada by the arm. "We will return to the cart," he said firmly, trying to hide his fear and concern when he saw the blood on her gown.

"Please, Drogo, just let me look at the women and children," Eada said as he tugged her toward his horse. She looked toward the chapel and realized that the women had used Lord Bergeron's arrival to slip inside with the last of the children. "Some of them were hurt, and I need to see that they are not badly injured and that what wounds they may have are being tended to properly."

He wanted to say *no,* to demand she get on his horse and let him take her back to safety, but the pleading look in her eyes weakened his resolve. "You are bleeding," he said.

"I am not dying. I just wish to assure myself that none of the terrified women and babes in that church are dying or soon will if they are not given aid."

His emotions too strong and confused, Drogo made no reply, just waved her toward the church. As he watched her hurry into the small chapel, he saw two pale faces appear briefly in the doorway. He nodded at Lord Bergeron then moved away to allow the man some privacy with Sir Guy and signaled his men to follow him.

Tancred dismounted, stood next to Drogo, and glanced

back at Lord Bergeron, who had his arm around Sir Guy's shoulders and was talking intently to the white-faced man. "Why is Lord Bergeron always so close at hand whenever you have the opportunity to finally kill that adder?"

"He is Sir Guy's uncle," Drogo replied in a tight voice, and then he took a deep breath to calm himself. "The man loathes Sir Guy but loves his sister, Guy's mother. For her sake, he does what he can to keep the fool alive."

"His sister's son?" Tancred could not fully hide his horror. "Then you can never kill Sir Guy."

"Yes, I can, and now I know that I must and I will. One day that fool's protective uncle will not be near or will finally decide that even his love for his sister is not enough to make him save Sir Guy."

"Why would Guy try so hard to kill Eada? From the look of both of them, there was quite a battle here."

"Who can say why Sir Guy does anything? After all the years he has hated me, I have yet to understand why. He was clearly here killing the women and children of this village. Why should killing Eada trouble him? And he may wish to see her dead just to strike a blow at me. Then, too, I am sure that Eada rushed here to save those innocents and spared Sir Guy none of her scorn and fury."

Tancred grinned. "No, she would not think to hold her tongue." He frowned at the chapel. "Do you think she will be long?" He looked around at the death and destruction in the village and grimaced. "If we linger here for too long, someone might think we had a hand in all of this."

"I will allow her a few more moments and then I will go in and bring her out. She has wounds of her own that need tending, and I wish to know all that happened here."

"Or why she even came here."

* * *

Eada finished tying the bandage she had wrapped around the old woman's wounded arm and sat back on her heels to look around. There were only six women in the church, including the old one she had just tended, but there were at least a dozen children. Three of the children cowered near the altar, and Eada suspected that they were now orphans. Sadly, there would undoubtedly be a lot more by the time the fighting was over.

"Whose children are those?" she asked a plump, dark-haired woman who helped the old woman sip water from a goatskin.

"They are Edgar the swineherd's children. He died from a fever in the spring, and their mother is the woman that Norman killed outside the door."

"Is there anyone who can take them in and care for them?"

"Take them in where? All our homes are in ashes. And when this army leaves, I do not think they will leave much behind save corpses."

There was no denying that hard truth, and Eada asked, "How old are they?"

"The taller boy is Edgar and he is twelve. His sister Hertha is ten, and the little boy is Gar and he is five. Why do you need to know?" the woman asked.

Eada heard the suspicion in the woman's voice and tried not to be hurt by it. "Are you sure no one in the village can care for them? That they have no kinsmen left?"

"Very sure."

"Then I will take them."

"And give them to those murderers?"

"Not all of the Normans are killers of children and helpless women. Did you not see that I was saved from one Norman by another?"

"I also heard you speak in their tongue," she said, and there was a murmur of angry agreement from the other women.

"As I now speak in your tongue. My mother could speak both French and English and she taught her children to do the same."

"And you ride with the Normans."

"I was captured in Pevensey, but God smiled upon me and I am held by a man who holds both honor and mercy in his soul."

The woman shrugged. "That does not mean he will welcome and care for Saxon children, children who were orphaned by his own countrymen."

Eada started to find their suspicions irritating. "Did I not help you? Did I not save your lives? I have already taken in a babe and a youth. I do not need more mouths to fill and the man who holds me does not need them either. And none of you are offering to care for them, so why do you argue with me? At least I can offer them a chance to survive. Can you?"

There was a long, heavy silence as the women looked at each other and then at the three terrified children. "No. Take them."

The agreement was made in such a sullen tone of voice that Eada decided she had better leave. Part of her understood their feelings, but another part was deeply hurt. As she urged the children out of the church, she realized that many of her people would distrust her now, for she rode with the enemy. It was not going to be easy to help her people if they all began to see her as the enemy, too.

Once outside the church, she cautiously approached Drogo. He looked at the children, then at her, but said nothing. Silently he gave each of his men a child to place in front of him on his horse, then grabbed her and tossed her up in the saddle. She could feel his anger, see it in the tight line of his jaw, as he swung into the saddle behind her. She just prayed that most of that anger was for Sir Guy and not her.

When they returned to their carts, they discovered that

William had ordered camp to be made. Ivo was waiting at the edge of the camp to lead them to Drogo's tent, which he had already prepared. Eada was not sure she wished to spend the night so close to the burned village, but one look at Drogo's frown was enough to make her swallow her objection.

It was not until they were inside his tent that he spoke. "I cannot become the shelter for every orphan in England," he said, as he helped her disrobe and then gently washed the cuts Sir Guy had inflicted.

"I know," she replied quietly. "If we can find a village that is not destroyed, there may be someone there who will take them in."

"You rushed blindly into danger again," he said, breathing an inner sigh of relief when he saw that none of her wounds was deep enough to require stitching.

"I know that, too." When he sat back on his heels, she slipped on her chemise. "I am trying to wait, to not answer the cries the moment I hear them; but, Drogo, this time I heard the cries of children. I heard their fear and their pain and I just ran to them. I think I knew that there was no time, that I had to get to them right away or they would die."

He took her into his arms and lightly kissed the top of her head. "And what good would you have been to them if you had died before you could even reach them?"

"None," she mumbled against his chest. "When I saw Sir Guy kill that woman at the very door of the church, I fear I allowed my fury to rule me."

"You attacked him?" Drogo asked, staring at her in surprise.

"Yes. I pulled him from his horse. We fought, and none of the other men interfered until I got hold of Sir Guy's sword. I almost defeated him. If his fellow knight had not put himself and his horse between us and had not earlier taken away the sword, I might have won. I did keep them all so distracted that the women and children were able to get inside the church." She frowned when Drogo began to laugh. "I do not see what is so funny."

"No? You, a tiny woman with no weapon, almost defeated one armored knight." He shook his head as the seriousness of the situation overcame his humor. "Sir Guy will now hate you as much as he hates me."

"I realized that as we fought. At first I think he wanted to kill me because I am with you, but then he wanted to kill me alone. But, why would he be cutting down women and children? They were not fighting him. They were no threat to him at all."

"I fear I cannot explain such brutality as I do not understand it myself. It seems to come from a pure love of killing. It is said that some men are maddened by the scent of blood, and yet Sir Guy does not appear mad."

"No. He does like the killing, and I think he especially enjoys cutting down the helpless and the terrified. As he killed that poor woman he smiled, as if it were all just some mild amusement, of no more importance than watching a minstrel play. I believe that is one reason I grew so angry. He took a person's life away with no more concern than he might show if he swatted a fly."

"It is at times like these that I wish I had had the courage to leave you behind in Pevensey. I only soothe that guilt by reminding myself that it was little safer there." He sighed and shook his head. "You are seeing all the black deeds and the evil many women of good birth are protected from."

She reached up and caressed his cheek with her now-bandaged hand, the fight with Sir Guy having left it covered in scratches. "Neither of us had much choice. And how can we be sure that I would have been saved from seeing the horror and the evil? Old Edith's gift has made it difficult for me to be blind to the troubles all around me." His eyes narrowed and she immediately regretted

reminding him of her strange skill, a skill that had caused
her to disobey him and put herself in danger yet again.

"You must cease running toward these voices alone."
He touched a kiss to her lips to silent her protest. "I understand what makes you do so and I cannot fault that.
But, Eada, you have this gift for a reason—to help others,
to save people. Would it not be a sin and a waste if you
got yourself killed because you cannot find the wit and
strength to wait but one moment to get one of us to go
with you?"

She thought about that and realized that he was right.
Although it was hard to ignore the pain and the urgency
of the cries she heard, she had to find the will to hesitate
before responding to them. When she had thought his
objections stemmed just from his concern for her safety,
she had shrugged them aside. She suspected that was still
the only real reason he wanted her to learn how to wait,
but his reasoning was faultless. She did have a valuable
gift, valuable and possibly life-saving for some of the innocents caught in the war. It was foolish to waste it. Dying to
save children was honorable, but that honor was dimmed
if it meant that she had robbed her people of a gift that
had, thus far, helped them.

"You are right. It would be foolish to waste it when all
I need to do is pause for one moment and get a man
with a sword to take me where I must go."

Drogo inwardly breathed a hearty sigh of relief. He had
not wanted to tie her to the cart, to restrain her in any
manner, but he had begun to think that it was the only
way to keep her alive. He could not silence what she
called her voices and he could not stop her from helping
someone who was in danger or in pain, but it was far
past time for her to begin to practice caution. It was even
more important now that she had Sir Guy as an enemy.

"Now, you must rest," he urged as he pressed her down
onto the sheepskin before the fire. "Your wounds were

not severe, but you should take care. I think you will also discover that a great many parts of you will soon begin to ache."

She grimaced as he gently spread a blanket over her. "They do already."

"You can expect nothing else when you fight with an armored knight with no more than your bare hands," he drawled.

"Sir Guy will never forget that I have humiliated him, will he?"

"No, never."

"It seems as if I do little more than cause you trouble at every turning."

"Oh, there are a few pleasant moments," he murmured, and grinned at her sleepy smile before kissing her cheek. "Sleep."

"I should see if I can help some of the wounded, and there were some who were suffering some most uncomfortable maladies."

"Men on the march often suffer very uncomfortable maladies. As for the wounded, you will not be allowed back into the village tonight; and any man who was wounded while he burnt the village and murdered the people there deserves to suffer his wounds."

"The church says we should forgive," she said but smiled at him, agreeing with his sentiments about the men who were hurt while indulging in destruction.

"Forgive them on the morrow. You have shown a true skill at healing and the word has been carried throughout the army. There will be many a time when you can show them the depth of your mercy."

He smiled when she stayed awake long enough to laugh, and then he sighed. A large weight had been lifted from his shoulders when she had finally agreed to be more cautious. Drogo knew she had not really heeded his warnings and pleas before. He was going to make sure that one man capable of defending her with a sword was always close at hand, however, for he suspected that while she might now hesitate before running to answer cries for help, she would not hesitate for long.

After one last check that she was warm and completely covered by the blanket, he slipped quietly out of the tent. The first sight that caught his eye as he stretched in front of his tent was the three children she had brought into his camp. They sat huddled together as May served them each some stew. He felt a true sympathy for the orphans, but he also wished they were not in his camp.

"More mouths to keep filled," drawled Serle as he stepped up next to Drogo.

"I was just thinking on that." He shook his head. "God alone knows how many more there might be before we reach London."

"Mayhap we can find a monastery or nunnery where we can leave them."

"The monastery will not take the girl-child, and the nunnery will not take the boys. I may wish they were not added to my number, but I cannot separate them."

Serle watched May gently wipe the smallest boy's chin with a corner of her skirt. "And soon you will not be able to tear them from that woman's arms."

"May does have a soft heart concerning children. So does Ivo. When I gain my lands, I think I shall have to make sure that they have a very large house." He smiled when Serle laughed then bent to pat Eada's hounds before they slipped into his tent.

"And how fares Eada?"

"She will be fine. Her wounds were small."

"But the hatred Sir Guy now holds for her is large."

Drogo grimaced and scratched his head. "Maybe even greater than the hate he holds for me." He told Serle everything Eada had told him about her fight with Sir Guy. "She humiliated him before his companions. She may have even cost him one or two of the very few followers he has."

"And I am sure that his uncle observed most of his humiliation as well, and I know Lord Bergeron well enough to promise you that he will never let Sir Guy forget it. He may save the fool for the sake of his sister, but he makes no pretense of liking his nephew and the man can have a biting tongue."

"So now I must watch *her* back as well as my own."

"And you had better get her to be more careful. If she keeps running headlong into trouble, someone might begin to wonder how she knows where that trouble is. She can only perform so many sudden rescues before people will begin to ask how she knows who is in danger."

"I know. And I shudder to think what trouble Sir Guy could stir if he discovered that she hears voices."

"Is that what she does?" Serle asked in honest curiosity.

"That is what she calls it—her voice or voices. The cries she hears are in her head as is the truth she can sometimes say without warning."

"Ah, I had thought that she had dreams."

"I know of only one—the warning she gave me about Sir Guy." He started toward the fire where the others had gathered. "I think we had best get something to eat before May pours it all down the throats of those children."

"How are the children?" Eada asked the moment Drogo entered the tent.

She felt that she had been lying awake and alone for hours even though May had come to see her briefly and Godwin had slipped away from Sir Guy long enough to assure himself that she was all right. Once she had gotten up to relieve herself, and it had proven to be a painful chore, every inch of her body protesting the movement.

Although she had cursed her weakness, she had quickly eased her aching body back down onto the soft sheepskin.

"The children are fine," Drogo replied as he sat down beside her and offered her a goatskin filled with wine, frowning when she groaned as she propped herself up to have a drink. "You are in pain?"

"Yes. Being thrown to the ground and having a full-grown, armored knight fall on you clearly causes one's body to suffer." She rubbed her throat; swallowing the wine painfully reminded her that Sir Guy had also tried to strangle her. "I had better feel less of this pain on the morrow or I think I shall be very unhappy."

"And will make others most unhappy as well, I suspect."

"You can cease to suspect it. It will be a fact hard to ignore. I have never endured pain or illness with any grace."

He shed his jupon, boots, and hose and, still wearing his shirt, eased his body beneath the blanket. Very gently, he turned on his side and slid his arm around her waist, edging closer until their bodies touched. Her ill humor both amused him and relieved him. It showed that her injuries were not serious.

"It will be a few days before the aches and pains fade, but they will fade."

She sighed and slowly snuggled closer, the warmth of his body helping to ease some of her aches. "You said the children are fine?"

"Yes. May has taken them to her heart, and they seem to have taken to her as well."

"And Brun?" she asked and felt a slight tension come and go in his body.

"He is also fine. As I have said, you have a true skill for healing and he now begins to find his weakness and confinement a great irritation. I believe he will soon be on his feet again."

A yawn forced itself upon her and she was surprised,

for she had already slept for hours. "I think I am about
to go to sleep again."

"Good. You need the rest to heal."

"There is one thing I must tell you before I do go to
sleep and, mayhap, forget what I wanted to say come the
morning."

"What?" he prodded when she closed her eyes and did
not continue.

"Godwin came to see me for only a brief time, but he
told me something about Sir Guy that he felt you should
know. He said the man could do little more than rant
and curse me when he returned to his camp. Godwin
does not understand French, not even as well as May, for
I have little chance to teach him, but he said the tone of
the man's words was alarming."

Drogo sighed, rested his cheek against her hair, and
only briefly thought on giving her some empty but soothing words. "I fear the man now hates you as much as he
does me. He only thinks I have humiliated him and he
wants me dead. You have actually done so."

"I know, and I think I may have cost him an ally. One
of his companions was thoroughly disgusted by Sir Guy,
by the way he behaved, refused to listen to reason, and
especially by the fact that he could not defeat me without
help."

"You once told me that you saw him as a dark and
threatening shadow at my back. Well, I think that threat
is now at your back, too."

Eada nodded, afraid and yet resigned. "Do not fear,
Drogo. I will keep a close watch, and I have one thing
to help me that you have never had."

"And what is that?"

"Godwin. A sharp-eyed spy within the very heart of our
enemy's camp. All I have to do is teach the boy French."

Sixteen

"Ivo, who is the knight who watches over me today?"
Eada demanded as she walked up to Drogo's burly servant.

When Ivo cringed and turned to look at her, his face
revealing his sudden timidity, Eada almost laughed, but
her humor was tinged with a hint of regret. She knew
she had been in an ill temper in the week since she had
fought with Sir Guy—and not only because of all of her
bruises, aches, and pains. It had not taken her long to
see that she was under constant guard. Drogo had not
completely accepted her word that she would be more
cautious. Even while she had to admit that she had been
reckless on several occasions, she still felt that Drogo was
being too protective and far too suspicious.

"Serle is here," Ivo responded carefully.

"Where? I do not see him."

Ivo pointed to a large group of men standing in a circle
looking down. Although she had had no trouble within
the camp except for occasional hate-filled looks from Sir
Guy, Eada was wary about approaching so many Norman
soldiers. Everyone, except Sir Guy and his companions,
appeared to respect her as Drogo's woman and appreciate her healing skills, but she had never placed herself
within reach of so many men before. She needed Serle,
however, for no one else was around. Even her dogs were
missing, and Eada suspected one of the knights had bor-
rowed them to go hunting again.

"Are you sure, Ivo? I do not see him there."

"He is on the ground, playing dice."

Eada took a deep breath to restore her suddenly wavering courage and walked toward the boisterous group of men. As she drew nearer, she was able to discern five men kneeling at their game. The soldiers seemed to be fonder of gambling than of fighting, she thought crossly as she nudged her way through the crowd. Some of the looks cast her way were not friendly and some were leering, but no one touched her and she began to relax.

"Serle," she called as she circled to the older man.

"Ah, little Eada," he called back cheerfully. "Hold but a moment. It is my throw, and I think this one shall make me a rich man."

She had to bite the inside of her cheek to keep from replying with sharp words. He could not know why she needed him and she certainly did not want to tell him that she was being pulled somewhere again, not in front of so many people. When he won the toss and, amid great cheering and loud complaints from the losers, collected his winnings, she did feel pleased for him. She also reached out to pluck at the back of his jupon to remind him that she was there before, caught up in the joy of victory, he began to play again.

"Drogo sent me to find you," she said when he glanced at her, frowning as he idly rolled the dice between his fingers.

Serle quickly left the game, amiably promising the losers a future chance to regain their coin. He took her by the arm and tugged her a distance from the men until they were too far away to be overheard. When he looked at her expectantly, she grimaced.

"I lied," she muttered.

"What?" he stared at her in a mixture of surprise and annoyance. "There had better be a good reason for such deceit, child. Did you not see that I was winning?"

"Yes, and you should be grateful that I pulled you free before your luck fled you. Now you have a pocketful of coin. A few moments from now, a few more tosses of the dice, and you could have been in debt." She shrugged when he put his hands on his hips and eyed her with an almost-fatherly indulgence.

"You need me for some reason, do you?"

"Yes." She glanced around to be certain that no one could hear her and said softly, "I must go into that village."

"Nothing has happened there. How can you hear cries when all is quiet, no one has been attacked, and no cottage has been set alight?"

"There are other things that can cause tragedy, Serle."

"Eada, sweet girl, you begin to make me very suspicious."

"I need to go to the village."

"Your *needing* to go is not enough reason for me to take you."

"I wish I could tell you more, but that is all I know. I was quietly mending Drogo's shirt when suddenly I got the strongest feeling that I must go into the village."

"This had better be good, child," he said, as he again took her by the arm and led her toward the horses.

"At least there is no trouble brewing there."

"True," he agreed as he mounted and pulled her up behind him. "That does not mean it will not appear the moment you ride onto the scene."

She clung to him as he nudged his mount into a trot and headed toward the village they had camped near. "You make it sound as if I carry that trouble around with me, sprinkling it about as we march to London."

"At times one must wonder. I have never known a girl to find trouble as easily as you do, nor one who is so adept at hurling herself right into the midst of it."

"I do not do it on purpose," she grumbled then rubbed

her stomach as it began to knot tighter the closer they drew to the village. "Oh, mayhap there is trouble ahead."

"Have you heard something now?" he asked, glancing back at her and frowning at how pale she had grown.

"No. I still hear nothing, only feel it. The closer we draw to the village, the stronger the feeling becomes. My belly is in knots and my heart has begun to pound so swiftly I am surprised you cannot hear it."

"Ah, now that is good," he muttered.

"Good? What is good about it? I am most uncomfortable."

"I do not mean what you suffer is good." He pointed to their right. "I see Drogo returning from his meeting with William and he has seen us."

Eada softly cursed and ignored Serle's bark of laughter. She did not really see any harm in Drogo's coming along except that waiting for him was delaying them and that delay was adding to her growing discomfort. It was a message of some sort, but it was going to be difficult to explain it to Drogo.

"And where do you two travel to?" He frowned and leaned closer to Eada. "You look ill."

"I feel ill, and I think I may soon be more so if I do not get to the village."

Drogo signaled Serle to continue and rode alongside him, keeping a close watch on Eada. She had never looked so grey or uncomfortable before, so physically affected by one of her sendings. Drogo wondered if they were getting stronger, too strong for her to endure.

"What is in the village?" he asked as he handed her a goatskin filled with sweet cider.

Eada took a long, slow drink and handed the goatskin back to him. "I do not really know. Something is demanding I go there, but I do not hear a voice or see anything; I just feel this almost painful need."

He reached over and patted her tightly clenched hand.

"Then we will go there. Do you know where in the village you are supposed to go?"

She stared at him yet did not really see him. His innocent question had stirred something within her. One soft word whispered its way through her mind.

"I must go to the nunnery."

"There is a nunnery in the village?"

"At the far end of it," replied Serle.

"What could there be within a nunnery that would draw you?" Drogo muttered.

"I wish I knew."

By the time they reached the sprawling nunnery, Eada was so unsteady that Drogo had to help her off Serle's horse and support her with an arm around her shoulder. As he led her toward the heavy iron gates which opened into a courtyard, she realized that what unsettled her was a fierce sense of hope and anticipation. She was struggling to understand what she might find there to cause her to feel that way when she heard a painfully familiar, high, boyish voice.

"Ethelred," she whispered.

Eada broke free of Drogo's light hold and ran toward the sound of the voice. The same anticipation that had made her dizzy and weak now gave her strength. She ignored Drogo's and Serle's curses and could hear them following her as she ran around the corner of the long, low, stone building. When she saw what she had been running toward, she stopped so abruptly that the two men stumbled in their attempts not to bump into her.

A woman sat on a stone bench mending a small shirt. At her feet sat a little boy. Eada did not need to see the woman's face to know that she was looking at her mother. Just as she gathered the strength to call to Vedette, her sister came out of the building and walked toward their mother. Averil's gaze settled on Eada; her eyes widened, and her steps faltered.

"Eada," she screamed a heartbeat later, and hiking up her skirts, she ran straight into Eada's open arms with such force she nearly sent them both tumbling to the ground.

Over Averil's shoulder Eada saw her mother rise slowly to her feet even as her little brother gave a cry and ran to her. Eada rocked as Ethelred bumped into her legs and wrapped his arms tightly around her. Vedette approached with more calm and dignity, but as she drew near, Eada was surprised to see that her mother was crying. A soft word from Vedette was enough to make Averil and Ethelred step away, and Eada found herself tightly clasped in her mother's arms.

"Sweet merciful God, you are alive," Vedette whispered in a hoarse, unsteady voice.

"I have feared that you might be dead," Eada said, brushing away her tears as her mother stepped back and looked her over. "Old Edith said that you, Averil, and Ethelred would survive, but sometimes I was afraid to believe it."

"I have lived in terror that some ill befell you since the moment I had to leave you behind. You do understand why I had to do that?"

"Of course. I will confess that, for a short time, I was angry and hurt, but reason soon cured me of that. And with each village I have watched burn, I have become more understanding, even glad that you had the strength to do it." She felt Drogo step up next to her and lightly touched his arm. "This is Sir Drogo de Toulon, Mother. I ride with him," she added carefully in English, pausing before slipping into French to include Drogo in their conversation, and saw by the slight widening of her mother's eyes that Vedette understood what she was saying.

"Is he kind to you?"

"Very. I know that I would be dead or badly hurt if not for him. And Old Edith said he is my mate. She is dead, Mother."

"We can speak of that later." Vedette held her hand out to Drogo and said in perfect French. "I thank you for keeping my daughter safe."

Although Drogo felt embarrassed facing Eada's mother, he bowed slightly and touched a kiss to the back of her hand. "It has not always been easy," he drawled.

"I have no doubt about that."

"You two can share your complaints about me later," said Eada as she tugged a strangely silent Serle forward. "This is Sir Serle, Mother."

Eada frowned when her mother stared at Serle and slowly grew alarmingly white. She looked at Serle and saw that he looked little better. As she turned back to her mother, she gave a cry of alarm and was relieved when Drogo moved quickly enough to catch the collapsing woman before she hit the ground.

The next few minutes were confusing. Eada was not sure how her mother went from Drogo's arms to Serle's, but as Serle sat down on the stone bench with Vedette in his arms, she dampened a strip of her underskirt in water from the well and began to bathe her mother's face. It was a few minutes before Vedette began to stir.

"Are you ill?" Eada asked, kneeling by the bench and taking her mother's hand in hers.

Vedette's gaze was fixed on Serle as she whispered, "No. I but thought that I was seeing a ghost."

"No ghost, Vedette," Serle replied, not releasing her as she carefully sat up.

As she got to her feet, idly patting her little brother on the head, Eada said, "You two are not strangers to one another."

With an obvious reluctance, Vedette slid off Serle's lap, sat next to him, and took his hand in hers. "No. We knew each other many years ago in France."

Eada opened her mouth to give her opinion that they had obviously known each other very well when Drogo took her by the arm and tugged her aside. He gave Ethelred and Averil one sharp signal to follow him, and after a brief hesitation, they did. Eada looked at her mother and Serle talking fervently and too quietly to be overheard and then eyed Drogo with annoyance.

"Do you know something about this?"

"No. Are you going to introduce me to the rest of your family?" He had to smile at the polite way she did so and the equally polite way her siblings replied despite the suspicious glare all three of them cast at him.

"If you do not know what that is about, then why did you pull us all away from them?" Eada demanded.

"Because it is evident that those two need a moment or two alone to overcome their shock at seeing each other again and, mayhap, to say a few things it might be best that you children do not hear."

He was right, but Eada decided he did not need to be flattered by her saying so. She was also irritated that he had referred to her as one of the children. As she watched her mother and Serle, their heads close together as they talked, she felt a confusing swirl of emotion inside her. There was jealousy that her reunion with her family had been usurped, hurt that her mother had allowed that to happen, and anger that her mother seemed able to forget her father with such ease. Embarrassed by her own selfish and somewhat childish emotions, she forced her attention to Drogo, who was valiantly trying to keep her siblings occupied.

"We were very afraid for you," Averil said quietly as she stepped closer and took Eada's hand in hers.

"I was very afraid for all of you as well," Eada replied.

"Each and every night I have suffered from dark dreams about all that might have happened to you. At times, I was very angry with our mother, asking her and myself how she could have left you alone and with an army landing on our shores."

"I hope you then answered yourself that she had no choice."

Averil smiled briefly. "Most of the time. Are you sure you are unhurt?" She cast a wary and suspicious look Drogo's way.

"Yes. I am hale and not unhappy. My heart is sore for our king is dead and we shall soon have to live under a new rule, but fate has decreed it and I am too tiny a person to argue with fate."

"Our father is dead."

"I know. Old Edith told me. How do you come to know for certain?"

"One of the men who fought with him came through the village and told our mother. He was marching to Hastings to fight William, and so I suppose he is now dead, too."

Eada hugged her sister, sensing the sadness in Averil, one she shared. "He probably is, although many did escape that battle. And those who did not made a fine accounting of themselves."

"But they did not win, and I believe that there will be no more fighting."

"Have the Saxons given up then?" asked Drogo.

When Averil hesitated, Eada nudged her and the girl finally said, "I think they believe this is some punishment. The news that William carries the Papal banner and holy relics has spread far and wide, as has the news of the loss at Hastings. The fight has left the ones we have spoken to, and they do not speak of any other army preparing to fight William. How can one fight God's will?"

"I was afraid that revealing that we had the blessings of the Pope would do that, and I confess I do not like to win because of it."

"You would rather the crown was won with only bravery and skill in battle?" asked Eada. "The blessing of the church is no small weapon."

"I know, and it may be sinful vanity, but I want to win because I am a skilled warrior."

"I am sure that if you were not, the battle could still have been lost."

"Mother is finally done talking to that man," announced Ethelred even as he hurried toward his mother.

Eada smiled at her mother who, still holding Serle's hand as if she feared he would disappear, stepped up to her and kissed her cheek. For now, she would not trouble her mother with questions or ill humors. They might not be able to visit each other for long, and she did not want to ruin their short time together with unpleasant accusations or recriminations. She was not sure her mother deserved them anyway.

"We have a great deal to talk about, Eada, but now is not the time or the place. Mayhap we could take our evening meal together?"

"Yes. Here or in the camp?"

"Here and—" she glanced at Drogo. "—I do not mean to offend, but I think we need some time alone."

"I take no offense, mistress," Drogo said, bowing slightly as he took Eada's hand in his. "I will bring her to you as the sun sets and return to collect her in three-hours' time."

Vedette nodded, but Eada could see the tension in her mother's expression. Now that she was over the shock of seeing the daughter she had had to leave behind, she was clearly upset about the relationship between Drogo and her eldest child. Eada began to feel nervous. One thing she had not considered in her joy at finding her family again was how it might change her life.

All the way back to camp she said nothing and was glad that both Serle and Drogo were silent as well. What should have been solely a source of happiness was suddenly looking like a great deal of trouble. When Drogo led her into the tent they shared, she turned to look at

him, and her increasing uneasiness was not soothed by
the frown on his face.

"It must please you to know that your family has survived," he finally said as he crouched by the fire and took
a long drink from the wineskin.

"Yes," she answered in a careful tone as she sat down
beside him, "but I was not often afraid for them. At first,
I felt guilty that I had not suffered as Averil said she had.
Then I realized that I did not worry much because Old
Edith had said that they would all survive. I had not seen
how deeply I believed in Old Edith until then."

"She could have lied to ease your fears."

"No. She told me too much else on that day that deeply
upset me. I am not sure, but I think she may have been
incapable of lying. However, she told me that my father
was doomed and that England was doomed, so I do not
believe she would have saved me from any other harsh
truth about my family."

"I am glad that her prophecy was borne out. I have
been worried, fearing that you would discover that my
people had killed them."

"And what if I had? Their blood would not have been
on your sword."

He smiled at her as he sat down more comfortably and
draped his arm around her shoulders. There was one
more thing he worried about—a new fear, born the moment he had seen her family. Now Eada did not need his
protection. Now she had some choice. She could stay with
him or stay with her family at the nunnery that had
proven to be a safe haven. Drogo wondered if he would
have the strength to offer her that choice and what he
would do if she chose her family.

"Is Eada almost ready?" Drogo asked May as the maid
stepped out of his tent. "I told her mother that I would

bring her when the sun set and it has already begun to do so."

"Yes, she will be out in a moment," replied May in halting French.

"You are getting very good at speaking our language."

She blushed. "Once I learned some, it has been easier to learn by just talking to Ivo. I had better go and help him with the children," she murmured and fled back to Ivo's small tent.

Drogo walked over to Serle, who sat beneath the tree a few feet in front of his tent and silently accepted a drink from the wineskin the man held up to him. "Do you not go to visit with the woman? We will break camp at dawn and march away."

"I know. I am to visit her after Eada has left," Serle replied. "Has she said anything about me and her mother?"

"Not a word. I was quite surprised that she did not even ask me. I think she has decided to ignore it or wait until her mother tells her. You said it was twenty years ago when you and Vedette were in love. Are you still?"

"Yes. I am as surprised as you look. How can such a thing remain alive when two people are as far apart as she and I were? It would seem that love should require some word or look or touch to stay alive."

"I would have said so, but I am not learned on the matter." He frowned as he gave Serle back the wineskin and then asked quietly, "What do you think I ought to do about Eada?"

"What do you mean?"

"Her family is alive and safe. She does not need my protection any longer. In truth, it would probably be safer for her to remain here with her mother than to march to London with me. The only real danger in this land at this time is us, and we will be leaving in the morning."

"But you do not wish to leave Eada behind."

"No, and that is selfish and shows little thought concerning what is better and safer for her."

"You are a man, Drogo, not a saint. I would not flay myself with guilt and remorse simply because you do not wish to be parted from Eada. Yes, it would be safer for her to stay here with her mother and siblings. Since I intend to try and convince Vedette to join me once I have reached London, you would not even be parted for so very long, not if we continue to be unopposed."

"Do you think Vedette will come to you?"

"Yes. But we talk on Eada now. My thought is that you should offer her the choice. After all, if she wishes to stay here and you make her go with you, I believe the warmth you two now share will disappear. And if you make her stay when she wishes to go with you, you may hurt her. The easiest thing to do is just ask her what she wants to do. And you had best make your decision quickly for she is now ready to go to her mother and I think you will be forced to it when you return to the nunnery to try and bring her back here."

As Drogo walked over to Eada and accepted the reins of his mount from Ivo, he thought over all Serle had said and knew the man was right. He grasped Eada by the waist and lifted her gently into the saddle. When he saw the little chest she clutched tightly in her hands, he was distracted from his concerns.

"You are taking Old Edith's box to your mother?" he asked as he mounted and nudged his horse into a slow walk.

"Yes." She rubbed her hand nervously over the time-worn carvings on the box. "I am hoping that she will give me the courage to look inside."

"I am sure it is nothing bad," he murmured, trying to dispel a pinch of jealousy that he would not be the one to make the discovery with her.

"Perhaps not, but I grew to womanhood listening to

Old Edith speak her truths and, sadly, not many of them
were good. That is all I can think of whenever I touch
this box."

"You have worried over that since she gave it to you.
It is time to put an end to that."

"So I thought."

When she grew silent, Drogo left her to her troubled
thoughts. He had a lot to think about himself. As he rode
toward the nunnery, he fought the sudden urge to
change direction and ride away with Eada, taking her out
of her family's reach. That urge grew even stronger when
he reined in before the gates of the nunnery and met a
waiting Vedette's gaze as he steadied a dismounting Eada.

"It was kind of you to allow her to come," said Vedette
as she held the gates open for Eada.

"She is your daughter," Drogo said quietly.

"Yes, she should be with her family."

"I will return for you in three hours," he told Eada
and turned back toward camp without waiting for her
reply.

A moment later, he kicked his horse into a gallop,
eager to put some distance between himself and the nunnery before he did something he might regret. Serle was
right, he reminded himself sternly. He had to give Eada
the choice of staying with him or staying with her family.
If he used his position as a knight in a conquering army
to hold onto her, he would soon find that all that was
good between them would be gone. When he returned
to the nunnery, he would give her that choice. All he
could do was pray that she would choose him.

Seventeen

As she sipped her wine from one of the elegant silver goblets her mother had fled Pevensey with, Eada idly touched the little chest on the bench next to her. She was still afraid of what Old Edith might have secreted inside, but that fear was beginning to annoy her. Drogo was right. It was far past time for her to face whatever truths the old woman had hidden within it.

"Eada, what is that?" asked Vedette as she watched Eada blindly move her fingers over the intricate carvings on the lid of the tiny chest as if she had done so a hundred times before. "I do not remember it being a part of our household."

"No, Old Edith bequeathed it to me when she died."

"I am sorry for the loss of your old friend."

"There is no need to be. She knew that her time here was done." Eada smiled. "It did upset those Normans when they found that she had already prepared her grave." Eada was surprised when her mother returned her smile, for she had always felt that her parents had not liked Edith, had even shared the fears others had. "I have been afraid to open it, and I was hoping that you would give me the strength to do so."

"Why should you be afraid?"

"Because she told me I was to read the truth within it and I dread seeing any more of her harsh truths." Eada frowned when her mother paled.

"Children," Vedette said to Averil and Ethelred, her voice tight and soft. "I believe it is time for you to seek your beds."

"But," protested Averil even as she stood up and took Ethelred by the hand, "I wanted to see what is in the box."

Vedette kissed their cheeks as they stopped at her side. "I will tell you all you need to know in the morning."

Eada also kissed their cheeks, but asked, "What harm could there be in their sharing my discovery?"

"As you said, Old Edith's truths were often harsh. I think these two children have had enough sad and upsetting news. I would feel more at ease if I could at least see what the woman has left before I show or tell them."

Although she nodded and gave a final wave to her siblings as they left the small central room of her mother's quarters, Eada was troubled by her mother's behavior. It was clear that Vedette had not hidden the news of their father's death and had expected them to understand why she had left their eldest sibling behind in reach of the enemy. How much worse could the truths within the box be? Her mother was also looking uneasy, as if she suspected what truth Edith had spoken of; but that made no sense to Eada either. As far as she knew, her parents had had nothing to do with the old woman and had often expressed the wish that Eada did not visit Edith.

"Do you open it now?" Vedette asked in a small voice, turning on her seat to face Eada squarely and twisting her hands in her lap.

"I begin to think that you are more afraid of what is inside than I am," Eada muttered as she slowly unlatched the little chest.

"Eada, that poor old woman was not cast out of Pevensey because everyone delighted in her truths. She chilled everyone's blood. Of course I am uncertain about what last and, quite possibly, dark truth she has left behind her."

That answer did not really satisfy her, but Eada took a deep breath and opened the box. What was inside was almost disappointing, although Eada doubted she could have explained why even upon pain of death. It just seemed that, after so many weeks of being afraid, she ought to be faced with more than documents.

"Can you read, *Maman?*" she asked as she carefully placed the scrolls and a small dagger on the table. "I suddenly cannot remember if you can or not."

"Only a very few words, and I had to fight to get your father to teach me them."

"Then I shall read them to you."

"You can read?" Vedette's shock briefly diverted her from the collection of things on the well-scrubbed wooden table.

"Old Edith taught me."

"I am not sure that was a good thing for her to do, and God alone knows where she learned."

"I never thought to ask. I just accepted it as another of her odd gifts." Eada frowned as she smoothed out the scrolls. "I suppose I shall have to tell Drogo that I can since he will wonder how I could look at these papers and know what they said."

"We can speak of your Norman knight later."

There was a sharpness to Vedette's tone that warned Eada that that talk would not be a pleasant one. She turned her full attention to the documents, and absently rubbing the carved wooden handle of the little dagger, she began to read. Each word she read chilled her blood. As she read the last, she nearly cried out from the shock and pain. Slowly she looked at Vedette, realizing that she had said nothing to the woman, reading the horrifying truths in complete silence. The pale, fearful look on

Vedette's face told her that the woman was fully aware of what dark secrets Eada had just learned.

"You know what these documents say," she finally said, her voice hoarse and heavy with accusation.

"Only because of the horror on your face." Vedette reached for Eada's hand and winced when Eada yanked it out of her reach.

"I am not your child. Old Edith was my mother."

"Yes."

Eada closed her eyes and tried to calm the swirl of emotion within her. A part of her had hoped that Vedette would deny it and would convince her that it was all lies made up by a lonely old woman. Another part of her was strangely calm, however, as if this did not come as any surprise. Eada swallowed the anger she was suddenly afflicted with, knowing that flinging it at the woman she had called mother for so long would not answer any of her questions. Old Edith had left her the truth, but only as seen through her eyes and in old, written words. Eada prayed that Vedette could soften that harsh truth with a few explanations.

"She told me that she once had a husband, a child, and a finer life. My father was that husband; I was that child, and most of the lands to the west of Pevensey were part of her finer life. How did she lose them?"

"She did not tell you that?"

"She did. There is a letter here." Eada picked it up, but quickly put it back down when the crinkling of the parchment revealed how badly her hands were shaking. "I wish to hear how you tell the tale."

Vedette rubbed her unsteady hands over her face, took a deep, trembling breath, and looked at Eada. "They were all taken from her because of her strange gift. I do not seek to excuse my part in this deception, but I swear to you that I did not know of it until I was wed to your father for nearly eight years."

"But you did not tell me."

"Your father commanded me to keep it secret. I never really forgave him for making me a part of that cruel lie," she added in a whisper, her eyes briefly clouding with grief and sad remembrance before she shook it aside. "As his wife I had to support him."

"But, why did he have to keep it hidden? His marriage to Edith was annulled, so there was no crime to hide."

"I never did understand completely. I think he was suffering from a great burden of guilt. Edith was much older than he, but she had been a good wife. He never said a harsh word about her except to curse her gift and, occasionally, that he had lost all he had gained because of it. Those lands and riches he always spoke of having lost were, in truth, Old Edith's lands and wealth."

"It says here that Edith was the daughter of an earl. If Father was so poor, why did they even allow her to marry him?"

"Because she was almost past childbearing age and no other man would take her. I do not have the full truth of why, with all she had for a dowry, she remained unwed. I do not think your father did either. He married her and, for a while, all was well. They lived in our home in Pevensey while planning to build a castle on her lands. In his way, I do believe your father grew quite fond of her. Then, despite her age, she gave birth to you."

Eada suffered and conquered a surge of guilt. It was birthing a child that had brought Edith her gift, the very gift that had lost her everything. That was not her fault, but it took her a moment to accept that.

"Your father did not immediately cast her aside," Vedette continued. "He tried to make her keep it a secret, but she was unable to. He then hoped it would fade. It did not. It grew stronger and she began to better understand what was happening. No matter how often he begged her to be quiet, she could not keep the truths she learned to herself."

"And she was punished for that."

"Yes. The fears of the people in town grew dangerous. Your father feared that soon even you would be in danger. He warned her one last time, but she did not heed the warning. That was when he cast her out. She wanted to keep you with her, but then agreed that you would be safer with him. It was not hard for him to get an annulment, but when the marriage was ended, so was his wealth. All he got to keep was the house in Pevensey, and he could not even hand that to Ethelred upon his death. It was his only while he lived."

"I often saw the fear of the people, yet it never seemed that strong. They simply stayed away from her."

"Yes, because now they could. She was no longer in the village; they did not have to see her every day, and they did not have to fear that they were the next ones she would see some truth about. Even Edith's father turned away from her, which hurt him as much as it must have hurt her, for she was his only child, his only living family." She reached out to cover Eada's small clenched hand with hers, relieved when, this time, it was allowed. "Old Edith terrified people, Eada. If she had not had such a powerful father, she would have been killed. Although he turned away from her, her father would have killed anyone who hurt her. Even after he died, people feared she might still have powerful kinsmen who would avenge her death; and then, after years had passed, I believe they just fell into the habit of seeing her only on market day and ignoring her the rest of the year."

As she struggled to understand, Eada covered her face with her hands. It was not until she heard Vedette refill her goblet with wine that she shook free of her shock and confusion. She took a long, hearty drink to steady herself then carefully put everything back into the box.

"You are now a wealthy woman. Edith held claim to a lot of land."

"Which some Norman will soon claim," Eada murmured as she closed the chest.

"Your Norman?"

On the tip of Eada's tongue was a sharp reminder to Vedette that she was not her mother, but Eada hastily swallowed the angry and hurtful words. Even if they were not of the same blood, Vedette was her mother. Old Edith had always called her that—and, Eada now recalled, without any bitterness. If Edith could accept it, so could she. She could even forgive Vedette for being part of the lie. The woman had not really had much choice. The ones who were to blame were the people who had let fear rule them. Eada knew that, although she still loved and missed her father, it would be a while before she could forgive him for casting her mother aside.

"Yes. *My* Norman. He is the reason I am still alive and that I am not one of those poor, sad creatures dragging themselves along after the army and lying down for any man."

"But you do lie down for him."

"I do, but there was no rape."

"Eada!"

"Old Edith said that Drogo was my mate. She said that when he and I both crouched by her as she was dying, mortally wounded after she hurled herself in front of his war-horse. Even then, filled with anger and grief as I was, I sensed the truth of it. He has never forced me."

"Does he mean to marry you?" Vedette gasped with shock when Eada simply shrugged.

"He has come here for gain, for lands and a title. He is a younger son with little hope of gaining land or position in France. That is what he marches for. He has ever been honest about that. He has offered me no promises, but he has also given me no sweet lies. And I have been safe with him. He has even allowed me to gather into his camp Saxons who are orphaned or hurt."

"You could now be safe with us."

"Perhaps. I think I prefer to stay safe with Drogo."

"Eada, it is wrong to remain in his bed. You are not married to the man and you have just said that he has never even implied that he will marry you at the war's end. And what if the Saxons win this war? How will it be for a woman who has claimed a Norman knight as her lover?"

"If some miracle visits us, one even Old Edith did not foresee, I do not think the men of this land should be too condemning or they might find that there are few women left to wed. I have been treated kindly, like a lover and not a captive; but each place the army goes, it leaves behind women raped or made love to. Too few of the latter, I fear. I doubt that, once the Normans reach London, there will be many women left along their route that have not been touched by Normans. I am surprised they have not invaded this nunnery, for the holiness of such a place has not stopped all of them."

Vedette shook her head. "I do not understand. You do not have to stay with the man now. You could stay here. Is it because of what you now know?" she asked softly.

"No. I have already begun to forgive you, although it may be a long time before I forgive my father. Drogo is my mate. I know this in my heart and mind. True, I do not know if he will marry me; but until he has exchanged vows with another, I will stay with him. I love the man, *Maman,* although I have not told him so; and I am trying to make him love me. I cannot do that if he and I are not together. He does not seem to realize that we are mates, and I have not told him that Old Edith said we were. It would be best if he came to that realization himself. It is also best if he comes to that realization before he learns that I hold the lands he seeks."

"But then he would marry you."

"Yes, for my lands. I want him to marry me for me. So, now *I* ask you to keep a secret. Tell no one about this bequest from Edith."

"I will not if you truly love the man. You are not simply accepting what Edith told and twisting your feelings to match her prophecy?"

"No. I truly love the man. As you love Serle?" she asked quietly and watched her mother blush.

"I did love Serle many years ago, and yes, I think a part of me still does. I loved your father, too. Oh, not at first, for I was told to wed him and, at that time, I had given my heart to Serle. But your father had more wealth and the house in Pevensey and a better bloodline. Serle turned to selling his sword, and I came to England. As the years passed, I came to care for your father as a wife should."

"I am not condemning you. Yes, when I first saw how you two looked at each other, I was angry. That has passed and, no, what I now know about my father's lies is not the reason I have grown so understanding. You are still young and have two children to care for. It would be most cruel, and foolish, if I tried to make you remain ever faithful to my father."

"Good, for I am going to join Serle when he reaches London and we will be married."

"Oh." Eada blinked, stunned, for while she had been ready to accept Vedette and Serle's renewing their old love affair, she had not thought it would all be decided so quickly. "You do not need time to, well, come to know each other again?"

"Or to properly mourn your father?" Vedette smiled faintly when Eada grimaced, revealing that that thought had been lurking in her mind. "No. I looked into Serle's much-battered face and knew the love I had felt for him years ago had merely been pushed aside. I cared for your father, never doubt that, and I was happy; but Serle was the man I loved, and still do. Some of our haste may come from a need to try and regain all we lost when we were separated, but I see no real need to wait. I am a widow and, strangely, knew I would be the moment your father marched away. A lot of my grief was spent in those first few days after Waltheof left to join Harold."

"I remember. Averil and Ethelred may not be as quick to understand."

"I will try to make it easy for them, and I believe Serle is a good man and will soon win them to his side."

"He is and he will."

A novice tapped lightly on the door of Vedette's quarters and announced that Sir Drogo and Sir Serle were waiting outside. Eada was almost able to smile at Vedette's blush and obvious eagerness as they both donned their cloaks and went out to greet the men. She frowned when she saw Drogo's face, for even the shadowed light from the torches near the gate could not disguise his serious expression.

"Is something wrong?" she asked as he took her by the arm and led her a few feet away from Serle and Vedette.

"Your family is safe," he said, as he began to pace in front of her. "I also know that this nunnery is safe from attack by Normans and will remain so. It seems the abbess is a distant cousin of William. You could stay here with your family. You no longer need my protection to survive this war."

"Do you wish me to stay here?" she asked quietly, trying not to be hurt, for she was not yet sure if he were giving her a choice or a command.

He stopped to look at her and lightly caressed her cheek. "I am giving you a choice. We both know that you are no prisoner and never have been. I will not make you one now just to please myself. Yes, I want you to stay with me, but I will not make you. If you prefer to stay here with your family, I will understand."

Eada bit back a smile as relief flooded her. He might

understand, but the tone of his voice and the tight, unhappy look on his face told her that he would not like it
at all. Although he still offered no words of love or promises that they would always be together, she knew that he
really wanted her to stay with him and that was enough
for now.

"I believe I will travel to London with you," she said
and smiled against his chest when he hugged her, apparently oblivious to the fact that the little chest she held
was digging into his hard stomach. "I just wish to ask my
mother if she will take in any of the children and if she
will keep my dogs with her."

"Are you sure you wish to leave your hounds behind?"

She nodded as he led her over to her mother. "This
long journey is wearying them, as is all the hunting trips
some of your fellow knights take them on. I think for
now they will be happier and safer with my family. In
truth, they are the only ones I am sure the dogs will stay
with. If I tried to leave them anywhere else, they would
try to follow me."

As Drogo and Serle stood back to allow her and her
mother a last moment of privacy, Eada hugged Vedette.
A lot of anger still churned around inside her, but she
knew Vedette did not deserve it. The woman had raised
her as her own, never slighting her in any way in favor
of the children of her body. For that alone, Vedette deserved forgiveness and understanding.

"You must tell Averil and Ethelred," Eada said, stepping away after Vedette agreed to take in any children
who wished to come to her and to keep the dogs. "I
think it is past time that we put aside this lie." When
Vedette nodded, Eada added quietly, "There is one good
thing that has come from this revelation. Now I understand how Old Edith could give me her gift. We were
blood. It was simply a mother passing her skills on to her

daughter." She smiled at the look of horror that passed over Vedette's pretty face.

"You have Old Edith's gift?" Vedette asked.

"I am afraid I do. Ask Serle. He knows. And Drogo knows, too, and does his best to protect me, so do not fear for me."

She kissed her mother's cheek and hurried to join Drogo, who had already mounted his horse. He grasped her by the hand, and she neatly swung up into the saddle behind him. As he turned his horse toward the camp, she quickly waved at Vedette, confident that Serle would soothe whatever upset Vedette still suffered from.

"Your mother is not happy about your choice," Drogo said as they rode away.

"No, but she is not really upset about that."

"There was bad news in the chest?"

"At this moment it still feels as if it were bad news."

"Eada, if you do not wish to tell me what you learned, I will understand."

"I am not Vedette's daughter. I am the daughter of Old Edith." She tensed when he said nothing. "Old Edith was a woman of good blood despite the poor life she lived."

"I was not suddenly worrying that my lover was a common woman," he drawled, understanding her sudden suspicions. "I was wondering what, if anything, I should say, for I could not judge how you felt."

"I am sorry. I did not mean to inflict any insult." She shook her head. "I do not know what I feel. I am angry, but at whom and why, I am not completely sure. It hurts to think of how little time I spent with my own mother, of how alone she was because of this dark secret and the dangerous fears of foolish people." Omitting all mention of earls and lands, she told him everything about her birth, Old Edith's banishment, and the lies her father and Vedette had told, if only by their silence.

"It was wrong not to tell you the truth when you were

of an age to understand, but it could have put you in danger. So, their reasons for secrecy might not have been all bad. I suspect that most people soon forgot that you were not Vedette's child. That could well have kept you safe, if only from the cruel suspicions some might have had."

"What suspicions?"

"That you also had Old Edith's gift."

"Ah, yes. They could have thought that what afflicted the mother would also afflict the child. As it now does. At least that has been explained. I have been puzzled about how Edith could give me her skills. Perhaps she did not give them to me as much as awaken the ones already within me."

"Did you tell Vedette that you now have the old woman's gift?"

"Yes, and she looked quite terrified, but not of the gift, I think. She knows how much it cost Edith and must fear that I will suffer a like fate."

They came to a halt before Drogo's tent and he helped her down. She sagged against him when he held her, silently trying to soothe her. There was only one thing he could do to wash away the sudden fear that had gripped her, a fear that she would end up alone and forgotten as Old Edith had, and that was to tell her that he would stay with her always. Eada knew he would not say it and, trying to hide her sudden anger at him, she slowly pulled away and went into the tent.

As they prepared for bed, she said nothing and was glad when Drogo respected that silence. Despite her confused emotions, she cuddled up to him when they climbed into bed. He was warm, strong, and felt a true sympathy for her; and she needed that.

"Did your mother tell you about Serle?" he asked as he combed his fingers through her hair.

"Yes." Eada sighed. "It will be some time before I can say I am happy about that. For all of the anger I now feel for my father, I find that I do not like the idea that she could turn to another so soon."

"It is not really another man, just one that she loved before she wed your father."

"I know and I am ashamed of how I feel. Do not worry. It will pass, if only because I like Serle and think he is a good man. He will care for Vedette and the children. There is one other thing that I believe adds to my sadness and anger."

"What is that?" he prodded when she fell silent.

"I still cannot think of Old Edith as *mother,* and yet I find that I am already thinking of Vedette as Vedette and not Mother. It is as if, by finding this out, I have lost my mother, and that makes no sense."

He brushed a kiss over her forehead. "It is born of your confusion. This is a hard truth to be told, and it will take you time to become accustomed to it. Vedette was your mother in all ways save blood, and Edith was the woman who gave you life. Perhaps, in time, you can begin to think of it as having two mothers—a blood one and a foster one."

"That would ease some of my turmoil." She raised herself up enough to brush a kiss over his mouth. "I believe I shall try to place that idea firmly in my mind."

"Eada, how could you know what was said in those documents? Did one of the nuns read it all to you? It might be wise if I had a word with the woman. This is not a tale you will want told far and wide."

"Only Vedette and I know. We were the only ones who looked at the scrolls, and we do not intend to tell very many people."

"Vedette can read?"

"No. I can."

She sat up slowly when she felt him tense. It was hard to see his expression in the dim light of the tallow candles. Eada struggled to wait and hear what he had to say before she judged him. He was understanding about her voices, but she could not be sure how he would react to her knowledge of something only men and a very few women of the church knew.

"Why did you not tell me?" he asked quietly.

"I do not know. I think that, since the occasion to display that skill never arose, I really gave it very little thought. Old Edith was most adamant that I should only do it when it was truly necessary and that I should not let it be widely known."

"She was right," he said, as he tugged her back into his arms. "It is just another thing that could cause you trouble. I should have guessed, for you were clearly very close to the old woman and she revealed the skill of writing when she marked her own gravestone. It is a good skill to have, but one can never be sure who might find it appalling that a woman has it. Some churchmen might even consider it a sin or worse. I know this may upset you, for you have tasted the sting secrets can cause, but will ask you to try and keep this a secret as well."

"You do not mind that I can read and write? Oh, and cypher?"

"No. I have often wondered why more people are not taught the skill. No one has ever explained to my satisfaction why such things are held so tightly by so few."

Eada felt herself go limp with relief. A moment later she realized how weary she was and yawned widely. Her emotions had run wild today and that had drained her of strength.

"I believe I will cease to worry about all this." She wrapped herself around Drogo, rubbed her cheek against his chest, and closed her eyes. "It will all still be there in the morning."

Drogo kissed the top of her head as he heard her breathing grow slow and even with sleep. She was right. It would all still be there in the morning. Her strength and spirit astounded him, as did her capacity for forgiveness and understanding. It was good that she had such a character, he thought with a sigh as he held her closer and thought of how many more miles they had to travel and all the destruction and death she would be forced to see. She would probably need a lot of that in the days ahead.

Eighteen

Eada woke with a cry of fear on her lips. She clutched the heavy blanket around herself as the sweat on her body dried and left her chilled. When she felt Drogo's hand touch her back, she shivered and curled up in his arms.

It had been five days since she had left her family behind to continue on to London. By the third day she had begun to wonder if she had made a mistake. The death of innocents and the destruction the army left behind haunted her dreams. She loved Drogo, and desperately wanted to stay at his side, but she feared the sadness around her and the horrors she was witnessing were beginning to twist her mind.

She took several deep breaths to try and calm herself, to look carefully at what had made her wake up shaking and afraid. When she remembered seeing Godwin, she tried even harder. This time it might not have been some remembered misery of the day that caused her night terror, but a warning of danger.

"Are you all right, *cherie*?" Drogo asked, idly kissing her neck.

"Wait," she whispered, willing to be diverted by lovemaking only when she was certain it was a normal fear that had awaken her. "This time my dream may have been more than dark memory."

"You have foreseen something?"

Drogo propped himself up on his elbow and watched

her. He was uneasy, as he always was when she revealed her gift, but he was willing to hear what she had to say. She had been proven right far too often for him to ignore. Although he wanted her skill to fade, he knew it was wise to make use of it while she had it.

"I am not sure," she answered cautiously as more and more of her dream became clear. "I think Godwin may be in danger."

"Can that not wait until morning?"

Suddenly Eada saw it all and understood what she saw. Godwin was sprawled in the dirt and Sir Guy, his hands drenched in blood, stood over the youth with a twisted smile on his face. It was night, dark mists swirling about both figures in her dream, and the fear that caused her heart to beat so fast told her that it was this night. Sir Guy was going to kill Godwin soon, could even be murdering the boy now. With a cry of renewed alarm, she leapt from the bed and began to pull on her clothes.

"Godwin is in danger now?" Drogo asked even as he climbed out of the bed and began to dress. "From whom?"

"Sir Guy," she replied as she tugged on her gown and struggled to do up at least enough of her laces to maintain her modesty. "Sir Guy is going to kill Godwin."

"Eada, we cannot go racing into Sir Guy's camp in the dead of night crying murder simply because you have had a dream about the boy."

"I thought you believed in my dreams and sendings?"

"I do, but we still cannot go and declare Sir Guy a murderer without more than a dream to strengthen our claim. We will both be thought mad or worse."

"But we have to go now."

"The dream told you it was happening now? Right now?"

"Not exactly," she replied as she fought to calm herself again. "The dream showed me Sir Guy standing over

Godwin with blood on his hands. It was night and all my instincts told me it was this night."

"Which is but half over. What you saw could happen at any time in the next four or five hours."

She thrust her fingers through her hair as she struggled to think of something they could do. He was right. There was still a lot of the night left and they needed a good reason for being awake and able to catch Sir Guy committing the crime. Her affection for Godwin made it difficult for her to think, however, and she looked helplessly at a tousled Drogo, who was lacing up his padded jupon.

"I cannot go back to sleep," she said. "I know Godwin is in danger of losing his life tonight. I have to do something to save him."

"I know. We can go outside now and walk by his camp. The man has been kind enough to set himself next to us so that we need not walk too far," he drawled, his irritation with Sir Guy's constant proximity clear in his voice. "We can always say that you needed to relieve yourself and that I felt you should not stumble about the camp alone."

"And what if nothing is happening yet? What if this murder is to be done later?"

"If we see nothing, you will come back inside the tent and I will watch Sir Guy's camp. Even if someone saw us wander into the wood the first time, they would not question my saying I had to go again. Too many are afflicted with a sickness of the bowels that has them squatting more than standing. They can think I suffer as well."

She nodded, and after throwing on her cloak, she gave him her hand and let him lead her out of the tent. "I just pray that I am still seeing what is or will happen and have not dreamed of something that has already come to pass."

"Be at ease, my love. You have yet to be wrong, only uncertain from time to time. We will save Godwin—this time."

Eada grimaced; she had to acknowledge the unpleasant truth. This time they might save Godwin, but they would not be able to free him from Sir Guy. That meant that Godwin would always be in danger. She could not be sure if the warning she had dreamt was only for now, for this one night, or if she should see it as a warning that Godwin would now be in constant threat of dying at Sir Guy's hands. There was no way she could keep a perpetual guard upon the youth.

As they walked closer to Sir Guy's camp, they heard his angry voice. Drogo increased his pace, and a moment later Eada saw her dream acted out before her eyes. Sir Guy was in a rage, pounding on Godwin with his fists. Even as Drogo released her hand to hurry over, Godwin fell to the ground and Sir Guy brutally kicked the defenseless youth. Several men stood nearby, frowning in disgust, yet hesitant to stop such a highborn knight. When Drogo ran into Sir Guy's camp, two of the men watching moved to assist him. They clearly felt that they could safely help one highborn knight restrain another. Any blame or displeasure that might result would fall on Drogo's shoulders and not theirs.

The moment Drogo pulled Sir Guy away from Godwin, Eada rushed in to help the youth out of the enraged knight's reach. She knelt in the dirt, holding the barely conscious boy's head on her lap and trying to clean the blood from his battered face with a strip torn from her undertunic. Her instincts told her that she and Drogo had been in time to save the boy. She just wished she could be certain that there would not be another time.

"What right have you to stop me from disciplining the stupid boy?" bellowed Sir Guy, swaying as he faced Drogo, his unsteadiness and slurred speech revealing his drunken state.

"I stopped you from killing the boy," said Drogo, his hand held cautiously over the hilt of his sword.

"I can kill him if it pleases me. He is a Saxon prisoner."

"That he is, but he is also little more than a child. What has he done that is worthy of beating him to death?"

"He keeps those cursed children around. He is a Saxon. What reason do I need?"

"You need a better one than this, fool," drawled a half-dressed Lord Bergeron as he walked into camp and eyed Sir Guy with blatant disgust. "Especially if it means I must rise from my warm bed to put an end to the disturbance."

"You have no right to tell me what to do," yelled Sir Guy, swinging his fist at his uncle.

Eada gaped when Lord Bergeron backhanded Sir Guy with such force the younger man fell to the ground. The look on Sir Guy's face as he stared up at his enraged uncle told her that he was as shocked as she was. It was clear that Lord Bergeron was rapidly losing his patience with his nephew, that he was past the point of merely scolding.

"I do not like to be roused from my bed because a drunken sot is taking out his frustrations on a child. And do not trouble yourself to think of lies to excuse your actions. Do you think I do not know why you are in such an ill temper?" Lord Bergeron watched his nephew stagger to his feet and brush himself off, but spoke to Drogo. "This idiot lost his last woman in a game of dice, Sir Drogo. Now, as he returns to an empty cot, he pauses to kick at a poor boy to try to sate his anger."

"Why is everyone so concerned about the spawn of our enemy?" snapped Sir Guy.

"Because you have taken this particular Saxon into your household. He is under your rule and thus under your protection. He does not deserve to be beaten to death because you have lost your whore to another man."

"If you find the boy so troublesome, I am willing to take him into my care," said Drogo.

"No. He may not be much good, but he at least tends my camp with some skill." Sir Guy smiled nastily as he wiped the blood from his lips. "Since you are such a kind man, Sir Drogo, and have such a deep love for your enemy, I will allow you to take the children."

"Thank God," whispered Godwin.

Eada knew the words were heartfelt, for the youth slumped against her, the last of his strength leaving him as relief swept over him, but she still felt compelled to ask, "Are you certain, Godwin? You told me you were fond of them."

"They are no longer safe here," he answered.

Seeing that Drogo was looking her way, she nodded, then turned her full attention on Godwin while the Normans discussed what to do with Hilde's children. "Are *you* safe? That is the question I should like an answer to."

"I think I will be now. Sir Guy spits a lot of venom about his uncle, but he is terrified of the man. Lord Bergeron has just expressed his disgust over this behavior and that will temper Sir Guy's brutality toward me. And he has never beaten me like this before. Tonight he was furious over his losses and I was near at hand. At first he tried to beat the children, but I put myself in his way."

"And have suffered for that bravery." She finished checking his injuries as well as she could under the circumstances and said, "I can see and feel nothing that will not heal. If you find anything needs more treatment than a good cleaning, come to me or call to me, whichever is safer."

"I will. I think that, with the children gone, I will be all right. They have learned to be very quiet, but they cannot hide completely and it was the sight of them which started Sir Guy raging. I think they remind him that he once had two women he could force to his bed. I just wish someone would kill the stinking pig."

"Someone will."

Godwin's swollen eyes widened slightly as he looked up at her then sat up with her help. Eada thought over the words that had just left her mouth and then nodded. It was not a wish from deep in her heart, but a truth that had suddenly emerged in her mind. Sir Guy would never see London.

"I pray you are having one of your sendings," muttered Godwin. "It would give me something to wait for. I belong to Sir Guy and the thought of doing so for very long, of enduring the man for years to come, leaves me chilled."

"You will soon be free of him. All you need to do is not let him kill you before he is cut down. I dreamt of this attack on you. That is why Drogo and I were at hand. I believe that means that if you call to me when you are in danger again, I will probably hear you. So, if that drunken beast starts to beat you or threatens your life, call out to me in your head and make the feeling behind the call as deep and as strong as you can."

"And that will bring you?"

"It brought me to Brun's cousin and then to Brun."

"Then I shall try." He looked toward the Normans as Sir Guy thrust the two scared children at Drogo. "If you do not come quickly enough, I pray you do not see it as a lack of faith if I just start screaming aloud."

"No," she said and smiled at him. "I am surprised you did not this time."

"I was caught by surprise for the man has never treated me this badly before and I did not think anyone would or could come to my aid."

"I will, and so will any of Drogo's people. I think that, since Lord Bergeron has made his disapproval so open, so will others. It took me awhile to look beyond all the killing and burning to understand that not every Norman behaves in such a cruel way. Drogo and his men are not the only honorable knights in William's army. They are as varied in their ways as are our men."

She stood up slowly as Drogo approached, the terrified children stumbling in front of him. As Godwin explained

to the children that they had to go into Drogo's camp,
Eada stepped closer to Drogo to allow Godwin some privacy with his charges. She felt sad that the blind cruelty
of one man had caused this separation, for they had already lost their family and now they would think that they
were going to lose Godwin as well. It did not surprise her
to see that both of the children were crying when they
returned to her side.

With one last look at Godwin, she ushered the children
into Drogo's camp and found a sleepy-eyed May hurrying
toward her. The yelling in Sir Guy's camp had roused a
number of people.

"I will take them, mistress," May said.

"You will soon need another tent," Eada murmured as
she nudged the children toward May's open arms. "I truly
thought the three I had saved from Sir Guy's sword would
stay with my mother, but they would not leave you. You
will now have six children to watch over. I could keep
them with me."

"No. Ivo and I do not mind. He is already sewing together another tent, for he is sure there will be more
children. And these two will not be staying long with me,
not unless Godwin dies or is forced to remain with that
beast for all his days."

"But that will hurt you. You are quick to love the children you take to your arms."

"I am, but I know I can never claim these. Godwin is
their family, and they will always want to be with him. You
go back to bed, mistress, and do not worry about them."

Eada watched May take the children to her crowded
tent and then looked up at Drogo. "I do not think I am
the only one you must speak to about collecting every
hurt and orphaned child," she drawled.

Drogo shook his head as he tugged her into his tent.
"Ivo was the same about animals. You saw how he loved
your hounds, nearly weeping when we left the dogs with

your mother. The man's heart is as big as his body. I will speak to him, but he will not heed me. He cannot turn away from anything or anyone in trouble or in pain. And such a command will make May unhappy. That is also something Ivo can never do." He laughed as he started to undress. "I fear I shall soon have an army of children."

"Who will grow to make you a strong army of loyal soldiers and servants," she said, as she hastily shed the last of her clothes and jumped beneath the warm covers to escape the chilled air.

"Yes, I suppose they will." Drogo slid in beside her and tugged her into his arms. "But do not forget that I must feed and shelter them until they are of a size to be of some use. Maybe I could convince you, Ivo, and May to take in only the older children."

Eada laughed and punched him lightly. "You already have Brun and will soon have Godwin. They will make fine soldiers. Brun already is one, and Godwin is of an age to begin training."

Drogo grew serious and, propping himself up on his elbow, he brushed a kiss over her mouth in hopes of softening his words. "I would like to save Godwin from Sir Guy, but I do not think I can. The moment Sir Guy suspects that I want the youth, he will hold on to Godwin all the tighter. If I were a rich man, I could dangle enough coin in front of the fool to make him forget his hate long enough to sell me the boy, but I do not have that heavy a purse."

"I know. I was not meaning that you must try to take Godwin from Sir Guy. You are right. The man will keep him just to spit at you. No, I just mean that soon Godwin will be free of that beast and, since he is a Saxon, you can claim him. He certainly will not be allowed to run free."

"No, but how do you know that Godwin will soon be free of Guy?"

"One of my voices told me. It said that Sir Guy would never live to see London."

"I hope to God that is the truth. No man deserves death as much as that one does. I do not suppose they told you if I would have the pleasure of killing him?"

"No. That would cause you trouble with Lord Bergeron, would it not?"

"No longer. Did you not see how frightened Sir Guy was? Lord Bergeron is but one ill deed away from turning his back on the fool. For all that Sir Guy resents Bergeron's constant interference, he has enough wit to know that it is that man's high place in William's court that helps to keep him alive."

"Then he may begin to behave himself."

He saw the doubt on her face and shook his head. "I am glad to see that you recognize how little chance there is of that happening."

"One likes to occasionally grasp at even the thinnest of hopes. If Sir Guy is to die, and my voices say he is doomed, I pray that he does so before all his lies cause you very much trouble."

"No one can pray for that any harder than I do. The number of people who heed his whispered lies and insults is still quite small. Something William said in one of our talks yestereve tells me that he is aware of what is going on, has probably even heard some of the talk, but he heeds it not. He just wondered why Sir Guy was trying to blacken my name."

"Then, perhaps, we do not need to worry about the man and his insults."

"Now, no. Tomorrow? Who can say? Right now, Sir Guy's own ill reputation is working to take the sting from his words, but that could change."

"It is all most unfair," she murmured as she slipped her arms around his waist and rubbed her cheek against the warm, hard skin of his chest.

"Yes, but I grow weary of talking of the ills of the world—and especially of that adder Sir Guy."

"Ah, you wish to sleep now."

She laughed when he gently pinned her to the bed beneath him and gave her a mock look of disgust. The kiss he gave her not only confirmed the passion he felt, already revealed by his body, but stirred her own. Eada was more than willing to let desire smooth away her worries. It could not cure them, but it was a most pleasant way to gain a brief reprieve.

Eada yawned widely as she pulled herself up into the cart. She made herself as comfortable as she could and looked at May, who sat next to her with Alwyn cradled in her arms. At her feet sat Welcome and Eric. It was not only another tent they would need if they kept collecting children, she mused.

As Ivo started the cart moving over the badly rutted road, she looked toward Sir Guy's camp. Godwin was tossing the last of Guy's belongings into a small cart. Although the youth moved stiffly, it appeared that he had not suffered any dangerous injuries from the beating he had endured. He waved at the children, who waved back before the crowds of camp followers blocked him from their sight.

"How are the children?" she asked May in French.

"Unhappy. They want to be with Godwin," May replied, her French still a little rough but understandable.

"I know, but they are safer with us and it will make it safer for Godwin."

"Sir Guy is just like my old master, Hacon."

"Yes, but his reign of brutality will be as short-lived."

"I pray your voices continue to be correct."

"So do I, and not solely for Godwin's sake. I want Sir

Guy's mouth shut before his insidious whispers can hurt Drogo."

"It would be a sin if such an evil little man could hurt an honorable knight like Sir Drogo with no more than lies and hints of suspicious acts. I would like to think that the man we must now call king was wiser than that."

Eada would have liked to have thought that as well, but she dared not put her hope in William. The man had his brutal side and he was quick to see treachery at every turning, for it had often been there. She suspected that, at times, it had been William's suspicious nature that had kept him alive. London was getting nearer, and if her voices spoke the truth, so was Sir Guy's well-deserved death. All she could do was pray that it came soon enough.

"I heard you had another confrontation with Sir Guy," said William as he paused by a stream to allow his mount to drink.

Drogo tensed as he edged closer to William's side so that Faramond could also drink. "Yes. The man was beating a boy to death."

"A Saxon boy."

"Yes, my liege, a skinny, unarmed Saxon boy of but fourteen years. I was not the only one who felt that the attack should be stopped," he said quietly and inwardly grimaced, hoping he did not sound too defensive.

"That drunken fool blackens all our names. Be wary of the man, Drogo. The hate he holds for you is a dangerous thing."

"I know. I watch my back most carefully."

"It is said that you have added two more Saxon babes to your household."

"I have. Ivo's woman cares for them, as does Ivo."

"And your woman?"

"She does as well, yes, my liege." He shrugged in an

attempt to look as if he felt it was no more than a minor inconvenience. "Women ofttimes find it hard to ignore a child in need."

William nodded as he nudged his horse to cross the rocky, ice-cold stream. "That is their nature and they must be honored for it. If you gathered Norman babes to your breast, then it would be seen as honorable; but these are Saxon children or, as some call them, the spawn of our enemy. There are those who begin to wonder over your kindness to Saxons."

"I know. I am confident, however, that those who have the wit to do so will see that children are no threat." When William gave him a quick, narrow-eyed glance, Drogo prayed he had not gone too far, but knew he had to finish what he had planned to say. "The worse they can do is eat all my food and leave me poorer than I am now." He felt relieved when William laughed. "I also think that it is not particularly wise to kill too many of the common people. After all, if they are all dead, who will plant the fields come the spring or build our homes or tend our animals?"

"The thought of a knight strapping himself into a plow halter is not a pleasant one," William drawled.

Drogo gave an exaggerated shudder. "Not at all."

"Just be wary, old friend. I see no harm in children or even that young Saxon boy. Others will, if only because you treat them so kindly. Perhaps your years with the monks gave you a more generous spirit. Do not let that generous nature of yours put a knife to your throat."

He nodded and watched William rejoin his brother and the closest members of his entourage. Drogo was still trying to decide exactly what William had been trying to say when Serle rode up beside him. One look at Serle's frowning face told him that the older man had seen him talking to William. That brief conversation had obviously looked serious from a distance.

"It was hard to be certain, for William's expressions change like the weather in this cursed place, but was that a pleasant talk or a warning?" Serle asked.

"A little of both, I believe. William seems to think my years with the monks is the cause of my soft heart."

"It did little to soften Bishop Odo," Serle drawled, nodding toward the armored churchman riding at William's side.

Drogo laughed, but his good humor did not last long. "I cannot turn aside children and boys."

"No, not even if it would be the wisest thing to do, at least until William actually sits upon the throne of England."

"I wish I could say that there will be no more fair-haired Saxons added to my entourage, but I have three within my camp who gather all the forlorn to their breasts with an ardor I cannot fight, even if I wished to."

"Since William thinks your kindness is due to your time in the monastery, it might be wise to remind others of it as well. It would be easy enough to make some think that you are more a monk than a warrior." He grinned when Drogo raised his eyebrows in an expression of exaggerated doubt. "I know that Eada's place in your bed makes you look more sinner than holy man, but I do not think that will matter. We both know that not all churchmen hold to their vows of chastity. They still tend the poor and nurse the ill, however."

"I know what you are saying, and it cannot hurt to try and steal some of the sting from Sir Guy's lies with such a reminder. It is no lie and I am not really trying to defend myself when I use it. That I will not do, for I have done no wrong."

"I know, son. I just pray that others have the wit to know it, too, and to continue to treat Sir Guy's lies with the scorn they deserve."

Nineteen

Tancred laughed heartily and clapped a grinning Unwin on the back. The good humor they shared was suddenly lost in shadow as the land they rode over was bathed in darkness. Tancred's smile faded, replaced by a look of horrified surprise and pain. Unwin disappeared into a swirl of blood red. Slowly, through the mists, Sir Guy appeared, his scarred face twisted with a gloating smile and his sword dripping with blood.

Eada woke so abruptly she nearly fell out of the cart. She clutched at the rough wooden sides of the cart and struggled to calm herself. Still badly shaken, but fully awake, she turned to find May staring at her with concern. Eric and Welcome also looked worried and Eada fought hard to give them a comforting smile.

"Are you all right?" asked May, leaning close enough to Eada to whisper so that the children could not hear what she said. "You cried out as if you were in pain or very much afraid."

"It was that accursed Sir Guy again," Eada replied. "I swear before God, May, that if that man does not cease to darken my thoughts and dreams, I shall kill him myself."

"I think you should wait and let a Norman kill him," May said with a false calm, her expression of fear contradicting her tone of voice.

Eada laughed and shook her head. "Poor May. Do not look so terrified. All I have at hand is an eating knife and a tiny dagger. I have never hefted a sword either. No

matter how much I want Sir Guy to embrace death, it
will not be I who sends him there." She smiled when May
sagged with relief.

"What is Sir Guy going to do now?"

"I think he is going to try and commit murder." Eada
looked around in a vain attempt to find Tancred and
Unwin, but saw only a now-recovered Brun following
closely in their second cart.

"Are you certain?" pressed May.

"Yes, but I could always just ask him," Eada muttered
as she caught sight of Sir Guy riding toward them.

"No, please," begged May as Eric and Welcome finally
saw Sir Guy and hastily moved closer to May.

"A poor jest," Eada said and reached over to pat May's
shoulder in an absent gesture of comfort.

When Sir Guy rode up beside the cart, Eada gave him
a sweet smile of greeting. The man looked so startled and
suspicious she almost laughed. He cast a quick look at
Ivo, who kept looking his way and scowling, then fixed
his cold gaze upon Eada. She wondered what game he
planned to play now.

"Is there something you want, Sir Guy?" she asked him,
amazed at how sweet and courteous she sounded even as
her stomach churned with fear and dislike.

"I but wished to get a closer look at the Saxon whore
who has stolen Sir Drogo's manhood," he drawled.

It was hard not to respond to that insult with the fury
he so clearly tried to arouse in her. If that were the kind
of remark he whispered in people's ears, Eada was astounded that anyone would even listen. Drogo de Toulon's manhood, strength, and bravery should be clear to
anyone who looked at him. It did not really surprise her,
however, that a man like Sir Guy would see kindness as
a weakness.

"Is there another Sir Drogo riding with William, for I
know you cannot mean the man who leaves me so ex-

hausted after a night in his arms that I must sleep the day away in this cart?" She was startled when her words made Sir Guy flush with rage.

"Enjoy your little jests, woman, for your good humor will not have a long, prosperous life. Once Sir Drogo is gone, you will be taken up by another who knows well the dangers of coddling a woman."

"And where might Sir Drogo be going, sir?"

"To that place all men who have allowed a woman to steal their strength must go—a cold grave. You have changed him into nothing more than a nursemaid to a pack of Saxon whelps. He is becoming the source of many jests. A man whose name causes only laughter does not live long."

"Then I should watch my back very closely if I were you, Sir Guy."

He raised his hand to strike her, but one long, hard look from Ivo halted his blow. After one cold, enraged glance at her, Sir Guy rode away. Eada slumped against the side of the cart and took several deep breaths to try to slow the rapid beat of her heart.

"He just said that he is going to kill Sir Drogo." May whispered in horror, speaking in French to hide her words from the frightened children.

"No, I am afraid that he did not say that. Oh, I know that is what he meant, but he did not say it clearly enough. If we repeated his words, others would surely hear the insults flung at Drogo, but they would not see the threat. We could certainly anger Drogo, and all who stand with him, by repeating Sir Guy's slurs upon his manhood, but no more."

"Are you going to tell Sir Drogo what was said?"

"Yes. Drogo is not a fool. He may even wish to challenge Sir Guy, but he will know he cannot safely do so on no more than the word of his Saxon lover or even

Ivo. It will show him how dangerous Sir Guy has become, however, and that can only be for the good."

"He wants to kill Sir Drogo," said Ivo.

"Very badly, but he will not do so fairly. He will either strike from the shadows or try to get William to believe that poison he has been spitting out, thus turning Drogo's liege lord into the sword that cuts Drogo down."

"Then I must kill Sir Guy."

May cried out in fear and Eada quickly patted her cold, trembling hand. "I fear you cannot do that, Ivo."

"He is a danger to Sir Drogo."

"Yes, a very big danger; but if you kill the man, you could cause Drogo a trouble of a different kind. You would also pay for it with your life, and that would greatly sadden Drogo. I do not believe Sir Guy will strike at Drogo until he is sure that his lies have failed to get him what he wants. London draws near and my voices say that so does the end of Sir Guy. No, what we must look for now is some plot against Tancred and Unwin."

"He did not speak of them."

"No, but my dream did." She related her dream to May and Ivo. "I was looking for them when I saw Sir Guy slither over here."

"They ride with Drogo, who rides ahead with William."

Eada whispered a curse. "As do Serle and Garnier, so there is no way for me to warn them."

"They will return when we stop to make camp in a few hours."

"If they do not, then I will have to go in search of them. The attack I saw in my dream came in the dark of night, and I must warn them of the danger they face before the sun sets."

Tancred laughed and Unwin hesitantly joined him as they rose from their places around the fire, where they had enjoyed another of Ivo's hearty meals. Eada put her hands on her hips and glared at both the men. They were treating her warning as no more than a woman's baseless fear and she could not fight such disbelief. Drogo believed her when she spoke of such things, but he and Serle were dining with William and could not make the two younger men listen to her.

The two men were young and strong and emboldened by a sense of victory. Even though they knew that Sir Guy was a treacherous adder, they were too cocksure to believe that he could kill them. At least Tancred was, and that insured that Unwin would never admit to the concern she had briefly glimpsed upon his face. She wondered if her dream had been warning her of this problem when it had shown her the two young men laughing.

"Why will you not heed me?" she snapped.

"You wish us to tell William that we cannot ride out to forage as we have been commanded to because Eada of Pevensey has had a bad dream?" Tancred asked as he shook his head. "He will think that we are mad or, worse, that we are cowards."

"It would do you no harm to try and be more cautious," advised Garnier as he caught the wineskin Tancred tossed his way.

"That is something we can do."

Eada watched them mount the horses Ivo had readied for them and cursed under her breath. She had not anticipated having to conquer their pride to get them to listen to her. The belief of others that she had warned had left her too unprepared to deal with such openly displayed disbelief.

"For all that they laugh and jest, they will be careful," Garnier said as, after the two young men had ridden away, Eada sat down and faced him across the fire.

"One cannot always guard oneself against treachery," Eada said.

"True. I am not sure I believe in dreams and voices, but you have been proven right each time you have spoken. Tancred and Unwin know that, and they will be watching their backs more closely."

"If warning them was all that I was meant to do, then why did my dream show me that they were dead?"

"It could have been showing you what would happen if you failed to warn them."

"Or it could have been showing me what will happen because they have scorned my warning. My dream could have been saying that warning them would not be enough to save them."

"But why would Sir Guy kill two Norman knights? It can gain him nothing but trouble."

"Not if no one knew that he had done it." She nodded when his eyes widened with sudden understanding. "Think on how easy it would be to blame their deaths upon the Saxons. There have been many such attacks. Vengeances mostly for men killed or villages burned. It would be no cause for alarm if two young knights did not return from a foraging journey."

"I will go and speak with Drogo," Garnier said as he stood up.

Eada watched Garnier ready his mount with Ivo's help and leave. She was not sure if there were time to get Drogo and then ride to find Tancred and Unwin before they were murdered, but it was better than doing nothing at all. Just as she began to resign herself to waiting and filled a bowl with some of Ivo's hearty stew, a panting Godwin stumbled up to her.

"What are you doing here? This will surely gain you a harsh beating and you have not yet recovered from the last one," Eada said as Godwin fell to his knees at her side and struggled to catch his breath.

"She is right, boy," said Brun as, still afflicted with a slight limp, he sat down on the other side of Eada.

"Sir Guy has ridden off with several of his treacherous friends," Godwin reported as he accepted the wineskin Eada held out to him and took a few deep swallows.

That news caused Eada's heart to skip with alarm. It was beginning. The trap was being set, and she had yet to get anyone to believe that there was a trap.

"Did he say anything and were you able to understand it?" she demanded, praying that Sir Guy was just going on another fruitless search for some poor woman he could force to his bed.

"My French is still weak so I am not sure that I know all of what they said."

"Tell us what you do know or what you just guess at. I believe it will be enough."

Godwin dragged his fingers through his hair. "They went in search of two men. I think they mentioned Sirs Tancred and Unwin, but I cannot swear to it. I dared not reveal that I was listening and so walked about the camp doing my work. At times that meant that I was not close enough to them to hear everything clearly."

"Do not worry on that. You were acting with great wisdom."

"The men they seek are riding toward London, foraging ahead I think they said. Sir Guy and his friends planned to ride hard and get ahead of these men. They were going to do something upon the road once they found them. I fear I did not recognize the word they used."

"Repeat it." Eada frowned when he did so and it took her a moment to recognize the poorly pronounced word. "The word is murder." She hastily told Brun and Godwin about her dream. "My dream was true and those two fools refused to listen to me. They only said that they would be careful."

"Sir Guy took five men with him. I would think that it

would be difficult to defeat six men intent upon murdering you no matter how careful you were."

"I saw Garnier leave," said Brun. "Did he not go to join them?"

"No, he went to speak to Drogo and Serle. Drogo dines with William, and Serle attends him."

"Drogo will believe in your dream."

"Garnier will have to wait until he and Drogo can speak privately. Drogo has made his men swear that they will do all that they can to keep my gifts a secret. It could be a long time before Garnier can draw Drogo aside."

"Then there is nothing you can do."

Eada looked at the horses. "Yes, there is. We must try to stop this murder."

"If we try to ride out of camp, it will be we who are put to the sword," said Brun, although his expression revealed his eagerness for such an adventure. "And Godwin cannot go. It would put him in danger, for he would be facing the very man he must call master."

"We will not be stopped if Ivo rides with us." She looked at Godwin. "You need not join us. If we can catch Sir Guy trying to murder Tancred and Unwin, I believe we can free you from Guy's brutal grasp. He will be sunk in disgrace because of this crime and you will be the one who revealed his treachery, thus saving the lives of two Norman knights. If we arrive too late and he finds you gone from his camp or sees you riding with us, he will know who betrayed him and that could put you in danger."

"I will ride with you," Godwin said.

"Godwin—"

"I know what risk I am taking. I also know that I could finally be free of that man. For that, no matter how small the chance, I believe I would willingly ride to the gates of hell itself."

"Should we not wait a little longer to be certain that

Sir Drogo will not be in time to save his friends?" asked Brun.

"If he has not ridden after them by now or within the time it will take us to saddle those horses, he will be too late," Eada replied as she leapt to her feet and strode toward Ivo, Godwin and Brun quickly following her.

It took longer than she liked to convince Ivo that it was necessary that they try to save Tancred and Unwin. Ivo had such a deep faith in Drogo that he found it hard to believe that the man could fail to save his friends. May finally convinced him to go, pointing out that no one was saying that Drogo would fail, only that there was a chance he might not even know of the danger until it was already too late. Eada gave May a brief, fierce hug of gratitude when Ivo nodded and began to saddle three horses with the help of Brun and Godwin.

"I do not like this," said May, the children huddling closer to her as they sensed her unease. "It could be very dangerous. Ivo is but a servant. He could stir a great deal of trouble if he has to fight a knight."

"If there is any fighting it will be because we have arrived in time to save Drogo's friends," Eada said. "They will say what happened and no one will question their word. If we are too late, then we will just return to camp and tell Drogo what has happened. We will not even pause to collect the bodies, no matter how much it will pain us to leave them behind."

"And what if Drogo returns here first, before he rides to aid his friends?"

"Then tell him what we have done. I do not believe he will be very angry, May. I am doing all he has asked me to. I told only those closest to us about my dream and I am not riding away alone, rushing blindly into the heart of danger. In truth, I believe there will be little fighting. This is not something Sir Guy wishes known, nor will his companions. I feel sure that, if they see someone coming, someone who could tell others of their crime, they will flee."

May relaxed after offering Eada a shaky smile. "You are right. Such men want no witnesses, and because they are cowards, they will all run from an equal fight. It also eases my mind to know that if Sir Drogo comes here, I can tell him the full truth."

"Oh, yes, please do, and as quickly as you can. Now, I will tell you what I can about where I saw this murder happen." Closing her eyes to try and see her dream again, Eada described the road and its surroundings as precisely as she could.

"Now that you have us mounted and prepared to ride *ventre à terre* to save Normans, do you think you might join us?" called Brun.

"If I had known what a sharp wit you had, I would have left you beside that river," Eada told him as she walked up to the men. "Whom do I ride with?"

"Me," Brun replied as he reached down and helped her swing up into the saddle behind him. "Ivo's mount can carry no more weight, and Godwin says he is not very skilled upon a horse."

Eada grabbed him around the waist as he nudged his horse into a slow trot to follow Ivo out of the camp. She noticed that although Ivo wore a sword, neither Godwin or Brun did. Slung over Ivo's saddle, however, were two swords. If the need arose, Tancred and Unwin would be joined by three armed men, and that eased her mind. She was comforted even more when they were allowed out of the camp with little more than a frown of curiosity from the guards. Few wanted to argue with a man the size of Ivo.

"There is only one question I have," said Brun.

"Only one?" Eada murmured.

He ignored her and asked, "Why are you riding with us?"

"Because it was I who had the dream." She met the disgusted look he sent her with a sweet smile. "I may be able to recognize the place where the murders are to be committed."

"If Tancred and Unwin are there, that would mark it well enough."

She fought the urge to hit him. "I am riding with you because no one thought to try to tell me not to." She grinned when he laughed. "I am surprised that you would ride to the aid of Normans."

"So am I, but the promise of a ride and, mayhap, a brief battle was more than I could refuse. The fact that I ride with the enemy to fight others of the enemy in an attempt to save the lives of more of my enemy makes this a foray I simply could not resist."

Eada laughed and shook her head, but then grew serious. "I will understand if you find it difficult to risk your life to save that of a Norman. You have suffered great losses at their hands."

"I have, but the men we race to save did not kill my family and would not do such a thing even if offered the chance. Yes, defeat is still a bitter taste in my mouth. At times I think that will linger until I die. But as I recovered from my wounds, I was forced to watch the men I only saw as my enemy. I can honor the ones you ride with, Eada. Yes, I would cheer if God suddenly swept them all into the sea; but if I must be ruled by Normans, I am grateful that I have stumbled into the hands of good, honorable men." He winked at her over his shoulder. "Now, you had best hold on tightly, for we must now ride hard and fast if we are to reach Sirs Unwin and Tancred before that murderous Sir Guy does."

A soft cry of surprise escaped her as Brun kicked his horse into a gallop. She clung to him tightly as Godwin and Ivo quickly moved to follow. They were an odd selection of rescuers—a captured Saxon warrior, a too-thin

Saxon youth, one small Saxon woman, and a large Norman servant; but she was suddenly confident that they could easily put an end to Sir Guy's murderous plot.

"What is so important that you pull me from William's side?" Drogo demanded as he finally left William's table in the great hall and walked over to an impatiently waiting Garnier. "Is Eada hurt?" he asked suddenly, concern swiftly overcoming his anger.

"She is fine. Can we speak privately?" Garnier asked in a soft voice.

"Come this way," said Serle, striding out of the great hall into the muddy inner bailey of the Saxon keep William had claimed for his quarters. "I think this is safe from unwanted listeners," he said, as he stopped in a shadowed corner of the bailey, a place that allowed them a clear view all around.

"Our sudden leave-taking could easily be viewed as suspicious," Drogo said.

"I believe you will find my news worth that risk. And I had to speak to you privately because this concerns a dream Eada had. She says that Sir Guy intends to murder Tancred and Unwin."

"Did she warn them?"

"Yes, but I fear they did not pay her much heed."

"Why did you not ride with them?"

Garnier grimaced and rubbed the back of his head, ruffling the new growth of hair there. "I fear I did not truly believe her either. I did warn Tancred and Unwin to be more careful, and that they did agree to. Whether they spoke true or just tried to soothe Eada, who can say?"

"At least Eada did not just rush off by herself," Serle said.

"Yet," Drogo said curtly. "When did she say this murder was to happen?"

"This night while Tancred and Unwin are out foraging as was ordered by William," replied Garnier.

"Wait, Drogo," advised Serle. "This makes no sense. Sir Guy wants you or Eada dead, not any of the rest of us. It is also a dangerous game he plays. He risks all, for William is treating any of his army who engage in such personal and deadly quarrels with a swift, harsh judgment."

"Eada said that Sir Guy will probably blame it on the Saxons," murmured Garnier. "It would work."

"It would," agreed Serle. "We have lost men who went out on small sorties or were caught out foraging."

Drogo cursed and strode toward the stables, only faintly aware of Serle and Garnier following him. He knew in his heart that Eada's dream was right—and not only because he believed in her gifts. It was the sort of cowardly thing Sir Guy would do. The man's other plots and games had failed to give him what he wanted, so now Guy meant to strike at all who were close to Drogo. Through his friends, Sir Guy would hurt him again and again. That was a game Sir Guy would greatly enjoy, he decided as the stablehand led out their saddled horses.

"Was Eada still in camp when you left?" he asked Garnier as they mounted and rode out of the bailey.

"Yes." Garnier hurried to keep pace with Drogo. "I told her that I was coming to speak with you."

"Then we had best return to camp as swiftly as we can."

"Should we not ride in search of Tancred and Unwin first?"

"Eada will know where the attack is to happen. I just hope that she is still in camp."

"Where else would she be?"

"Riding to stop Sir Guy."

Serle laughed heartily, and that was enough to stop Garnier's protest. Drogo was certain that if he did not reach the camp in time, Eada would be gone. She would wait only until she felt there was no time left, that she had to act to save Tancred and Unwin. All he could do was pray that he would arrive first or that, if he were too late to stop her, she would at least have the good sense to take someone with her.

Twenty

"She really has gone," Garnier murmured as he looked around the camp, astonished to see only May and the children.

"Where has she gone, May?" Drogo asked with a calm he did not feel as he leaned forward on the pommel of his saddle and looked down at the nervous young woman.

"She went to try to save Sirs Tancred and Unwin. She did wait for you, sir, but said that there was no time left."

"Did she go alone?"

"Oh, no, sir. She took Ivo, Godwin, and Brun."

"Godwin and Brun?"

May nodded. "Sir Guy had five men, so she felt Sirs Tancred and Unwin needed nearly that number as well."

"How did she know how many men Sir Guy rode with?"

"Godwin told her. He came here to tell her that he had heard Sir Guy and his friends plot against Sirs Tancred and Unwin. That was when Eada's voice told her that there was no time left to wait. This murder had to be stopped."

"Did she linger long enough to tell you where this murder is to occur? I had hoped that she could lead us to the place she saw in her dream." Drogo had to smile when May closed her eyes and carefully described the place Eada had seen in her dream. He could easily see Eada doing the same as she had related the information to May. "That was well done," he said when she finished and looked up at him. "I believe I know where that is. One last question—

did they intend to fight off six armed men with only their bare hands?"

"Ivo was armed, and he carried two swords with him."

Drogo nodded and turned his mount in the direction Eada had gone. With Serle and Garnier right behind him, he made his way through the crowded camp with as much speed as he could. The moment he was free of the tangle of people, carts, animals, and tents, he spurred his horse to a gallop. Although he felt certain that Sir Guy and his cohorts would flee once they were faced with any real opposition and once the chance of committing their crime in secrecy was gone, he was eager to reach Eada before she faced any real danger.

"Are you sure this is the place?" asked Brun as he looked around the wooded area where Eada had demanded they stop.

"Yes," she replied as she slid off the horse and rubbed her backside. "We must wait here."

"And this murder will be brought to us, will it?" Brun dismounted along with Ivo and Godwin and lightly tied his horse to a tree.

"You need not sound so scornful. We have arrived first, that is all." She smiled at Brun. "You ride very fast."

He ignored her flattery. "Mayhap your gifts allowed you to find the quickest way to reach this place. I will admit that there were a few times I thought you were mad when you insisted that I had to take that turn or follow that route."

"Since I have never been here, I think it was my inner voices directing me."

"Do you think those voices will be kind enough to tell us what to do when six battle-hardened and armed knights ride into view?"

Eada glared at Brun, Godwin, and Ivo when they all

laughed. She was not really angry with their teasing, but
she did wonder how they could be in such a good humor.
Her instincts told her that being there would be enough
to stop the attempt at murder, but she could not know
that for certain. Neither could they. They could also be
facing a hard battle, even death or wounding. It seemed
an odd time for teasing and laughter.

"Do not look so worried, Eada," said Godwin.

"Someone needs to worry, I think."

"Sir Guy will flee like the coward he is as soon as he
knows that Sirs Tancred and Unwin have been warned
and that they are not alone."

"That is what I think, but then I wonder if we can be
so certain of how the man will act. This attempt to murder two knights is madness, is it not? This is nothing more
than an act of spite. How many men do you know who
would kill two people just to hurt one?" She nodded
when her three companions began to frown. "Maybe Sir
Guy's hatred of Drogo has turned his mind. It is hard to
know what a madman will do."

Ivo nodded and took the swords from his saddle, handing them to Godwin and Brun. "You may need these."

"It would be a blessing if we could kill Sir Guy here
and now," muttered Brun as he buckled on his sword.

"It would be," agreed Eada. "I cannot be sure if tonight is the time of his death or not. The fact that I do
not feel sure probably means that he will escape the justice he deserves at least one more time."

"Someone comes," Brun whispered, pushing Eada behind him as he crept closer to the rutted path that was
the road to London.

Eada edged around him only enough to get a clear
view. The horses were coming down the road, and she
knew that it had to be Tancred and Unwin. It also meant
that Sir Guy and his men had to be close at hand, yet

she saw no sign of them. She began to fear that she had led her group to the wrong place.

"Look over there, Eada," whispered Brun, pointing to a thick grouping of trees just across the road. "I believe our enemy lurks within. You have brought us within feet of them."

"I wish I could be pleased about that," she murmured as she caught the glitter of moonlight on armor glinting through the trees. "What should we do?"

"Put ourselves somewhere between them and those blind fools riding down the road," he said, hurrying toward the approaching Tancred and Unwin.

She, Ivo, and Godwin quickly followed him. He darted out onto the road just past a sharp turn which hid them from Sir Guy and his friends. Eada followed him, her heart pounding so hard and fast she feared Sir Guy would hear it. She was not sure why Brun was trying to keep Sir Guy unaware of their presence, but decided to bow to his wisdom in such matters.

Tancred and Unwin were talking and laughing as they came into view. It did not look as if they were taking any extra cautions, she thought a little sourly. They halted so abruptly, their horses reared, kicking up a lot of dust. Eada coughed and glared at them.

"Eada?" Tancred said in a small, hoarse voice as he rode closer to her. "What are you doing here?" he asked as he looked at her and her three companions. "Are Brun and Godwin wearing swords?"

"Yes," she replied sharply. "It might be wise if you spoke more softly. Voices can travel a long distance on such a still night, and you will warn the men waiting for you around the bend in the road."

He and Unwin quickly placed their hands on the hilts of their swords. "Your dream was true?"

Eada made no attempt to hide her exasperation. "It was, and if you had paid more heed to it, I would not be standing here in the dark and the cold, forced to the ungrateful task of saving your lives."

Tancred ignored that and turned to Brun. It annoyed Eada to be so completely overlooked as the men discussed what they had to do next. It annoyed her even more when she was ordered to stay behind with Godwin as the other four went to face their enemy.

"You will be safer here," said Godwin as he tugged her to the edge of the road.

Before she could give her opinion on that, she heard the distinct sound of swords clashing with swords. Godwin held her back when she took a step toward the sound. After a brief moment of trying to tug free, she gave in and stayed where she was. Although she wanted to see what was happening, to assure herself that her friends were all right, she realized that she would only be in the way. She was so intent on listening, on trying to guess what was happening by the sounds she heard, that she was startled into crying out when a horse suddenly snorted behind her. It fleetingly pleased her to hear Godwin gasp as well and know that he was caught equally unawares. Her heart in her throat, she turned around slowly and nearly gaped when she found Drogo, Serle, and Garnier right behind her.

"You are very quiet horsemen," she said and met Drogo's steady look with a wavering smile.

"And you are a very troublesome woman," he drawled.

"I remembered to bring someone with me this time."

"Ye-es, and I will have to talk to you about arming Saxons. Do not move from this place," he advised her as he moved around her and galloped down the road, a grinning Serle and equally amused Garnier right behind him.

Eada waited a few minutes before following them, a softly cursing Godwin right behind her. She knew that Sir Guy and his men would never linger to face three more armed men. It did not surprise her to find Drogo and the others standing around in the road. Two of Guy's companions had paid dearly for his plot, and she quickly hurried past the two bodies sprawled on the ground.

"I thought I told you to stay back there," Drogo said even as he draped his arm around her shoulders and tugged her close to his side.

"I did until the danger was past," she replied. "Sir Guy?"

"Fled with his remaining friends. I am not sure, but I think one more of them will fall before he can reach camp."

"It would have been a true victory if we could have ended that adder's life here," said Brun as he relinquished his sword to Tancred.

"He may yet pay for this. Even if his uncle can save him from William's punishment, this will destroy him." Drogo nodded toward the two dead men Serle and Garnier were securing to the back of the horses left behind. "I have all the proof I need that he tried to murder you. We all saw him, even if it was only as he fled for his life, and everyone knows these two are his men."

"But you do not think he will be punished harshly by William?" asked Eada.

"Tancred and Unwin are still alive. That could be enough for his uncle to win him a reprieve. But I promise you, he will be as nothing and he will never be able to cast aside the disgrace he has brought upon himself with this black deed."

"Which means he will truly be mad with hate for you."

It did not comfort Eada at all when Drogo's answer was a shrug. She remained lost in her worry as they returned to camp, almost glad that he had to leave her there and immediately return to William's court. As she sat down before the fire, she closed her eyes and tried to will her voices to tell her something, but they remained silent.

"All will be well," said Godwin as he sat down beside her.

She managed a smile for the youth. "It will be for you. That is a victory in itself."

Godwin smiled as Welcome and Eric cuddled up to his side. "Drogo feels certain that no one will argue with his claim to me. He feels sure that he can ask any price to soothe the insult Sir Guy has delivered tonight and he has sworn that the price he will ask is me."

"I believe Sir Guy delivered more than a mere insult tonight."

"Yes, but his uncle is a powerful man and has given William a lot of help with this battle. It takes a heavy purse to bring such an army here and a lot of the coin came from Lord Bergeron."

Eada nodded, disappointed but understanding how that could keep Sir Guy from suffering the punishment he deserved. "Where is Brun?"

"He has already sought his bed." Godwin caught her lightly by the arm when she started to rise. "Do not worry. He has not hurt himself. He is just tired. He is healed but he has yet to regain his full strength. At least he has the wisdom to recognize the need to rest."

"True. I wish this night had been the end of Sir Guy."

"We all do."

"I know. It is just that I have a very bad feeling about him. I cannot be sure if it is a warning from my voice or just the hate I have begun to feel for the man."

"That confusion will clear."

"I pray it will. I believe I shall have a great need for my voices to be exact and loud in the days to come."

Drogo waited impatiently as William and Lord Bergeron talked. The man's gestures and pale, tight expression made it obvious that Lord Bergeron was in the unenviable position of pleading for Sir Guy's life. Drogo also knew that William would give the man what he wanted this time for he owed Lord Bergeron a great deal. He just wished they would hurry and settle the matter. He had yet to ask for Godwin and he was eager to get back to camp, back to Eada.

When Lord Bergeron finally stepped back from William, Drogo walked over even as William signaled him to join him. He could tell by the dark look on William's face that none of this pleased him. Drogo prayed that he was not entangled in that anger. Although Drogo was not at fault, William could not always be counted on to be completely fair.

"I cannot punish Sir Guy except to banish him from my court." William held up his hand when Drogo started to speak. "You took the life of two of what few friends the fool had. Let that be enough. Also, this cowardly act will not be kept a secret, so he will pay in many other ways." He glanced at Lord Bergeron. "And the fool has lost all his protections as of this night."

Out of the corner of his eye, Drogo saw Lord Bergeron nod and felt a sense of relief. He could now act openly against Sir Guy. The man had thrown away the shield he had been able to hide behind for so long.

"I was not going to argue your decision, my liege," Drogo said. "I wish to ask a blood price of Sir Guy. My men survived, but murder was what was planned."

William frowned. "Sir Guy does not have much coin."

"It is not coin I ask for. I want the boy Godwin."

"You want Sir Guy's young prisoner?" William asked in surprise.

"Yes. It was Godwin who warned us of Sir Guy's murderous plots. I believe it is no secret that the boy is badly treated by Sir Guy. That treatment could worsen dangerously now and I wish to save him from that. I owe him the lives of my men, and it is the least I can do for him."

"Done. Do you have any objection, my lord?" William asked Bergeron, who shook his head. "Then when you tell that fool nephew of yours that you have managed to save his miserable life one last time, you may also tell him that he is to allow that boy to stay with Sir Drogo and had better never again lay a hand on the youth."

Lord Borgeron bowed and strode out of the great hall. Drogo felt sure that when his lordship found his nephew, Sir Guy would pay dearly. Not dearly enough, but it would do for now.

"You are free," Drogo announced as he sat down beside Eada and smiled across the fire at Godwin.

He laughed when Godwin thanked him profusely. The boy then gathered up the sleepy children and hurried away to find the bed Ivo had prepared for him. Drogo looked at Eada, who only smiled her gratitude, and he knew immediately that something troubled her.

"Tell me, what is wrong?" He draped his arm around her shoulders and kissed her cheek. "Your friend is free of Sir Guy's brutal grasp. That should please you."

"It does. I just wish we were also free of the man."

Drogo sighed and then nodded. "We are free of all that has made us hesitate to act. Not only has Lord Bergeron saved his nephew for the last time, but William himself has torn away all protection. Now, if Sir Guy threatens us, we can act without restraint."

"That is good news."

"But his body hanging from a tree would have pleased you more."

"Yes, and I am a little ashamed at my bloodthirsty feelings."

"They could never equal the ones I have toward the man." He glanced toward Sir Guy's camp. "Have you seen him?"

"I saw Lord Bergeron drag him inside the tent not long before you returned. Neither man has emerged."

"Maybe we shall have some luck and Lord Bergeron will kill him in a fit of rage and disgust."

Eada suddenly laughed. "I think I would have heard that."

"It was just an idle hope."

Drogo stood up and held out his hand. Smiling faintly, Eada rose and slipped her hand into his. It had been a long and eventful night and she would welcome her bed. Glancing up at Drogo's face and seeing the way he was looking at her caused her smile to widen. It would be awhile before he would let her go to sleep.

The moment they stepped inside the tent, Drogo began to undress her. Eada laughed and tried to undo his laces even as he was tugging her clothing off. He tumbled her down onto the sheepskin bedding before the fire and she greedily welcomed him into her arms.

"You are beautiful," he said when they had finally cast off all their clothes and he crouched over her, studying her by the warming light of the fire.

"You are most fair yourself," she murmured, smoothing her hands over his chest.

Drogo slowly kissed his way down her soft body. "If I tell you that you taste as sweet as the richest honey, are you going to say that I, too, am sweet?"

She laughed and threaded her fingers through his slowly growing hair. When he curled his tongue around the hardened tip of her breast, she purred her pleasure and arched into his caress. Her passion swept over her with a dizzying speed and strength. Eada wondered if the excitement of the night had helped to fire her blood. She cupped his head in her hands as he lathed and suckled her breasts, stirring her desire until she found it hard to remain still.

When his kisses slid lower, she murmured her regret

as he moved out of her reach. He touched a kiss to the inside of her thigh and she opened to him without shyness or hesitation. A hoarse cry of delight escaped her as he gave her the most intimate of kisses. She surrendered completely to the pleasure he stirred within her, arching to the strokes of his tongue. He cupped her backside in his hands and took full advantage of her openness. Eada could feel her body crying out for release but she fought it. The feelings racing through her body were so exquisite she wanted to savor them for as long as possible.

When her body broke the restraints she had imposed upon it, she cried out for Drogo to join her, but he held her close, praising the sweetness of her body. Eada had barely begun to recover from the blinding pleasure that had torn through her body when Drogo restirred her passion. This time when she called to him he joined her, uniting his body with hers even as she shuddered with the power of her release. As she sank into the mists of desire's highest reward, she heard him call her name and felt him bury himself deep within her.

Eada slowly opened her eyes as Drogo finished gently bathing her. She watched him walk to the bucket of water, and hastily rinse himself off—and decided that he was a beautiful man. When he returned to their bed and pulled her into his arms, she curled herself around him.

She waited for embarrassment and shame to taint the warmth still heating her blood, but it did not come. Eada realized that she no longer worried if something they did was a sin. Her modesty was not completely dead, for she always covered herself when the passion faded and doubted that she would stop blushing when Drogo made love to her in the light of day as he sometimes was inclined to do; but she knew she was now free of the shyness that had often restricted their lovemaking. That change within herself pleased her, and she smiled against his chest as she smoothed her hand over his stomach.

"Do we continue to march on the morrow?" she asked, toying with the dark curls below his navel.

"Yes. As the sun rises. I must ride to the fore of the army with William again."

"He obviously wants your sword skills near at hand."

"I would like to think so."

"If it is so then your reward when he is crowned should be very good."

"That would also please me. At times my greed for such gain shames me, but it does not cure me. After a moment or two of self-chastisement, the greed returns."

"It is not greed. You merely seek a better life than being a hired sword. No one can fault you for that."

She touched a kiss to his chest, suddenly wanting to divert him from talk of rewards and what would happen when they reached London and William was declared king. She wondered if he had even thought about what would happen to her, but she did not really want to know. If he had not, that would hurt her as much as the lack of love-words did. The safest thing was to avoid all talk of the future.

"I would have thought you would be very tired," he said in an increasingly husky voice as she began to cover his chest with soft kisses and light, teasing strokes of her tongue.

"I think riding to battle has left me with very hot blood," she drawled and smiled when he shuddered beneath the kisses with which she covered his hard stomach.

"You had nothing to do with the battle except to show us where it would be."

"Do you mean to talk me out of my boldness?"

When she slid her hand down to stroke his hardening manhood, he groaned and shook his head. "No. That would be madness."

Eada laughed against his stomach, slowly praising every inch of his strong body with her mouth, kissing her way down one strong leg and up the other. The way he trembled and shifted beneath her gave her a heady sense of power that fired her blood. His hoarse cry of delight when she finally turned her attentions to his manhood inspired her.

Drogo struggled to keep control of his passion when he felt her warm lips against him. The fact that they had already made love helped him. It was a moment before he realized that Eada was trying to help him linger in that place where he could enjoy her attentions yet not have to end them because of the demands of his body. That she had learned his body so well only added to his pleasure.

He slowly sat up, threading his fingers through her hair. His breathing was almost painfully hard and fast as he watched her love him. He caressed every inch of her he could reach as she pleasured him, struggling to control the pace of their lovemaking with as much skill as she was revealing. The way she kept him on the sharp edge of passion's abyss astounded and pleased him. Drogo had never experienced anything as sweet or as beautiful.

Finally, when he could wait no longer to bury himself in her warmth, he lifted her in his arms. They both shuddered as she eased their bodies together. Drogo held her by the hips and moved her slowly, still trying to prolong the sweetness of their desire. He took the hard tip of her breast deep in his mouth and felt her shudder against him and knew they could wait no longer to satisfy the demands of their bodies. For one brief heady moment, their movements grew fierce, and then she cried out, clutching him as she tried to pull him closer, pressing herself down. He held her tightly as his own release ripped through his body, leaving him gasping and shaken.

Drogo looked down at the woman in his arms. She had fallen asleep even as he had cleaned them off. His body still tingled from the delights they had shared and he felt pleasurably weary, yet sleep was proving elusive.

Try as he might, he could not stop the thoughts that crowded into his mind. Soon they would be in London. The end of their journey was but days away. All the decisions he had tried to avoid would be there waiting for him. It was probably past time that he gave his future some thought.

One thing he was sure of was that he did not want to lose Eada, but he feared he might not be given any choice in the matter. He wanted her so badly that he knew he would willingly shame them both just to hold her at his side. He also knew that she would fight such shame, that her pride would not allow her to be no more than his leman.

Drogo feared that the choices he would have to make would be painful. He needed Eada and he needed lands. Common sense told him that he would not be able to have both.

"William was right all those days ago in Pevensey," he murmured as he touched a kiss to her hair. "He said I had captured myself a troublesome bundle. But, troublesome as you are, I pray that I can keep you."

Twenty-one

"This is madness," muttered May as she followed Eada into the deserted village.

Eada cautiously entered the little cottage and, after assuring herself that there was no one inside, turned her attention to the constantly complaining May. "We need supplies. On the morrow we will reach London, and I am sure that there will be very little for us there."

"How do you know there is anything for us here? The soldiers have already crawled all over this village, taking all they could lay their hands on."

"I know, but they do not always know where to look. They take only what is right in front of their eyes. Sometimes, as with the animals, they even lose some of their bounty in their eagerness to grab all of it at once. I am confident that Ivo, Godwin, and Brun will find something hiding in the wood; and they know how to catch pigs, chickens, and sheep."

"At least Godwin and Brun have a Norman at their side. I cannot feel it is safe for us to be beyond the camp without a Norman with us."

"May, everyone knows who we are. Did you not hear the guards greet us by name as we walked out of the camp?"

"They were men even I recognized. That does not mean that every Norman knows we belong to Sir Drogo."

Eada suspected May was right, but she was not about to

admit it. They were taking a chance wandering around the village with no guard, but she could not wait any longer for Drogo or one of his men to return to camp. The sun was already setting and soon it would be too dark to glean anything from whatever the soldiers had left behind. Their supplies were growing dangerously low. She could not ignore this opportunity to replenish them.

"The faster we find what we need, the faster we can return to camp," she said and smiled when May muttered under her breath but began to search the cottage.

It was almost dark by the time they left the village. Eada felt torn between guilt over stealing from the people who had fled the village and delight in how much she had found. She prayed that the villagers had had the foresight to take enough supplies with them to hold off starvation through the winter. With the land in such turmoil, they would have a chance to help themselves to the bounty of the forests and streams without fear of reprisal from the new lords of the land. She clung to that thought to comfort the guilt she could not fully repress.

A soft cry of alarm from May pulled her from her thoughts and alerted her to trouble. Eada looked ahead and cursed. Between them and the camp stood Sir Guy and the two men who had survived the attack on Tancred and Unwin. Even as he started to move toward them, she set her bounty beneath a tree, silently commanded May to do the same, and ran. She was pleased to see that May had no trouble keeping up with her. As she ran, Eada searched for some place to hide or to turn so that she could get around Sir Guy and head back to the camp. They were staying out of Sir Guy's reach for the moment, but they were also getting farther and farther away from safety and she knew that could prove to be a fatal error.

For what felt like hours, Eada and May ran from their enemies. No matter how often they darted and turned, however, they could not get back on the path that led to the camp. Eada could outrun any man, but May did not have her stamina. As they hid behind a tiny cottage and struggled to catch their breath, she realized that May would soon be too exhausted to flee. The woman's breath was coming in fast, rasping gasps and the short rests they could steal from time to time were no longer enough.

"I think you should stay here, May," she whispered, peering around the corner of the house and keeping a close watch on the three men searching for them.

"No. I will not leave you." May's voice was little more than a croak and it shook badly, revealing how weak the woman was.

"You will soon leave me anyway, for you are close to collapsing."

"I just need to catch my breath." May frowned at Eada. "I do not understand why you are still so strong."

"I have always been able to run fast and for a long way." Eada scowled at the men who were drawing closer to their hiding place. "I had never considered it a very useful skill until now."

"Are they coming?"

"They are still a few houses away. I want you to stay here, May. You are so weary that you will probably not get more than a few steps before you stumble and fall. That will get us both captured."

"But—"

"No, listen to me. I will run when they draw near and pull them after me. It will probably take them a few minutes to realize that you are no longer with me. I want you to sneak back toward the camp. That may actually give us a chance."

May bit her lip as she considered Eada's plan. "Are you sure you can stay out of their grasp?"

"Yes, unless fate decides otherwise. If I can just keep running, these fools will all be heaps upon the ground before I even begin to tire." She winked at the uncertain

May, then nudged her in the direction of the camp.
"Go."

Before May could offer any more arguments, Eada
darted back out into the road. An immediate cry went
up from Sir Guy and his men, and she took them on a
merry chase, trying to keep them from seeing that May
was not with her and giving May a chance to get back to
the camp and find help.

Eada was chuckling over a particularly clever move that
had put her behind Sir Guy's friends when a scream put
an abrupt end to her amusement. She realized, even as
she began to turn around, that only two men had been
chasing her for the last few moments. A sense of helplessness swept over her as she saw Sir Guy holding a knife to
May's throat.

"Did you think you could fool me?" he demanded as
he moved closer, dragging a terrified May along with him.

"Let her go," Eada said. "She is nothing to you."

"She is something to you, though, is she not? Enough
to make you stop running and allow yourself to be captured."

"And what do you think capturing me will bring you?"

"Drogo de Toulon."

"Do you really think he will walk into your arms just
to save his Saxon whore?" The way Sir Guy just smiled
as he stopped right in front of her while his two friends
moved to stand behind her chilled her blood.

"You are more than that to the fool. He has made the
mistake of letting others see that and thus putting a
weapon in their hands."

"Only you would use a woman as a weapon." She cried
out in pain as, in one swift move, he pushed May aside
and backhanded Eada across the face.

Eada studied him through the tears of pain stinging
her eyes and felt a deep fear chill her heart. Even in the
faint light of the moon she could see the glitter of mad-

ness in his eyes. He blamed all his woes on Drogo, refus-
ing to face his own weaknesses and mistakes. There would
be no reasoning with the man.

"Charles," he ordered the thinner of the two men with
him, "I want you to go to Sir Drogo and tell him that I
hold his woman. He is to come to this village, alone and
unarmed, and hand himself to me. Peter, help me tie these
two whores up."

Eada watched the man called Charles head back to the
camp as she and May were roughly bound together. This
time she had not just put herself in danger, but May and
Drogo as well. Even the thought that her voices had said
Sir Guy would die before seeing London was not enough
to comfort her. Those voices had never told her if Drogo
would live or die.

She cried out in pain as Sir Guy pushed her and May
down onto the ground. He stood over them, grinning as
she tried to right herself and May; finally, awkwardly, she
propped their bound bodies against the side of a cottage.
Anger seeped through her fear. There was no reason for
this. No crimes had been committed against the man
other than the ones he imagined in his twisted mind.

"Drogo will kill you," she said, glaring at Sir Guy, then
leaning away from him when he crouched in front of her.

He grabbed her chin in a tight hold and forced her to
face him. "Drogo will run to try to save you. That is his
way. I should have recognized that weakness in him before.
I might have won my battle with him before he disgraced
me."

"You disgraced yourself. Drogo was not the one that
made you hide in those trees with murder on your mind.
If you suffer now, your suffering is all of your own making."

"No. It is Drogo de Toulon's fault," he screamed as he
leapt to his feet. "He has always made me look the fool.
He is the one who has turned my own family against me.

Now, after all these years, I can finally make him pay for the insults he has done me."

Eada said nothing, for nothing she might say would make any difference. The man's own words confirmed his madness. Her fate was in Drogo's hands. She prayed he could think of a way to save them both.

Drogo stared at Charles, his fists at his side, clenching and unclenching as he fought the urge to beat the skinny, long-faced man. "Tell Sir Guy that I will come."

"I think he meant for you to return with me," Charles said, the squeak in his voice revealing his nervousness.

"As you wish."

"Wait!" Charles pointed to the sword at Drogo's waist. "You are to come unarmed."

"Of course, Sir Guy would never invite a fair fight," he murmured.

As Drogo slowly removed his sword, he drew closer to a furious Serle. He had only a moment to tell his men what he wanted them to do. His head bowed, he used the removal of his sword to hide the fact that he talked to Serle.

"I leave it to you to get me free of this trap," he whispered, daring one quick glance at his man to see Serle nod in understanding. "Use the two Saxon boys if you need to. The more men you have, the better the chance that you can stop this madman without injury to Eada or me."

"A quick attack and swift disarming or death is what is needed," Serle murmured, lowering his head to hide his face as he answered. He accepted the sword Drogo handed him and raised his head to glare at Charles.

"I am ready," Drogo said, and he walked past Charles and headed toward the village.

"They will all pay dearly for this, lad," Serle called after Drogo and smiled coldly when Charles looked his way.

Drogo silently laughed as Charles quickened his pace, hurrying to get away from Serle. It did not surprise him that the men Sir Guy gathered around him were as cowardly as he was. His own helplessness angered him, but he did not really fear the man he was about to face. Sir Guy was fool enough to think that he had won, and that would give Serle and his men the chance to come up behind him.

A sharp taste of fear stung the back of his throat when he saw Eada and May tied and sitting at a grinning Sir Guy's feet. It was quickly replaced by rage. As he drew nearer, he could see the dark stain of blood at the corner of Eada's lip and knew Sir Guy had struck her. It took all his willpower not to leap at the man.

"Your cowardice is only surpassed by your stupidity," Drogo said in a tight, cold voice and he calmly eyed the sword Sir Guy suddenly held at his throat.

"Your life now sits on the tip of my sword, Sir Drogo," he said. "I would be wary of spitting out too many insults."

"Oh, you are certainly able to kill me now, but have you given any thought to what will happen when you do?"

"What more can happen to me? I have been cast aside by my own family, shunned as a disgrace. There is no hope of gain for all the fighting I have done. Even my fellow knights turn away from me, treating me as little more than dirt upon their boots."

"But you are alive. I can promise you that if you kill me and the women, you will not live out the night." He noticed a sudden sheen of sweat appear on Sir Guy's upper lip and realized that the man was not as confident of victory as he tried to appear. "My men hold a greater loyalty than any of the dogs you have sniffing at your heels. They will hunt down the man who has my blood upon his hands.

There is no place in all of England or in France where you will be safe."

"Shut your mouth!" Guy screamed.

Drogo easily dodged the wild swing of Sir Guy's sword, but before he could move to disarm the man, Sir Guy's two friends grabbed hold of him. He fought to free himself of their grasp until Sir Guy placed the tip of his sword at Eada's throat. Enraged by his own inability to help her, he grew still and glared at Sir Guy.

"Let the women go," he said in as calm a voice as he could muster. "They gain you nothing. It will only blacken your name more when it is known that you killed two helpless women."

"This whore of yours is far from helpless," Sir Guy drawled and roughly kicked Eada, smiling coldly at the way Drogo jerked in his friends' hold.

Drogo stared at him, aching to kill the man. He prayed that his men would act soon, but resisted the urge to look for some sign of them. Forcing back all his fury, he tried to get Sir Guy to move his sword away from Eada.

"This will not regain you your uncle's favor," he said and breathed an inner sigh of relief when Sir Guy stepped past Eada to focus his attention on Drogo.

"My uncle never favored me. He favored my mother. Now even that bond has been severed, and you cut it."

Eada watched Drogo, wondering why he was bothering to talk to this madman. Nothing he could say could save them. The waiting to die was beginning to be too much. Just as she considered telling Drogo to just try to kill this fool who was blaming him for every small wrong he had suffered, she felt a faint tug on the ropes that bound her and May. She grit her teeth against the urge to look and see who was trying to save her.

"Eada," May whispered.

"Hush. We must not pull Sir Guy's attention our way."

"What a clever woman," whispered a voice to their right

that she recognized as Brun's. "I should not worry too much. That fool is holding himself enthralled by his litany of woes, and his men are too busy trying to hold Drogo."

Trying to keep her lips as still as possible so none of Guy's men could see that she was speaking, she asked, "Where are the others?"

"Do not look."

"We will not."

"Serle is but a step away from Sir Guy; and Tancred, Unwin, and Garnier are very close to bumping into the two fools holding Drogo. This will soon be over. There, you are freed; but do not move until you know it is safe."

That moment came but a heartbeat later. Drogo's men sprung upon Sir Guy and his friends so swiftly and fiercely that they had no chance to flee or defend themselves. With Brun's help, she and May moved out of the reach of the men. Eada rubbed her wrists as she saw Drogo step over to Sir Guy, who was locked tightly in Serle's grasp.

"I am going to give you a chance to die with some scrap of honor," Drogo said as he accepted his sword from Unwin and, once Serle released Sir Guy, handed his enemy his weapon. "It is more than you deserve, but I feel I owe it to Lord Bergeron."

Eada did not want to watch, but she found herself unable to look away as a coldly furious Drogo began to fight with a terrified Sir Guy. A desperate need to live was all that kept Sir Guy alive for the few minutes he managed to successfully defend himself against Drogo. There was no hope of his winning, however, and he knew it. His skill with a sword was no match for Drogo's. Eada winced as Sir Guy screamed, his life ending with one clean stab to the heart.

"Are you hurt?" Drogo asked as, after wiping his sword clean on Sir Guy's jupon, he turned to face Eada. "He struck you," he murmured as he stepped closer and wiped the blood from her lip.

"I am fine," she said, hoping the anger she could feel in him was the remainder of what he had felt for Sir Guy and not aimed at her.

"Why were you here—alone?"

"Because I am a witless fool?" She was relieved when he laughed.

"We will discuss the truth of that later," he drawled and touched a gentle kiss to her mouth before turning his attention to the two men who had ridden with Sir Guy.

Eada spared a brief smile for Brun when he stood beside her. Obviously, Drogo's men had recognized his worth and were willing to include him in their number. That promised a good future for Brun and she was glad. He would serve Drogo well.

She winced as Drogo's two captives cried for mercy even as Tancred and Unwin led them away. William would not be merciful. It might have been better if Drogo's men had killed them, but she forced all concern for them from her mind. They had earned their punishment. She was sure this was not the only crime they had committed, and since they had ridden with Sir Guy for a long time, she knew they had the blood of innocents on their hands. When Drogo put Sir Guy's body on his horse, she walked over to him.

"What are you going to do with him?" she asked.

"Give his body to his uncle. Lord Bergeron did not deserve the shame this fool brought to his name, but Sir Guy is his blood and he will want to bury him properly."

"Of course. If it is all right with you, perhaps Brun can walk May and me back to camp. I was able to find some food and would like to collect it. I set it aside when Sir Guy began to chase us."

"It was my fault that he caught us," May said quietly as she joined them. "I could not run as fast as Eada."

"I have an idea of how fast and how far Eada can run, May. I would not feel shamed by your inability to keep

pace with her." He looked at Eada and then nodded.
"Brun and Serle will take you back to camp. I will see
you after I have spoken to Lord Bergeron and William."

Eada watched him ride away and sighed. She was going
to have to suffer a scolding about leaving camp without a
guard, but she decided it was a small price to pay for her
life. In the end, her error in judgment had brought only
good. They had all survived and the threat of Sir Guy was
gone forever. As she walked toward the supplies she had
collected, she wondered idly if she could get Drogo to see
it all in such a pleasant light.

Drogo fought to hide his disgust as he watched Sir Guy's
friends hanged. Their punishment was long overdue, but
he had always considered hanging a brutal death, slow and
horrifying to watch. A clean cut with a sword would have
been a far more merciful death. He tried to console himself with the reminder that these two men had never shown
anyone mercy. The moment it was over, he turned to a
grim-faced Lord Bergeron, who had stood silently at his
side throughout the hasty judgment and the executions.

"I am sorry, my lord," he said.

"You did what you had to. My nephew would not have
hesitated to kill you and the two women."

"In truth, I was not asking pardon for his death. I am
sorry that you may suffer in some way for his crimes. You
do not deserve that."

Lord Bergeron grimaced and glanced toward William,
who sat with his closest friends and family. "It will cost
me, but not too dearly. It was clear a long time ago that
most men simply pitied me my relation with the young
fool. The most I will suffer from is my sister's grief; but
that, too, is long past due."

"You did more than many men would have to try to
save her from that."

"Your woman is unhurt?"

"Only a bruise."

"Good. I am not one of those who sees all Saxons as the enemy, and I think you have gathered a fine group who will serve you well in the years ahead." He clasped Drogo on the shoulder. "Because all my nephew's interest has been in you, it has allowed me the chance to watch you closely, especially during this campaign. Will you accept a word of advice from an older and, hopefully, wiser man?"

"Of course, my lord."

"We will be in London on the morrow, and I have no doubt that William has won this war. You will be faced with many choices, my young knight. Weigh them carefully. When you reach for something, be sure it is what you truly need. Do not forget that you could live a long life, and what youth and ambition demand now could turn to cold dross in the years ahead. Regrets are a torture to live with."

Drogo nodded but frowned as soon as the man left. He was not sure what Lord Bergeron had been trying to say. As he walked to join Tancred and the others where they waited with the horses, he tried to shrug aside the man's confusing words and realized that they would not be dismissed so easily. It was not until he vowed to look more closely at them later that they ceased to plague his thoughts.

"I am glad that we were not asked to watch the hanging," Tancred said as Drogo reached them and they all began to mount their horses.

"I wish I had been so fortunate," murmured Drogo as they rode back to camp, "but I was the one who brought them to William for punishment. It was my duty to see it carried out."

"Hanging has always turned my stomach," agreed Serle, "but I can think of few others who deserved it

more. They were always in the thick of it when the innocents were killed or brutalized."

"And I found myself struggling to remember that."

"There is one thing I should like to speak about before
we reach London and it is forgotten or you are kept too
busy to consider it."

"And what is that, Serle?" Drogo smiled, for his old
friend looked very serious.

"It is about Brun. I know you do not know what, if
anything, you will receive as a reward from William. I
have faith that it will be a demesne of some size. Even if
the gift is but a small holding, you will need men at your
side to hold it, for there are certain to be troubled days
ahead. I believe you should carefully consider accepting
Brun as one of your men-at-arms."

"You think he is that good and that he will be loyal?"

"Yes. The boy is no fool. He knows the Saxons have
lost, and he has sworn fealty to you. He would serve you
well and he is already an able warrior."

"He is that," agreed Tancred and Unwin and Garnier
nodded.

"Then I will do as you advise," said Drogo. "Take the
youth into your care, Serle, and hone his skills. I just pray
that I will gain a holding worthy of such soldiers."

Eada quickly swallowed the piece of apple in her mouth
and smiled at Drogo when he entered the tent. His raised
eyebrows told her that she had not completely succeeded
in hiding her feelings of guilt. He helped himself to one
of her apples and sat down next to her before the fire.
The way he watched her as he ate the crisp, tart fruit
made her uneasy.

"Have Sir Guy's friends been punished?" she asked in
an attempt to ease the building tension between them, a
tension she began to suspect was all on her side.

"They were judged and hanged."

"Oh." She grimaced, knowing that they were deserving of their fate, but hating such brutal judgments. When Drogo said nothing else, she finally snapped, "If you are intending to chastise me, I wish you would hurry and do so."

Drogo laughed and shook his head. "At first I wanted to—badly. Now it does not seem so important. I can only hope that you remember how close death came, not only to you but to May as well."

"And you," she whispered and shuddered.

"I was not very concerned about myself. Sir Guy was so sure that I would walk blindly to my death that he did not ask me to swear to anything in an attempt to protect himself, only that I face him alone and unarmed. He thought that I would walk to him like a lamb to the slaughter. I had not realized that the man thought of me as such a weak fool."

"The man saw honor, bravery, honesty, kindness, and all such fine qualities as weaknesses. If someone thinks you are weak, if he has nothing but contempt for all that you hold dear, then he will begin to see you as a witless fool. He only feared you when you had a sword in your hand and I think that is why he hated you so deeply. If you were the witless fool he believed you were, then his fear of facing you, sword to sword, must have constantly enraged him."

Drogo stared at her for a moment then slowly smiled. "At times, Eada, the way you can see into people's hearts so clearly is truly frightening."

She returned his smile and heartily wished he spoke the truth. At times she did seem able to see into people's hearts and minds, but that skill utterly failed her when she tried to use it on Drogo. They would ride into London on the morrow, and she still had no idea of what he felt or planned.

Twenty-two

Wrapped tightly in a heavy blanket, Eada stared out the narrow, dirty window at the streets of London. Drogo had had to make use of his position in William's court to get the small room in which they were quartered. Everyone else with them had had to make camp outside of the city. In the past three days, she had rarely seen him. He slipped into bed late at night, rousing her only enough so that she knew he was there, and then he was gone by the time she woke in the morning. She missed him and she missed their lovemaking. The knowledge that her time with Drogo might be coming to an end made these lost moments even harder to bear.

She also hated London, she decided, grimacing at the noises that rose up from the already-crowded streets. The city was filled with people—Norman, Saxon, and foreign mercenary. Many of William's army and its followers had had to camp on the outskirts of the city, but they crowded its streets all day and most of the night. Hundreds of fires kept the air thick with stinging smoke and dimmed the light of the sun. The roads winding around the closely packed buildings were thick with mud, manure, and human waste. Rats were everywhere, fat and bold. At times she had felt a need to escape the confines and ills of Pevensey. London was a hundred times worse.

Eada knew, however, that what truly soured her mood was the sense she had that Drogo was already pulling away from her. He had said nothing and done nothing to make her feel that way, yet she could not shake free of the fear. The war was won. William was soon to be crowned, and then he would reward his followers, taking from the Saxons to profit the Normans. Drogo was certain to be favored, and Eada suspected that was the root of all her fears. Once Drogo had the lands and the riches they would bring him, would he then cast her aside and reach for a bride who could further enrich him? He had still offered her no promises and no words of love, so she had nothing she could use to push aside the fear gripping her heart.

A rap at the door dragged her from her dark thoughts. She wondered why May, who had come to her every morning, was arriving so early. Hitching the blanket up so that it would not drag on the floor and trip her, she made her way to the door, smiling over the tiny steps she had to take because of the blanket.

Her smile vanished abruptly when she opened the door. It took her horrified mind a moment to accept that it was not May she was looking at but Drogo and William, the man who would be crowned king in just a few days. The soft laughter of Tancred, Unwin, and the two large men escorting William finally pulled her out of her speechless shock.

"To what do I owe this great honor?" she asked, pleased that her voice revealed none of her embarrassment or nervousness.

Drogo grinned. Eada looked beautifully tousled, her thick, fair hair tumbling over her slim shoulders in a wild, unbrushed cascade of curls. Little more than her head, her small hands, and her tiny, slippered feet were revealed by the thick blanket she had wrapped around her. Her lovely face was delicately tinted pink by her blushes. Only her wide lavender eyes revealed the embarrassment she was feeling. He suspected he would hear a lot about that later, but the vision before him made the threat of a scolding easy to bear.

A grinning William reached out to gently detach one of her hands from the blanket and kissed the back of it. His grin widened at the way she hastily moved to hold the blanket closed with only one hand. Eada found the men's amusement extremely irritating. The moment he released her hand, she tugged the blanket back up from where it had slipped down off one shoulder. *At least they have now seen the strap of my chemise and know I am not completely naked beneath this blanket,* she thought as she struggled not to glare at the man she would soon call her king.

"Lord William has come to take your oath of fealty," Drogo said.

"Now?" she gasped, and then she frowned, suspecting she was the butt of some jest. "Women do not take oaths of fealty."

"For you, Lord William has decided to make an exception."

Eada suddenly remembered what she had said to William on the shores of Pevensey and she gave him a nervous smile. "That is most kind of you, my lord."

Drogo was amazed at the grace Eada revealed, despite her strange attire, as she knelt before William, kissed the ring upon his hand, and swore a very pretty, if not completely correct, oath of fealty. He was relieved to see the look of charmed amusement on William's face, for when William had suggested the visit and asked for the oath, Drogo had not been sure just how serious the man was. It had made him uneasy to know that William had recalled what Eada had said to him on the day of their landing. His concern faded as William helped her stand and kissed her hand again.

"Your French is perfect, child," William said. "Your mother taught you well."

Although Drogo had assured her that William had understood her small deception all those months ago, his mention of it made her nervous. "My liege," she began, struggling to think of the appropriate words of apology.

"Do not seek my forgiveness. You have it. In truth, I understand what you did better than most. It was but a tiny, harmless rebellion. It will also give me a tale to tell my wife when she joins me, one she will take great delight in."

After a few more pleasantries, the men left. Eada stared at the door before staggering to the bed and collapsing on it. When she heard the door open again, she groaned. What more could happen to her? She scowled up at Drogo when he walked to the side of the bed and grinned down at her.

"If I were not so weak with mortification, I would hit you," she said.

Drogo laughed, sat down on the edge of the bed, and brushed a kiss over her mouth. "I am sorry, *cherie,* but what could I do? He is my liege lord. I did try to say that you might still be abed, but William can be a most determined man."

"He did not do this because he mistrusts me, did he? I began to think he was just amused, but I find it hard to know what he thinks or feels."

"He is a difficult man to judge, but do not worry. There was no dark meaning behind this. I believe he suddenly remembered what you had said that day in Pevensey and decided he would do this, partly as a jest and partly because he merely felt inclined to."

"I do not believe William forgets anything," she murmured.

"Good. Then he will not forget your pretty words of loyalty."

"It would have been better if I could have given him those words dressed in my finest, with my hair brushed and my face washed."

Drogo smiled as he stood up and moved to open the chest at the foot of the bed where they stored their clothes. "I begin to think it was best just as it happened. The more I consider it, the more I think that William will never forget what happened here, if only because it is a droll tale."

"Well, I am so glad that I could provide him with some amusement." She frowned when he ignored her cross words and held out her soft, grey gown. "You do not need to tend to me. May will soon be here."

"No, she will not. She is helping your mother dress for her wedding to Serle."

Eada sat up slowly and gaped at him. "My mother has already reached London?"

"She did not have far to travel and decided not to wait until Serle sent for her but began her journey here within days after we left her behind." Drogo pulled her to her feet, tugged off the blanket, and tossed it on the bed.

"And she means to marry Serle right now?"

"Within the hour."

She was so stunned by the news that she blindly allowed Drogo to dress her, brush her hair, and even wash her face. It was not until they were on his horse and trotting toward the large encampment outside the city that her confusion began to clear. She easily dismissed the pang of hurt she felt that her mother had gone to Serle first upon her arrival. If nothing else, Vedette could not know where she and Drogo were. Other things troubled her, however, such as the speed of the marriage and how her siblings might be feeling about it. She realized that the talk she had had with her mother when she had found her again had not resolved all her questions.

"There has been no courtship," she said.

"They courted each other twenty years ago," Drogo said.

"And both of them have grown and changed a great deal since then."

"True. Eada, there are more things that are good about this marriage than bad. Do not forget that Serle and your mother are not children anymore. Who would know better what they want or need than they? Also, your mother is a widow in a land that will bear the scars of war for years to come. Not only has she lost her husband, but her home. Do you wish her to spend the rest of her days hiding in a nunnery?"

"No, but that does not mean she must do this right now. Averil and Ethelred should be given time to come to know Serle."

"They will have to do that after the wedding. Your mother needs the protection of a man. I know you are aware of Serle's worth even though he is not a rich man and will probably never hold any lands."

"It is not Serle's worth I question. I like Serle."

"Then your brother and sister will, too. Even though Serle is surprised that love could survive all the years they have been apart, he does love your mother. Let that ease your mind. He will protect her and provide for her and for the children. Your mother clearly needs and wants that, for she traveled here to find him, not even waiting for him to send for her or help her make the journey."

Eada was still mulling over his words when they halted before Serle's tent. She dismounted, chuckling at how nervous Serle appeared, but he ceased his pacing and hurried to greet her and Drogo. She greeted him politely but then went to talk to Averil and Ethelred, who sat with Brun, Godwin, and the increasing number of children May and Ivo were collecting.

"How many do they have now?" Eada asked as she sat on a log next to Brun, her siblings on the ground in front of her. "By the time we reached London, May and Ivo had taken in nine children. There are more than that here."

"I believe there are fourteen—if you do not include Welcome and Eric, who stay mostly with Godwin," replied

Brun. "I told Drogo that he had best get his lands and flee to them before he needs to build a castle just for May and Ivo and all the orphans and cast-off babes they have taken in."

"Cast-off babes?"

"They have stepped out in the morning to find babes left in front of their tent. Three so far. I believe they are the unwanted spawn of the women who follow the army."

Eada shook her head, saddened by the tale, but only briefly. May and Ivo would give the babes all the love they would need. She turned her attention to her siblings and was not surprised to see them constantly looking toward Serle.

"He is a good man," she said, and they both looked at her and flushed with guilt.

"Does it not trouble you that she can wed another so soon after our father's death?" asked Averil, her hurt and confusion trembling in her voice.

"Father has been dead for many months; but, yes, it does, a little. I will cure myself of that, however, for Mother's sake. As I rode here, I was torn by many emotions, none of them good; but, I am overcoming them. This is not the land we once knew and everything is going to be changing. You cannot go home again. Some Norman will soon preside over all we had. Mother needs the protection of a man; she needs a place to live and someone to provide for her. She is now a Saxon woman alone living in the midst of a huge Norman army. If she is the wife of a Norman knight, she will be as safe as she can be in such troubled times. So will you."

"She says she loves him."

"I cannot judge the truth of that; but if she says so, then it must be so. Come, Averil, she loved and honored our father while he was alive. What harm is there if she now turns back to a man she loved in her youth?"

"Do you really feel that way?"

After looking deep into her heart, Eada nodded, realizing that talking to Drogo and then her siblings had finally calmed her doubts, hurts, and fears. "Yes. And trust me when I say that Serle truly is a good man, kind and honorable. If you but give him a chance, you can have a good life with him."

"That is what Brun told us," Ethelred said, nodding at Brun.

"Such kind words for a Norman," Eada murmured, smiling at a frowning Brun.

"I speak the truth when I see it." He grinned when she laughed at his petulant tone. "It is not always easy to say, especially about a Norman. I still fight with my anger."

"But you can see beyond it, and that is good." She looked back at Averil. "It is a lesson you should learn."

"I will try," Averil murmured. "It has to be a better life than the nunnery."

Eada suddenly realized that Averil was not looking at her as she spoke. Her sister was not looking at Serle either. When Averil blushed faintly and smiled shyly, she followed the direction of her gaze and nearly gasped. Averil was exchanging glances with Unwin, who stood at Drogo's side. Eada turned to look at Brun, who grinned widely, laughter filling his eyes.

"I think she will soon recover from her anger at Normans," Brun drawled.

"It would appear so." She laughed with him.

"And what do you two find so amusing?" Drogo asked as he stepped up next to Eada, but before she could answer, he frowned at all the children crawling and playing in front of Ivo's tents. "Are there more of them or do I miscount?"

As Brun told Drogo about the latest additions to Ivo's growing family, Eada had to laugh at the look on his face. "You are going to have to speak to them."

Drogo sighed and then laughed. "I have. It does no

good. I think Brun's advice was the best I have heard. I must try and get my lands and then flee to them."

The mention of the bounty he waited for swept away Eada's good humor, but she managed a smile as he took her by the hand and pulled her to her feet. "Is it time for the marriage to begin?"

"Yes. The priest is just arriving," he added as he pointed to the man dismounting in front of Serle's tent.

Taking Ethelred by the hand and signaling Averil to come along, Eada went with Drogo. Once inside the tent, Eada studied her mother carefully and felt the last of her qualms ease. Vedette looked every inch the eager-yet-nervous bride. The reasons to marry so quickly might be ones of necessity, but it was clear to see that she also married for love. Serle's battered face held the same look of happy anticipation and Eada knew that everything would be fine.

It was not until the feasting was over and she and May were helping Vedette undress that Eada actually had a chance to talk to her mother. "Did you tell Averil and Ethelred the truth about me?"

"Yes," Vedette replied. "They felt badly for Old Edith, but that was all. It was a great deal easier than I had thought it would be. They think of you no differently than they always have."

"I wondered, for they said nothing to me."

"I believe they simply do not think about it. Because you share a father, you are still their sister, and that was all they really cared about."

"It would be nice to see things in that simple way again. I think it is the only thing I miss about being a child."

"Yes," agreed Vedette as she fingered the ribbon laces on the front of her night dress. "As one ages, everything become so very complicated. I feel silly in this. It is but the early afternoon."

"The afternoon of your wedding day," Eada reminded

her. "If you tie the tent closed and do so tightly, you will not even notice. It is also for the best that we cannot indulge in a full day of feasting, for it would be a sinful waste at this time. And do not forget that Serle must greet the dawn on the morrow. If you waited until later, your wedding night would be a short one."

Vedette laughed then quickly grew serious. "Did Averil and Ethelred talk about how they feel? They did not know if they approved of this, Averil especially."

"They will be fine. Averil might take a little while to set aside all ill feeling, but I think Ethelred has already. Brun told him that Serle was a good man, and that seemed to be enough."

Vedette smiled. "It would be. Ethelred worships Brun."

"Oh, dear," Eada said with such exaggerated concern that May laughed, but then she saw the confusion and worry on her mother's face. "I jest, *Maman*. Brun is a good man. Do you think Serle would be training him if he were not? Brun has the wit and the heart to recognize good men even amongst the army that defeated him. He fought bravely at Hastings and now he will fight bravely for Drogo."

"Ah, yes, Sir Drogo. I think we should talk about him."

"Another day, *Maman*. This is your wedding day. And, in all honesty, there is nothing more to say. Nothing has yet changed."

"I will allow you this reprieve, but only for a little while. The war is over and William will be crowned king in the new year, which is but days away. There must be some decision made concerning you and Drogo."

"I know. For now, just pray that, when it comes, it is the one that will make me happy."

Vedette kissed her cheek. "I will, for I want you to know the happiness I feel right now. You are worthy of it." She sighed as she glanced nervously toward the tent opening. "I just wish I were not so old. There is little chance that I can give Serle a child."

For once Eada was not disturbed by the abrupt arrival of her voices. She stared at Vedette, unable to think of the woman as anything but her mother; and once the feeling had passed, she smiled. "You will give Serle two fine sons." She laughed at the look that settled on Vedette's small face. "You look as if you do not know whether to be pleased or terrified."

"I am pleased that I can give Serle children. I am sorry, but the fear was because of what you just did." She shivered slightly. "It was just like Old Edith. I could almost see her, almost hear her. Does it not frighten you when that happens?"

"A little. Less and less each time." She heard Serle cough nervously just outside the tent and hastily kissed her mother's cheek before grabbing May by the hand. "Be happy, *Maman,*" she said and slipped out of the tent, tugging May along behind her.

To Eada's delight, Drogo had work to do within the camp and she was able to visit with Averil and Ethelred as well as with her other friends. She took careful note of how often Unwin found an excuse to wander by, looking only at Averil, who readily returned his looks. May and Ivo surprised her with the news that they had taken advantage of the priest's presence in the camp and gotten married. She felt sorry that the war had stolen the chance of their having any real celebration; but it was a fleeting regret, for the war had also brought them together and they were both quite content with what they had.

It was not until Drogo collected her to take her back to London that Eada realized she had been using the company of family and friends to stop herself from thinking. She hated to admit it, for she was happy for her mother and for May, but she was also painfully jealous. Both of those women had found the happiness they needed, and hers remained out of her reach.

She scowled at Drogo's back as they rode, letting anger

conquer her pain and sadness. He did not even notice how the uncertainty he left her to wallow in was tormenting her. As long as she welcomed him into her bed, he seemed to think that nothing was wrong.

For one brief moment she considered kicking him out of bed and demanding some answers. It would solve nothing, she decided quickly. It could even end what little she shared with him sooner than it needed to end. The answers he might give her could be the wrong ones, forcing her to leave him. There was so little time left before those harsh decisions would have to be made that she was willing to wait a little longer. She dreaded the thought of losing even one day because she had allowed pride to make her impatient.

By the time they returned to their quarters, she had her errant emotions back under control. Her stomach still full from all the food she had consumed at the wedding, she declined the bread and cheese Drogo offered, undressed, and crawled into bed. Warm and comfortable beneath the covers, she watched him prepare for bed and decided that he was worth sacrificing some of her pride.

"I miss Unwin's help," Drogo said as he slipped in beside her and tugged her into his arms. "I am not sure I understood why he needed to stay in camp for a little while longer."

Eada laughed. "To gaze longingly at my sister." She met his surprised look knowingly.

"Unwin was exchanging glances with Averil?"

"Every time he could find an excuse to walk by."

"She is a little young."

"Thirteen. She will grow. That might not matter. If Unwin's family—"

"Unwin's family had nothing to give him save the armor he wore. They sent him here hoping he could become more than a mercenary or a monk. He has already done that, having been knighted by William himself when we arrived in London. I shall have to have a talk with him, however. As you have said, Averil is thirteen and will grow, but not for a few years, and I cannot have him neglecting his duties to exchange glances for that long." He grinned when she giggled. "I saw you talking to Brun. How does he fare?"

"His limp is gone and a lot of his anger has faded. He is also truly honored that Serle has offered to train him."

He shook his head. "I do not even have my lands yet and I have a household larger than most lords have."

"And growing every day," she added, fighting down the pain any mention of his promised lands had begun to cause her.

"So many babes, yet Ivo and May seem to manage them all well. And even if I can get them secured somewhere before that number is added to, I am sure they will quickly begin to breed their own." He laughed. "They make a good match. I was worried that Ivo would spend his days alone because he is slow."

"A man with a heart as full of love and kindness as Ivo's can never be alone."

"True." He pulled her closer, rolling so that she was beneath him. "I think that is enough talk. I have not been here to see you awake for too many nights."

"Far too many nights," she agreed and welcomed his kiss, determined to savor as much of their passion as she could before it was torn from her grasp.

Twenty-three

Eada fought the urge to scream and wail, to hurl herself at Drogo's feet and beg for his love. It was not only her pride that held her back. She knew she would only deeply shame them both and gain nothing for it. Her inner voices told her not to worry, that Drogo was her mate, but she did not really trust them. This time they could be the echoes of her own shattered heart and not the truth. She sat on the edge of the bed in their room, her hands clasped tightly together, and watched Unwin help Drogo dress for his meeting with William, all the while fighting to keep her emotions subdued, her expression one of calm and acceptance. He had told her that he would do this from the moment they had met and she could not, by word or by deed, condemn him for it now. Especially not when he had waited with growing impatience for six weeks since the triumphant arrival in London.

It did not help her control her sorrow to think about how happy everyone else was despite the bitter sadness of the Saxon defeat. Her mother was with Serle, her first love. May was now a free woman and married to Ivo. The way Unwin and Averil looked longingly at each other told Eada that, as soon as her sister was of age, she and Unwin would marry. That left only her. She would be alone. Soon she might suffer from the fear and the scorn Old Edith had. The mere thought of the loneliness she would have to endure sent chills down her spine.

Some had tried to soothe her fears by reminding her that she was wellborn and assuring her that, when Drogo got the lands he sought, it did not mean that he would cast her aside. She knew otherwise. William not only had to reward his knights but to placate the highborn Saxons he now tried to rule. Already there was talk of Norman knights marrying Saxon ladies, the kinswomen of Saxons who had bowed to William or those of the Saxon noblemen whose lands the Normans now claimed. It was the quickest, firmest way to bind Saxon and Norman together. There was a good chance that, when Drogo was given his lands, he would be offered a wife as well. She would not, could not, remain with Drogo if he married another.

"How do I look?" Drogo asked Eada.

"Like a lord," she replied and forced a smile. "All of William's court will feel as if they have been lost in the shadows when you walk in."

"Well said," he drawled, grinning briefly over her elaborate flattery.

"They were pretty words, were they not?"

He laughed as he buckled on his sword then grew serious as he looked at her again. "And have your voices told you what my future now holds?" He frowned when she visibly tensed.

Eada forced herself to relax. His question had simply startled her, for it was the first time he had asked about her sendings and he had done so in such a calm, easy manner that she knew he now fully accepted her strange gift. She thought it almost amusing that, after cursing Old Edith's bequest from the moment she had first realized she had it, she should now regret not hearing anything at all. Drogo wanted some assurance that all would be well, that William would give him a wealthy boon, and that he had finally gained all he had fought for, but her voice was strangely quiet.

"I fear I have not heard even a whisper for days," she finally replied.

"Do not look so forlorn, *cherie,*" he said, as he stepped over to her and brushed a kiss over her forehead. "Better no word at all than some dark warning."

"True." She trailed her fingers over his cheek. "Watch your back."

"I always do, and Tancred waits outside to do the same. I will return as soon as I have met with William."

Eada smiled in reply, but the moment Drogo and Un-win left, she flopped back onto the bed and fought a fierce battle against the urge to weep. Her soul mate had left to get his reward for conquering her people, uttering no promises, no words of love, not even a hint of what the future might hold for her.

"Well, fool," she scolded herself, "Old Edith said I would meet my mate, but I do not recall her saying that I would keep him."

"You do talk to yourself a lot."

A soft screech escaped Eada as she abruptly sat up then she scowled at May, who quietly shut the door behind her. "And you walk too quietly," she complained. "You frightened away a year or two of my life."

"I thought you might wish some help to prepare for your lord's return," May said as she opened the chest at the foot of the bed.

"I am not sure I should be here when Drogo returns."

May dropped the gown she was unfolding and gaped at Eada. "But he will be returning with his gift from our new king. He will wish to share his new honors with you."

"Will he?" Eada shook her head when May's expression of shock changed to one of confusion. "May, William is a king on an uneasy throne, a Norman claiming he has the right to rule Saxons. He knows this will not be easy and he needs to cover his new lands with allies. He

will give the lands to the Normans and he will soothe his
Saxon allies by wedding those Normans to Saxon ladies."

"But you are a Saxon lady."

"I have no lands." Eada felt guilty about telling May
such a lie, but she did not want the truth to be known
yet and May might not be able to keep such a big secret.
"If Drogo wed me, it would please none of William's
Saxon allies, for they are no kin of mine, and since my
father fought with Harold, it could anger his Saxon and
his Norman allies."

"You swore allegiance to William."

"That was but a game. Yes, I will hold to my vow and I
have no fear that William doubts my word, but it serves
no purpose. I cannot fight for him and I cannot enrich
his purse. He only wished my allegiance because of what
I had said that day I met him on the shores of Pevensey.
I am sure I am now forgotten." Eada stood up and signaled
May to help her dress, for, whatever she decided she must
do, she wanted to be attired in her finest. It would feed
her courage.

"Then what is to happen now?" May asked as she unlaced the simple brown gown Eada wore.

"I am not sure. It depends upon whether or not William offers Drogo a bride with his land."

"Lord Drogo will not accept a bride."

"Of course he will," Eada snapped, but the sharpness
of her reply was dulled as May tugged her embroidered
blue gown down over her head. "If his king says that he
must wed the girl to gain the land, Drogo will do it. He
has made no secret of why he joined this battle—to gain
lands and a title."

"Then you can be Lord Drogo's leman. I am certain
he will want you to stay with him."

"No, I will not become his whore. William is king now
and the war is over. I can no longer claim that I need
his protection, either."

"What will you do?"

"I have many choices. After all, I can speak both French and English. Few others can." She managed a smile as she looked at May. "I will survive."

May nodded as she laced up Eada's gown. "I know you will, for you are very strong; but will you be happy?" She frowned at Eada. "I thought the old woman told you that Lord Drogo was your mate."

"She did, but that does not mean that I will wed him, bear his children, and win his love. I was reminding myself of that when you walked in. Come, do not look so forlorn. We cannot know what will happen until Drogo returns from William's court." She sighed. "I should not be surprised that my fate rests in William's hands. That, too, was foretold."

Drogo paced the cool stone hall of the great tower, realized what he was doing, and stopped, only to begin again a moment later. He could not understand his sudden uneasiness and confusion. This was what he had waited for, fought for, and hungered for. The only thing he should be feeling was an intense curiosity about what his reward should be.

"Will you cease?" asked Tancred in exasperation.

A quick glance at his friend revealed that, despite the tension in his voice, Tancred was slouched against the wall with his customary grace and languid air. "You do not appear to be distressed," Drogo said as he forced himself to stand still in front of Tancred.

"My neck has begun to ache from watching you go back and forth. What ails you?"

"Nothing ails me."

Tancred shook his head and made a sharp, mocking noise. "You do not behave like a man who is about to gain all he seeks."

"And how should I behave on such an important occasion?"

"Certainly not as if you are about to face imprisonment. *Merde*, you act as if you are about to face some ordeal. The most you should be doing is trying to guess what lands you may soon hold, what title you might gain, and where in this damp mist-shrouded land you might rule. So, again I ask, what troubles you?"

"I do not know," Drogo replied in a soft voice as he slumped against the wall next to Tancred and tried to smile reassuringly at an uneasy Unwin.

"Are you afraid that you will not be given all you deserve?"

"No. Whatever our king chooses to grant me will be more than I have now. I will be thankful for whatever lands I might be given." He nodded. "Yes, even as I speak the words I know, in my heart, that they are the complete truth."

"Well, if you do not know what gnaws at you, I cannot help you. I would advise you to calm yourself before you meet with our king, however. William may see your mood and wonder on it. I do not believe you want to try and explain yourself to him."

"No." Drogo shuddered at the thought. "I shall thank him most graciously for what he gives me and leave. I will collect Eada and the others and go to my lands as soon as I am able. I wish to place some distance between myself and this court. There is too much intrigue, and I do not wish to be caught in its web. Will you travel with us?"

Tancred nodded. "Just this morning I was granted a small holding near Hastings. If your lands are in that direction, I will be most pleased to travel with you."

Drogo clasped Tancred by the shoulder. "I am pleased about your good fortune, but I shall miss you at my back. It will be strange not to have you always at hand."

"Mayhap I will not be too far away. Mayhap fate will

smile upon us and our granted lands will be close together.''

"That would be good. Who is your liege lord?"

"I do not know. The king is trying to find out who held
the lands I now claim a piece of, but no one seems to
know. The earl is known but not how the lands were held
under him or by whom. It may be months, even years,
before that is known." Tancred lightly bit his bottom lip
and glanced warily at Drogo. "Are you certain you should
take Eada with you?"

"Of course. She is my woman. Why should I cast her
aside?"

Before Tancred could reply, a man called for Drogo.
With a last frown directed at Tancred, the unanswered
question sitting uneasily in his mind, Drogo followed the
man. The tension that had been subdued by his talk with
Tancred now returned in full and Drogo felt his insides
knot up. This was the moment he had waited for, yet he
dreaded it. That made no sense, and that confusion only
added to his tight uneasiness.

Drogo bowed as he confronted William, idly thinking
that the man sprawled in the huge oak chair looked more
the warrior than the king. He smiled his gratitude for the
honor when William waved him toward a bench on his
right. As he sat down and faced his liege lord, Drogo
fought to hide his confused feelings. The room was filled
with the smoke of tallow candles and a fire as well as William's large entourage. There were also Normans, Saxons,
and even some of William's mercenaries, all awaiting their
rewards or a chance to argue their fate. Drogo hoped all
of that was enough to keep William from looking too
closely at him or keeping him at his side for too long.

"I am pleased that you and all your men survived the
war, Drogo," William said.

"So are we, my liege," said Drogo, and he returned
William's quick grin.

William sighed, his mood changing quickly as he frowned at the people gathered in the hall. "I fear that, although the victory came more swiftly and easily than I had planned, it will not be easy to discover exactly what I rule. I do not fully understand the Saxon ways and laws, and since they do not fully understand mine, I fear we often talk a great deal yet learn nothing from each other. They do not understand what I ask and I do not understand their replies and explanations. With so many Saxons dead or in hiding, it is also impossible to gather all the information I need." He shook his head. "It could be years before I know all I now lay claim to, but everyone wishes to know today what their fate is or what they have gained."

As he prepared himself to graciously accept the news that he would have to wait to know what lands would be his, Drogo murmured, "And one cannot expect the defeated to rush to hand over all they have lost."

"True, my old friend. But for you, I do have good news. In truth, this boon became known to me but an hour ago. Do you see that pretty Saxon woman trying to hide in the far corner of the hall?"

His heart sinking, Drogo looked where William pointed. The woman was fair, blonde, and shapely. When she saw the king pointing her way, she looked up briefly and blushed, quickly averting her gaze and revealing a becoming modesty. As he had stood upon the shores of France months ago, he would have considered such a woman a true prize, an excellent choice for a bride. Now he was almost terrified that William was going to suggest that he marry the girl.

"She is very pretty," was all Drogo could bring himself to say.

"And alone. Her father and brothers fell at Hastings, leaving well-marked, rich lands. The man who takes her to wife will be both powerful and wealthy."

"But only if he takes her to wife."

William nodded. "The bond of Saxon with Norman, the old ruling blood with the new, will ease resentment and anger. If that Norman is a fair and honorable man, I will have at least one island of peace in this sea of anger I must try to calm."

Drogo knew he should say yes without hesitation. This gave him all he had come to England to gain. This was far more than he had any right to expect. He would rise from little more than a mercenary knight to a lord with lands to rule, power, and wealth. Such a gain would also help his men, especially Serle and Unwin, who had little hope of any gain for their service. Even recalling his debt and responsibility to those who served him could not bring the word yes to his lips. The strange advice Lord Bergeron had given him the day of the hangings no longer seemed so strange. This was the decision the man had been referring to, this was when he had to choose between ambition and happiness. He did not want the woman. He did not want any woman but Eada. The woman was the choice of ambition; Eada was where his happiness would be found. Suddenly, nothing William could offer was alluring, not if it would cost him Eada.

"You hesitate?" William asked, watching Drogo closely.

"I do not want the woman," Drogo replied quietly, wondering how he could refuse such a gift without causing insult.

"I fear the woman comes with the lands. There will be anger aplenty when the people see that not only their king will be foreign. That will be eased some if marriages are made."

"I know and I agree, but I cannot take the woman." He suddenly realized that the look upon William's ruddy face was not one of anger or outrage but of amusement. "You are not surprised by my refusal."

"No. We have marched together for months, Drogo. I believe I know what lies in your heart. I but wondered if you craved the lands and wealth more than the woman. Do not fear to insult me. I accept your refusal with but one regret. I have nothing else to offer you. Not now. Mayhap not ever."

"I understand." Drogo was surprised at his lack of disappointment or regret.

"Keep your little Saxon lady, my friend. Wed her and breed an army of sons with your strength and her spirit, and you will be much respected and honored. What I *can* give you is all she and her family lay claim to. All I ask is, when you learn what that is, you let me know. At least I will have a full accounting of one holding."

"Thank you, my liege," Drogo said, standing and bowing.

"I pray that you will still thank me in the years ahead. I hope she is worth what you might be giving up."

"She is. I am but ashamed to admit that I did not see it before. Now, if I may be given leave, I believe I shall go and discuss my discovery with Eada."

William's hearty laughter followed him as he walked out of the hall. William understood his choice, but Drogo was not sure his men would. When he met up with Tancred and Unwin and saw the eager, expectant look upon their faces, Drogo inwardly grimaced. They were going to think he was mad.

"I now understand why you asked if I would be taking Eada to my new lands, Tancred," Drogo said as he stood before his two friends. "William is handing out wives with some of the lands."

Tancred sighed and nodded. "Our king spoke of it briefly. He even asked if I thought you would accept one particular woman, an earl's daughter."

"He did not offer her to you?"

"I am not as highborn as you or as lauded a knight. He was seeking her equal. Did he find him?"

"No." Drogo smiled when Unwin gaped at him in

shock, but he noticed that Tancred was not surprised. "I told him I did not want the woman."

"Was she so hideous?" asked Unwin.

"No. She was most fair. I simply did not want her."

"He wants Eada, boy," Tancred said to Unwin, clapping the youth on the back.

"Mistress Eada is a fine woman, brave and very fair," said Unwin. "She is also poor and landless."

"Very true," agreed Drogo. "Although she does hold that fine house in Pevensey and her family was not actually poor."

"I meant that she is no earl's daughter. I am not sure she is even a thane's daughter."

"No, but she is mine; and now, all that her family laid claim to is mine."

"Can you be satisfied with that?" asked Tancred. "You sought a great deal more when you sailed here."

"I know, and I continued to want it until it was offered to me and I saw what I had to sacrifice to gain it." He laughed ruefully and shook his head. "William was not surprised; and, I think, Tancred, neither were you. I was stunned. There it was, all I craved or thought I did. All I had to do was marry the woman. I could not do it. Even reminding myself of all I owe those who ride with me could not make me do it."

"You owe us nothing."

"I do. You have all stood at my back, fought at my side. You have lost little, Tancred, for you have always had the chance to gain from this. All you had to do was survive the battles. Serle, Garnier, and young Unwin are not so fortunate. Their fortunes have been tied to mine. For that reason I regret my choice, but only for that reason. And that regret was not strong enough to make me cast aside Eada." Drogo draped his arm around Unwin's slim shoulders. "I fear you have bound yourself to a poor knight. I may yet gain, but William could make no promises."

"You made the choice you had to, sir," Unwin said. "I have enough. My first battle was long and fierce, yet I survived and gained honor. Without you, I would have been sent back to France, untried and with no one to fight for or with. I would have missed this great battle. I have been part of the army that won William the crown of England. No, you owe me nothing. And there is always the chance that you and the rest of us may still gain more."

"Ah, the never-dimmed hopes of the young," murmured Drogo, smiling when Tancred laughed and Unwin blushed. "You are right, Unwin. There is always the chance for greater gain, and if I see that chance before me, I will grasp it firmly. Now, let us return to our rooms as I feel a great need to grasp something else most firmly, something a great deal softer and sweeter than coin and land."

"Do you think Mistresse Eada will be disappointed over how little you have gained?" asked Unwin as he hurried to keep pace with Tancred and Drogo when they left the tower and walked along a narrow, winding road.

"No, and that may be the only thing I am sure of concerning that lavender-eyed woman," replied Drogo. "Eada will have all she had before, no more, no less, except that she will have it through me. She is not a woman who hungers after riches or power."

"She just hungers after you," drawled Tancred as he paused before Drogo's quarters.

Standing next to Tancred, Drogo frowned up at the tiny window to the room he shared with Eada. "I pray you are right. I am suddenly possessed by a teeth-clenching apprehension. I have never done any more with a woman than bed her or treat her with courtesy, depending upon who she was. Curse the girl. I have bravely faced the whole of the Saxon army screaming for my blood and wielding battle-axes, yet quail at the thought of speaking my heart to one woman."

"I fear this ordeal is one Unwin and I cannot face with

you." Tancred gave Drogo a light shove toward the door. "We will be ready to celebrate or commiserate with you, however."

Drogo cast his grinning companions a sour look then started into the house. With each step he took toward his room he struggled to regain his lost confidence and courage. He had just refused a rich gift from a king. How much more difficult could it be to speak of love and marriage with a tiny Saxon lady?

Twenty-four

"You still have not told him?" Vedette cried in surprise, and she gaped at her daughter, who was sprawled on Drogo's bed looking an odd mixture of sullen and forlorn. "You have let him go to William to seek lands when you hold more than enough to please him?"

Eada sighed. For the first time since she had found her again, she was not really pleased to see the woman she still thought of as her mother. She did not want to talk about Drogo or her lands or why she continued to keep her inheritance a secret. She had resigned herself to accept what fate would give her, and her mother was intruding upon the sense of sad but calm acceptance.

"I told you why I will not tell Drogo about the land," she said, as she sat up and smoothed her gown.

"Yes, and I agreed with you when you told me, but *not now*. Child, William is besieged by Saxons who fought with him and by ones who have surrendered. To secure a place for themselves under his rule they are fighting to bind their bloodlines to that of a Norman noble. Do you know what that means?"

"Of course—marriage. I have heard the talk." Eada wished she did not sound so sulky, for it weakened her claim that she was ready and willing to accept what fate offered her.

"And yet you send your man off to William, possibly to be handed a wife with his gift of land?"

"He does not need to accept the lands or the wife who comes with them."

"Oh? Is he to refuse all for love of you?"

There is no need to sound so scornful," Eada snapped, scrambling off the bed only to pace the room.

"Such foolishness deserves scorn. He is a knight, Eada. If he is to have any life at all, he must have land. This is not a matter of simple greed. It is far more intricate a choice he must make."

"But, if he loves me—"

"If he loves you, and I believe he does even if he does not realize it, he will still choose the lands even if he must marry some other woman to gain them. Eada, he has spent his whole life reaching for this bounty. It is what blood and breeding demand. It is all he could have had if he had just been born first. You should have told him that you have the land he seeks."

Eada began to think that she had made a very big mistake. There was so much truth to what Vedette said that it was hard to ignore or deny. Drogo was wellborn, probably holding as good a lineage as the man he now called king. He could not make simple choices. There were also other people he had to consider, ones whose futures depended upon the choices he made. Men had sworn their swords to him. Unspoken had been the agreement that Drogo would do all he could to better his position in life, thus improving theirs. She was being selfish in thinking that he could ignore all of those obligations to be with her. She was thinking only of herself. Drogo could not and would not do that. She cursed.

Vedette's eyes widened. "I think you have ridden too long with the army."

Ignoring the reprimand, Eada pulled her bag out from beneath the wide, rope-strung bed and threw it on top. She walked to the chest at the foot of the bed, opened it, and removed her few possessions. Frowning, Vedette

moved closer as Eada tossed her clothes onto the bed
and then into her bag.

"What are you doing?" demanded Vedette.

"Packing." Eada scowled when Vedette grabbed a gown
she was stuffing into her bag, but after a brief, silent tug-
of-war, she managed to wrest it free and pack it.

"You are going to run away."

"I am going to free Drogo of what is now an incon-
venient obligation—me."

"I have always thought that you had more wit than was
good for any woman to have, yet all sense has fled you
now. Where can you go?"

"To my lands. Old Edith's cottage can be made most
comfortable."

"William is claiming all Saxon lands. He may wish to
give yours to some Norman knight."

"Then he will give me to the knight, too, will he not?"

"You would marry another man?"

Eada tied her bag shut with only a few quick, angry
movements. "You have just told me that I have sent the
man I want into the arms of another woman, so what
does it matter?"

"But you told me that Old Edith said Drogo was your
mate."

"The mate of my heart and my soul. She did not say
that we would be man and wife." Eada sat down on the
bed and gave Vedette a sad smile. "I realize that I was
asking something of Drogo that he could not do, no matter
how much he might wish to. He is not a man alone. He
cannot simply follow his heart and cast all else to the four
winds. You were right. I was being foolish, foolish and very
blind. I did not look beyond my own needs and wants."

Vedette patted Eada on the shoulder. "It is good that
you see that now, but that does not mean that you must
leave."

"Would you have me stay and become Drogo's whore?"

A light blush colored Vedette's pale skin and she nervously twisted the ties on the side of her pale-grey gown. "No. That would please no one, and you would soon be most unhappy. Yet there is the chance that Drogo will not be offered a wife. You should at least wait until you are certain."

Eada stared at Vedette for a full minute and then said quietly, "He will be offered a wife."

Vedette shivered and rubbed her arms. "I do not think I will ever grow accustomed to the way you do that. Have you just seen Drogo wed to another?"

"No. I just know that he will be offered a wife." She grimaced. "The curse of this gift is that it tells me that yet will not tell me if he accepts or not."

"Then wait."

"No. If I wait until he returns and he has chosen to accept but wishes me to stay, I fear I might not have the strength to leave. And, yet again, you are right; that would make me very unhappy."

"But how can you get to Old Edith's tiny house? It is a very long journey."

"It is, but I do not believe it will take as long as it did to get here, for I am not an army and will not be pausing to lay waste to villages."

"You sound as if you have grown to hate the Normans," Vedette said quietly, watching Eada closely and making no effort to hide her concern.

"No, *Maman,* I have grown to hate armies and wars. And—" she lowered her voice, an innate caution making her somewhat secretive as she added, "I am not fond of kings and those men who hold great power. They are the ones who lead those armies and cause those wars. They care nothing for the soldiers or the innocents, only for power and riches." She shook her head as she stood up and donned her cloak. "There are people who say these tragedies are a punishment from God, but the devastation I saw was wrought by earthly hands.''

Vedette hugged Eada and looked at her with a mixture of sympathy and sadness. ''I wish I could have saved you from seeing such horrors. They have made you bitter.''

''No, not truly. Wiser, mayhap wary, but not really bitter. My lack of power makes me ache with sorrow, but I am not weighted down with that every day of my life. Now, I really must go or I will still be within reach when Drogo returns.''

''Have you thought about what will happen if Drogo does not accept a wife and returns here to find you gone?''

''If he remains unwed, unpromised to another, and he wants me, he can come and get me. I am not hiding. You need not keep this a secret. There is only one thing I ask you to remain quiet about.''

''Your lands.''

''Yes. You are probably right to say that I erred in not telling Drogo about my lands before he went to see our new king. Now he will have made his choice, and knowing about the lands I hold will not change that. If he is still free to choose a wife, I do not want that choice to be made because of my new wealth.'' She grimaced as she pulled up her hood and picked up her bag. ''I am not being too clear.''

''Clear enough,'' Vedette said as she followed Eada to the door. ''You cannot go alone.''

''I know. I also know that I cannot take any of Drogo's men.'' As she and Vedette made their way out of the small house, Eada kept a close watch for Drogo and his men. ''Brun would take me.''

''He has sworn fealty to Drogo. He would go with you, but he would have to break his bond to do so.''

''And I will not ask that of him. That leaves Godwin.''

''He has to worry about the children he cares for.''

Eada stopped and stared toward the camp where the

lesser knights, mercenaries, servants, and army-followers stayed. "This is becoming very complicated," she muttered then looked at her mother. "If Godwin does not think the children should make the journey, could you care for them? It need only be until Drogo knows I am gone, then, if you wish, you can give them into May's care."

"You are right. This does grow complicated. And how will you make this journey? You have neither a cart nor a horse."

"Godwin can take the cart and pony Drogo took from Old Edith's. If Drogo feels I have no right to them, I will return them when I am back in Pevensey. Now, tell Godwin that I will be waiting for him at the east gate of the city."

Even as she muttered about ill-thought flights and the folly of pride, Vedette kissed Eada on the cheek and started toward the camp. Eada smiled faintly, amused by her mother's complaints, then sadness overcame her amusement. A touch of fear crept into her heart as well as she realized the enormity of what she was doing. Not only was she leaving the man she loved, she was preparing to ride over a countryside ravished by war with only a youth for protection. Most of William's army was in London, and she prayed others would be too busy trying to find shelter and food before the winter weather grew too harsh to trouble her and Godwin.

By the time she reached the east gate, Eada had decided that the road to Pevensey had to be safer than the dark streets of the city. She was exhausted from hiding from and fleeing the lustful attentions of soldiers and mercenaries. The men wandering the streets of London saw a woman alone as easy game, especially when that woman was a Saxon. Standing a safe distance from the guards at the gate, but keeping a close watch on them, Eada waited for Godwin, praying that he would not be too long. The way the guards watched her made her fear that it would not be long before their lusts overcame their sense of duty and they left the guarding of the city gates to chase her.

Godwin had barely brought the cart to a halt beside her when Eada leapt into the seat beside him. She spared a brief greeting for the two children and hastily patted her hounds before ordering Godwin to get moving. She did not relax until the gates of the city and the leering guards were out of sight.

"This is madness," Godwin finally said with a scowl.

"It may be, but it is also necessary. You decided you would rather have the children with you?"

Godwin glanced back to wink at the children. "They decided." Since the two children were occupied with all they could see and paid him no heed, he added quietly, "It will be some time before they cease to fear losing me as they have lost everyone else they knew. They love May and Ivo, but when I must leave them in their care, they are afraid and cling to me when I return for them."

"This may be good for them then. They will be in a home."

He made a scornful noise. "You grasp for reasons to explain this mad flight."

Eada found Godwin annoyingly insightful. "Did my mother not tell you why I am returning to Pevensey?"

"She did, and I do understand why you wish to leave Drogo's side until you know what place you might hold in his new life. What I do not understand is why you must take yourself so far away. Why not just go and live with your mother?"

"Because I am weak," she replied, making a face when he looked at her in surprise. "I do not think I can ever break the bond I have with Drogo. If he is near at hand, I will go to him, even if he is wed to another. Distance will never kill the feelings I have for the man, but it will stop me from shaming myself. I will be no mans leman. Yes, I have lain with him without the sanctity of marriage, but we were both free. Fate and destiny have said that he is my mate, but they have not said that I must commit adultery. That is one sin I refuse to indulge in."

Godwin nodded then asked, "And what will you do when William discovers your lands and gifts some knight with them?"

"I will decide on that when it happens."

"Have you decided on how we will survive? The Normans took everything."

"Not everything. Old Edith had some stores which I did not give them and a few of her chickens and pigs fled. They may still be around." She glanced into the back of the cart and smiled at Godwin. "I also see that you have helped yourself to more than the cart."

"With your mother's gracious assistance. She was most concerned about our survival. When she realized that the children were coming, too, she put in even more. I believe she is praying that Drogo will come and seek you out."

"I hope that as well, but only if he is still a free man. I will accept him now only as a husband." But Eada wondered if she had the will to hold to that vow.

Drogo frowned as he entered the room he shared with Eada. Even before he had opened the heavy oak door he had sensed that something was wrong. It did not really surprise him to find her gone as she spent a lot of time in the camp with her mother, May, and young Godwin. Not until he opened his chest and saw that all her clothes were missing did he begin to grow concerned. His sense of urgency, heavily flavored with fear, grew when he looked under the bed for the bag that was no longer there.

As he stood looking blindly around the small room, he realized she had left him and he fought back a sense of panic. Drogo slowly calmed himself, and as his heartbeat eased and his mind cleared, he chided himself. Eada was

a proud woman, yet he had not allowed himself to think
very long on how she might feel. Despite all the talk of
William giving brides away along with the land he handed
out to his loyal followers, despite the visual proof all
around them that Saxons were trying to wed their kinswomen to Normans in order to tie their families to the
victors by blood, he had offered her no assurances that
her place in his life would not change. In fact, until he
had turned aside William's generous offer, he had not
really given much thought to what would happen between
him and Eada after he had received all he had fought
for. He should have realized that Eada was not a woman
who would sit quietly and wait to see what he would decide about her future.

Cursing his blindness and unintentional cruelty, he
marched out of the empty room. Drogo did not want to
think about how much he might have hurt her. He
headed straight for the camp where everyone who could
not afford or find quarters within the city now lived.
There was no doubt in his mind that Vedette would know
where her daughter had gone. He was disappointed when
he reached the tent Vedette shared with Serle and did
not find Eada there.

"Ah, greetings, my lord Drogo," Vedette said as she
ushered Drogo inside. "How fared your meeting with William?"

Drogo looked at her sweet smile. Although Vedette was
not Eada's blood mother, there were some distinct simi-
larities between her and the girl she had raised. Except
for the way Vedette toyed with the laces of her gown, she
gave no sign that she knew something was wrong. He
reminded himself that this was a woman who had successfully fled an advancing army, saving herself, most of
her family, and most of her valuables. She was not as
delicate and as soft as she looked.

"I am well pleased," he replied, crossing his arms over

his chest and watching her closely. "You may not be. I was given your home in Pevensey and all that goes with it. Do not look so concerned. I shall count as mine only what was there when I arrived." He almost laughed at her visible relief that he would not claim all she had fled with as well.

"That seems a small payment for your loyalty and service."

"That it does," said Serle as he stepped inside and nodded a greeting to Drogo.

"I was offered a far richer prize, but I could not accept it," explained Drogo.

"Why not? You are a lord by blood if not by title."

"The land came with an encumbrance I was not willing to accept—a wife." He smiled when Vedette's eyes widened then grew serious as he looked at Serle, a man whose fortunes were tightly bound to his. "I pray you can forgive me, old friend. I have acted selfishly. The lands and the wealth and power they carried were heady prizes, but I turned them away. As they were dangled before my eyes, I fear I did not consider the ones who depend upon me. To gain that prize I had to take the woman and, at that moment, I saw clearly that I could bind myself to no woman save Eada."

"Do not beg pardon from me, lad. I ask no more than a roof, a warm fire, and food in my belly." He put his arm around Vedette's slim shoulders. "If I had been given such a choice many years ago or now, I would have done the same. I am also acutely aware of all you would have suffered had you not made that choice. It pleases me that you saw the truth for yourself before it was too late." He frowned and looked around. "What puzzles me is—where is Eada? Do not say that the girl has refused you after you made such a sacrifice?"

"No. She has not refused me, for I have not had the

opportunity to speak to her." Drogo fixed his gaze on a blushing Vedette. "I returned to find Eada gone."

"Vedette." Serle said his wife's name in a stern voice as he stared down at her. "Where is Eada?"

"You can see for yourselves that she is not here," Vedette replied as she slipped out of Serle's reach, and she wondered frantically if Eada had had enough time to get beyond Drogo's immediate reach. The young lovers would be well served by a few days of separation, she decided.

"Vedette, this man is your liege lord and intends your daughter no harm or disgrace."

"He has not said what exactly he does intend for her."

"I intend to wed her if she will have me for her husband," Drogo said in a grave voice, but he could not fully suppress a smile at Serle's confusion and dismay.

"While your passion is still new and hot that may please you well enough. But what happens if you gain in power and wealth? Will you begin to think you have erred in taking a Saxon wife, one who can bring you no lands or coin?"

"No, and I say that knowing that I may yet gain more lands, wealth, and power. William understood why I refused his generous offering. He was not even surprised. He also said that, once he knows more of the lands he now seeks to rule, he will try to better my prize. Where is Eada, Vedette?"

Nervously, for she knew Drogo would be furious, she replied, "She went back to Pevensey."

"Alone?" was all Drogo could say as he fought back a sudden surge of anger born of his fear for Eada's safety.

"No. Godwin is with her."

"And those two babes of his, too, I have no doubt."

"They refused to be left behind. They are terrified that he will leave them as so many others have."

"So, Eada is traveling over a land torn apart and devastated by this war with a boy, her hounds, and two babes. How could you let her indulge in such madness?"

"She was not prepared to heed my warnings or pleas. Both were weakened by the fact that I understood why she had to leave. Drogo, all signs pointed to your being offered a wife. Eada knew it for fact in that way she has of knowing things others do not. Unfortunately, her gift would not tell her if you would accept the wife. She knew that if she stayed and you returned with a bride but still wanted her, she would not be able to refuse you. Being nothing more than your leman would slowly kill her. I knew that as surely as she did. What choice did I have?"

Drogo did not know enough about Eada's feelings for him to argue that. "Where can she go in Pevensey? And how can she survive? The army took almost everything."

"I am sure there are still things the army could not find, not in the short while they stayed in the town." Vedette blushed and sent him an apologetic smile. "I also gave them some supplies."

"Do not look so afraid. I am glad that you did. Where in Pevensey will they go?"

"To Old Edith's house. What are you going to do?"

"Follow her." Drogo paced the tent as he tried to sort out his plans. "I must inform William that I will be leaving. Since my lands are in Pevensey, I believe I will gather up all I own and travel to them. All we can do is pray that the weather does not worsen or I may not be able to reach her until the spring."

Drogo cursed as he and Unwin carried his belongings out of his room and down the narrow, dark stairs. It had taken a week to gain an audience with William only to have the man request one last duty of him. Aiding yet another group of Normans who had arrived to see what they could gain now that the fighting was over had stolen away another eight days. There had been two bad storms, but the weather had cleared again and he was eager to leave London. By the time he reached Pevensey, it would have been three weeks or longer since he had last seen Eada. His insides were knotted with fear for her. At the moment, he could not even be sure that she was still alive.

"We will find her," Brun assured Drogo as he loaded the heavy chest and Drogo's armor into the cart.

"You feel certain of that, do you, despite all of the dangers she must face throughout the journey and probably in Pevensey itself?"

"Yes. She is small and pretty, but she is Saxon. She is like the land you now claim. It will allow you to rule it and change it, but you will never truly conquer it. In truth, I think Eada will be far less compromising," he added with a grin, laughing heartily when Drogo was unable to argue.

Twenty-five

"God save us, but it is cold," Godwin muttered as he entered Old Edith's cottage and hurried to warm himself by the central hearth.

Eada stirred the pot of stew cooking over the fire. It had been almost a month since they had left London, and she felt they had succeeded in making themselves secure and comfortable for the winter. Godwin had hunted down eight chickens and four pigs, which meant that they could use a few for food and still have enough for breeding in the spring. Most of what Edith had stored away was still there, and although it was not much, it would certainly keep starvation from their door. Although they occasionally saw soldiers, no one troubled them, the little cottage promising no gain to anyone with a covetous eye. If her heart did not ache so for Drogo, she would have been happy.

"Have you heard anything today?" Godwin asked as Welcome crawled onto his lap.

She grimaced with a mixture of irritation and her own deep sense of unhappiness over the apparent failure of her unwanted gift. "Nothing. No warnings, no promises."

"I really thought he would come after you."

"He has what he came to England for. I can give him nothing. Godwin, even people like us do not always have the freedom to follow our hearts. A man like Drogo has even less. He is chained by birth and obligation. Yes, I am

heartsore that he has not come; but if he now has a wife,
I am glad that he has shown the kindness to leave me
alone."

"And you have had no warning that someone would
come to claim these lands?"

"None." She looked at the small box she had set on
a shelf near the door. "I think that when spring comes
I will go to William myself and tell him of these lands."

"But if he does not know, why should you tell him?"

"Because he will learn of them some day. There is no
stopping that discovery. If I go and tell him myself, I will
lose nothing and I might actually gain some say in my
future."

"As you say, you can lose nothing." He set Welcome
aside and stood up. "I will just fetch some wood and make
certain that our stores of firewood are still full and dry."

Eada watched him leave and sighed. He was good company, as were the children, yet she still ached with a loneliness she suspected nothing could cure. Nothing except
Drogo. She missed him so much that some nights she
could not sleep she was so twisted with longing. Even
though all their time together had been spent in the very
heart of the war, of the defeat of her own people, she easily
recalled quiet times, happy times, and, especially, passionate times. She tossed some herbs into the stew and once
more tried to convince herself that she would never see
Drogo again. Eada knew that, as long as she still hoped,
she would still hurt. One day, she prayed, she would be
able to think of Drogo without pain.

Godwin cursed and, after tossing the kindling into the
small shelter on the side of the cottage, he tried to pull
the splinter out of his palm. He was so intent upon ex-
tracting the sliver of wood from his wind-chilled hand that
the sudden loud snort of a horse right behind him startled

him and he whirled around so quickly he stumbled and fell. As he slowly got to his feet, he stared up into the grinning faces of Drogo and Serle. Godwin felt a confusing mixture of elation, caution, and fear. Eada would be happy that Drogo had come after her, but only if he had come for the right reasons. In the back of his mind Godwin was also painfully aware that he had walked away from a Norman knight's household without permission.

"Sir Drogo," he began and hastily cleared his throat when his voice cracked embarrassingly.

"Actually, son, it is now Lord Drogo," drawled Serle, idly tugging forward the extra horse they had brought with them.

"Oh." Godwin bit his lip, but thoughts of Eada's happiness gave him the courage to ask, "I am pleased that you got the reward you sought and deserve, Lord Drogo, but have you come here as a free man?"

Drogo stared at the youth with surprise and an increasing amusement. Godwin was still a slightly built youth, and his skin was pink with cold and his own blushes. He stood firm, however, prepared to protect Eada. The boy had to know how easily he could be brushed aside, and Drogo admired his courage as well as his loyalty to Eada. He wondered if the Saxons in his household would ever be as loyal to him as they were to Eada, doubted it, and immediately decided that it did not matter. Once Eada pledged herself to him, he knew she would never turn that deep loyalty against him.

"I am free, boy," he answered. "Very free, but not very wealthy." Drogo decided that the boy deserved the full truth. "I was offered an earldom, Godwin, with all the lands, wealth, and power any man could want."

"An earldom?" Godwin was stunned, and intimidated. "Are you an earl now?" he asked in a small voice.

"No. I refused it." He laughed at the look of openmouthed astonishment on the youth's face. "To gain that

I had to take the earl's daughter as my wife. There is only one woman I want, and that is why I stand before this meager cottage in the cold and argue with you."

Godwin grinned. "So what did you gain, my lord, besides a fine title?"

"All that Eada and her family hold." He frowned when Godwin just grinned wider.

"Eada is within, my lord."

"There is one thing we must do first."

Eada frowned at Godwin as he slipped into the cottage and went immediately to the children. "What are you doing?" she asked when he began to put cloaks on the children.

"There is a lot of kindling upon the ground," Godwin replied. "The strong winds of last night gleaned a lot of deadwood from the trees. I thought the children could help me collect it."

"Do you wish me to help as well?"

"No, there is no need, and I know that you would not wish to leave the meal unattended." Godwin shepherded the children and her dogs toward the door. "It will be good for them to help and to get outside."

"Do not let them become too chilled," she called after him.

Barely a minute had passed when Eada heard the door creak open again. She turned to ask Godwin what was the matter and gaped. It took another full minute for her mind to accept what she saw. Drogo shut the door, removed his cloak and tossed it over a heavy chest near the wall, and then sat down next to her. He smiled and reached over to gently close her mouth. Eada struggled to say something.

"Where is Godwin?" she finally managed to ask, her voice hoarse with surprise and emotion.

"He, the children, and your dogs have gone to Pevensey with Serle," Drogo answered as he took the wooden spoon from her lax hold and helped himself to a taste of the stew. "Good. I am glad to see that you are not yet in danger of starving."

Eada gave him a weak smile. She was both elated and afraid. He had come after her, but was he free? As she looked him over with a greed she was sure was reflected in her face, noticing that his thick, black hair now hung to just below the neck of his heavy jupon, she realized that she felt something else—a strong need to be in his arms. Although she knew it was a poor time to be seized by her passions, she was unable to push the feeling aside. Since she had ridden away from him, her thoughts and dreams had been crowded with sweet memories of their lovemaking. As it became increasingly difficult to think of anything besides how badly she needed him, Eada decided that, at the moment, she needed the answer to only one question.

"Are you married?" she asked, startled at how low and husky her voice was, and the way Drogo's eyes grew even darker told her that he was fully aware of what afflicted her.

"No. I have no bride," he answered and leaned closer to her, removing the pot of stew from the fire.

"You are promised to no one?"

"No. I am a free man."

"Then I believe we can do all the rest of our talking later."

"I have always considered you the cleverest of women."

Eada laughed shakily and flung herself into his arms.

A soft sigh of contentment escaped Eada as she stretched and smoothed her hand over the broad, hard chest of the man at her side. Old Edith's bed had never been so comfortable. A brief grin touched her face as she looked at their clothes strewn all over the room. They had cast them off so quickly and blindly, she suspected that only good luck had kept any of them from landing in the fire.

When Drogo turned, draped his arm around her waist, and kissed her shoulder, she fought to shake free of passion's lingering mists. It would be nice to simply spend the night making love to each other; but she could not allow that to happen, at least not until they had talked. Sensing that he was watching her, she cautiously met his dark gaze. The seriousness of his expression told her that he had come to the same decision.

"That was very rewarding, but it was not what I came here for," he said and then laughed when she quirked one delicately arced brow. "Not fully. Why did you leave London, Eada?"

She found his habit of surprising her with blunt questions irritating. "It was evident that William was eager to marry Saxons to Normans. Saxons were eager to marry their women to one of the victors. The chance that you might have to take a bride to gain the land you sought was so great that I could not ignore it."

"And your voices told you that I would be offered a bride."

"So, you did speak to my mother," she murmured, shifting closer to his warmth as he combed his fingers through her hair. "Yes, I was told that you would be offered a bride. As is its wont, my voice chose not to tell me whether or not you would accept that bride."

"And so you fled?"

"I felt that I had no other choice. As you can see, I have a certain weakness for you—" she ignored his grin, "—and I knew that I could easily become trapped into being your leman."

"You would consider that a trap?"

"That is exactly what it would be. The moment I became your leman, all of my other choices would be gone. The war made us lovers and, strangely, it made it acceptable to most people. I was a captive in their eyes, and if they gave the matter any thought at all in the midst of all of that death and destruction, it was only with a touch of sympathy. Once the war was over, once I became a leman and not a captive, that acceptance would have been pulled away. Then it would have been seen that I had made a choice and that that choice was to be your whore, to be a partner in adultery. I would see myself in the same way and I would find that very hard to bear. It is almost funny. I would stay because of this great passion we share, yet eventually, it would be that passion which would destroy me."

"It was that same fear that made your mother reluctant to tell me where you had gone," he said, as he touched a kiss to her forehead. "I wish I could say that I would never have asked that of you, but that weakness you speak of is a shared one."

"And was I right? Were you offered a wife?"

"Yes, and a very fine one, too," he replied as he sprawled on his back and crossed his arms beneath his head. "She was fair, had a firm, full shape and a becoming modesty."

Eada slowly sat up, clutching the coverlet to her breasts, and frowned down at him, fighting a touch of jealousy. "If she was such a beauty, where is she?"

"Right now she is probably on her father's vast lands becoming acquainted with her new husband."

"Vast lands? You were offered vast lands?"

"An earldom." He grinned at her look of astonishment, a look that closely matched Godwin's.

"You are an earl?" she asked in confusion.

"No. The title of earl only came if I wed the woman, and I said no."

She rubbed her forehead as she struggled to understand what he was telling her. "You refused William when he offered you an earl's seat with all of the lands, wealth, and power that goes with it?"

"And the woman. Do not forget the woman. I could not accept one without the other."

The amused look on his face began to annoy her. "Why do you not just tell me all that happened in your meeting with the king. This conversation has become so confusing that I have an aching head."

He laughed but told her about his meeting with William. Eada could not believe it. William had offered Drogo everything he had fought for, far more than he could have ever hoped for, yet Drogo had said no. It was clear that he had said no because he did not want to marry the woman. Eada was almost afraid to guess what that meant.

"Was William angry that you refused him?" she asked quietly, a stab of fear briefly pushing aside her other concerns.

"No. He expected it. At first, I feared that I would insult him by turning aside such a generous gift, but then I saw the amusement on his face. He was not surprised and said his only regret was that, at that time, he had nothing else to offer me."

"So you got nothing?"

Eada was torn between elation and utter dismay. It truly appeared that Drogo had done exactly what she had convinced herself he would never do. That made her heart pound so hard and fast it was almost painful. What upset her was the enormity of what he had turned aside. It also frightened her. If he had refused such a wealthy prize for love of her, would it become a poison that would finally kill that love?

"Drogo, why?" she asked before he could answer her first question. "It was all you had fought for; it was why you came here; why you risked dying in a strange land."

He sat up slowly, grasped her by the shoulders, and kissed her. "Eada, my sweet, when William offered me that woman as my bride, I knew only one thing for certain. I could not bind myself to another woman. She could have held the crown in her soft, white hands and I would still have had to say no."

She placed her unsteady hand over his heart and prayed that she continue to restrain the tears that were choking her. "But to cast aside so much—"

"The cost was too high. Eada, I could not take the woman. I knew, at that very moment, that I could only pledge myself to one woman and no other." He smiled when she fell into his arms, but his smile faded when he felt the dampness of her tears on his chest. "This makes you weep?"

"It makes me afraid."

"Afraid? Afraid of what, *cherie?*"

She took a deep breath to control her tears and looked up at him. "What if, one day, you decide that I was not worth such a great sacrifice? What if you are never able to gain all you have sought and the realization that you pushed aside your only chance for such gain because of me becomes a slow poison to all we share?"

"Eada, my mind and heart were clear when I said no. I have no regrets now and I will never have any regrets. In truth, the only thing that has troubled me since that day is the knowledge of how cruelly I have treated you. I gave you nothing." His eyes widened when she placed her fingers over his mouth.

"You gave me honesty. I have known since the day I first met you that you were here seeking all that birth had denied you. If I hoped to have some part in that, it was not because you led me to think so. You gave me no false promises, no empty assurances. No, it was not what I wanted or longed for; but then again, it was. You treated me most fairly."

"You are too forgiving."

"Not at all. You are just too determined to don a hair shirt."

He grinned and hugged her before growing serious again. "I heartily cursed William for each day that I was forced to linger in London. I was never sure what I feared, yet each day that passed made me even more afraid. I had seen what I wanted and I needed to tell you, yet you were not there and I could not pursue you." He brushed the last of her tears from her cheeks. "You seemed surprised to see me. Did your voice not say that I would be coming after you?"

"Yes, but it did not say when or if you would be free. And when it tells me things that I desperately wish to hear, I am not able to trust it."

"And why did you desperately want me to come after you?"

Eada blinked and stared at him. She suddenly realized that, for all of their talk and emotion, neither of them had said the three little words that would ease any lingering doubts and fears. What he had done certainly showed that he loved her and she was sure that he could sense how she felt, but it was far past time that they spoke openly about what was in their hearts. She smiled inwardly, prepared to tell him of her love for him, but curious if she could get him to do it first.

"Why did you refuse an earl's daughter, title, and lands?"

Drogo traced the delicate lines of her face, amused at how timid he suddenly felt, even shy, both feelings he had not suffered since he had been very young. All the emotion she had revealed told him that he had nothing to fear, yet he hesitated. Taking a deep breath to steady himself, he cupped her small face in his hands and brushed a kiss over her upturned mouth.

"I did it because I love you, because I knew that I could never speak my vows to another woman no matter how

weighty her dowry or fair her face. I but regret that I was
so slow to see it and that my ignorance may have served
to hurt you."

"You saw it in time and you came to me," she whispered. "Nothing else matters except that I love you as
well, Sir Drogo." She readily accepted his fierce kiss, returning it in full.

"We must be wed as soon as possible," he said when
the kiss ended, his voice hoarse from the strong emotion
coursing through him.

"I wish I had some dowry," she murmured, recalling
her lands and suddenly not sure that he would be able
to keep them. William would still have to be told about
them and, despite the high favor in which he held Drogo,
it was possible that he would have to give her lands to
another. "You should not be left poor and landless after
all you have done."

"Oh, I am not poor and landless; I am now a baron.
William gave me your home in Pevensey and said that I
could lay claim to all you and your family held." He
frowned when she suddenly tensed, staring at him with
her mouth slightly agape. "Your mother was not upset by
the news, especially when I told her I would claim only
what was there when I arrived, that she could keep all
she had fled with. Because she had married Serle and I
was hopeful that you would marry me, I saw no harm in
accepting," he added, afraid that she was angry and feeling a need to justify himself.

Eada waved aside his explanations with one sharp gesture of her hand. "Our home was certain to go to some
Norman. I am pleased that it was you. Only one thing you
just said concerns me. William granted you all that I or
my family holds claim to? Are you certain that he said it
just that way, that *everything* which is ours is now yours?"

"Yes. I now hold *all* that was your family's or yours. All
he asked was that I send him a full accounting when I

discover what that is. Did Old Edith grant you this cottage?"

"Yes," she replied absently as she picked her chemise up off the floor and tugged it on.

"Where are you going?" he asked as she hopped out of bed and walked away.

"Do you remember that small carved chest that I carried with me?" she asked him as she reverently took the box off its shelf, carried it back to the bed, and held it out to him.

Warily, Drogo took it, frowning as she climbed back onto the bed and wrapped the heavy coverlet around her chilled body. "It was when you finally looked inside this that you found out Vedette was your foster mother."

She nodded, her stomach twisting itself into knots as she worried about how he would react to her news. "There was more than that in that little box. See for yourself."

It was hard to sit quietly as he carefully looked over everything in the box then looked it over again. What made Eada really nervous was the lack of expression on his face. No matter how good her reasons had been for keeping silent, she had deceived him. She was not sure how he would judge her.

"You have lands," he finally said in a flat, tightly controlled voice. "Why did you never tell me?"

"Because I wanted you to want only me and not my lands." When he looked at her as if he were having difficulty deciding whether she were mad or an idiot, she cursed softly. "Drogo, from the moment you set your feet on English dirt, you spoke of needing and wanting land. I never told you, but Old Edith said that we were fated to be mates." She saw his eyes widen as the ghost of a smile touched his lips and decided with an inner sigh of relief that he was not as angry as she had feared he would be. "I was thinking of fate and destiny, and you spoke only of lands and wealth. When I realized that I loved you, there was still no word from you about what part I might play in your life once the war had ended."

"Eada, I—"

"No," she said and shook her head, silencing his apologies. "I am neither condemning you nor blaming you. I am just telling you what was in my mind and my heart when I decided not to tell you about those lands. As I have said, you were always honest with me, Drogo, and I never told you any of what I felt, so how could you have acted upon it?

"When I first learned of Old Edith's bequest, my first thought was to run to you. Then pride and, mayhap, vanity possessed me. I did not wish you to keep me just because I had the lands you craved. I wanted some sign from you that I was in your heart. Do you understand?"

"Very well."

The tenderness of the kiss he gave her made Eada tremble. She clung to him before carefully putting everything back into the box. It was difficult to believe that she could be so blessed. Drogo loved her and, through him, everything her father and Old Edith had left behind would still be hers. She set the little box on the floor and laughed when he pulled her back into his arms, playfully wrestling with her until she was gently pinned beneath him.

"Do you think William will be angry that I have kept such a secret?" she asked, a hint of worry intruding into her sense of contentment.

"No. I believe William will be both amused and relieved." He touched a kiss to the tip of her nose. "After all, you have given me the boon he feared he might not have to give me and he will have an exact accounting of a very large area of his new kingdom. Now, my little and very wealthy bride, I am not in the mood to speak of kings and lands and conquests."

Eada grinned as he moved against her suggestively, but

then grew serious. "You have conquered me, my fine, dark Norman."

"No, and I do not wish to. All I ask of you, my lavender-eyed Saxon, is your love."

"And that you have in full, for now and for forever."

ABOUT THE AUTHOR

Hannah Howell is an award-winning author who lives with her family in Massachusetts. She is the author of over thirty Zebra historical romances and is currently working on a new historical romance featuring the Murrays, HIGHLAND AVENGER, coming in April 2012! Hannah loves hearing from readers and you may visit her website: www.hannahhowell.com.

New York Times *bestselling author Hannah Howell returns to the fateful realms of the Scottish Highlands, where a man's destiny lies in the heart of the woman who once betrayed him . . .*

Beaten and left for dead, Sir Lucas Murray is a man wounded in body and soul. He has brought himself back to becoming the warrior he once was—except for his ruined leg and the grief he feels over the death of the woman he once loved . . . the same woman who led him into enemies' hands.

Dressed as a masked reiver, it is Katerina Haldane who saves Lucas as he battles for his life—and for revenge. Shocked that she still lives, Lucas becomes desperate to ignore the desire raging through his body. And Katerina becomes desperate to regain his trust, trying to convince him of her half-sister's role in his beating. Lucas is reluctant to let down his guard, but his resistance melts once Katerina is back in his arms . . . and his bed. Now he must learn to trust his instincts—in battle and in love . . .

Please turn the page for an exciting sneak peek at Hannah Howell's HIGHLAND SAVAGE!

Scotland
Spring, 1481

His robes itched. Lucas gritted his teeth against the urge to throw them off and vigorously scratch every inch of his body he could reach. He did not know how his cousin Matthew endured wearing the things day in and day out. Since the man had happily dedicated his life to the service of God, Lucas did not think Matthew deserved such an excruciating penance. A mon willing to sacrifice so much for God ought to able to do so in more comfortable garb.

"This may have been a bad idea, Eachann," Lucas murmured to his mount as he paused on a small rise to stare down at the village of Dunlochan.

His big brown gelding snorted and began to graze on the grass at his hooves.

"Weel, there is nay turning back now. Nay, I am but suffering a moment of uncertainty and it shames me. I have just ne'er been verra skilled in subterfuge, aye? 'Tis a blunt mon I am and this shall require me to be subtle and sly. But, 'tis nay a worry for I have been practicing."

Lucas frowned at his horse and sternly told himself that the animal only sounded as if it had just snickered. On the other hand, if the animal could understand what he

said, snickering would probably be an appropriate response. Yet, he had no choice. He needed revenge. It was
a hunger inside him that demanded feeding. It was not
something he could ask his family to risk themselves for,
either, although they had been more than willing to do
so. That willingness was one reason he had had to slip away
under the cover of night, telling no one where he was
going, not even his twin.

This was his fight and his alone. Surrounded by the
strong, skilled fighting men of his clan, he knew he
would feel deprived of satisfying the other need he had.
He needed to prove to himself that his injuries had not
left him incapable of being the warrior he had been
before he had been beaten. He needed to defeat the men
who had tried to destroy him and defeat them all by
himself. His family had not fully understood that need.
They had not fully understood his need to work so hard,
so continuously, to regain his skills after he had recovered
from the beating, either. He knew the praise they had
given him as he had slowly progressed from invalid to
fighting man had, in part, been an attempt to stop him
from striving so hard to regain his former abilities, to overcome the stiffness and pain in his leg. He desperately
needed to see that he was as good as he had been, that
he had not been robbed of the one true strength he
had. He had to prove himself worthy of being the heir to
Donncoill.

"Artan would understand," he said, stroking Eachann's
strong neck as he slowly rode down the hill toward the
village.

He felt a pang of lingering grief. His twin had his own
life now, one separate from the one they had shared
since the womb. Artan had a wife, his own lands, and a
family of his own. Lucas was happy for his twin yet he was
still grieved by the loss of the other half of himself. In his

heart Lucas knew he and Artan could never be fully separated but now Artan shared himself with others as he had only ever shared himself with Lucas. It would take some getting used to.

"And I have no one."

Lucas grimaced. He sounded like a small sulky child, yet that feeling of being completely alone was one he could not shake. It disgusted him, but he knew part of it was that he had lost not only Artan; he had lost Katerina. She had betrayed him and did not deserve his grief, yet it lingered. No other woman could banish the emptiness left by her loss. No other woman could ease the coldness left by her vicious betrayal. He could still see her watching as he was beaten nigh unto death. She had made no sound, no move to save him. She had not even shed a tear.

He shook aside those dark memories and the pain they still brought him. Lucas decided that once he had proven to himself that he was the man he used to be, he would find himself a woman and rut himself blind. He would exhaust himself in soft, welcoming arms and sweat out the poison of Katerina. Even though it was not fully a fidelity to Katerina that had kept him almost celibate, he knew a lingering hunger for her, for the passion they had shared, was one reason he found it difficult to satisfy his needs elsewhere. In his mind he was done with her, but it was obvious his heart and body were still enslaved. He would overcome his reluctance to reveal his scars and occasional awkwardness to a woman and find himself a lover when he returned to Donncoill. Maybe even a wife, he mused as he reined in before the small inn in the heart of the village. All too clearly recalling Katerina's dark blue eyes and honey-blond hair, he decided that woman would be dark. It was time to make the cut sharp and complete.

Dismounting, Lucas gave the care of Eachann over to

a bone thin youth who quickly appeared at his side. The lad stared at him with wide blue eyes, looking much as if he had just seen a ghost and that look made Lucas uneasy. Subtly he checked to make certain that his cowl still covered the hair he had been unable to cut. Although he had told himself he would need the cowl up at all times to shadow his far too recognizable face, Lucas knew it was vanity that had made him reluctant to cut off his long black hair and his warrior braids. Deciding the boy might just be a little simple, Lucas collected his saddle-packs then gave the lad a coin before making his way into the inn.

After taking only two steps into the building, Lucas felt the chill of fear speed down his spine and stopped to look around. This was where he had been captured, dragged away to be savagely beaten and then left for dead. Despite the nightmares he still suffered on occasion, he had thought he had conquered the unreasonable fear his beating had left him with.

Annoyance over such a weakness helped him quell that fear. Standing straighter he made his way to a table set in a shadowy corner at the back of the room. He had barely sat down when a buxom fair-haired maid hurried over to greet him. If he recalled right, her name was Annie.

"Father," she began.

"Nay, my child. I am nay tonsured yet," Lucas said, hoping such a tale would help explain away any mistakes he might make. "I am on pilgrimage ere I return to the monastery and take my final vows."

"Oh." Annie sighed. "I was hoping ye were looking for a place to serve God's will." She briefly glared at the men drinking ale near the large fireplace. "We could certainly use a holy mon here. Dunlochan has become steeped in sin and evil."

"I will be certain to tell my brothers of your need when I return to them, child."

"Thank ye, Father. Ah, I mean, sir. How can I serve ye?"

"Food, ale, and a bed for the night, lass."

In but moments Lucas was enjoying a rich ale, a hearty mutton stew, and thick warm bread. The good food served by the inn was one reason he had lingered in Dunlochan long enough to meet Katerina. His stomach had certainly led him astray that day, he thought sourly. In truth, his stomach may have kept him at Dunlochan long enough to meet Katerina, but it was another heedless part of him that had truly led him astray. One look at her lithe body, her long thick hair the color of sweet clover honey, and her wide deep blue eyes and all his wits had sunk right down into his groin. He had thought he had met his mate and all he had found was betrayal and pain.

Lucas cursed silently. The woman would not get out of his life, out of his mind or out of his heart. That would not stop him from getting his revenge on her, however. He was not quite sure how he would accomplish that yet, but he would. First the men who had tried to kill him and then the woman who had given the order.

Another casualty of that dark night was his trust in people, in his ability to judge them as friend or foe. Lucas had believed Katerina was his mate, the woman he had been born to be with. Instead she had nearly been his death. It was hard to trust his own judgment after such a near fatal error and an ability to discern whom to trust was important to a warrior. How could he ever be a good laird to the people of Donncoill if he could not even tell friend from foe?

He sipped his ale and studied the men near the fireplace. Lucas was sure that at least one of them had been there that night, but the shadows cast by the fire made it difficult to see the man clearly. One of the things he recalled clearly was that few of the men had been fair like most of the Haldanes were. It had puzzled him that Katerina would hire mercenaries, but, perhaps, her own people would never have obeyed such an order from her. If those men were no more than hired swords it would make the killing of them easier for few would call out for vengeance when they died.

Six men suddenly entered the inn and Lucas stiffened. No shadows hid their faces and he recognized each one. It was hard to control the urge to immediately draw his sword and set after them. He shuddered faintly, the memory of the beating flaring crisp and clear in his mind and body. Lucas rubbed his left leg, the ache of shattered bones sharpened by those dark memories. His right hand throbbed as if it recalled each and every slam of a boot on it. The scar that now ran raggedly over his right cheek itched and Lucas could almost feel the pain of the knife's blade cutting through the flesh there.

He drew in a deep breath and let it out slowly. Lucas knew he needed to push those memories aside if he was to think clearly. The revenge he hungered for could not be accomplished if he acted too quickly or if he gave into the fierce urge to immediately draw his sword and attack these men. When he realized part of his ability to hold back was because he did not think he could defeat the six men with a direct attack, he silently cursed again. His confidence in his newly regained battle skills was obviously not as strong as he had thought it was.

"Annie!" bellowed one of the men as he and his companions sat down. "Get your arse o'er here and pour us some ale, wench!"

There was an obvious caution in Annie's steps as she approached the men with tankards and an ewer of ale. "Hush, Ranald," she said. "I saw ye come in and was ready. There is nay need to bellow so."

Lucas watched as the young woman did her best to pour each man a tankard of ale even as she tried to avoid their grasping hands. Unlike many another lass who worked in such a place, Annie was no whore easily gained by a coin or two, but the men treated her as if she was. By the time she was able to get away from their table, she was flushed with anger and her eyes were shining with tears of shame. Lucas had to take a deep drink of the strong ale to quell the urge to leap to her defense. He gave her a small smile when she paused by his table to refill his tankard and wondered why that made her eyes narrow and caused a frown to tighten her full mouth.

"Have ye been here before, sir?" she asked as she suddenly sat down across the scarred table from him.

"Nay, why should ye think so, child?" he asked.

"There was something about your smile," she said then shrugged. "'Twas familiar."

Lucas had no idea how a smile could be familiar but told himself to remember to be more cautious about doing so again. "Mayhap ye just see too few, aye?"

"Certainly too few that show me such fine, white teeth."

"A blessing I got from my family and God. That and cleaning them regularly."

She nodded. "The Lady Katerina taught me the value of cleaning my teeth."

"A good and Godly woman is she?"

"She was, aye."

"Was?"

"Aye, she died last Spring, poor wee lass." She glared at the men who had treated her so badly. "They and the ladies at the keep say my lady killed herself, but I dinnae believe it. She would ne'er have done such a thing. Aye, and the lovely mon who was courting her disappeared on the verra same day. No one has an answer for where he went." She suddenly looked straight at Lucas. "That is who your smile reminded me of, I am thinking. A bonnie lad he was. He did make my lady happy, he did."

Lucas was too shocked to do more than nod. He could not even think of something to say to turn aside the dangerous comparison Annie had just made. Katerina was dead. The news hit him like a sound blow to the chest and it took him a moment to catch his breath. He told himself that the sharp grief that swept over him was born of the fact that he had lost all chance to exact his revenge upon the woman for her betrayal, but a small voice in his mind scoffed at that explanation. He ruthlessly silenced it.

"Is it a sin to visit her grave e'en though she is buried in unconsecrated ground?" Annie asked.

"Nay, lass," he replied, his voice a little hoarse from the feelings he was fighting. "Her soul needs your prayers e'en more than another's, aye?"

The thought of Katerina resting in the cold ground was more than Lucas could bear and he hastily pushed it aside. He also ignored the questions swirling in his mind, ones that demanded answers. He could not believe Katerina would kill herself either, but this was not the time to solve that puzzle. As he sought his revenge on the men who had beaten him he could ask a few questions, but that revenge had to be the first thing on his mind for now. When that was done he would discover the truth about Katerina's death. No matter what she had done to him, he knew he would never be able to rest easy with the thought of her lovely body rotting in unconsecrated soil.

"Do ye think ye could pray for her, sir? Would that be a sin?"

Lucas had no idea and fumbled for an answer. "'Tis my duty to pray for lost souls, child."

"I could take ye to where she is buried," Annie began and then scowled when Ranald and two of his companions came up to the table. "If ye want more ale, ye just needed to ask."

"I came to see why ye are sitting and talking so cozily with this monk," said Ranald.

"What business is it of yours, eh?"

"Ye waste your time wooing a monk, lass. If ye are hungry for a mon, I am more than willing to see to your needs." He grinned when his companions laughed.

"I but wished to talk to someone who has traveled beyond the boundaries of Haldane land," she snapped. "Someone who doesnae smell or curse or try to lift my skirts." Annie suddenly blushed and looked at Lucas. "Pardon me for speaking so, sir."

"'Tis nay ye who must beg pardon, child, but the men who compel ye to speak so," Lucas said, watching Ranald closely.

"Here now, I but woo the lass," said Ranald, glaring at Lucas.

"Is that what ye call it?"

"What would ye ken about it, eh? Ye have given it all up for God, aye? Or have ye? Are ye one of those who says vows to God out of one side of his mouth whilst wooing the lasses out the other?"

"Ye insult my honor," Lucas said coldly, wishing the man would leave for the urge to make him pay now, and pay dearly, for every twinge of pain Lucas had suffered over the last year was growing too strong to ignore. "I but question your skill at wooing."

"Do ye now. And just what are ye doing in Dunlochan? There is no monastery near here."

"He is on a pilgrimage ere he takes his vows," said Annie. "Leave him be and go back to your friends and your ale."

"Ye defend him most prettily, lass. I have to wonder

why." Ranald scowled at Lucas. "What is he hiding under those robes?"

Even as Lucas became aware of the sudden danger he was in, Ranald yanked back his cowl and exposed the hair Lucas had been too vain to cut. For a brief moment, everyone just stared at Lucas, their eyes wide and their mouths gaping. Lucas actually considered attacking the man Ranald immediately but good sense intervened. The man's friends were already rising from their seats and inching closer.

Taking advantage of everyone's shock at seeing what they thought was a ghost, Lucas leapt to his feet, grabbed his saddlepacks, and bolted for the door. He gained the outside and turned toward the stable only to stumble to a halt as someone grabbed his robe from behind. Cursing, he turned and kicked the man in the face. Knowing he would not make it to his horse in time, Lucas tossed aside his saddle packs and yanked off his robes. By the time Ranald and his friends had finished stumbling out of the inn, Lucas was facing them with a sword in one hand and a dagger in the other.

"So, it *is* ye," said Ranald as he drew his sword and he and his companions moved to stand facing Lucas. "Ye are supposed to be dead. We threw ye off the cliff and saw ye just lying there."

"And ye ne'er went back to see if I stayed there, did ye," Lucas said, his scorn clear to hear in his voice.

"Why trouble ourselves? We had beaten ye soundly, ye were bleeding from several wounds and we threw ye off a cliff."

Lucas shrugged. "I got up and went home," he said, knowing his family would groan to hear him describe the many travails he had gone through to return to Donncoill in such simple terms.

"Weel, ye willnae be crawling home this time, laddie."

"Nay, I intend to ride home in triumph, leaving your bodies behind me to rot in the dirt."

"I dinnae think so." Ranald sneered as he glanced at Lucas's left leg. "I watched ye run out of the inn and ye limp and stumble like an old mon. We left ye a cripple, didnae we."

Lucas fought down the rage that threatened to consume him. He had to exact his revenge coldly, had to fight with a clear head and think out every move he made. It was this man's fault that Lucas could no longer move with the speed and grace he had before, and it was hard not to just lunge at the man and cut him down. Before the beating he would have not been all that concerned about the other men, knowing he could turn on them with an equal speed and have a good chance of defeating them all. Now, because of these men, he had to weigh his every move carefully if he had any hope of coming out of this alive.

"E'en that wee wound willnae stop me from killing ye," Lucas said, his voice almost cheerful even as he noted with a twinge of dismay how the men began to slowly encircle him.

"Still arrogant," said Ranald, grinning as he shook his head. "Weel, soon ye will be joining your wee whore in the cold clay."

"So, Annie spoke true when she said Lady Katerina was dead."

"Aye, she joined ye or so we thought. Tossed her right o'er the cliff and into the water with ye."

That made no sense to Lucas, but he pushed his sudden confusion and all the questions it raised aside. How and why Katerina had died was of no importance at the moment. Staying alive had to be his only priority. A quick glance toward the inn revealed a white-faced Annie and several other Haldanes watching and listening. Lucas had to hope that, if he failed to win this fight, they would find out what happened to Katerina, although why he should care about that was just another puzzle he had no time to solve.

"I dinnae suppose ye have the courage to face me mon to mon, without all your men to protect your worthless hide," Lucas said as he braced himself for the battle to come.

"Are ye calling me a coward?" Ranald snarled.

"Ye needed near a dozen men to capture me, beat me nigh unto death and toss me off a cliff, and then ye murdered a wee unarmed lass. Aye, I believe I am calling ye a coward and weel do ye deserve the name."

"'Twill be a joy to kill ye, fool."

Glancing around at the men encircling him, Lucas had the sinking feeling that it would also be a quick killing, but then he stiffened his backbone. He had been in such tight spots before and come out nearly unscathed. All he needed to do was regain that arrogance Ranald found so irritating. Lucas was a little concerned that he would fail at that. It seemed his heart was beating so hard and fast that he could actually hear it. Telling himself he was imagining things, he readied himself to win and, failing that, to take as many of these men with him as he could. This time, killing him was going to cost them dearly.

Embrace the Romance of
Shannon Drake

When We Touch
0-8217-7547-2 $6.99US/$9.99CAN

The Lion in Glory
0-8217-7287-2 $6.99US/$9.99CAN

Knight Triumphant
0-8217-6928-6 $6.99US/$9.99CAN

Seize the Dawn
0-8217-6773-9 $6.99US/$8.99CAN

Come the Morning
0-8217-6471-3 $6.99US/$8.99CAN

Conquer the Night
0-8217-6639-2 $6.99US/$8.99CAN

The King's Pleasure
0-8217-5857-8 $6.50US/$8.00CAN

Available Wherever Books Are Sold!

Visit our website at **www.kensingtonbooks.com.**